Praise for *New York Times* bestseller
The Heir

"Burrowes debuts with a luminous and graceful erotic Regency… a refreshing and captivating love story that will have readers eagerly awaiting the planned sequels."

—*Publishers Weekly*, starred review

"The heroine of Grace Burrowes's erotically charged romance is a woman of such mystery that both the hero and the reader become obsessed with her."

—*USA Today*

"A witty, sensual, Regency romance featuring complex characters who ring true to the time period, leaving readers saying huzzah!"

—*Booklist*

"Burrowes's enchanting romance charms from the beginning… tenderness and sensuality, lighthearted verbal battles, and tense moments combine to delight."

—*RT Book Reviews*

"With tons of intrigue, searing seduction, and wonderful humor, Grace Burrowes's first book is a... must read for fans of Georgette Heyer and Regency romances."

—*Night Owl Romance*, Top Pick

"A scorching, romantic novel; it is both hot and sweet, and it is sure to touch readers' hearts."

—*Romance Reviews Today*

"An irresistible love story... Ms. Burrowes's smooth writing style engages all the senses."

—*The Long and the Short of It Reviews*

"A blooming author who promises to become a household name... the lovemaking is highly passionate and fiery, and utterly enthralling."

—*Romance Fiction on Suite101*

"A sweet, sexy, tender romance between two characters so vibrant they seem to leap off the page. Burrowes's fresh, gorgeous writing held me riveted from start to finish."

—Meredith Duran, author of *Wicked Becomes You*

"Fascinating, mysterious, and engaging... The book was researched well to bring out the Regency flavors that make reading this genre so much fun."

—*History Undressed*

"Regency romance at its best... With lots of humor and steamy romance, these books are always a delightful read."

"Enthralling... Ms. Burrowes's character development, use of imagery, and her ability to create a strong sense of place make *The Soldier* a breathtaking love story that lingers in the mind and heart."

"Burrowes has a real knack for writing sensual and emotional love scenes that mean something."

LADY SOPHIE'S
CHRISTMAS WISH

GRACE BURROWES

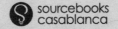

sourcebooks
casablanca

Published by Sourcebooks Casablanca, an imprint of Sourcebooks, Inc.
P.O. Box 4410, Naperville, Illinois 60567-4410
(630) 961-3900
FAX: (630) 961-2168
www.sourcebooks.com

Printed and bound in the United States of America
QW 10 9 8 7 6 5 4 3 2 1

*This book is dedicated to my dear sister, Maire.
Like other Notables (our mother) she arrived
in December, and she is the closest thing to a saint
I ever hope to meet on earth, being good, fun,
and easy to love. No family ever received
a better holiday present.*

One

"AIN'T A BLEEDIN' BEDAMNED ROOM T'BE HAD IN ALL A bleedin' Lun'nun, guv!"

The innkeeper raised his voice to holler over the racket created by one screaming infant. "Stables is full up too, and more bleedin' snow on the way! Beg pardon!"

He hustled away and started bellowing over the din in the common for somebody to mop the bleedin' floor. Not surprised at the lack of accommodations, Vim moved off in the interest of sparing his bleedin' ears.

Though moving wasn't easy in the crowded confines of the common.

The floor was a slick expanse of that particular type of mud created when snow, horse manure, and dirt were tracked in from the semifrozen quagmire of the inn yard, and yet it was hardly the worst feature of the crowded room. The stench rising from the floor blended with the aromas of wet wool, unwashed bodies, and overcooked mutton stew to offend even the lowliest nose.

Overlaying it all was the incongruous scent of cinnamon, as if a little spice would confer on the scene some sense of seasonal good cheer.

Which was not bloody likely.

Piercing the noisome air, over the cursing and muttering of stranded travelers, over the scrape of boots and the swearing of the hostlers in the yard beyond, came that sound most capable of driving Wilhelm Lucifer Charpentier to madness.

A crying baby.

Vim had noticed the little blighter when all the passengers on his stage had been told to debark here in the very heart of London, because the weather was precluding further progress on the journey south. Like benumbed sheep, they'd all stumbled into the inn, toting their belongings with them only find an assault on their ears was to be the price of thawing their toes.

The child's crying ratchetted up, from indignant to enraged. The next progression would be to inconsolable, which might last hours.

Happy bedamned holidays.

Vim knew people in London. People who would act pleased to see him. People who would smile and welcome him as an impromptu guest for the duration of the foul weather. Happy people, offering him wassail while they laughed their way through the same hopeless madrigals and selections from Handel's *Messiah*.

He shifted his gaze from the scene beyond the window to the woman holding the unhappy baby a few feet away.

"I beg your pardon, madam. May I be of assistance?" He tipped his hat and had to fist his hands at his sides, so strong was the urge to pluck the offending infant from her arms. "The child appears distressed."

She bobbed a curtsy while holding the child. "I've

explained to him that such a tantrum is hardly seemly, and I do apologize for the noise." She focused her gaze on the child. "You are a naughty fellow, young Kit, banging your tankard and shouting down the rafters…"

She went on softly remonstrating the baby while Vim recovered from the prettiest pair of green eyes he'd ever beheld. Overall, she wasn't a pretty woman—she had a full though solemn mouth in the usual location, underscored by a definite chin and a nose somewhat lacking in subtlety. Her hair was dark brown and pulled back into a positively boring bun at her nape. But those eyes…

And her voice. It was the voice of a pretty lady, soft and luminous with good breeding and gentility, though she was using it to try to gently scold the child into better behavior.

"May I?" He held out his arms, meeting those green eyes when she looked faintly puzzled. "I have some experience with children."

She passed him the child, moving close enough to Vim that he realized she was not particularly tall. She had a dignity about her, though, even holding a bellowing baby.

"His mama should be right back. She just went around to the back for a moment." The lady cast a hopeful look at the door—a hopeful, anxious look.

Vim took the child, who appeared distracted by the change in venue—though likely only temporarily.

"You will hush," he said to the baby. This pronouncement earned him a blinking, blue-eyed stare from his burden. "This good woman is tired of your fretting, as is the entire room and likely half the block. Behave your little self, or we'll call the beadle to haul you off to gaol. That's better."

He put the baby to his shoulder and began to gently pat and rub the small back. "He just finished his luncheon, didn't he?"

The woman colored slightly. "I believe he did."

Still on the breast then, which was going to be a problem.

"I don't believe his mother will be returning." He said it calmly, an observation about the weather, nothing more.

"I beg your pardon?"

"Voice down, madam, lest His Highness start to fretting again, hmm?" He turned his body to provide the woman a little privacy, his larger frame effectively blocking her from the rest of the room.

"Sir, you just said you aren't sure his mother will be coming back. A trip to the necessary will hardly keep her until spring." She hissed the words, suggesting she lacked a parent's instinctive capacity for dissembling before children.

"The necessary is not in the direction of Piccadilly. She took off at as smart a pace as this footing will allow."

"You must be mistaken." Except a certain shift in the lady's expression told him the mother's behavior might not be entirely out of character.

"She's a solid young woman, blonde, attired in a purple cloak?" The baby rooted on his shoulder. "I have a handkerchief in my pocket. Would you be so good as to extract it?"

Again he'd spoken calmly, babies being fiendishly perceptive even before they learned their first words.

The lady was perceptive too. She stuck a hand into the pocket of his greatcoat and produced the handkerchief without further comment.

"Lay it on my shoulder."

She had to go up on her toes to do that, which meant amid all the stink and filth of the common, Vim caught a whiff of something... lovely. A hint of late spring. Cool, sunny, sweet... pink-throated roses and soft climbing vines of honeysuckle.

She stepped back to watch him warily.

"I suspect his recent meal has left him a tad dys"—the baby burped loudly and wetly—"peptic."

"My goodness." She blinked at Vim's shoulder, where the infant was now beaming toothlessly at all he surveyed. Vim shifted the child and retrieved the handkerchief, which had protected his greatcoat more or less from carrying the scent of infant digestion for the rest of the day.

He hoped.

"How long do you intend to wait for his mother?" The child swung a tiny hand and caught Vim's nose.

"Joleen was to board the Portsmouth stage." Another anxious visual sweep of the surrounds.

Vim took a step back so the lady might have a view out the window. He also disengaged his proboscis from the baby's surprisingly strong grip.

"I was told the coaches are all putting up for the duration, madam. My own travel has been interrupted because of it." The baby knocked Vim's high-crowned beaver straight at the woman beside them. She caught it deftly in one hand. When Vim dipped his head, she positioned the hat back where it belonged.

"That is a naughty baby," she said, eyeing the child.

"He's a boy baby. They all have more energy than they know what to do with, until they sleep like the dead, restoring themselves for their next round of mischief."

This recitation seemed to please the little fellow, for he smiled directly at Vim, a great drooling expression of benevolence disproportionate to his tiny size.

"I think Kit likes you."

"He likes having food in his tummy and a warm place to cuddle, the same as the rest of us. You can linger here, but I honestly do not think the mother will return. May I have your coach brought round for you?" Though the pandemonium in the yard suggested it would be far simpler to escort the lady to her conveyance.

"I only brought the gig, and it's right around the corner." She reached for the baby, but Vim took half a step back.

"I am happy to carry him for you."

"But he's..." She fell silent, regarding the baby gurgling contentedly on Vim's shoulder. "He does seem quite happy there."

"And I am happy to enjoy his company, as well. If you'd lead the way?" He nodded toward the door to encourage her, because her eyes bore a hesitance, suggesting she knew better than to allow a strange man to accompany her down the street.

"I neglected to introduce myself," Vim went on. "Wilhelm Charpentier, at your service." He left off the title, as he usually did with strangers, but he did bow with the baby tucked against his chest. The child laughed, a hearty, merry baby-chuckle calculated to have Vim bobbing around the room for the pleasure of My Lord Baby until one or both of them succumbed to exhaustion.

"I'm Sophie Windham." She dipped another curtsy while Vim cast around mentally for why the Windham name sounded vaguely familiar. "I should have known Joleen—his mama—was up to something when she took her valise to the necessary."

"You were occupied with a certain unhappy little gentleman. Shall we be going? I don't like the look of that sky."

She glanced out the window and got moving. It took some minutes to navigate through the crowd; then they had to pause inside the door for Miss Windham to wrap the child in a thick woolen shawl.

"My conveyance is just around that corner." She pulled on her gloves, nodding to the north, toward Mayfair. "We're not far from home, but with Joleen's valise, I thought the carriage would save us effort."

She wasn't wearing a bonnet, which allowed her to wrap a knit scarf around her head in such a way that her ears and neck and some of her hair were covered. Vim was relieved to get shut of the commons, relieved to breathe the relatively fresh air of the out-of-doors. They hadn't gone very far when Vim stopped abruptly.

"God in heaven. What is that?"

"Not so loud." Miss Windham turned to frown at him as the boy holding the reins darted off toward the inn. "You'll hurt Goliath's feelings. He's a very sensitive pony."

Her sensitive pony was almost as tall at the withers as the top of Vim's head, which put the beast at something over eighteen hands. Such an animal would be able to cut through the snow without breaking a sweat, but his kind were seldom kept in the confines of Town.

"Did he escape from in front of some beer wagon?" Though escape was hardly the appropriate term. A horse that size went where he pleased—fences, stone walls, and human wishes notwithstanding.

"He did not enjoy a sanguine existence before joining our stable, but he's the best of horses in bad weather. I'll take the baby." She turned to Vim as he noticed three fat, lazy snowflakes drifting down from the sky. He did not pass her the child.

"I don't see a driver, Miss Windham. How will you manage to guide the horse and hold Kit?"

"I can put the reins in one hand," she said, brow puckering. "Goliath knows the way home."

"No doubt he does." Or he knew the way to his barrel of oats. "Nonetheless, I would be more comfortable if you'd allow me to drive you. It seems we're to be treated to yet more snow, and I would not want a lady and her very young charge relying on the good offices of her horse when a gentleman was on hand to see to her safety."

It was a courteous, gentlemanly speech, calculated to reassure her and let him attend to an errand of conscience, though he'd meant what he'd said: he wanted to see her and the baby safely ensconced in a well-heated home before he set about finding his own accommodations. Call it vestigial chivalry or a rare manifestation of seasonal charity, but he wasn't going to abandon her to her own devices just yet.

"It's only a few blocks, Mr. Charpentier." She gave his name the same emphasis he did, Shar-pen-tee-ay, in deference to his father's distant Norman antecedents.

"Then you won't mind if I drive you." He tossed his haversack into the back, and with his free hand, he took her elbow, guiding her over to the gig. The angle of her chin suggested she had a stubborn streak, which was about to come inconveniently into evidence, but a chilly breeze came along at just the right moment— sporting more snowflakes—and her chin dipped.

"If you insist, then. I do appreciate it."

He boosted her into the gig and glanced at the sky in silent thanks. If there was one thing he did not regard as a productive use of his time, it was arguing with a strange woman in the street while a blizzard bore down on the city and the baby in his arms grew closer to that moment when...

"My goodness." Miss Windham wrinkled her nose where she sat on the bench. "Something..."

"Not something." Vim handed her the baby. "Someone. He ate, he burped, and now he must treat us to a demonstration of the health of the other end of his digestion." He climbed into the gig and unwrapped the reins from the brake. Beside him, Miss Windham was holding the baby slightly away from her body.

"I say." She frowned at the child. "I do say. You're sure they do this regularly?"

"With appalling regularity, if you're lucky. I'd guess the boy's getting some solid food too, which will make his situation a great deal easier if you can't locate the mother."

She didn't ask him how he came to such a conclusion, though the evidence presented to Vim's nose was unassailable. A child subsisting exclusively on mother's milk wasn't half as odoriferous as Kit had just been.

Vim flicked the reins, and the chestnut behemoth in the traces moved off. "Where are we heading?"

She rattled off an address on one of the great squares of Mayfair, prompting Vim to wonder just whom he was escorting.

Sophie Windham was well spoken, but she was also driving herself around London in the dead of winter. Her clothing was well made but not fancy enough to suggest wealth. She had the brisk competence of a housekeeper, and a position in service would explain her lack of familiarity with child care, as domestics seldom married.

"You were traveling today, Mr. Charpentier?" She'd relented and was holding the child against her body, despite the baby-stink emanating from the bundle in her arms.

"Heading to the family seat for the much-vaunted holidays." The family seat, such as it was, for the holidays, such as they were. His tone of voice must have given him away, for she shot him a look. He could feel her scrutinizing his profile and see her female brain choosing the most delicate way to frame an awkward question.

But she said nothing.

"What about you?" He glanced over at her. "Is London home, or should you be traveling somewhere to join your family for Christmas?"

"My brothers are coming through Town later in

the week. We'll journey to Kent together, assuming they all arrive safe and sound."

"How many brothers do you have?"

"I had five. Thanks to consumption and the Corsican, I now have three." Her voice hadn't wavered, hadn't revealed any particular sentiment, but she cradled the child closer.

"I am sorry for your losses."

She was quiet for a moment, while around them, the flurries were becoming a light, regular snow. She spoke just when he'd thought the topic closed. "My brother Victor died this time of year. I don't think my parents will spend another Christmas in Town for some time. We're still trying to find our balance with it."

He had no idea what to say to that. The lady fell silent, as well, suggesting the admission wasn't comfortable for her either. "This is a fairly recent loss?"

She nodded. "You can turn up that alley there; it will lead to our mews two blocks up."

Not surprisingly, the alley was relatively free of snow. The neighborhood was such that droves of servants would be available to move snow, to dig out the stables, to shovel off and then sweep the walks and garden pathways.

"My father died at Christmas, as well," he said as the horse trotted along. "He was not a well man in my lifetime. I think my mother was relieved to see him at peace." The baby fussed, which provided a distraction. "Try patting his back."

She did, gently and awkwardly.

"You aren't accustomed to children, are you?"

She paused in her attention to the child. "I am an

aunt, but it's hardly a role that prepares one for…" She wrinkled her nose tellingly.

"Dealing with a baby is usually a matter of trial by fire. Is that your mews?"

The stable doors bore an emblazoned crest, something with a unicorn and a lot of vinery, which again tickled the back of Vim's memory. A groom came out amid the thickening snow to slide the stable door back so Goliath and the gig could be parked right in the barn aisle.

Vim brought the horse to a halt and alighted, turning to take the baby from Miss Windham's arms. "You'll want to be seeing to his nappy."

She opened her mouth as if to say something, then drew her brows down. "His nappy?"

The wizened little gnome of a groom looked up from where he was coiling the reins then quickly went back to work.

Vim brushed a finger down his own nose. "His nappy. I can show you if you would like."

The offer was made before his brain had a chance to truss up his idiot mouth. The baby made another fussy noise, blinking up at Vim owlishly. So little, and the boy's mama had just abandoned him. A clean nappy wasn't too much of an imposition, really.

Miss Windham's expression had cleared. "Higgins, Goliath stood for a bit in the cold. Perhaps he should have a bran mash?"

Higgins paused in the unbuckling of the harness straps to pat the horse. "Of course, Miss Sophie. Nothing's too good for our lamb."

"Precisely." The smile she sent the groom would

have felled a brace of sober stevedores. Holding the baby just a few feet away, Vim watched as her mouth curved up into the very arc of sweetness, her eyes lit with warmth, and her whole countenance beamed appreciation and approval at the groom.

Or perhaps at the horse.

She petted the gelding on his tremendous stern then moved toward to the animal's bow and planted a kiss on his enormous nose. "Thank you, precious. Stay nice and warm tonight."

The horse blinked at her or perhaps batted its eyes. When Miss Windham straightened, she wasn't smiling.

"I suppose we should get the baby out of this weather. Higgins, you're settled in for the night?"

"Right and tight, Miss Sophie. Any word from your brothers?"

"They're due any day, though the weather might slow them down. Thank you for asking."

She swept past Vim, so he fell in step behind her. Miss Windham did not float nor mince, as a society lady would have. She clipped along, all business, until she got to the barn door, where she stopped so abruptly Vim nearly collided with her.

"This snow means business," she observed. "It will be difficult to send anybody out to search for Joleen as long as the weather is so foul."

"Are you sure you want to do that?"

She moved off again, casting him a curious look over her shoulder. "She fell prey to a footman, Mr. Charpentier. Joleen was old enough, but she was innocent and not overly bright. I don't hold it against her that she gambled her heart on a losing hand."

She clearly held it against the footman, however. Vim pitied the man if Miss Windham ever laid eyes on him again.

They passed through a gate into a walled garden that backed up to nothing less than a mansion. In some parts of the city, the old great houses built in the reign of the last king had been broken up into multiple dwellings, each with its own narrow strip of back garden.

This house took up roughly half the block, with no divisions of the back lots to suggest it had been split into rental properties. There would be a ballroom in a dwelling this size, parlors, music rooms, and enough cheery fires to keep a baby nice and warm.

The baby squirmed in Vim's arms just as both wind and snow became more intense.

"This way." Miss Windham led him to a back door. As soon as Vim stepped inside, he was hit with the scents of clove, allspice, cinnamon, and yeast. A wave of nostalgia for Blessings up in Cumbria, with its big kitchens and familiar retainers, passed through him as the child began to squawk in earnest.

"He is telling us he has been patient as long as he's going to be, Miss Windham. We'll need clean nappies, a clean flannel, and some warm water."

She paused in the act of hanging her cloak on a hook. "The fires in the nursery have likely been allowed to go out because Kit was to have been on his way south by now."

"A servants' parlor might do." If any room in the house was kept cozy this time of year, it was the servants' parlor.

"Follow me."

She led him through a spotless kitchen and down a short, dim hallway that looked to be lined with pantries. The servants' parlor at the end of the hallway was indeed snug and comfortable and enjoyed a view of the snowy back gardens. A fire burned cheerily in the hearth, though the room was with without occupants. The cradle sitting near the hearth suggested Kit had already spent a substantial amount of time here.

Vim spoke to his hostess over the baby's increasingly loud fussing. "This will do. If you'll bring flannel and warm water, I'll get him unwrapped."

She withdrew a little quickly, her expression suggesting a distraught baby unnerved her every bit as much as it did Vim.

"We can get down to business," Vim informed the child. "But I need to get you unswaddled first, so be patient." As soon as he set the baby down, the little fellow started kicking his legs out and waving his arms around.

"Getting bored, are we? Flail around all you like, little man. You'll be off to sleep that much sooner."

The habit of talking to people too small to join in the conversation was ingrained. Babies liked being talked to, just the way they liked music boxes and twittering birds and running water. In some ways, babies were the easiest people to like.

But as the warm air in the parlor picked up the scent of soiled nappy, Vim revised his judgment: *clean* babies were easy to like. He tossed his coat on a chair, slipped his cuff links in a pocket, and started rolling up his sleeves.

He soon had the child naked on a blanket before the hearth, the dirty nappy neatly folded and tucked aside. Fortunately, the mess was minimal.

At the soft click of door latch behind him Vim glanced up from where he knelt on the floor. Miss Windham stood there, some folded cloths in one hand, a steaming bowl in the other. Her eyes went to the baby, surprise registering at the child's state of undress.

From her expression, Vim considered that the baby on the floor was very likely the woman's first encounter with a completely naked male.

Two

SOPHIE WINDHAM FREQUENTLY DESCRIBED HERSELF AS a well-read, intelligent woman in an age when neither attribute was much encouraged among her peers. Coming upon the scene in the parlor, all that came out of her mouth was, "My goodness!"

And then... nothing. She frankly gaped at the tableau before her: the baby naked on a nest of rugs and blankets, cheerfully kicking and squirming at nothing in particular, and the great golden length of Mr. Charpentier, curled indolently above the child, long, elegant fingers playing with the child's feet.

Sophie did not know how to change a diaper.

She did not know how to comfort a fussy baby.

She did not know the particulars of feeding such a small child.

But she did know that these matters were the province of *women*, a fact of which Mr. Charpentier was apparently ignorant.

"Is it good for him to be... unclothed like that?" she asked.

The man rose smoothly to an imposing height—he

was every bit as tall as Sophie's brothers—and cocked his head at her. "Be a little difficult to get him cleaned up otherwise, wouldn't it?"

Stupid, stupid, stupid. Sophie felt a blush rising up her neck. "Suppose it would. So how does one…?" She gestured with the clean nappies at the baby.

"It isn't complicated." He took the cloths and basin from her. "I shall demonstrate. By the third one, you'll be an expert. The trick is to be fast and calm, as if you were dealing with a nervous horse or an injured cat."

He folded himself down to his knees, leaving Sophie no choice but to join him and the baby on the floor.

"Why does he kick and wiggle about like that?"

"Because he can. My guess is if we put him on his tummy, he'd be just about at the stage where he's getting up on all fours and rocking but not quite crawling yet." As he spoke, Mr. Charpentier wrung out a cloth in the warm water and started using it to tend to the child… who was quite completely and utterly naked.

Sophie's blush threatened to become permanent. There were certain body parts not intended for exposure to the broad light of day, much less such gleeful exposure. The baby was grinning and cooing as Mr. Charpentier deftly used the rag to clean what needed to be cleaned. When he seized both of the child's ankles in one hand and lifted the baby partly off the rug to reach a little farther back, the infant started laughing, as if being handled like that was great, good fun.

Mr. Charpentier set the nasty rag aside and tickled

the baby's tummy. The child grabbed at the man's hand and caught one long index finger in his tiny fist.

"I've been taken prisoner by a fierce pirate." He shook his finger gently, which inspired the baby to kick madly. "If you'd slide the nappy under the pirate's bottom, we'll see to his attire."

Bottom. Well, what else was there to call it?

She attempted to comply, when Mr. Charpentier again half raised the child by the ankles.

"Other way, Miss Windham. We'll use the tapes to fasten the thing on him. As much energy as he has, a snug fit is called for."

She repositioned the diaper but had to move in close to man and baby to get it done. Kneeling side by side with Mr. Charpentier, she made the mistake of glancing over at him.

At the coaching inn, she'd been nigh distraught over the baby's increasing discontent. Joleen had been gone long enough that Sophie had begun to worry, and thinking what to do over the baby's crying had been impossible.

And then a quiet, calm male voice right beside her. "May I be of assistance?"

She'd wanted to snap at him something to the effect that it was the baby needing assistance—she was perfectly fine—then stomp away with the dratted child before she started yelling herself.

Except the gravity of his voice, coupled with blue eyes so full of kindness and concern, had her passing him the baby without further question.

She'd never realized babies were so heavy. It wasn't that they were large; it was that one could never put them down for a moment—or if one did put them down, one assumed a burden of anxiety of greater weight than the actual child, which had one picking the little person up again, no matter how tired one's arms were.

"Watch carefully, Miss Windham. This is an arcane and closely guarded Portmaine family secret."

He picked up both the tapes on one side, but the child thwarted the adult's attempt to secure the nappy by dodging south with one small hand and grabbing stoutly onto his own…

"My goodness!"

The baby grinned, the man smiled as well, and Sophie wished the floor would swallow her up immediately and permanently.

"He's just a baby, Miss Windham. He knows only what feels good, and there's no harm in it, really." Gently, the man disentangled the child's hand from that portion of the male anatomy for which Sophie's brothers had endless names.

And Sophie herself had not a one she'd speak aloud.

Mr. Charpentier leaned in close over the baby, so close his wheat-blond hair fell forward over his shoulders. "You are scandalizing the lady, young Kit. Desist, I say." He shook his head from side to side, making his hair swing. The baby cooed his delight, barely missing Mr. Charpentier's chin with a small heel.

And all the while, the man had been deftly tying the nappy closed at the sides with two neat bows that would be easy to untie when the need arose.

"How often is this necessary?" Sophie asked.

"Very often." The man leaned forward, crouching

on all fours over the child. "Because we are a very healthy, busy baby, aren't we, Master Kit?" He shook his hair for the infant again, provoking more squealing and kicking and grinning.

It wasn't dignified in the least, the way the grown man crouching on the floor played with the child—made a fool of himself to entertain a stranger's abandoned baby.

Not dignified, but it was… oddly endearing.

Sophie felt an urge to get up and put some distance between herself and this tomfoolery on the floor, and yet she had to wonder too: if she brushed a lock of her hair over the child's nose, would the baby take as much delight in it?

She sat back. "How is it you know so much about babies?"

"My half sisters are a great deal younger than my brother and I. We more or less raised them, and this is part of the drill. He'll likely nap next, as outings tend to tire them when they're this young."

He crouched low over the child and used his mouth to make a rude noise on the baby's belly. The child exploded with glee, grabbing wildly for Mr. Charpentier's hair and managing to catch his nose.

It was quite a handsome nose in the middle of quite a handsome face. She'd noticed this at the coaching inn, in that first instant when he'd offered to help. She'd turned to find the source of the lovely, calm voice and found herself looking up into a face that put elegant masculine bones to the best possible use.

His eyes were just the start of it—a true pale blue that suggested Norse ancestry, set under arching blond brows. It was a lean face, with a strong jaw and well-defined chin—Sophie could not abide a weak chin nor the artifices of facial hair men sported to cover one up.

But none of that, not even the nose and chin and eyes combined, prepared Sophie for the visceral impact of more than six feet of Wilhelm Charpentier crouched on the floor, entertaining a baby.

He smiled at the child as if one small package of humanity merited all the grace and benevolence a human heart could express. He beamed at the child, looked straight into the baby's eyes, and communicated bottomless approval and affection without saying a word.

It was… daunting. It was undignified, and yet Sophie sensed there was a kind of wisdom in the man's handling of the baby she herself would lack.

"He'll get drowsy soon." Mr. Charpentier shifted back onto his heels. "That's the best part, when they're all sweet and snuggly. Little buggers wrap us around their fingers without even trying."

"You sound pleased about this."

He turned his head, his smile fading as he regarded her. "When a fellow is likely to end up in a foundling home through no fault of his own, or left on the church steps in the middle of winter, he'd better have a mighty lot of charm stored up if he isn't to die before he learns to walk."

He'd spoken quietly, but Sophie had to look away. Her gaze scanned the snowy back gardens, a sight as bleak as the prospect Mr. Charpentier described.

"I don't know how to change a nappy, Mr. Charpentier. I don't know what Kit likes to eat, I don't know how to… entertain him, but I do know he won't be going to any foundling home. Not now, not ever."

He regarded her with an odd gravity for a man seated on the floor. "You're sure about this?"

She nodded. "If the family didn't turn Joleen out when her difficulty became apparent, if we didn't turn her out when the child came along, if we provided for the child thus far, and we provided coach fare home for Joleen, we'll not be turning our backs on Kit now."

The decisions had been hers, the matter tacitly left to her discretion by Their Graces' inaction, just as all the family strays eventually ended up in Sophie's care. Sophie had decided the holidays were a fine time to let Joleen and her child make their way home, though Joleen herself had seemed reluctant to go.

"I expect Joleen's family would not have welcomed her, much less her child," Sophie said, the conviction growing even as she spoke.

"And she could not bring herself to consign him to a slow death by black drop, courtesy of the parish." Mr. Charpentier's tone was mild as he began slipping a dress over Kit's head, but something in the angle of his jaw suggested anger. "Joleen gambled her child's life on your kindness."

He had Kit dressed in no time and was soon slipping wool socks over the baby's chubby feet. "Would you like to hold him, Miss Windham?"

"Me?"

"You did well enough at the inn and on the way home." He tucked the shawl around the baby and picked him up. "He'll likely nod off to sleep if you take the rocking chair."

"I suppose it can't be too difficult."

"Easiest thing in the world." He got to his feet, holding the baby without the least awkwardness, and even extended a hand to assist Sophie to her feet.

It was a large hand, clean and elegant—also warm. Maybe that was why Kit liked it when Mr. Charpentier played with his toes.

"Take the rocker. I'll hand him to you."

She complied, feeling an odd bolt of nervousness as she did. She'd held this baby—not for long, not very confidently, but she had.

"He likes to be right near you, skin to skin if possible. He likes the warmth, and he even likes to hear your heart beat."

"He told you this, did he?" She accepted the bundle of baby from Mr. Charpentier's grasp, a maneuver that had him leaning in close enough she could catch the scent of bergamot about his person. Bergamot and soap, maybe a little laundry starch, nothing more. No tobacco, no sweat, no horse, nothing. The baby probably liked that about him too.

"Support his head." Mr. Charpentier slipped his hand beneath Sophie's where she'd wrapped hers around the back of the baby's skull. "We'll put him on his tummy next time he's romping on the floor and see how strong his neck is. If he's about to crawl, he'll have no trouble holding his head up. Ah, there. Going for the thumb. That's a sure sign a nap is on the way."

The child slurped on his own left thumb stoutly, while Mr. Charpentier remained kneeling beside the rocker. It should have been a prosaic, unremarkable moment, but holding the baby in her arms, the man at her side keeping watch over woman and child both, what Sophie felt was a profound and strange intimacy.

⁓

Wilhelm Charpentier had spent a substantial portion of every one of the past fifteen years sailing for purposes of trade. He'd kept mainly to the Baltic and North Seas when his siblings had been young, then branched out to the Mediterranean, until he'd eventually made his way to China, the Antipodes and a circumnavigation of the globe.

He'd heard dozens of languages, eaten unpronounceable dishes by the score, learned of all manner of exotic practices between men and women, but he'd never before seen a woman truly, visibly fall in love.

While he knelt on the carpet beside a scarred old rocking chair in a lowly servants' parlor, he *saw* Sophie Windham fall in love. It came over her in a matter of moments, put a soft sparkle in her eyes and a warmth in her smile, and most of all, it changed the way she touched the object of her affection.

Little Kit went from being a potentially malodorous bundle of trouble to the one person on earth she'd die to protect. She laid him in her lap, taking both of his wrists in her hands, leaving him free to kick his shawl away, grinning and cooing at her while she steadied him with her hands.

"Such a strong fellow you are." She smiled down at him, bringing his hands together then gently spreading them wide again. "I applaud your strength, Master Kit.

A sturdy young man like you will be riding to hounds by his second birthday."

Vim had the sure conviction Sophie Windham had never voiced such nonsensical utterances in her life. He tore his gaze from the lady and child and sat back to catch a glimpse of the weather through the windows.

Ye almighty gods. He needed to be leaving. The light would soon be gone, the temperature would drop, and the snow would only get deeper as darkness fell. It seemed like a metaphor for Vim's life, but he could at least take with him the knowledge Kit would be safe and loved and as happy as one devoted female could make him.

"I think he's tiring," Miss Windham said softly. She tucked the shawl around the baby and cradled him in her arms. "How long is he likely to nap?"

Vim went to the hearth to poke up the fire—just the thought of going out in the storm made his insides curdle—and considered the question.

"However long you think he should sleep, he won't. If he's been larking around all day, and you think he's entitled to sleep for hours, he'll catnap. If you think he slept late in the morning and has hardly stirred from his blankets, he'll go down after luncheon and barely be up in time for his dinner. Babies delight in confounding us, and it's their God-given right to do so."

"His eyes are closing."

Vim had to smile. She hadn't heard a word he'd said, so fascinated was Sophie Windham with one rather ordinary baby.

Except there were no ordinary babies. Not in England, not on the Continent, not among the natives on any continent in any culture. There had never been an ordinary baby—not to the child's mother, in any case.

"Miss Windham, I really must be going."

That got her attention. She peered up at him, her expression disgruntled.

"Must you? Will you at least let me feed you before you go? The taverns and public houses will be full to the brim, and you have been quite kind to both Kit and me. I haven't even offered you a decent cup of tea, so you really cannot be going just yet, Mr. Charpentier."

She rose with the child, her hold on him as confident and relaxed as if this were her fifth baby. She was perhaps old enough to have had five babies—she wasn't a girl by any means—but her figure belied the notion entirely.

Sophie Windham was blessed with a body a courtesan would envy. Devoid of cloaks and shawls and capes, Vim could assess her womanly charms all too easily.

"I appreciate the offer, Miss Windham, but the sooner I'm on my way, the sooner I'll be able to find lodging with friends. Your offer is much appreciated nonetheless." He reached for his greatcoat, still draped over a chair, but she advanced toward him, determination etched on her features.

"Sir, I am virtually alone in this house with a helpless child dependent on me for his every need. I have no idea how to feed him. I know not how or when to bathe him. I haven't the first idea when his bedtime should be or what do with him upon waking. The least you can do is impart some knowledge to me before you go wandering the streets of Mayfair."

The angle of her chin said she'd stop him bodily. Maternal instinct, whether firsthand or vicarious, was nothing a sane man sought to thwart.

"Perhaps just a cup of tea."

"Nonsense." She eyed him up and down. "You've likely had nothing to eat since dawn, and that was probably cold, lumpy porridge with neither butter nor honey nor even a smidgen of jam. Come along."

He once again fell in step behind her, but this time he was free to admire the twitch of her skirts. If she wasn't the housekeeper, she was likely a personal companion to the lady of the house. She had that much self-possession, and no woman her age would have been left unchaperoned by her family were she a member of the actual household.

"Have a seat," she said, nodding at a plant table in the middle of the big kitchen. "I'll put us together a tea tray, and you can tell me what Kit will eat."

She was bustling around the kitchen with the particular one-handed efficiency parents of a very small child developed. The boy would be attached to her hip in a few days, or her back…

"Give me the baby." He held up his arms and saw she was tempted to argue. "If you're working around boiling water and hot stoves, he's safer with me."

She relented, handing him the baby then tucking the shawl more closely around the child. She hovered for a moment near Vim and the baby now cradled in his arms, then straightened. "If you'll hold him, I can put together a bit more than a cup of tea."

She took an apron down from a hook and tied it around her waist in practiced moves, which made for another piece of the puzzle of Sophie Windham: a lady's maid would never condescend to kitchen work, though in the absence of the cook, a house-keeper might.

"Has the family closed the house up for the holidays then?" He rubbed Kit's back, not for the child's comfort—the little shoat was fast asleep—but for his own.

"They went down to Kent early this year and gave most of the staff leave. Higgins and Merriweather will bide over the carriage house to keep an eye on the stock, and they'll bring up more coal from the cellar if I ask it of them. Would you like an omelet? There's a fine cheddar in the pantry, and the spice rack is freshly stocked."

He needed to be going, true, but negotiating the weather on an empty stomach would be foolish. "An omelet sounds wonderful, but don't go to any trouble."

She smiled at him as she bustled into the pantry. "I like to cook, though this is a closely guarded secret. What should I be feeding Kit?"

"Bland foods, of course. Porridge with a bit of butter and a dash of sugar, though my nurse always said honey wasn't good for babies. Mashed potatoes with a touch of butter. Boiled vegetables, plain oatmeal."

"What about meat?"

He cast back over more than two decades of memory. "Not yet, and not much fruit, either. Strawberries gave my youngest sister hives when she was a baby, so I wouldn't advise them. Pudding was always very popular in the nursery."

"If the weather weren't so foul, I'd send one of the

grooms over to fetch Nanny Fran from Westhaven's townhouse. Do you like onions in your omelet?"

"A few."

The kitchen was soon full of the scent of good, simple cooking. He watched as Miss Windham cut slices from a fresh loaf of bread then slipped them onto a tray for toasting. She moved with a competence that spoke of time served in the kitchen, and yet she could not possibly be the cook: if the entire household had been given leave, there was no point in the cook remaining for just two grooms.

"Where do you hail from, Mr. Charpentier?"

"Here and there. The family seat is in Kent, though I was raised at my stepfather's holding in Cumbria. I'm a merchant by profession, trading mostly with the Americans and the Scandinavians these days."

"I've never seen Cumbria, though I'm told it's lovely." She spoke as she worked, the epitome of domestic tranquility.

"Cumbria's lovely in summer. Winter can be another matter altogether."

"Will you be with family for the holidays?"

He was distracted momentarily from answering by the picture she made standing at the stove, watching the omelet cook as she occasionally peeked at the toast and also assembled the accoutrements of a tea tray.

Why wasn't she with family? He barely knew the woman, but seeing her here, cooking for him, making him feel welcome with small talk and chatter while the snow came down in torrents outside, he felt a stab of something... poignant, sentimental.

Something lonely?

"I'll be with my uncle and his family. I have half siblings, but my sisters have seen fit to get married recently, and one doesn't want to impose on the newlyweds."

"One does not. Three of my brothers have married, and it can leave a sister not knowing quite how to go on with them. Pepper?"

"A touch."

"Is he asleep?"

"Never ask. If he is, it will wake him up. If he isn't, it will let him know you're fixed on that goal, and he'll thwart you to uphold the honor of babies the world over."

She smiled at the omelet as she neatly turned it in the skillet. "Her Grace raised ten children in this house. She would likely agree with you."

A ducal household? No wonder even the domestics carried themselves with a certain confidence.

When he might have asked which duke's hospitality he was imposing on—his half brother had regular truck with titles of all sorts—she brought the tea tray to the table, then cutlery and a steaming plate of eggs and bacon. She set the latter before him and stood back, hands on hips.

"If you'll give me the baby, I can hold him while you eat."

"And what about you? As a gentleman..." But she was already extricating the child from his arms and taking a seat on the bench along the opposite side of the table.

"Eat, Mr. Charpentier. The food will only get cold while we argue."

He ate. He ate in part because a gentleman never argued with a lady and in part because he was starving. She'd served him a sizeable portion, and he was halfway through the omelet, bacon, and toast when he looked up to see her regarding him from across the table.

"You were hungry."

"You are a good cook. Is that oregano in the eggs?"

"A little of this and that."

He paused and put his fork down. "A secret family recipe, Miss Windham?"

She just smiled and pretended to tuck the shawl around the sleeping baby; then her brow knit. "Earlier today you mentioned a Portmaine family secret. Is this your wife's family?"

It was a logical question. It could not possibly be that this brisk, prim woman was inquiring as to his marital status. "My mother remarried when my father died. Portmaine was my stepfather's family name. It is not my good fortune to be married."

She nodded, and Vim went back to devouring the only decent food he'd had in almost a week of traveling. Yes, he could have taken the traveling coach from Blessings, but Blessings and all its appurtenances belonged to his younger half brother, who might have need of the traveling coach himself.

So Vim hadn't asked. He'd taken himself off, traveling as he often did among the common folk of the land.

"Did you ever want to marry, Mr. Charpentier?"

He looked across the table at Miss Windham to see she was again pretending to fuss with the baby, but a slight blush on her cheek told him he'd heard her question aright.

"I always expected to marry," he said slowly. His uncle certainly expected him to marry—ten or twelve years ago would have suited the old man nicely. "I suppose I haven't met the right lady. You?"

"What girl doesn't expect to marry? There was a time when my fondest wish was to marry and have a family of my own. Not a very original wish, I'm afraid." She shifted the baby and reached across the table to pour them each a cup of tea. As long as she'd let it steep, Vim could smell the pungent fragrance of the steam curling up from his cup.

"Darjeeling?"

"One of my brothers favors it. How do you take your tea, Mr. Charpentier?"

"My friends call me Vim, and I will be fixing the tea for you, Miss Windham, seeing as your friend is yet asleep in your arms."

She frowned, but it was a thoughtful expression, not disapproving. "My friends call me Sophie, and my siblings do. You may call me that if you like."

It wasn't a good idea, this exchange of Christian names. Watching some subtle emotion play across Miss Windham's—Sophie's—face, Vim had the sense she allowed few to address her so familiarly. He wouldn't have made the gesture if he weren't soon to be leaving, never to see this good lady again.

"Sophie, then. Miss Sophie. Will you eat now? I can hold Kit."

"You're sure you've had enough?"

"I have eaten every crumb, so yes." He rose and came around the table, reaching down to retrieve the baby. She didn't hand him up, though, so when Vim reached for the child, his arm extended a little too far, to the point where his hand slid a few inches down Miss Windham's breastbone before he could get a decent grip on the child.

Down her breastbone and along the side of one full breast.

The contact lasted not even a second and involved the back of his hand and her bodice, nothing more, but Vim had to work to keep the frisson of lust that shot through him from showing on his face—a moment of sexual awareness as surprising as it was intense.

The lady, for her part, took a sip of her tea, looking not the least discomposed.

"Best eat quickly," Vim said, settling the child in his arms. "You never know when My Lord Baby will rouse, and then the needs of everyone else can go hang. It was a very good omelet."

"Is there such a thing as a bad omelet?" She ate daintily but steadily, not even glancing up at him while she spoke.

"Yes, there is, but we won't discuss it further while you eat." He resumed his seat across from her, the weight of the baby a warm comfort against his middle. Avis and Alex could both be carrying already, a thought that sent another pang of that unnameable sentiment through him.

"What else can you tell me about caring for Kit, Mr. Char—" She paused and smiled slightly. "Vim. What else can you tell me, Vim?"

"I can tell you it's fairly simple, Miss Sophie: you feed him when he's hungry, change him when he's wet, and cuddle him when he's fretful."

She set down her utensils and gazed at the baby.

"But how do you tell the difference between hungry and fretful?"

Her expression was so earnest, Vim had to smile. "You cuddle him, and if his fussing subsides, then he wasn't hungry, he was just lonely. If he keeps fussing, you offer him some nourishment, and so on. He'll tell you what's amiss."

"But that other business, at the coaching inn. You knew he was uncomfortable, and to me it wasn't in the least obvious what the trouble was."

"And now you know he needs to be burped when he's filled his tummy. Your tea will get cold."

She took a sip, but he didn't think she tasted it, so fixed was she on the mystery of communicating with a baby. She continued to pepper him with questions as she finished her meal and tended to the dishes, not untying her apron until the kitchen was once again spotless.

By that point, Vim had been making slow circuits of the kitchen with the child in his arms. He had less than an hour of light left, and it really was time to be going.

"I thank you for the meal, Miss Sophie, and I will recall your cooking with fondness as I continue my travels. If you'll take Kit, I'll fetch my coat from the parlor and wish you good day."

He passed her the baby, making very sure that this time his hand came nowhere near her person.

∽

He was leaving.

This realization provoked something close to panic in Sophie's usually composed mind. She told herself she was merely concerned for the baby, being left in the care of a woman who had still—still!—never changed a single nappy.

But there was a little more to it than that. More she was not about to dwell on. Mature women of nearly seven-and-twenty did not need to belabor the obvious when they fell prey to unbecoming infatuations and fancies.

"I wish you'd stay." The words were out before she could censor herself.

"I beg your pardon?" He paused in the act of rolling his cuffs down muscular forearms dusted with sandy, golden hair. How could a man have beautiful forearms?

She bent her head to kiss the baby on his soft, fuzzy little crown. "I have no notion how to go on with this child, Mr. Charpentier, and those old fellows in the carriage house likely have even less. I realize I ought not to ask it of you, but I am quite alone in this house."

"Which is the very reason I cannot stay, madam. Surely you comprehend that?"

He spoke gently, quietly, and Sophie understood the point he was making. Gentlemen and ladies never stayed under the same roof unchaperoned.

Except with him—with Vim Charpentier—she wasn't Lady Sophia Windham. She'd made that decision at the coaching inn, where announcing her titled status would have served no point except to get her pocket picked. Higgins was old enough to address her as Miss Sophie, and being Miss Sophie was proving oddly appealing. A housekeeper or companion could be Miss Sophie; a duke's daughter could not.

"This weather will be making all manner of strange bedfellows, Mr. Charpentier. And if we're alone, who is to know if propriety hasn't been strictly observed?"

"This is not a good idea, Miss Windham."

"Going out in that storm is a better idea?"

She let the question dangle between his gentlemanly concerns about propriety and the commonsense needs of a woman newly burdened with a small baby. When he turned to stand near the window, Sophie sent up a little prayer that common sense was going win out over gentlemanly scruples. The baby whimpered in his sleep, which had Mr. Charpentier sending her a thoughtful look.

"I can stay, but just for one night, and I'll be off at first light. There is some urgency about the balance of my journey."

"Thank you. Kit and I both thank you." She had the oddest urge to kiss his cheek.

She kissed the baby instead. "Come along, and I can show you to a guest room."

He retrieved his haversack from the back hallway and followed along behind her, a big, silent presence. She could feel him taking in the trappings of a duke's Town residence but hoped he saw the little things that made it a home too.

The servants had decorated before leaving for the season—pine boughs scented the mantels, red ribbons decorated tall beeswax candles that would have been lit at the New Year and on Twelfth Night were the family in residence. Cinnamon sachets and clove-studded oranges hung in the hallways, and wreaths graced the windows facing the street.

"Their Graces must take their holidays seriously," Mr. Charpentier observed. "Is that a Christmas tree?"

Sophie paused outside the half-open door of one of the smaller parlors. "Her Grace's mother was German, like much of the old king's court. The Christmas trees were originally for Oma, so she wouldn't be as lonely for her homeland."

She wondered what he'd say if he knew he was peering around at a duchess's personal sitting room. Mama served her daughters and sons tea and scoldings in this room, also wisdom, sympathy, and love.

Always love.

Sophie stood for a moment, the baby cradled on her shoulder, Mr. Charpentier close by her side in the doorway. She was going to associate bergamot with this moment for a long while to come, the first time she'd shown a visitor of her own around the house—a visitor of hers and Kit's.

She waited for Vim to step back then continued their progress. "Your room is on the first floor. The servants' stair goes right to the back hallway, though the main staircase is the prettier route."

She took him through the front entrance with its presentation staircase of carved oak. The whole foyer was a forest of polished wood—the walls and ceiling both paneled, the banisters lathe turned, and half columns with fanciful pediments and capitals standing in each corner of the octagonal space. The wood was maintained with such a high shine of beeswax and lemon oil that sunny days saw more light bouncing around the foyer than in practically any other part of the house.

"I take it Their Graces entertain a fair amount?" He was coming up the stairs behind her, as a gentleman would.

"His Grace is quite active in the Lords, so yes."

"And Her Grace?"

"She keeps her hand in. They also have the occasional summer house party at the family seat. This room ought to serve for the night."

She'd taken him not to a guest room but to her brother Valentine's old room in the family wing. The wood box would be full, the coal bucket filled, a fire laid, and the bed made up in anticipation of his lordship's visit to Town to collect his sister.

"I'm sorry it's so chilly. I'll bring you up some water for the room. Let me show you the bathing chamber. As far as I know, the fire under the boiler should still have some coals."

The bathing chamber was across the hall, a renovated dressing room having had the ideal location between cisterns and chimneys.

"This is quite modern," Mr. Charpentier said. "You're sure Their Graces would not mind your sharing such accommodations with a virtual stranger?"

They'd mind. They wouldn't begrudge him the best comforts the mansion could offer, but they'd mind mightily that he had Sophie's exclusive company.

"A duke's household doesn't skimp on hospitality, Mr. Charpentier, though by rights we should be providing you a valet and footmen to step and fetch."

"I'm used to doing for myself, though where will I find you should the need arise?"

"I'm just down the hallway, last door on the right."

And it was time to leave him, but she hesitated, casting around for something more to say. The idea of spending another long, cold evening reading by firelight seemed like a criminal waste when she could be sharing those hours with Mr. Charpentier. The baby let out a little sigh in her arms, maybe an indication of some happy baby dream—or her own unfulfilled wishes.

"Shall I bring the cradle up from the servants' parlor, Miss Sophie?"

The cradle?

"Yes. The cradle. That would be helpful. I suppose I should get some nappies from the laundry and clean dresses and so forth."

He smiled, as if he knew her mind had gone somewhere besides the need to care for the baby, but he said nothing. Just set his bag down, went to the hearth to light the fire, and left Sophie standing in the door with the child cradled in her arms.

"You'll find your way to the bathing chamber if you need it?"

He rose and began using a taper to add candlelight to the meager gloom coming from the windows. "I've made do with so much less than you're offering me, Miss Sophie. Travel makes a man realize what little he needs to be comfortable and how easily he can mistake a mere want for a need. I'll be fine."

His circuit of the room brought him back to her side. He blew out the taper and speared her with a look. "Will you be fine?"

She liked standing close to him, not only because he wore a pleasant scent, but also because something about his male presence, the grace and strength of it, appealed to her dormant femininity. If all men had his manners, competence, and sheer male beauty, being a woman would be a much more appetizing proposition.

Sophie took her courage in both hands and gazed up at him. "I'd like to hear about those travels, Mr. Charpentier. About the worst memories and best memories, the most beautiful places and the most unappealing. I've lived my entire life in the confines of England, and tales of your travels would give my imagination something to keep when you've left."

He studied her for a moment then lifted one hand. Her breath seized in her lungs when she thought— hoped?—he was going to touch her. To touch her cheek or her hair, to lay his palm along her jaw.

He laid his hand over the baby's head. "If My Lord Baby gives us a peaceful evening, I'll tell you some of my stories, Miss Sophie. It's hardly a night for going out on the Town, is it?"

It was better than if he'd touched her, to know he'd give her some tales of his travels, something of his own history and his own memories.

"After you've settled in, then. I'll see you in the parlor downstairs. We'll see you."

Except the baby in her arms was seeing nothing at that moment but peaceful, happy baby dreams.

Three

VIM'S LITTLE TRIP THROUGH THE DUCAL MANSION revealed a few interesting facts about the household. For example, money was not a problem for this particular ducal family.

The servants' parlor was a comfortable place for furniture, carpets, and curtains that had seen some use, but it was far from shabby. The bathing chamber was a gleaming little space of pipes and marble counters that spoke of both available coin and a willingness to enjoy the fruits of progress.

The main entrance was a testament to somebody's appreciation for first impressions and appearances. The whole house was gracious, beautiful, and meticulously maintained.

Also festooned with all manner of seasonal decorations, which usually struck Vim as so much wasted effort. Pine boughs quickly wilted and dropped needles all over creation. Clove-studded oranges withered into ugly parodies of their original state. Wreaths soon turned brown, and Christmas trees had to be undecorated as carefully as they were decorated—assuming they didn't catch fire and set the entire house ablaze.

A lot of bother for nothing, or so he would have said.

But in this house...

He finished his bath and found a clean pair of pajama trousers as well as a clean pair of winter wool socks. Though the vast canopied bed beckoned, Vim instead appropriated a brocade dressing gown from the store in the wardrobe and made his way back through the house to the little servants' parlor.

He opened the door without knocking and found Miss Sophie within, on her feet, the baby fussing in her arms.

"I don't know what's wrong." Sophie's voice was laden with concern. "He keeps fussing and fretting but he isn't... it isn't his nappy, and he doesn't want for cuddling. I don't think he has to settle his stomach either."

Vim sidled into the room, closing the door behind him. "He's probably hungry again. Marvelous accommodations upstairs, by the way." And a marvelously warm silk lining in the dressing gown.

The child quieted at the sound of his voice, turning great blue eyes on Vim. Vim peered down at the baby cradled against Sophie's middle. "Are you hungry, young Kit, or simply rioting for the fun of it?"

The child slurped on his little left fist.

"Hungry it is. Have you any cold porridge in the kitchen, Miss Sophie?"

"No doubt we do, but he just ate not three hours ago. Are you sure he isn't sickening for something?"

In those same three hours, Sophie had apparently

gone from benevolent stranger to mother-at-large, capable of latching onto every parent's single worst, most abiding fear.

Vim laid the back of his hand on the baby's brow. "He's only yelling-baby-warm, not fevered, so no, I don't think he's sickening. Often when they're coming down with something, they grow a bit lethargic. He's at the mercy of a very small belly and has to eat more often than he will later in life. This belly here."

He poked the baby's middle gently, which provoked a toothless grin.

"Why didn't I know he'd like that?"

"Likely because you yourself would not react as cheerfully did I make the same overture to you. Why don't I take him while you hunt him up some tucker? A bit of warm milk to mix the porridge very thin and a baby spoon will get us started."

Sophie nodded and stepped in close. It took Vim a moment to comprehend that she was handing him the baby, and in that moment, his eyes fell on her hair. Some women thought an elaborate coiffure adorned with jewels and combs and all manner of intricacies would call attention to their beauty.

Others cut their hair short, attempting boyish ringlets and bangs and labeling themselves daring in the name of fashion.

Still others went for a half-tumbled look, presenting themselves as if caught in the act of rising from a bout of thorough lovemaking.

Sophie's hair was a rich, dark brown, and she wore it pulled back into a tidy bun. For the space of a heartbeat, Vim was close enough to her to study her hair, to admire the simple, sleek curve of it sweeping back from her face to her nape. He could not see any pins or clasps, nothing to secure it in place, and the bun itself was some sort of figure of eight, twisting in on itself without apparent external support.

Which was quietly pretty, a little intriguing, and quite appropriate for Miss Sophie Windham. And if Vim's fingers itched to undo that prim bun and his eyes longed for the sight of her unbound hair tumbling around her shoulders in intimate disarray, he was gentleman enough to ignore such inconvenient impulses entirely.

"I've got him," Vim said, securing his hands around the baby. "Though I have to say, I think a certain baby has gained weight just since coming home from his outing."

Sophie's smile was hesitant. "You like to tease him."

"He's a wonderful, jolly baby." Vim raised the child in his arms so they could touch noses. "Jolly babies are much better company than those other fellows, the ones who shriek and carry on at the drop of a hat."

His nose was taken prisoner once more, which had been the objective of the exercise.

"I'll see to the porridge."

But she'd been smiling as she left the room, which had also been an objective. To be a mother was to worry, but a worried mama made for a worried baby.

"And we cannot have you worrying," Vim informed the child. "Not like I'm worrying in any case. I was supposed to be at Sidling last week—much as I dread being there this time of year—and there will be hell to pay for my lingering here, though have you chanced a look out the window, My Lord Baby? See all that snow?"

Kit kicked both legs in response and gurgled happily, then slapped his fist back to his mouth.

"I last saw snow like this in Russia. Damned place specializes in cold, dark, snow, and vodka, which explains a lot about the Russian character. And because it's just us fellows, I need not apologize for my language. Can you say damn? It's a nice, tame curse, a good place to start. Nobody curses as effectively as a Russian. Nobody."

And nobody could lament like a Russian either, to the point where Vim had left the country with a sense of relief to be going back to England. Long faces everywhere, sad tales, sad songs, sad prayers, and vodka.

"Nearly drove me to Bedlam, I tell you."

Africa hadn't been any better though, nor Tasmania. The Americas were reasonably cheerful places, provided a man didn't venture too far north or south, nor too far inland.

Kit whimpered and swung his fist toward Vim's nose again.

"You want your supper or your tea or whatever. Don't worry, Miss Sophie will be stepping and fetching for you directly. You're going to be a typical male, relying on the women for all the important things— though you're a little small yet for that discussion."

"Mr. Charpentier, are you having a conversation with that child?"

Sophie stood in the doorway, a tray in her hands and her head cocked at a curious angle.

"He won't learn to speak if all he hears is silence." Though Vim had to wonder how much Miss Sophie had heard. "Do you want that cat in here?"

An enormous, long-haired black animal was stropping itself against her skirts.

"That's Elizabeth. He's earned a little nap by the fire." The cat continued to bob around her hems, its gait a far cry from a feline's usual sinuous movement.

"What's wrong with him?"

She nudged the door closed with her hip and set the tray down on a coffee table. "Nothing is wrong with him; he's simply missing a front leg. How do we feed that child?"

Indeed, upon closer inspection, under all the hair, the cat was managing on only three legs, and that in addition to the burden of being a tom named Elizabeth. "Let's use the sofa. I'll demonstrate, and then you can take over."

He settled with the baby then waited while Sophie took a seat just a few inches away. The cat—lucky beast—curled himself up against her other hip.

"This is a messy proposition, but it's all in good fun," Vim explained. "You can't load up the spoon with too much—his mouth is quite small, and he'll manage to get the excess all over creation. You also have to prop him up a bit to help him get the food down rather than up. When he starts batting at the spoon or using the spoon like a catapult, you know he's through for the time being."

"How does a new mother learn all of this?"

"The baby teaches her, and I expect a mama's sisters and cousins and grandmothers lend a hand. In my experience, the younger a man is, the more the ladies admire him. Isn't that right, Kit?"

His use of the baby's name had the child turning to regard him, which opportunity Vim used to slip a spoonful of porridge into the infant's mouth.

"Success. There, you see? He was hungry."

The baby kicked in agreement and opened his little maw again, fists waving while Vim navigated another spoonful of porridge down the hatch.

"We're off to a great start. Would you like to try the next one?" He passed her the spoon and saw her expression shift to one of determination.

"It's as you said earlier, isn't it?" She dipped the spoon into the porridge. "One should be quick and calm, like with the animals."

"Precisely." She had the knack of it immediately, slipping the child his food without little fists or little feet interfering.

And she was so absorbed in her task, leaning over the child and talking to him of his great appetite and wonderful manners, that she was apparently oblivious to her full, warm breast pressing continuously against Vim's arm.

She wasn't his usual type—a bored wife looking for a casual diversion or a professional willing to spend an evening with a foreign lord. But then, it had been a long time since he'd indulged his sexual appetites.

Sophie would call them his base urges, if she referred to them in any manner. Except her breast against his arm didn't feel base. It felt soft and lovely and almost as comforting as it was arousing.

He didn't examine the problem in any detail

because he was a man who'd long since learned to govern his lust. Neglecting his sexual recreation had simply taken a toll, catching him unaware before a warm fire with an attractive woman.

Not pretty, precisely, but attractive.

Sophie sat back, regarding the baby. "Is he finished?"

Vim glanced at Kit, who was wearing some porridge around his rosy cheeks. "Give it one more try."

She got the spoon into the baby's mouth, but Kit spit his porridge right back out again.

"My goodness. Rude but effective." She produced a rag and got Kit's little phiz cleaned up with a few brisk swipes. "Will he go back to sleep?"

"Is that hope I hear in your voice, Miss Sophie?"

She smiled sheepishly. "I don't suppose it can all be cooing and sleeping, can it?"

"At first there's a great deal of sleeping, but then they start to notice their world, and the fun begins. Let's let him romp a bit, shall we?"

He rose with the baby before the urge to put an arm around Sophie's shoulders overpowered his good sense. Babies did this. They created a capacity for maudlin sentimentality in all who beheld them. It was a response determined by God to give the little blighters a fighting chance in a world with little enough tolerance for sentiment.

Vim couldn't resent the child for it, but neither would he fall prey to the baby's charm. He was leaving in the morning, and that was that.

"How does a fellow romp at his age?" Sophie remained on the sofa, one hand stroking lazily over the cat. Vim could hear the animal purring from several feet away.

"We'll see." He patted Kit's back gently on the off chance a burp was brewing. "I don't think Kit is quite able to crawl yet, for which, God be thanked."

"Crawling is bad?"

"Crawling is dangerous." As he spoke, Vim arranged an afghan on the carpet then spread the baby's shawl on top of the blanket. "I expect crawling is half the reason the Elizabethans strapped their infants to cradle boards, chamber pots, and cribs."

A very small burp emerged from the very small baby.

Sophie glanced around the room, frowning. "How could it be dangerous to crawl? I thought it was a necessary prelude to walking."

"Come down here with us." Vim settled on his side along the blanket and patted the carpet. That she couldn't see the dangers was vaguely alarming. As of tomorrow, she'd be on her own with the child until her brothers showed up—and they, being men, were a dubious source of aid at best.

She sat beside him, her legs tucked around to the side. "He's getting up on all fours."

He was, his little nappied fundament pointing skyward until he got his chubby arms braced under him. When he gained his hands and knees, Kit looked around, grinning gleefully.

"Well done." Vim tapped the child's nose gently with one finger. More grinning and even some rocking in place. "He hasn't quite got it figured out yet."

"He will soon?"

"Any day, but consider that he'll soon be rollicking about and view the room from his perspective."

"What do you mean?"

Vim stretched out on his belly. "Join me."

She looked around dubiously then shifted to stretch out on the other side of the child.

"What do you see, Sophie?"

"I see the fireplace."

"Kit will see it too. He'll see the dancing flames and bright colors; he'll feel the warmth; he'll hear the hiss and pop of the occasional log; he'll see the shower of sparks."

"My goodness."

"What else do you see, Sophie?"

She was quiet a moment while Kit started babbling his pleasure at life in general. "I see the set of hearth tools, ready to come crashing down on a curious baby. I see standing lamps and nice frilly table runners, all ready to be pulled over by a fat little fist. I see things a fellow could put in his tiny mouth, and things that could strike him on his precious little head. I see... trouble."

She rolled to her back, eyes going to the baby. "How do they ever survive? How did Her Grace raise ten children?"

He shifted to his side to face her, so they were separated by one grinning, cooing baby. "She had help, I'm sure, but this is part of the reason the little ones are kept in the nursery. My guess is the hearths are raised there, so nobody can crawl into the ashes, and the shelves are built into the wall, so nothing can come crashing down on a fellow's head."

"They are." She sighed, eyes going to the ceiling. "And there are no table runners, no pretty little glass bowls full of flower petals, only toys that are quite sturdy."

"And a crib?"

"There are cribs up there, though Kit still fits nicely in his cradle."

"Except he'll soon be able to climb out of his cradle, won't he?"

"My goodness." She closed her eyes. She kept them closed when she resumed speaking. "I went to the maid's quarters to see if Joleen left anything for Kit."

"And?" Vim moved again, to lift the baby straight up over his chest. The child squealed with delight, paddling the air with both arms and legs.

"All of Kit's dresses and socks and little blankets were in a tidy pile on her bed. She meant to leave him."

He knew better. He should have pretended to be absorbed in the child's play, but he could hear something in Sophie's voice that had him bringing the baby down to his chest and regarding Sophie where she lay a couple of feet away.

"This upsets you."

She nodded, eyes still closed. While Vim watched, a single tear leaked from the corner of her eye and made a silvery track into the dark hair at her temple.

"Sophie, do you cry for the child or for the mother?"

"I never cry."

If he weren't lying nearly beside her, he might have believed all the starch in her voice despite the evidence of his eyes. He secured the baby to his chest with one hand and reached over with the other, brushing the back of one finger from the corner of her eye to her temple. "Never?"

She turned her head toward him so his hand ended up trapped under her cheek. He did not retrieve it.

"I'm in charge of strays." She spoke evenly, the tears still kept sternly from her voice. "All of my life, I was the one who could be counted on to nurse a rejected lamb, to find a litter to accept an orphaned kitten. Joleen went astray, so she became my charge to deal with. She should not have left Kit this way."

"Maybe she should not have had Kit, and this was the only way she could cope. How old was she?"

"Sixteen."

"Old enough to know better, Sophie." He ran his thumb over the smooth skin of her cheekbone and withdrew his hand. The gesture had been meant to comfort her; it had in fact comforted him.

"Take the baby." He lifted Kit high again. "He's in fine fettle, ready to conquer the world."

She glanced at Vim as if she suspected his suggestion was a tactic, which it was, but she took the child and cradled him on her sternum. "He is quite stout, isn't he?"

"He's just right for a man of his years, or months."

"And what shall I do with him now that I have him?"

"That's what's bothering you, isn't it?" Vim lay on his side, his head propped on a fist braced by his elbow. "You see the uncertainty Joleen introduced into his life with her decision, and responsibility for this stray is daunting."

She lifted the baby up, touched noses with him, and set the child back on her middle. "Daunting about sums it up. He could crawl into the fire, take a chill, pull the bookends down on himself... all in the space of moments. His life should last decades, but only if I can keep him safe and teach him how to go on."

"You could foster him." Vim watched as Sophie stroked a finger down the baby's cheek. The child turned to investigate the sensation while Sophie repeated the caress on the other cheek.

"I *should* foster him. I should find some nice lady with an infant of her own and pay handsomely for Kit to have lots of love and attention, other children to play with…" She closed her eyes again, a gesture Vim realized was Sophie's way of composing herself.

"Sophie, he's old enough to be weaned, if needs must."

"Is he? I don't even know when that would be. I've seen children larger than Vim still…" She fell silent and blinked at the baby.

"At the breast." Vim finished the thought for her.

"I was going to say dependent on their mothers. Nanny Fran said Joleen never had much milk. She said the girl was too fretful to nurse properly."

"I suppose that's possible. A fretful mare sometimes lacks enough for her foal. Kit looks healthy nonetheless."

"He does." She frowned at the child and tried lifting him up over her chest. When she had him positioned on straight arms above her, he started wiggling and paddling again. A slight smile bloomed on Sophie's mouth, just as the child emitted a particular… sound.

"Oh, dear." She lowered him gingerly. "I believe it's time I learned to change a nappy myself."

"Have we a clean supply?"

"In the laundry. I can get…" She started to rise,

but Vim put a hand on her shoulder as he shifted to a crouch.

"You stay. I'll fetch the goods." He didn't give her time to argue, but rather was out the door in no time, a single candle in his hand. Yes, it was important to retrieve what the baby needed for his hygiene, but it had also become important to get off of that floor and away from the woman lying on her back before the fire.

She cried for stray babies and probably for the stray mother too. If Vim did not mind the dictates of common sense, he'd be tucking himself close to her sweetness and heat, and when he left, she might be crying for the occasional stray baron as well.

❧

"I've learned something." Sophie addressed herself to the baby, who was giving off a certain scent, suggesting a clean nappy was an urgent need.

She told herself it was just a healthy baby smell. The equivalent of the scent of a stall that needed mucking, nothing more.

Kit made a swipe for her nose, which pleased her inordinately.

"I've learned something about why my parents are still so enthralled with each other after more than thirty years of marriage. It's little fellows like you who are partly responsible."

She let him catch her nose this time. It was lovely, to be caught by the nose. She kept talking, talking right into his tiny palm. "Their Graces raised ten such as you. Can you imagine how many nights they spent sprawled on the floor like this with My Lord Baby or My Lady Baby? Both of them watching the child, both of them feeling these sentiments of wonder and terror? It's all your fault, yours and those of your ilk."

Kit held on to her nose and smacked her cheek with his free hand.

"It is too. You coo and babble and smile at the world, more helpless than you even know, and you make us helpless too, helpless not to love you. Mr. Charpentier—Vim—has fallen under your spell."

She rose with the child in her arms, which freed her nose from the pirate baby's imprisoning grasp. "Mr. Charpentier is very charming too, isn't he?"

Kit emitted another noise, a surprisingly loud noise for such a little person.

"That was not charming, Kit."

Though to her, even that was a little endearing. The child didn't care what sounds or smells came from his body. He cared that he was safe and warm, his tummy full, and people around him who would see to his well-being.

And thank God for Wilhelm Charpentier. Thank God the man was willing to breach propriety for the sake of the child. Thank God for snowstorms that allowed Sophie to ask for such a thing.

Because as much help as Mr. Charpentier was with the baby, there was a part of Sophie that was enjoying the man's company just for herself. In the privacy of her thoughts, when Sophie beheld Vim Charpentier, she let herself dream a few naughty dreams and wish a few silly wishes. There was no harm in it—she was a lady and he was a gentleman and wishes were ever a waste of time.

She heard footsteps in the hallway and took a seat on the sofa, laying the child in her lap.

"There was warm water on the hob," Mr. Charpentier said. It was difficult to say his first name—Vim—but not so hard to think it. Unusual, Teutonic, and consistent with a sense of energy and purpose. Vim.

"I want to try to do it myself this time."

"And I'll let you. Kit seems to enjoy healthy digestion." Vim pushed aside the coffee table to lay a receiving blanket on the sofa, took the baby from Sophie's lap, and laid the child on his back on the blanket. "Have at it, madam. I wish you every success."

He remained kneeling beside the sofa, resting on his heels. Sophie was at once glad for his proximity… and mortified.

She untied the tapes holding the nappy onto the child and lifted it away.

"Careful." Vim's big hand folded the cloth back up over the child loosely. "He'll make a mess all over you half the time if you don't take evasive maneuvers."

Sophie's face heated as she realized the child was… wetting the already soiled nappy.

"Something about fresh air seems to inspire them. Probably saves you a change in the long run. I think it's safe now."

So matter of fact! Sophie unfolded the now damp and odoriferous cloth.

"My… goodness."

"Quite a mess."

She glanced over to see the blasted man grinning at her. "You put him up to this, Mr. Charpentier. Corrupted the morals of a mere baby."

"Quit stalling. It isn't good for him to be messy. He'll get the nastiest rash and have to sport about in the altogether for days."

Not grinning now, smiling from ear to ear. Smiling like a naughty man.

Sophie smiled too, and peeled the diaper away from the child. Mr. Charpentier slapped a damp cloth into her hand, wrung out but still warm.

"Do a proper job of it," he said. "I wasn't kidding about the rash. Poor little things scream themselves to exhaustion with it. For the same reason, you'll also want to dry him thoroughly after his bath."

Sophie tended the baby, though looking at even such little male parts was mortifying. Worse yet, the child started grinning and kicking as she dealt with a certain area.

"He likes it, Sophie. Best be grateful for it too."

"Grateful?" Grateful the little beast had no more modesty than her brothers had had as adolescents?

"Can you imagine this same exercise if he didn't want you touching him? Coyness would hardly make the business easier or tidier."

He accepted the dirty nappy from her and passed her a clean one. Amid kicking feet and surprisingly agile little paws, Sophie managed to get the diaper changed. It took concentration and dexterity, and when she finished, the result was disappointingly asymmetric. "It doesn't look as tidy as yours."

"Looks hardly matter. He's just going to consign

the clean one to the wash the same as all the others. I'll take this one back to the laundry."

He rolled up the linen in his hand while Sophie busied herself slipping socks back on the baby's feet. She didn't want to see Mr. Charpentier grinning at her, because she was feeling foolishly proud of having changed her very first—very nasty—soiled nappy.

"Good job, Sophie Windham. You're off to a fine start."

He stroked a hand over her shoulder and rose, leaving the room with the dirty diaper.

A pat to the shoulder, nothing more, but Sophie felt as if it was the first real praise she'd ever earned. She leaned over and gently closed her finger and thumb over the baby's button nose.

"He said I did a good job. No thanks to you."

Kit grinned, cooed, and kicked her hand away.

Sophie and her baby were going to be fine. Vim assured himself of this as he lingered in the kitchen, washing his hands and putting together a tea tray. Foraging in the bread box yielded a supply of iced buns, which suited his appetite wonderfully. He found butter, honey, and the tea things, and made his way back to the parlor.

Maybe before he left in the morning, he'd show Sophie how to bathe the child. She was well on her way to mastering feeding, changing, and playing with the baby. A bath was about the only thing left Vim could demonstrate.

He'd take a peek at the nursery too, just to make sure it was safe.

And perhaps find the child some toys. A family with ten children had to have some toys gathering dust in a chest or closet.

And he could leave his direction...

He stopped just outside the parlor door.

He would *not* be leaving his direction. This little interlude was a function of bad weather, worse luck, and a wayward sense of responsibility for a woman and child he'd never met before and wouldn't likely see again.

Would *not* see again.

And if he'd left his address, it wasn't as if Sophie could write to him, or him to her. Proper conduct forbade such communication. And his conduct with Sophie *would* remain proper, no matter his common sense had lost its grip on his male imagination.

When he returned to the parlor, Sophie was once again on the floor with Kit. She sat cross-legged on the blankets, the baby on his stomach before her.

"My Lord Baby rang for a parlor picnic," Vim said, pushing the door closed with his heel. "The string quartet should be along any minute. If you'd like to wash your hands, I can attend His Highness."

"I don't know as it's safe to leave the two you alone together. You'll teach him drinking songs and ribald jokes."

"He already has a whole store of ribald jokes. One can tell this from his smiles and grins." Vim set the tray on the floor out of the baby's reach and settled so the child was between him and Sophie.

"Are all babies this jolly?"

"Heavens, no." He got comfortable, assuming the

same tailor-sit Sophie had. "I was in a Magyar camp once after a particularly hard winter, and the old women were muttering around the fire that the babies had stopped crying. They longed for the sound of a baby crying, a baby with enough hope and health left to bellow for his supper or his mama or his blanket."

Now why in the hell had he brought that up? The moment had haunted him, left him wishing he could scoop up all the silent, listless babies and bring them home to merry England to be cosseted and cuddled and stuffed with porridge.

Sophie ran her hand down the baby's back then tried to adjust a nappy that had been tied securely if not exactly prettily onto the child's body. "I'm going to wash my hands. You plot petit treason with Kit, and when I come back, I want to hear more stories of your travels. Not just the company stories that make people laugh, but the real stories—the ones that stayed with you."

She made a silent departure, leaving Vim to watch as the baby once again maneuvered to all fours.

"And you think exploring the world will be great good fun, don't you?" he asked the child. "You don't know yet that you'll see children starving and old women nigh freezing to death." He picked the child up and cradled him closely, speaking with his lips pressed against the baby's downy hair. "Don't be in a hurry to grow up, young Kit. It isn't all it's reported to be. You go wenching and drinking and carousing around the globe, and pretty soon, all you want is home, hearth, and a woman of your own to give babies to. You can find your way to any port on any sea, but you can't find your way to those simple blessings."

The baby let out a sigh and mashed his fist into his mouth. Vim set him down faceup on the blankets.

"Roll over, why don't you? It's one way to get a change in perspective." He rolled the baby slowly to his tummy just as Sophie came back to the room.

"Have you listed all the best taverns in Oxford for him?"

"There are no taverns in Oxford. It's scholars cheek by jowl, scholars on every street corner, composing poetry in Latin and Greek."

She sank to the floor, this time stretching out on her side near the baby. "My brothers said there was an entirely different sort of commerce being conducted on those street corners. Does that fist just taste better than the other, do you think?"

Vim took the opposite length of floor. "He favors the left. One of our old grooms in Cumbria said it's a function of how the child lies in the womb, so one hand is easier to maneuver than the other. Said horses are prone to the same tendency, more supple on one side than the other."

"When Kit learns to trot, we'll put the theory to the test."

A silence descended, broken by the sound of the cozy fire a few feet away, the bitter wind outside, and the baby's contented slurping. It wasn't like any silence Vim could recall—sweet, comfortable, and yet... poignant. He would be leaving in just a few hours, going out into the chill wind while the woman and child would remain here before the fire.

Four

"SHALL I POUR YOU SOME TEA, SOPHIE?"

"Yes, thank you. And I saw some cinnamon buns too. I'll take mine with butter."

Vim busied himself with the food, grateful for the distraction. Kit was up on his hands and knees again, occasionally rocking and bouncing as if he expected the floor itself to propel him along the carpet somehow.

Sophie took her tea, setting the cup and saucer up on the coffee table out of the baby's reach. "What story will you tell me?"

"What kind of story would you like?"

"An exciting story. One with an exotic climate and mortal peril."

He had to smile at the relish in her voice. "Do we have bloodthirsty warring factions in this story?"

"No war, please."

She'd lost a brother to the Corsican's armies. He'd forgotten that, though she never would. "You want a happy ending, then?"

She studied her teacup for a thoughtful moment. "I don't admit to my family that I still want the happy endings and wishes to come true. A mature woman should just take life as it comes, and I do have a great deal to be grateful for."

"But a mature woman should also be honest with herself, and with me. You're allowed to wish for the happy endings, Sophie. For yourself and for Kit too."

When he looked up from his teacup, she was studying him. "May I wish for a happy ending for you too, Vim Charpentier?"

She would. Regardless of her role in this grand household, Sophie Windham was decent enough—lady enough—to include him in her wishes, though he knew a fleeting frustration at not being able to divine what *exactly* her role was.

"Christmas approaches, and I'm sure you've been a very good girl. You may wish for anything you like."

Something flickered across her usually serene features, something feminine and mysterious and quite... attractive.

Vim launched into a tale of shipwreck on a tropical paradise, leaving out mention of flies, dysentery, and petty squabbling among the survivors. He described the noise and destruction of the hurricanes, the attempts to rebuild the boat, and the difficult voyage from the island back to some semblance of civilization, wondering why no one had ever asked for this story before.

Not that anyone asked him for any stories.

"You have entertained Kit marvelously," Sophie said when he'd brought the tale to its mandatory happy conclusion. "I can see him planning his first voyage."

Kit was sailing the expanse of Vim's chest, the baby's

back arched like a baby seal's. Vim tapped him gently on the nose. "I can see My Lord Baby succumbing to exhaustion following this very eventful day. If Miss Sophie and I are flagging, sir, then you most certainly are overdue for a visit to the arms of Morpheus."

Kit grinned hugely and thumped Vim on the chest with one fist.

"I don't think he agrees with you." Sophie finished this observation on a polite yawn.

"Shall I take his cradle up to your room?"

"That would be appreciated. I'd best grab some clean nappies, shouldn't I?"

"Forearmed and all that. I'll put the tea tray away."

"Leave it. I'll deal with it in the morning."

After you're gone. She'd left the words unspoken out of kindness, no doubt.

He cuddled the baby to his chest and got to his feet. The idea of leaving ought to fill him with relief. The longer he stayed, the greater the possibility some word of this interlude would reach the wrong ears. He was overdue to report to Sidling, and Sophie was managing famously with Kit. He really would be glad to be on his way once more, even on his way to Sidling at the Christmas season.

Sophie reached for the baby, and Vim passed him over without another word.

❧

"He thinks I've been a good girl." Sophie made sure Kit was resting comfortably in his cradle then went back to the task at hand, which was brushing out her hair at the end of the day.

Also coming to terms with Mr. Vim Charpentier's disturbing presence just a few doors down the corridor.

"I haven't been good, young Kit. I've been perfect. My conduct is held up to the young debs as exemplary. The fellows all know it's safe to escort me anywhere, my papa has been seen patting my cheek in public, and my mama is confident my portion of charity work will suffice for the entire family's good name."

She paused with the brush and peered at the baby. "You know how tiresome it is to be good all the time."

Kit sighed around his thumb. Sophie took it for a sigh of commiseration.

"Except I'm not perfect. I watch Mr. Charpentier's mouth when he speaks of the sun on the Caribbean waves being so bright it makes the eyes ache. He has a beautiful mouth and a gorgeous voice. It isn't all pomp and circumstance, like His Grace holding forth on the Catholic question. It's…"

She let go a sigh. She'd sighed a lot since closing her bedroom door. To her ears, those sighs were the sound of a grown woman admitting she wasn't nearly as done with wishes and dreams as she ought to be. "Vim's voice is warm. He has the knack of making me feel like I'm the only person who has ever listened to him. Like I'm the person to whom he must tell his stories."

That was so fanciful, she fell silent. Not even a baby should be told of the shifting about going on in Sophie's middle, from a woman of common sense to a woman who, for the first time in her life, understood what it was to be smitten.

"And to think I wanted as much solitude as I could steal this Christmas."

It had been wicked and daring and very bad of her not to go with her family directly out to Morelands. Every year she dutifully participated in the exodus to Kent for the holidays, and Sophie saw decades of Yule seasons spent with her aging parents, sharing fond reminiscences of nieces and nephews as they grew to adulthood.

"I want to be wicked, Kit. I want to crawl off my blankets and go exploring. I want to get into trouble, but I do not want to bring trouble to Mr. Charpentier."

Vim looked to her like a man who'd dealt with more than his share of trouble, as if beneath all the kindness and humor in his marvelous blue eyes, there was a weariness of spirit, a burden on his heart. She wanted to ease that burden, and she wanted to do it not just with polite, ladylike, kind words, she wanted to offer him the comfort of her very body.

She should not be thinking of Mr. Charpentier and trouble in the same breath. Sophie knew so little about getting into trouble—much less getting into trouble without making trouble—that she lay awake for a long time, wondering just how a proper lady might go about it.

A proper lady and a wonderful, unexpected gentleman with a beautiful mouth, a gorgeous voice, and an even lovelier heart.

❧

Vim had fallen into the luxurious bed, thinking sleep would follow immediately, and it did, only to depart a few hours later. The storm still raged outside, but his guest room was wonderfully cozy. There were several buckets of coal waiting to be added to the fire, the bed curtains were heavy enough to block out both cold and light, and the house was quiet in the way a solid structure could be even with a winter wind howling outside.

And yet, something woke him... a sound, a shift, something.

From down the hall he heard a faint, lilting melody. It came to Vim through the darkness, the tempo slow enough that a tired woman could walk the floor to it, a fussy baby in her arms.

He considered getting up, but there was no strident bawling from the child to pierce the lullaby. There was only darkness and warmth and a sweetness with the erotic edge to it men didn't speak of when considering a mother and baby.

He'd slept naked, a pleasure not always practical when traveling economically. And as Sophie's voice drifted to him through the darkness, he pushed the sheets aside and let his hand find its way to the burgeoning fullness of his cock.

He'd traveled too far and seen too much to feel guilt or awkwardness about a private moment like this. A slow, voluptuous pleasure claimed him as Sophie's voice died away in the warmth and darkness. It wasn't right or wrong, it made no difference in how Sophie would view him in the morning, but as pleasure inundated his body, Vim had to admit it was a solitary, even lonely, pleasure.

❧

"Do all male children like being naked?"

Sophie posed the question as dispassionately as she could, but Kit was in rare spirits as Mr. Charpentier unswaddled him in the kitchen.

"No." He lifted the child into his arms from the blankets spread on the worktable. "All males of any age like being naked, and I'm fairly certain it's true across species, as well. Test the water."

He said things like that to her, naughty things, things her brothers probably thought and didn't say—though they might have when they were younger.

Sophie dipped her fingers into the small washtub on the table. "It's warm but not hot."

"Then let the games begin."

The games were to comprise Kit's first bath in Sophie's care, and entailed heating two buckets of water over the kitchen fire, lining the edge of a tub with towels, and mixing hot and cold water just so, to just such a depth, and assembling blankets and nappies and flannels and socks, as well as the mildest soap Sophie could borrow from her mother's private chambers.

Mr. Charpentier was in shirt, waistcoat, and breeches, his cuffs rolled back to his elbows. He'd warned Sophie that bathing a baby was best undertaken in old clothing, so she was in a comfortable dress of maroon velvet, her sleeves turned back, as well.

"In you go, young Kit." He slowly lowered the baby into the tub, which provoked an immediate and deafening squeal of delight. Kit sat in the middle of the tub, smacking the water vigorously with both hands and crowing with glee.

"Told you it wasn't for the faint of heart."

There was gruff humor in Mr. Charpentier's voice,

the first humor Sophie had detected from him that
morning. "Now what do we do?"

"We play."

He lowered his hand into the water and used his
thumb and middle finger to flick the baby's chest with
water. The gleeful squealing stopped, and Kit stared at
the large male hand that had produced such a startling
new sensation.

"He wants you to do it again."

"You do it." Mr. Charpentier straightened and
grabbed a cloth to dry his hand, the baby's gaze on
him the entire time.

Sophie regarded the baby making a happy tempest
in the middle of the washtub. A duke's daughter did
not engage in tomfoolery... but she wasn't a duke's
daughter at that moment. She was a woman with a
baby to bathe.

"Kit." She trailed a hand through the water. "You
are having entirely too much fun in there. Perhaps it's
time we got down to business." She dribbled water
down the child's chubby arm, and got heartily splashed
as Kit expressed his approval of this new game. By
damp fits and starts, Sophie got him bathed, got the
entire front of her old dress wet, and only realized Mr.
Charpentier was largely dry when the man handed her
a clean blanket to wrap the wet, wiggling baby in.

"You were no help at all, Vim Charpentier. You
left me stranded at sea."

"You managed quite well with just your own oars,
Sophie Windham. Kit looks to be considering a career
in the Navy." He tucked the blanket up over the
child's damp head. "Watch he doesn't catch a chill

now. Some people think bathing unhealthy, though I can't agree. At Kit's age, it's fun too."

"But somehow, as older children, we get the idea a bath is not fun." She used the blanket to pat gently at Kit's face and hands then laid him blanket and all on the worktable.

Vim stood back, watching her as she put a clean nappy on the baby, dodging little feet and hands as she worked. She'd had some practice with this through the night—more practice than any tired woman wanted.

"What's not fun," Vim said, trailing a finger down the baby's cheek, "is being told what to do, whether it's a bath, sums, or Latin vocabulary. You're getting better at this."

"You're distracting him, which helps a great deal. Is someone telling you what to do?" She didn't look at him as she posed the question. His mood had been a trifle distant, though he'd been perfectly polite since joining her in the kitchen more than an hour ago. Polite but preoccupied.

"This storm is telling me what to do. It's telling me I won't be making any progress toward my family seat today."

She couldn't help it. She smiled at him, letting both relief and pleasure show plainly. "I was rather hoping you'd reach that conclusion."

His answering smile appeared reluctant, lifting one corner of his mouth then working its way to the other. "But you weren't about to lecture or nag or bully me. You just fed me an enormous breakfast then let Master Kit work his wiles on me." The smile faded. "I don't like to think of you here alone with him in this weather. What if you should need a doctor? What if you should burn your hand?"

"Worrying is seldom productive," she said, quoting her mother and sounding—to her horror—exactly like Her Grace. She sat Kit on the table amid his blankets and started working a clean dress over his head.

Vim tidied up the little makeshift bath, hanging the now damp towels on nails in the rafters near the hearth. "You didn't worry every time you got up with Kit in the middle of the night?"

"How did you know we were awake?"

He shot her a peculiar look from across the kitchen then went back to hanging towels. "You have a pretty voice, Sophie."

It made no sense, but his compliment had her blushing. She'd received compliments before, on her attire, her mare, her embroidery, but her voice wasn't something she'd purchased or made, it was part of her.

"My mother thought we should all learn an instrument," she said. "I tried piano, but my next oldest brother is so astoundingly good at it, I put him to use as my accompanist from time to time. My whole family likes to sing, except my father. He cannot, as they say, carry a tune in a bucket."

She finished bundling the child up, her gaze drawn to the way muscles bunched and moved under the skin of Vim Charpentier's forearms as he worked. "What awaits you at home, Mr. Charpentier?"

"Why do you ask?" He hung the last towel on a hook and crossed to the table. "Are we reusing this water, or should I dump it?"

"You can dump it in the laundry, and you're avoiding my question by answering it with a question."

The single glance he flicked at her confirmed Sophie's suspicion in this regard. He wasn't good at evasion or dissembling—something she had to approve of—and he did not want to make this journey down to Kent.

Did not want to even discuss it.

He came back into the kitchen, rolling his sleeves down as he did. Sophie found this mundane gesture on his part inordinately interesting.

"If you'd like to catch a nap, Sophie, I can watch His Highness for a bit."

A generous—and distracting—offer. Sophie let the topic of his journey home ease away. He hadn't pried regarding her status; she would return the consideration—for now. "I was hoping you would watch the baby for a just a little while, but not so I can sleep. I'd like to check on Higgins and Merriweather, bring in more milk and eggs, and take the grooms some cinnamon buns and butter."

He blew out a breath, and Sophie prepared to be Reasoned With.

"Have you looked out the window, Sophie Windham?"

"Occasionally, yes."

"Then you comprehend there's better than two feet of snow out there and more coming down?"

"I do comprehend this. I also comprehend Higgins and Merriweather shoveled out paths between the house and the mews. The least I can do is show my appreciation."

She lifted Kit off the table and perched him on her hip. A discussion of this nature required patience and determination, nothing more.

Vim took two steps closer to her, until she had to lift her chin to meet his gaze. "You aren't going to back down on this. What's the real reason you want to make this outing, Sophie?"

"What's the real reason you don't want to go home?"

The question was out of her mouth before she could consider its rudeness, but he was right: she was determined on her outing.

"It isn't home." His mouth was a flat line, his eyes bleak. "If you'll let me do some shoveling, I will escort you and My Lord Baby to the mews. If we bundle him up, he should enjoy the change of scene."

She considered that this was a Male Tactic, designed to keep her indoors out of guilt and concern for the child, but the disgruntlement in Vim's expression belied that notion. "You're sure the weather won't bother him?"

"No more than it's bothering me." He turned to leave, heading for the back hallway. She let him go, because their last exchange hadn't been quite as polite as everything that had gone before.

Still, she sensed it had been honest. She liked that it had been honest.

❧

Vim had heard a rumor regarding certain native peoples of far northern Canada. It was said to be an article of hospitality in those parts to offer a guest the intimate use of his host's wife, or to trade wives with friends for purposes of sexual recreation.

As Vim shoveled out paths thoroughly drifted over, he considered the hypothesis that excessive winter weather affected the humors such that prurient activity became even more enticing than usual.

Not that it had been enticing in recent memory. Not until he'd decided Sophie Windham and her foundling needed some supervision to get a proper start with each other.

He should not have given in to the urge to gratify himself the previous night, but the temptation had been rare of late, and a man didn't want to admit such a thing could be worrisome. He shoveled that thought off into the nearest drift.

He was getting old, and by God, he did not want to spend his holidays at Sidling.

He was clear enough on that to have a path reshoveled from the house to the stables in no time. The exertion had felt good, but another form of exertion wanted to crowd its way into his imagination, one involving naked bodies and cozy beds.

He could shovel his way to Kent in no time if he allowed his mind dwell there, so he put up the shovel and let himself into the mansion's back hallway.

"We're ready!" Sophie's voice sang out from the kitchen, and then she appeared in the doorway, the baby all but rolled into a rug, so snugly was he covered.

"I'll take Kit." Vim held out his arms, and Sophie passed along her bundle without protest.

"Thank you. Let me fetch the buns, and we can be on our way."

She disappeared into the kitchen, leaving Vim to realize Sophie had been feeling housebound too. It put him a little more in charity with life, to think he was doing her a service just by seeing her across the alley.

The bundle in his arms cooed.

"It's winter." Vim peeled away just enough blankets to expose baby-blue eyes. "Cold is part of it, but we're English, so we refer to this as fresh air. Repeat after me: fresh air."

"Gah."

"My sentiments, as well, truth be told, but there's a steaming bowl of porridge in it for you if you keep your nappy clean for the next fifteen minutes."

"Bah!"

Vim was still smiling when Sophie emerged from the kitchen. Her gaze went from Vim to Kit and back to Vim. "This looks like a conspiracy in progress. What have you two been up to?"

"Plotting a raid on the pantry. Shall we brave the elements?"

"Please." She wrapped a scarf around her ears and neck and followed Vim out the back door. When she stood with him for a moment on the back terrace, her cheeks rosy and her breath puffing white in the winter air, Vim considered handing her the baby and plunging headfirst into the nearest snowdrift.

The impulse to kiss her was that strong.

❧

Devlin St. Just, Colonel Lord Rosecroft, propped his stockinged feet on a scarred coffee table, took a sip of lovely rum punch, and listened to his younger brothers squabbling. It was a wonderful sound to a man who had only two younger brothers left.

"I say we wait another day." Westhaven was getting quite ducal in his pronouncements, which was an understandable tactic, if poorly advised when dealing with their youngest brother.

"I say you're full of shit," Lord Valentine replied with a diffidence no doubt calculated to aggravate. "The snow isn't that deep, we've already tarried here a day, and all we've seen is some flurries and a lot of low-hanging clouds. This is Sophie we're talking about, need I remind you?"

"Sophie." Westhaven pushed out of his wing chair and began to pace around the inn's private parlor, making a credible impersonation of their mutual father, His Grace the Duke of Moreland. "Sophie, the paragon of probity. Sophie, the delight and comfort of our parents' eyes. Sophie, the sensible. Sophie, named for wisdom herself. She isn't clinging to a tree in some enormous snowdrift, her lips too frozen to call for help. She's ensconced in Lady Chattell's parlor, being plied with chocolate and marzipan."

St. Just took another sip of his punch and exchanged a look with Val intended to limit the goading. Westhaven was worried. Worried enough to be counseling sense when sense wasn't necessarily going to carry the day. As heir to the dukedom, he'd refined worrying to a high art, and his siblings all loved him for it.

Mostly.

"Sophie is sensible," Val said, still affecting bored tones. "She's sensible enough not to get caught when she's visiting the Magdalene houses in the East End. She's sensible enough to take in every stray animal that ever pissed in a back alley and to put the vagrant humans she finds there to work in the stables. She's sensible enough to tat lace and embroider pillowcases while fomenting the rights of women with her pin money. The storm is reported to be worse in London, and I say we push on now."

St. Just intervened before they started yelling in the ducal tradition. "Both of you have some punch. The spices are excellent, and it calms the humors. Seasonal cheer never hurt a fraternal congregation."

Westhaven resumed his seat, running his hand through dark chestnut hair. They all shared height and green eyes, but St. Just and Val had darker hair. This plan to meet up in Cambridge had been Westhaven's idea, and as usual with Westhaven's plans, a sound notion. Val had been appraising some antique harpsichords in Peterborough, Westhaven lecturing at Cambridge, and St. Just traveling south from Yorkshire—and all of them had been cordially summoned by Her Grace to put in a holiday appearance at the ducal seat in Kent.

One could ignore a summons from His Grace. The duke would simply issue a louder summons or come deliver the next summons in person.

One ignored a summons from the duchess at risk of causing that dear lady disappointment, and Val and Westhaven were arguing over the sibling who, in all her twenty-some years, had likely caused Their Graces the least disappointment.

So far. Sophie was a different hairpin, though. She might not merit regular castigation like her brothers and sisters, but St. Just knew she puzzled her parents, and puzzlement was in some ways a more painful state of affairs than disappointment.

St. Just kept his features bland, as he'd learned to do when listening to half-drunk generals squabble over competing idiot plans while the sensible course lay in plain sight before them all, silently begging for notice.

"Valentine, you are agitating to push on in part because you are worried about matters at home in Oxford." St. Just passed his youngest brother a steaming mug along with a shut-up-and-hear-me-out look. "Westhaven, you are concerned we'll offend Sophie if we go to heroic measures to retrieve her from Town when she's perfectly capable of managing competently under all situations—at least to appearances."

He passed Westhaven a mug, and in deference to the man's standing and sensibilities, a please-hear-me-out look.

But Val was never one to take orders just because it made sense to do so. "A new wife is not a *matter*. She is my family. Their Graces have had thirty years to spend holidays with us, and this my first—"

Westhaven sighed, took a sip of punch, and glanced over at Val. "It doesn't get easier the longer you're married. You still fret, more in fact, once the babies start coming."

Val's head cocked, as if he'd just recalled his brother was also his friend. "Well, as to that…" Val smiled at his punch. Baby Brother sported a devastating smile when he wanted to, but this expression was…

St. Just lifted his mug. "Congratulations, then. How's Ellen faring?"

"She's in fine spirits, in glowing good health, and I'm a wreck. I think she sent me off to Peterborough with something like relief in her eye."

Westhaven was staring morosely at his grog. "Anna isn't subtle about it anymore. She tells me to get on my horse and not come back until I've worked the fidgets out of us both. She's quite glad to see me when I return, though. Quite glad."

For Westhaven, that was the equivalent of singing a bawdy song in the common.

St. Just propped his mug on his stomach. "Emmie says I'm an old campaigner, and I get twitchy if I'm confined to headquarters too long. Winnie says I need to go on scouting patrol. The reunions are nice, though. You're right about that."

Val took a considering sip of his drink then speared St. Just with a look. "I wouldn't know about those reunions, but I intend to find out soon. Dev, you are the only one of us experienced at managing a marching army, and I'm not in any fit condition to be making decisions, or I'd be on my way back to Oxfordshire right now."

"Wouldn't advise that," Westhaven said, still looking glum. "Your wife will welcome you sweetly into her home and her bed, but you'll know you didn't quite follow orders—our wives are in sympathy with Her Grace—and they have their ways of expressing their…"

Both brothers chimed in, "Disappointment."

A moment of thoughtful imbibing followed, after which St. Just went to the door, bellowed an order for another round of punch, then returned to the blazing fire.

"All right, then. It seems to me the clouds are hanging off to the south and west, but all the northbound and eastbound travelers are telling us the storm is serious business. Here's what I propose…"

Lord Val and Lord Westhaven listened, and in the end they agreed. The grog was good, the advice was sound, and Sophie was, after all, their most sensible sister.

Five

IT WASN'T A MEWS, IT WAS A MENAGERIE.

As Sophie introduced Kit to the end of Goliath's nose, Vim's gaze scanned the interior of what should have been ducal stables. For some reason, Miss Sophie held sufficient sway over the household that she could command space in the barn for a little brindle milk cow with one horn, another hulking draft horse which looked to Vim to be blind in one eye, and a small cat missing one eye, part of an ear, and all of a front paw. Vim had no doubt if he inspected the rest of the premises, he'd find yet more strays and castoffs in her keeping.

"Kit likes Goliath," Sophie said, taking the child's tiny fingers and stroking them over the largest Roman nose in captivity. "But then, who would not love my precious, hmm?"

She leaned over and kissed the horse's muzzle, a great loud smacker of a kiss that had the baby chortling with delight. Kit swung a fist toward the horse, but Sophie leaned away before the child could connect.

"Come meet wee Sampson, my other precious." She moved off down the shed row as Higgins came shuffling up to Vim's elbow.

"She'll be in here half the morning, dotin' on them buggers."

"Where does she find them?"

Higgins hitched his britches up and frowned. "She just does. She come upon Sampson at the smithy when they was blinding him for work at the mill. Miss Sophie wouldn't have none of that, no matter the colonel tried to explain to her a half-blind horse is worse than one with no sight at all."

"A horse that size could turn the millstone handily."

"Not if he's got sight in one eye, he can't. He'd fall down dizzy after an hour in the traces."

"Who's the colonel?"

"Her oldest brother. Good fellow with a horse. Was in the cavalry all acrost Spain and at Waterloo."

Sophie was making every bit as big a fuss over the second horse as she had the first. She held the baby up on the side of the horse's good eye and spoke quietly to horse and baby both.

"Why did she name her tom cat Elizabeth?" It was a silly question, but some part of Vim wanted to know this detail.

"Ye'd have to ask her. It's something Frenchified."

She knew French, and she had a brother who'd made the rank of colonel—not an easy or inexpensive feat.

"Mr. Sharp-an-tee-air?"

Vim glanced down at the little man standing beside him. "Mr. Higgins?"

"I know Miss Sophie has took the nipper in, and

that's a sizeable task for any woman, much less one
what hasn't got any nippers of her own."

Ah, the stable gnome was working up to a lecture.
Sophie didn't need to lecture Vim, she had minions
assigned to the task. "She's managing quite well, and
it's mostly common sense."

"And lord knows, the girl has got common sense."
Higgins's frown became more focused. "About most
things, that is."

"Spit it out, Higgins. Once she's done petting
that bedraggled cat, she'll turn her attention on you
and start ordering you to consume all those buns and
refrain from shoveling snow and so on."

"All I'm saying is her family sets great store by her,
and they'd take it amiss did any mischief befall our
Miss Sophie."

"I'm coming to set great store by the lady too, Higgins.
But for her, I'd be cooling my heels in some taproom,
nothing to occupy me but watered ale, cards, and occasional trips to a privy as malodorous as it was cold."

"Then you'll be moving along here directly, won't
you, sir? Wouldn't want the girl's family to come to
troublesome mis-conclusions, would we?"

Higgins's rheumy blue eyes promised a world of
retribution if Vim attempted to argue.

"Settle your feathers, Higgins. I stayed only at the
lady's express request in order to acquaint her with
some basics regarding care and feeding of an infant. If
you're equipped to step in, please do, because I'm on
my way as soon as the weather permits—tomorrow at
first light, if at all possible."

And he wanted to go. He just didn't relish the idea

of hours in a mail coach trying to slog its way through the drifts. Hours of cold, hours of the wheezing, coughing companionship of other travelers...

His gaze fell on Sophie where she was crouched in the aisle having some sort of conversation with the bedraggled little cat and the baby.

"Her hems will never come clean."

He hadn't realized he'd spoken aloud until Higgins snorted quietly. "And she'll never care a whit if they do, either. That is one smart bebby, that Kit. He's made a good trade."

"You didn't think much of the mother?" For God's sake, the girl had been only sixteen years old.

"She set her cap for young Harry, Joleen did, and damn the consequences. Their Graces turned Harry out, but they give him a character, see? He kept coming around here on the sly, meeting with Joleen and whispering in her ear, if you know what I mean. Last I heard, he was taking passage for Boston."

Higgins meant a pregnant girl couldn't get any more pregnant, so an enterprising and conscienceless young man would keep swiving her for his own pleasure.

"I seen Harry prowling around last week, that girl about shivering herself to death waiting for him in the garden. She's run off to her Harry and left little Kit to shift for hisself."

"He's shifting quite well. I'm not sure a baby ever found any better care than Kit is getting."

"Because Miss Sophie has a soft heart. Her family thinks she's sensible, but she's like Westhaven. They're sensible because somebody in the family has to be sensible, but neither of 'em is as sensible as all that."

Vim tried to translate what was and wasn't being said.

"You're saying sometimes one acts sensibly out of regard for one's family, not because one finds it a naturally agreeable course." And God help him, Vim could testify to the truth of that sentiment.

Higgins nodded. "That says it right enough. You'll be leaving in the morning?"

"Come hell or high water, I intend to."

Sophie was smiling at the baby, who was making a determined play for the cat's nose. Vim expected the beast to issue the kind of reprimand children remembered long after the scratches had healed, but the cat instead walked away, all the more dignified for its missing parts.

"He must go terrorize mice," Sophie said, rising with the child in her arms.

"You're telling me that cat still mouses?" Vim asked, taking the baby from her in a maneuver that was beginning to feel automatic.

"Of course Pee Wee mouses." Sophie turned a smile on him. "A few battle scars won't slow a warrior like him down."

"A name like Pee Wee might."

She wrapped her hand into the crook of his elbow as they started across the alley. "Elizabeth gets more grief over his name than Pee Wee does."

"And rightly so. Why on earth would you inflict a feminine name on a big, black tom cat?"

"I didn't name him Elizabeth. I named him Bête Noir, after the French for black beast. Merriweather started calling him Betty Knorr after some actress, which was a tad too informal for such an animal, and hence he became Elizabeth. He answers to it now."

Vim suppressed the twitching of his lips, because this explanation was delivered with a perfectly straight face. "I suppose all that counts is that the cat recognizes it. It isn't as if the cats were going to comprehend the French."

"It's silly." She paused inside the garden gate, her expression self-conscious.

He stopped with her on the path, cradling the baby against his chest and trying to fathom what she needed to hear at the moment. "To the cat it isn't silly, Sophie. To him, your kindness and care are the difference between life and death."

"He's just a cat." But she looked pleased with Vim's observations.

"And this is just a baby. Come." He took her gloved hand in his. "Kit has had his outing, and so have you. I was hoping the snow would stop, but it seems to be coming down harder again."

She kept her hand in his and let him escort her back into the warmth and coziness of the kitchen. As short as the daylight was in December, between the child's bath, the shoveling, and the excursion to the mews, the day was half gone.

Watching Sophie unswaddle the baby, Vim decided that was a good thing. This time tomorrow, he'd be across the river and headed for Kent, just as he'd promised Higgins.

❧

Sophie hadn't wanted Vim to see the collection of misfits she kept in the stables. She wasn't ashamed of them by any means, but she was... protective.

Each animal contributed somehow, to the best of its ability, but most people didn't see that. They saw only the ridiculousness of a draft animal who turned to a one-ton blancmange at the sight of a whip, or a mouser who was hunting with half his weapons dulled by injury.

Vim hadn't laughed.

She could not save every animal in the knacker's yard, she couldn't find a home for every cat yowling under the summer moon, but she could help those few in her care.

Vim finished getting out of his winter gear and peered down at the baby.

"I'd say stuff some nuncheon into his gullet and put him down for a nap."

"I wanted to do some baking this afternoon," Sophie said. "His nap would be a good time to do it."

"His nap would be a good time for you to rest, Sophie Windham. He'll keep you up half the night tonight too, you know, and I won't be around tomorrow to spell you if you need forty winks."

He gave her a fulsome look, as if willing her to acknowledge his impending departure.

"Then tomorrow Kit and I will practice napping at the same time. I boiled some apples this morning. Do you think he'd like to try them mashed into his porridge?"

Porridge had never disappeared more quickly, Sophie was sure of it, and it gave her a little dose of pleasure to think the apples had been her idea. While she fed the baby, Vim busied himself constructing a sort of sugar tit with a wad of clean sponge, a laundered handkerchief, and some sewing cord. Kit took to it easily, slurping away like he'd been doing it since birth.

Which he might have been, though Sophie couldn't recall seeing anybody feed the child except Joleen, and that not often.

"It's my turn to do a nappy," Vim said. "You burp him, and I'll bring his cradle down here then tend to his wardrobe, so to speak."

"You think he'll sleep in the kitchen?"

"It's warm, and you'll be here puttering about. He should sleep easily enough now that we've tired him out."

Sophie watched Vim disappear up the back steps, wondering how she'd cope when he wasn't on hand to discuss every little decision with her.

To add mashed apples or not?

To take the child outside or keep him in the house?

To put the cradle in the parlor down the hall or set it in the kitchen?

There had been a moment out by the back gate, when she'd been trying to explain about Elizabeth's name, and the kindness had come back into Vim's eyes. She'd wanted to trespass on that kindness, to beg the man to stay one more day. She could honestly say she wanted his help with the child, but the truth was, she'd almost gone up on her toes and kissed his cheek.

Or his mouth. She found the idea of kissing his mouth increasingly hard to ignore, as was the idea of running her hands over the muscles of his chest, or the thought of his bare skin under her fingertips.

She hadn't kissed him, because he'd be kind about that, as well. Then too, several other homes backed up to the alley, and at least two had a clear view to the Windhams' garden gate. Bad enough Sophie could be seen coming and going from the house on the arm of a strange man. How much worse if she'd been observed kissing him in broad daylight?

"The snow is trying to make up its mind," Vim said, bumping down the back stairs with the cradle held under one long arm. "It's coming down in fits and starts now, not as steadily as it did yesterday."

"Then it's sure to taper off soon." Sophie injected as much false cheer into her voice as she could. Not only would she have to say good-bye to Vim Charpentier when the snow stopped, she'd have to accept her brothers' escort out to Morelands and very likely turn Kit over the care of a foster family.

"What has put that look on your face, Sophie?"

"What look?" She laid the child in the cradle where Vim had set it near the hearth.

"Like you just lost your best friend."

"I was thinking of fostering Kit." And just like that, she was blinking back tears. She tugged the blankets up around the baby, who immediately set about kicking them away. "Naughty baby," she whispered. "You'll catch a chill."

"Sophie?" A large male hand landed on her shoulder. "Sophie, look at me."

She shook her head and tried again to secure Kit's blankets.

"My dear, you are crying." Another hand settled on the opposite shoulder, and now the kindness was palpable in his voice. Vim turned her gently into his embrace and wrapped both arms around her.

It wasn't a careful, tentative hug. It was a secure embrace. He wasn't offering her a fleeting little squeeze to buck her up, he was holding her, his chin propped on her crown, the entire solid length of his body available to her for warmth and support.

Which had the disastrous effect of turning a trickle of tears into a deluge.

"I can't keep him." She managed four words around the lump in her throat. "To think of him being passed again into the keeping of strangers… I can't…"

"Hush." He held a hanky up to her nose, one laden with the bergamot scent she already associated with him. For long minutes, Sophie struggled to regain her equilibrium while Vim stroked his hand slowly over her back.

"Babies do this," Vim said quietly. "They wear you out physically and pluck at your heartstrings and coo and babble and wend their way into your heart, and there's nothing you can do stop it. Nobody is asking you to give the child up now."

"They won't have to ask. In my position, I can't be keeping somebody else's castoff—" She stopped, hating the hysterical note that had crept into her voice and hating that she might have just prompted the man to whom she was clinging to ask her what exactly her position was.

"Kit is not a castoff. He's yours, and you're keeping him. Maybe you will foster him elsewhere for a time, but he'll always be yours too."

She didn't quite follow the words rumbling out of

him. She focused instead on the feel of his arms around her, offering support and security while she parted company temporarily with her dignity.

"You are tired, and that baby has knocked you off your pins, Sophie Windham. You're borrowing trouble if you try to sort out anything more complicated right now than what you'll serve him for dinner."

She'd grown up with five brothers, and she'd watched her papa in action any number of times. She knew exactly what Vim was up to, but she took the bait anyway.

"He loved the apples."

This time when Vim offered her his handkerchief, she took it, stepping back even as a final sigh shuddered through her.

"He loves to eat," Vim said, "the same as any healthy male. What were you thinking of baking today?"

Another seemingly innocuous question, but Sophie let him lead her by small steps away from the topic of Kit's uncertain future.

"I was going to make stollen, a recipe from my grandmother's kitchens. I make it only around the holidays, and my brothers will be expecting it."

"May I help?"

She was certain he'd never intended to offer such a thing, certain he'd never done Christmas baking in his life. "There's a lot of chopping to do, depending on the version we make. Do you like dates?"

They discussed Christmas baking and sweets in general, then various exotic dishes Vim had encountered on his travels. Sophie had to brush the white flour off Vim's cheek when he offered to take a turn kneading the dough, and Vim snitched sweets shamelessly. Sophie scolded him until he popped a half a candied date in her mouth, and when she would have scolded him for that, he fed her the other half.

While the baby, oblivious to the adults laughing and teasing and even getting some baking done around him, slept contentedly in his cradle.

&

"Now this is odd."

Percival Windham folded the copy of *The Times* he'd been enjoying with his late afternoon tea and peered at his duchess.

"What's odd, my love?" He topped off her tea and passed her the cup.

"Murial Chattell has written to say they just made it out to Surrey before the storm struck London, and the weather is being blamed for her daughter's early lying-in."

"Popping out another one is she? Old Chattell will be bruiting that about in the clubs until Easter."

His bride of more than three decades gave him the amused, tolerant look of a woman who could read her husband like the proverbial book. "Don't fret, Husband. Devlin and Valentine are both putting their shoulders to the wheel, so to speak. There will be more grandbabies soon."

And Emmie and Ellen were mighty fetching inspiration for a man to pull his share of the marital load. Her Grace, as always, had a point.

The point she'd been trying to make belatedly struck him. "Sophie was supposed to be spending time with Chattell's middle girl, wasn't she?"

Her Grace took a placid sip of tea. A deceptively placid sip of tea. "That was Sophie's plan."

"That girl takes entirely too much after her mother, if you ask me."

"Oh?"

What a wealth of meaning a married woman could put into one syllable.

"You, my love, are subtle. A braver man might even say devious when you want to achieve your ends. You agreed to Sophie's plan to linger in Town with friends because the Chattells boast a houseful of empty-headed sons whom Sophie could wrap around her dainty finger, were she so inclined."

"But Sophie is not with the Chattells, Percy." A small frown creased Her Grace's brow. Had they been anywhere but His Grace's private study, she wouldn't have given even that much away. "Muriel mentions how crowded the traveling coach was with the two younger girls and all their winter finery, and she goes on and on about the difficulty of traveling in such bad weather. She does not mention Sophie."

His Grace enjoyed very much the machinations necessary for parliamentary schemes. He enjoyed advising the Regent on national and foreign policy when that overfed fellow deigned to listen. His Grace enjoyed very, very much the company of his grand-children, and there was no greater joy in his life than his marriage.

He did not always precisely enjoy being a father, much less a father ten times over, much *much* less the father of five single females, all of whom were arguably of marriageable age.

"If Sophie were a boy, we would not worry," he pointed out.

"Yes, we would."

They'd buried two grown sons. Yes, they would worry. They would always worry.

"Shall I go back up to Town, my love? People always exaggerate descriptions of inconvenient weather. I'm sure the roads can't be as impassable as all that when there are only a few inches of snow on the ground hereabouts."

"No, you shall not." Her Grace put a little scold in her words. "We have three strapping sons who are on their way to collect Lady Sophia as we speak. If Sophie is up to something unsound, better her brothers sort her out at this stage than her parents."

"You're sure?" Something had shifted in Her Grace's relationship with their sons in recent months, possibly as a function of all three acquiring wives. If she was delegating management of Sophie to the boys, then it was only because Her Grace was well and truly not concerned about the girl.

"Percival Windham, you are proposing to go haring off in the dead of winter with a storm of biblical proportions raging just to the north and west, while I sit here and do what? Worry about you in addition to the four of our offspring who are not now under our roof? I think not."

"Just making sure, my love. More tea?"

She smiled at him, his reward for helping her make up her mind. If Sophie were up to mischief, His Grace was privately of the opinion it was about damned time, provided the mischief involved a suitable swain. Sophie was wasting her youth tending to the halt and the lame when she ought to be about snabbling a handsome specimen to help provide her dear parents with some chubby little… to help her fill her nursery.

His Grace opened the paper to the financial section. An attempt to read the contents thereof was about as soporific as a tot of the poppy, but it was a fine excuse to let his mind drift off to which young men of his acquaintance he might consider worthy of his most sensible daughter.

If any.

～

Some vital male brain function had been impaired during the few minutes Vim had held Sophie Windham in his arms. Badly impaired—impaired as if some part of him had been aching sorely for a long time, though it had taken the feel of that one woman in his embrace to make him aware of his own hurt.

And now he could not focus on much else.

He liked her, was the problem. Or part of it. The other part was he desired her, which made no sense. Of course he desired her the way any healthy male would desire any attractive woman, but this was… different.

Vim had been a sexual friend to any number of women, and they'd been happy to return the favor. Romping was merely… romping. A wink and a smile, and both parties could be on their way, an itch having been adequately scratched for the nonce.

Sophie was not a woman to romp with. She was a woman a man could spend years learning to cherish.

"You can put those in the batter now." She gestured with her wooden spoon as if to remind Vim they were trying to put the baby's nap to some use besides encouraging Vim's rampant sexual fantasies. He picked up the cutting board and shifted to scrape a pile of finely chopped dates into the bowl of pale batter.

Baking was an activity designed to part a sane—and mildly aroused—man from his wits. Sophie had him pouring things into her bowls, standing right beside her, brushing arms and bodies and hands. She asked him to taste the batter, putting a spoonful of sweetness right into his mouth before he could protest or move away.

While they worked, she gently interrogated him, and he let her, because it gave him something to think of besides the sensation of her soft, full breast pressing against his arm when she leaned across him to retrieve the cinnamon.

"Didn't you miss your family on all those long journeys?"

He accepted the tin of cinnamon back from her, their fingers brushing again as he did. "They are my half siblings, though we were all raised together. I missed them, but there was a sense too of not wanting to impose. The estate in Cumbria is theirs, not mine."

She stopped stirring for moment and frowned at him. "My oldest brother and sister suffer from this same affliction. It's as if Devlin in particular must always remind himself that he's half our brother, and therefore half not our brother. He has nigh broken my mother's heart with this nonsense. Nutmeg next."

"Broken your mother's heart, how?" He passed her the nutmeg, enjoying the little heat that sparked where their hands touched. He'd done it deliberately that time, and she wasn't exactly storming off with indignation.

"Mama loves Devlin, but she's not his mama, so she's kept her distance out of respect for his feelings for his real mama. It's gotten better since Dev married. Do you suppose there's such a thing as too much spice?"

Interesting question. "I don't know. We'll have to have a little taste."

Before his better judgment could interfere, Vim took Sophie's hand in his, dragged her index finger through the batter, and brought her finger to his mouth. He swirled his tongue around the end of her finger and withdrew it slowly from his mouth.

"Seems perfect to me." He kept her hand trapped in his own, abruptly aware that what he'd done was about as blatantly sexual as if he'd just dropped his breeches and started stroking himself before her very eyes.

She smiled at him, withdrew her hand, and passed him the nutmeg. "Then it's time to put it in the oven. Tell me about your home." She turned to pour the batter into a greased pan, and the moment passed, which was both a relief and a disappointment.

A relief, because her self-possession hinted she might have some experience, and an experienced woman was fair game—as housekeeper, companion, lady's maid, or whatever she was, Sophie might have allowed herself some discreet sexual recreation.

And she might allow herself just a little more.

The disappointment was because he'd like at that very moment to sit her up on the sturdy counter and step between her legs until those legs were wrapped around his flanks, urging him into her heat. He watched her bending down to put the—what was it they'd been making?—into the oven, and yet more lascivious images crowded into his mind.

She'd asked him something, though. Something about...

"I'm not sure I have a home."

She straightened and closed the oven door. "Surely you dwell somewhere when you're not on your travels." The look she sent him was far too serious for the concentration he could muster.

"I have properties. There's a lovely old place in Surrey where I spend a few weeks most years. I suppose that qualifies."

She began putting things away. "You travel all the time?"

Something in her manner suggested she wasn't finding the topic pleasant.

"I used to spend some of my winters up in Cumbria with one of my sisters. I've occasionally bunked in with my brother here in Town, and I often check in with my younger sister wherever she's governessing, but as I've mentioned, my sisters are married now and starting families."

Vim brought a kettle of hot water from the pot swing in the fireplace and poured half the contents into the dishpan, then added some cool water as Sophie began stacking dirty dishes by the sink.

Standing beside her, he tried to fathom what emotion was radiating from her and failed.

"Then what is this travel to Kent about?" she asked. "You seem quite intent on it."

Was that the bee in her bonnet?

"Kent is the family seat on my father's side. When my mother remarried, I went with her to Cumbria. I'm not sure my uncle was comfortable with the arrangement, but he never protested. Shall I wash while you dry?"

"I will not refuse a man's offer to wash dishes in my kitchen."

She still did not sound precisely happy.

"Tell me of your home," Vim suggested, using a rag to start washing the mixing bowl in the warm, soapy water.

"It's beautiful. Big but cozy. It will always be home."

"Do you miss it?"

She accepted the clean bowl from his hand, frowning as she did. "There comes a point where the familiar can feel more like a prison than a haven, though in truth it's neither. It's a home, a place laden with memories, nothing more and nothing less."

Vim stared at the water. "A place with obligations too."

"What sort of obligations?"

Now why had he brought up this mare's nest of unpleasant associations?

"My uncle is getting older, and he refuses to hire new staff. My aunt has never been a traditionally practical woman, and their daughters are no help whatsoever."

"Do you worry for them?"

"Oh, of course."

Something in his tone must have given him away. Sophie put a hand on his sleeve. "What aren't you saying? If you worry about them, you must love them."

"I hardly know them, Sophie. They're my only paternal family, but I've never…"

She was standing right beside him, her big green eyes holding a world of compassion Vim did not want directed at him. He did not deserve it, certainly not from her.

"Sophie, I want to kiss you."

He'd meant to state it as a problem, a small, troubling matter she needed to take into consideration when she stood so close. It came out sounding like a prayer, like the most fervent wish hoarded up in a tired, lonely heart that had long since lost the courage to wish.

She set aside the towel in her hand while Vim watched her mouth in anticipation of a gentle, even kind, rebuke.

And then the baby let loose with a loud, indignant squall.

❧

Sophie didn't want to kiss Vim Charpentier; she wanted to gobble him up like a holiday sweet, to gorge herself on the feel and taste and scent and sound of him.

Which was… disquieting. She'd been kissed before, fondled, groped, pulled into dark alcoves and promised all manner of outrageous pleasure when it became apparent she wasn't entertaining offers of marriage.

Some of it she'd found… intriguing, but not intriguing enough to risk the consequences.

Thank God for fussy babies. They gave a woman time to recover her balance and assess what it meant when a man did not kiss a lady but announced that he wanted to.

"Let me try." Vim took the small spoon from her hand—no flirtation there—and addressed himself to the baby. "If you refuse your victuals, young Kit, we will spank you soundly and send you to bed quite hungry indeed. I will eat them up myself, in fact. Yummy warm porridge with plenty of juicy apple mashed into it. How can a man—even such a wee man as you—refuse such ambrosia?"

"We will not spank you," Sophie interjected. "Not until you are at least as big as Vim."

When the baby spat out another mouthful of his dinner, Vim sat back, a puzzled expression on his face. "The boy is in a mood about something. We can try again later, and he'll probably eat a double portion."

He tried putting the baby back in the cradle, which provoked more fussing and kicking.

Sophie took Kit from Vim's arms. "He wants cuddling."

By the time darkness had fallen, they'd both had turns holding the infant, rocking him, and distracting him with trips to the window. While Sophie took the last of the cakes and muffins from the oven, Vim toured the kitchen with the baby in his arms.

"You never did tell me about your family seat," Sophie said. Thanks to Kit's fussiness, there had been no opportunity to revisit Vim's startling pronouncement regarding that other business.

That business about kissing her. About *wanting* to kiss her.

"It's a pretty enough place," Vim said. "The main part is a Tudor manor with sprawling grounds. My aunt is quite the landscaper. Uncle likes to fish, so we have two ornamental lakes and several ponds."

"And you will inherit this property?"

"For my sins, yes."

She paused in the middle of wrapping the bread in muslin. "Do I take it you have bad memories of this place?"

He touched noses with the baby, which Sophie accounted a stalling tactic.

"I have few memories one way or the other. My father died when I was quite young, and then we removed to Cumbria. I spent a few holidays in Kent when I was at University, but my uncle didn't issue many invitations. My siblings in Cumbria seemed to need some looking after, so I bided there more than anywhere else. That bread smells heavenly."

"When it cools, we'll have some. Kit seems quieter."

"Shall we try to feed him again?"

It was a good suggestion. Sophie didn't for a minute believe Vim had told her more than a superficial glossing over of the truth, but concern for the child won out over her curiosity.

Then too, if she pried too closely into Vim's situation, he might feel entitled to pry into hers, which would not serve in the least. A man might announce a desire to kiss a housekeeper or other domestic, but he'd never risk offending a duke's daughter with such forwardness.

Fortunately, the child ate prodigiously, as Vim had predicted. Sophie cut fat wedges of bread for her and Vim, added a dish of butter to the tray, and followed Vim and the child down the hallway to the servants' parlor.

They put the baby on his nest of blankets, and

while Kit seemed to enjoy the change of scenery, he made no move to get up on all fours but stayed on his belly or his back, content to watch as Sophie and Vim ate their buttered bread.

"I should have made you a proper dinner," Sophie said. "I wonder how women with large families ever get anything done."

Vim looked over from where he was letting Kit gnaw on his finger. "You're from a large family."

"My mother had scads of help. Does that child's diaper need changing?"

Vim inhaled through his nose. "Not yet. Will you be all right when I leave tomorrow, Sophie?"

She was glad he'd brought it up, but she would not ask him to stay. Men of a certain ilk could sit still only so long before all around them suffered for it.

And what difference would one more day make? Whether Vim knew it or not, she was still Lady Sophia Windham, with a baby to find a decent home for, and he was a man whom she was convinced never bided any one place long enough to call it home.

"We'll manage." She started tidying up the remains of their meal. "My brothers will show up in a day or so, and two of them are parents."

"I do believe His Highness is yawning."

Subject changed. He'd wanted reassurances that she'd be able to manage, nothing more. Well, she wanted some things from him too.

"Let's see if we can't read him to sleep," Sophie suggested. She went to the bookshelves and pulled down a volume of Wordsworth's poetry. There was a copy in the library as well, but that version would not have dog-eared pages or a spine cracked and creased with frequent readings.

She didn't realize Vim was standing behind her until she bumped into him when she turned around.

"Steady." His hands closed around her upper arms then dropped away. "What have you found for us?"

"Poetry. Nice, calm, pastoral poetry to read a fussy young man to sleep."

"What sort of household is this, Sophie, that the servants read poetry?"

"A proper English house. Bring My Lord Baby to the sofa." She sat a little left of the middle of the sofa, so Vim would have to sit either near her or very near her. He scooped Kit up in a blanket and obligingly took the place to her left, right next to her, which allowed him to prop his elbow on the sofa's armrest.

"I vote you read and we fellows will listen in rapt silence."

"And thus Kit is indoctrinated into the conspiracy to which all males belong," Sophie muttered.

"And you ladies don't have conspiracies of your own?" He brought the child to his shoulder and started rubbing Kit's little back. The sight sent odd tendrils of warmth drifting through Sophie's insides.

"We women are cooperative by nature; that's different from conspiratorial."

She chose a poem at random, not so much to have the last word as to distract her thoughts from the man beside her. Vim was holding Kit with just as much affection and care as if the baby were his own child.

Which he was not. Kit wasn't her child, either. She must not forget this. Sophie paused, blinked, and tried to recall her place. She had most of the book half-memorized, which meant it was little help when notions of parting from Kit came stealing relentlessly into her brain.

While she was making a pretense of choosing another poem, something warm settle on the back of her neck.

Vim's hand. He'd said nothing. His body hadn't shifted. He still held the child in the crook of his arm, but he was touching Sophie too. His thumb was making slow circles on her nape, sending a melting warmth down her spine and up into her brain.

"Read more slowly, Sophie. I think Kit's dropping off."

She nodded carefully so as not to dislodge the wondrous gift of his hand on her person. When she read again, she could barely focus on the words, so drunk was she with the sensation of Vim Charpentier's touch on the bare skin of her neck.

She'd wished for things from him before he left, things no decent woman admitted to wanting, things she could never have asked for in words.

And this slow, sweet touch was part and parcel of what she'd wished for.

⁓

There was something fundamentally aberrant about a man who could sit with an infant propped in one arm and still have erotic thoughts about the woman encircled with the other arm. Though they weren't truly erotic thoughts.

They were more the kind of thoughts that noticed

the way firelight brought out red highlights in Sophie Windham's hair, or saw how graceful the curve of her cheek was, or heard the sheer cultured beauty of her voice as she did Wordsworth proud. The poetry made Vim miss the Lakes, from whence the poet drew inspiration, where Vim's younger siblings were gathering for the holidays.

A man could breathe in Cumbria. He could ramble for hours on the fells with no company but the land, the sheep, the gorgeous sky, and his own thoughts. Mental images of the Cumbrian countryside had sustained Vim on many a journey, but they filled him now with a peculiar kind of loneliness.

Beside him, Sophie fell silent.

"He's asleep." Vim whispered the words, unwilling to disturb the child or the moment. When Sophie made no move to leave the sofa, he stroked his hand along the side of her head, reveling in the feel of her warm, silky hair.

She put the book aside, and the next time Vim caressed her hair, she sighed and turned her face into his shoulder. They stayed like that for a long time, while the fire burned down and both thought of what might have been and what could never be.

Six

SOPHIE WOKE TO THE FEEL OF VIM'S THUMB TRACING along the curve of her jaw. She didn't move, but he must have sensed her waking, because he uncurled his arm from her shoulders.

"You take the baby," he said quietly. "I'll bank the fire and collect his cradle. We'll have you both upstairs before he wakens."

That hand caressing her neck was to be a tacit touching, then. Better than nothing but little more than a memory. A pleasurable memory but not quite a happy one.

Sophie stood and took the baby from Vim, making no effort to avoid the slide of her hand along his abdomen as she did. Vim was warm and muscular, and sitting in the circle of that warmth had been a gift Sophie could not openly acknowledge. She had the sense as she cradled the child to her chest she was going to miss Vim Charpentier's warmth for a long time after she'd managed to wish him safe journey on the morrow.

He did a thorough job of banking the fire and

securing the hearth screen, but he did it quietly too. He took the cradle under one arm, picked up a single candle in his free hand, and led Sophie through the cold house to the family wing.

"Let me light your candles," he said, stepping back to follow her inside her bedroom. The room was wonderfully warm because Vim had kept the fire going all day.

"This is a nice room," he said, glancing around. "It looks both well appointed and comfortable."

Perhaps he was thinking it was a fancy room for a woman who had yet to acknowledge her relationship to the Duke of Moreland, but Sophie made no reply. When Vim set the cradle by the hearth, Sophie laid the sleeping baby down and tucked the blankets around him.

"He seems worn out," she said. Vim lit the candle by her bed then came over to light the two on each end of her mantle.

"You seem worn out, Sophie Windham. Kit can stay with me tonight, if you like."

"Not when you have to travel tomorrow. You need your rest, while I can nap when the baby does. Good night, Vim, and thank you."

He set his candle on the mantle and peered down at her, moving close enough that his bergamot scent tickled her nose.

"What I said earlier?"

She nodded. He'd said a lot of things earlier, but she knew exactly which handful of words he referred to.

"I can't offer you anything, Sophie. I'm dealing with problems in Kent I can't easily describe, but it's urgent that I tend to them. Even if I weren't being pulled in that direction, I have obligations all over the empire, and you're a woman who—"

She stopped him with two fingers to his mouth.

"I want to kiss you too, Vim Charpentier."

He looked briefly surprised, then considering, then a slow, sweet smile graced his expression. He lowered his head and touched his lips to hers.

A kiss, then. She'd at least have a kiss to keep in her heart. Sophie rose up on her toes and wrapped her arms around him while he slid his hands along her waist to steady her by the hips. His hold was careful, gentle even, and utterly secure. When she thought he meant for them to share something just a tad more than chaste, that hold shifted, bringing her flush up against his body.

She made a sound of longing in the back of her throat, and his hold shifted again. She realized a moment too late he was anchoring her for the real kiss, for the press of his open mouth over hers, for the startling warmth of his tongue insinuating itself against her mouth.

She'd heard of this kind of kissing, wondered about it. It hadn't sounded nearly as lush and lovely as Vim Charpentier made it. He didn't invade, he explored, he invited, he teased and soothed and sent an exotic sense of wanting to all quadrants of Sophie's anatomy.

He made her, for the first time in her female life, *bold*. She ran her tongue along that plush, soft space between his bottom lip and his teeth.

He growled, a wonderful, encouraging sound that had her tongue foraging into his mouth again, even as she laughed a little against his lips. The kiss became a battle of tongues and lips and wills, with Vim trying to insist on gentleness and patience, and Sophie demanding a complete melee.

Her hands went questing over the muscles shifting and bunching along his spine then up into the abundance of his golden hair. Bergamot stole into her senses too, a smoky Eastern fragrance that made her want to seek out the places on Vim's body where he'd applied the scent.

She undid his queue and winnowed her fingers through his hair, even as she felt Vim's arms lashing more tightly around her.

Against her stomach she felt a rising column of male flesh, and it made her wild to think she'd done that, she'd inspired this man to passion.

"Vim Charpentier…" She breathed his name against his neck, finding the pulse at the base of his throat with her tongue.

"Sophie… Ah, Sophie."

Her name, but spoken with such regret. It might as well have been a bucket of cold water.

The kiss was over. Just like that. She'd been devouring him with her mouth and her hands and her entire being, and now, not two deep breaths later, she was standing in his embrace, her heart beating hard in her chest, her wits cast to the wind.

"My dear, we cannot."

Vim's voice was a quiet rumble against her body. He at least did her the kindness of not stepping away, though his embrace became gentle again, and Sophie felt him rest his cheek against her hair. Her mind drunk and ponderous, she only slowly realized what he was saying. He'd contemplated taking her to bed—and rejected the notion. In her ignorance, she'd been so swept up in the moment she'd given no thought to what might follow.

What could have followed.

If only.

She tried to tell herself "if only" was a great deal closer to her wishes and desires than she'd been one kiss ago. There was "if only" in Vim's voice and in the way he held her, as if she were precious. It was a shared "if only."

It was better than nothing.

She realized he'd hold her until she broke the embrace, another kindness. So she lingered awhile in his arms, breathing in his scent, memorizing the way her body matched up against his much taller frame. She rested her cheek against his chest and focused on the feel of his hand moving over her back, on the glowing embers of desire slowly cooling in her vitals.

He'd experienced desire, as well—desire for her. His flesh was still tumescent against her belly. Before she stepped back and met his eyes, Sophie let herself feel that too.

If only.

❧

Vim drifted to awareness with jubilant female voices singing in his head. "Arise! Shine! For thy light is come!"

Too much holiday decoration had infested his dreams with the strains of old Isaiah, courtesy of Handel.

Though somebody was most definitely unhappy.

He flopped the covers back and pulled on the luxurious brocade dressing gown before his mind was fully awake. In the dark he made his way down the frigid corridor and followed the yowling of a miserable infant to Sophie's door.

"Sophie?" He knocked, though not that hard, then decided she wasn't going hear anything less than a regiment of charging dragoons over Kit's racket. He pushed the door open to find half of Sophie's candles lit and the lady pacing the room with Kit in her arms.

"He won't settle," she said. "He isn't wet; he isn't hungry; he isn't in want of cuddling. I think he's sickening for something."

Sophie looked to be sickening. Her complexion was pale even by candlelight, her green eyes were underscored by shadows, and her voice held a brittle, anxious quality.

"Babies can be colicky." Vim laid the back of his hand on the child's forehead. This resulted in a sudden cessation of Kit's bellowing. "Ah, we have his attention. What ails you, young sir? You've woken the watch and disturbed my lady's sleep."

"Keep talking," Sophie said softly. "This is the first time he's quieted in more than an hour."

Vim's gaze went to the clock on her mantel. It was a quarter past midnight, meaning Sophie had gotten very little rest. "Give him to me, Sophie. Get off your feet, and I'll have a talk with My Lord Baby."

She looked reluctant but passed the baby over. When the infant started whimpering, Vim began a circuit of the room.

"None of your whining, Kit. Father Christmas will

hear of it, and you'll have a bad reputation from your very first Christmas. Do you know Miss Sophie made Christmas bread today? That's why the house bore such lovely scents—despite your various efforts to put a different fragrance in the air."

He went on like that, speaking softly, rubbing the child's back and hoping the slight warmth he'd detected was just a matter of the child's determined upset, not inchoate sickness.

Sophie would fret herself into an early grave if the boy stopped thriving.

"Listen," Vim said, speaking very quietly against the baby's ear. "You are worrying your mama Sophie. You're too young to start that nonsense, not even old enough to join the navy. Go to sleep, my man. Sooner rather than later."

The child did not go to sleep. He whimpered and whined, and by two in the morning, his nose was running most unattractively.

Sophie would not go to sleep either, and Vim would not leave her alone with the baby.

"This is my fault," Sophie said, her gaze following Vim as he made yet another circuit with the child. "I was the one who had to go to the mews, and I should never have taken Kit with me."

"Nonsense. He loved the outing, and you needed the fresh air."

The baby wasn't even slurping on his fist, which alarmed Vim more than a possible low fever. And that nose… Vim surreptitiously used a hankie to tend to it, but Sophie got to her feet and came toward them.

"He's ill," she said, frowning at the child. "He

misses his mother and I took him out in the middle of a blizzard and now he's ill."

Vim put his free arm around her, hating the misery in her tone. "He has a runny nose, Sophie. Nobody died of a runny nose."

Her expression went from wan to stricken. "He could die?" She scooted away from Vim. "This is what people mean when they say somebody took a chill, isn't it? It starts with congestion, then a fever, then he becomes weak and delirious…"

"He's not weak or delirious, Sophie. Calm down." It took effort not to raise his voice, not to get angry with the woman for overreacting so egregiously.

Except the same fear gnawed at Vim's guts: the baby was warm, he was unhappy, his nose was running more than a little… God in heaven, no Mayfair physician was going to brave this weather in the middle of the night to come tend a tweenie's bastard foundling.

"He's quieter now, Sophie," Vim said, injecting as much steadiness as he could into the observation. "Why don't you sing to him?"

"I can't sing when he may be dying."

She'd lost brothers. One of them at this same time of year… Something was nibbling at the back of Vim's mind. Something to do with colicky babies and why panic wasn't warranted, but he couldn't focus on retrieving whatever it was with Sophie near tears, the baby fretting, and no one at hand to help.

"Then I'll sing, though that will likely have the child holding his ears and you running from the room."

This, incongruously, had her lips quirking up. "My father isn't very musical. You hold the baby, I'll sing."

She took the rocking chair by the hearth. Vim settled the child in his arms and started blowing out candles as he paced the room.

"He shall feed his flock, like a shepherd…"

More Handel, the lilting, lyrical contralto portion of the aria, a sweet, comforting melody if ever one had been written. And the baby was comforted, sighing in Vim's arms and going still.

Not deathly still, just exhausted still. Sophie sang on, her voice unbearably lovely. "And He shall gather the lambs in his arm… and gently lead those that are with young."

Vim liked music, he enjoyed it a great deal in fact—he just wasn't any good at making it. Sophie was damned good. She had superb control, managing to sing quietly even as she shifted to the soprano verse, her voice lifting gently into the higher register. By the second time through, Vim's eyes were heavy and his steps lagging.

"He's asleep," he whispered as the last notes died away. "And my God, you can sing, Sophie Windham."

"I had good teachers." She'd sung some of the tension and worry out too, if her more peaceful expression was any guide. "If you want to go back to your room, I can take him now."

He didn't want to leave. He didn't want to leave her alone with the fussy baby; he didn't want to go back to his big, cold bed down the dark, cold hallway.

"Go to bed, Sophie. I'll stay for a while."

She frowned then went to the window and parted the curtain slightly. "I think it's stopped snowing, but there is such a wind it's hard to tell."

He didn't dare join her at the window for fear a

chilly draft might wake the child. "Come away from there, Sophie, and why haven't you any socks or slippers on your feet?"

She glanced down at her bare feet and wiggled long, elegant toes. "I forgot. Kit started crying, and I was out of bed before I quite woke up."

They shared a look, one likely common to parents of infants the world over.

"My Lord Baby has a loyal and devoted court," Vim said. "Get into bed before your toes freeze off."

She gave him a particularly unreadable perusal but climbed into her bed and did not draw the curtains. "Vim?"

"Hmm?" He took the rocker, the lyrical triple meter of the aria still in his head.

"Thank you."

He said nothing. Now that Kit was quiet and Sophie calmer, he could enjoy the pleasure of rocking a sleeping baby, even as he also enjoyed the picture of Sophie Windham, her hair a surprisingly long, dark braid over one shoulder, her natural form patently obvious through the soft flannel of her nightclothes.

A woman's feet were personal. A man might take possession of her hand, buss her cheek, slide her arm through his, take her in his arms for the space of a waltz, and otherwise admire her attributes, but he never, ever saw her feet.

Nor she his. Vim glanced down at his own bare toes. *I was out of bed before I quite woke up.* Sophie's words came back to him. Kit had them both trained, and Vim hadn't even known the child a week.

Thank God and all His angels Vim would be

leaving in the morning. If he stayed much longer, no force on earth would be able to drag him away from Sophie or the baby.

~~~

Sophie awoke to a wonderful sense of warmth and a heaviness in all her limbs that bespoke an exhausted rest. She nuzzled her pillow, and the scent of bergamot wound through her brain.

She opened her eyes just as her pillow heaved out a sigh.

"My goodness."

Vim Charpentier slept beside her, his arm around her where she was plastered to his side. Light came through a crack in the window curtains, and a quiet snuffling sounded from the cradle near the hearth.

"He's awake." Vim's voice was resigned. "I'll get him. It's my turn."

"He's not fussing yet. You have a few minutes."

Vim sighed gustily, and his hand settled on Sophie's shoulder. "I do apologize for appropriating half your bed. Just a few more days rest, and I'll be happy to vacate it."

There was weary humor in his tone and something else… affection?

"Vim?"

He shifted a little, so Sophie might have met his gaze if she'd had sufficient courage.

"I've never awoken with a man in my bed before. It's cozy."

"And I've never been referred to as cozy before, but the Infant Terrible has reduced me to viewing

that state as worthy in the extreme. You're cozy too."
He kissed her temple, and a sweetness bloomed in
Sophie's middle.

Affection. It was different from passion and different
with a man than with, say, a sibling or friend.

It was *wonderful.*

"Sophie?" The hand that had been petting her back
stilled. "I seem to have lost my dressing gown."

"Have you now?" She let her fingers steal across his
flat middle, except they bumped something smooth
and warm arrowing up from his groin. She had half
gripped its length when she realized—

"My goodness." She snatched her hand back, her
face flaming.

She felt his belly bounce with laughter. "More than
you bargained for, hmm? Close your eyes, and I'll
vacate the bed."

She closed her eyes—almost—though she did
not want him vacating the bed. That he could joke
and tease about something so... personal. She slitted
her eyes in time to see Vim's long, lean male figure
completely naked, his back to her. The adult male
fundament was... attractive, she realized. Muscle and
naughtiness and masculine beauty, in a way.

And then he turned to rummage for his dressing
gown, and Sophie felt her breath seize.

"You're peeking," he said, casual amusement
lacing his voice. "Shame on you, Sophie Windham."
He shrugged into the dressing gown, taking from
Sophie her first and likely only glimpse of an aroused
adult male.

But he hadn't hurried, and she'd seen... God above,

it made her mouth go dry, all that virility and power and lazy grace. His male parts were only fascinating for their novelty, the rest of him being sufficiently impressive that Sophie finally understood her sister Jenny's preoccupation with sketching and painting.

"I'll be back in a moment, my girl. Put some socks on when you leave that bed."

He sauntered out, leaving Sophie to glance at the clock.

For God's sake, the morning was well advanced. She'd never slept this late in her adult life.

Never stayed up half the night with a fussy baby.

Never awoken with an aroused male in her bed.

Never seen an adult male naked and so gloriously unconcerned with it.

And had never before wanted to see more, touch more, taste more...

"You have addled my female wits," she said, slogging out of the covers and crossing to the cradle. "You and your coconspirator. Men."

Kit regarded her with blue eyes so guileless it was as if he hadn't kept both adults up most of the night. His nose was not running, which was more relief than Sophie would have imagined.

"You were in a state last night, my friend. And when you're in a state, I am in a state. I daresay Mr. Charpentier was in a state too."

Quite a state. They'd taken turns with the child. Sophie had sung until her throat ached, and Vim had paced and paced and paced with the baby. She only vaguely recalled the man climbing into bed with her, then climbing back out, then climbing back in.

He'd let her sleep, and he was leaving today.

What if he'd left yesterday and Sophie had had to contend with Kit's bad night all by herself? What if she'd fallen asleep when the child needed her? What if Kit were truly falling ill?

"My mother raised ten children," she informed the baby as she changed his wet nappy on the chaise. "No wonder she can handle Papa without ever losing her composure."

Or raising her voice, or ever, ever disagreeing with His Grace before others. One night with a fussy baby and Sophie was regarding her parents with quite a bit more respect.

A knock on the door heralded Vim's return. "How is His Highness?"

"He's quite well rested. Unlike you. You should sleep now, Vim, and I'll feed the baby."

His crossed to the window and peered out. Sophie shifted to stand beside him, Kit in her arms. The snow had stopped, though a bitter wind was sculpting enormous drifts in the back gardens. "The paths you and the grooms shoveled yesterday are all but obliterated."

"I'll dig some more before I leave. Those duffers in the mews aren't up to a task this size."

He was leaving. His arm came around her shoulders as if to silently acknowledge the pain of that reality. "You'll manage, Sophie. That child could not be in better hands."

She turned into his body, the child in her arms, and Vim embraced them both.

He said nothing, just held woman and baby while Sophie tried to tell herself she was lucky. She'd been well and truly kissed; she'd been declared cozy; she'd been held and cuddled and given a good start on learning to care for the baby.

But she was not a baby. Held and cuddled was lovely. It was not enough. She'd wished for so much more. Wished for it until she couldn't wish any more, and then Vim Charpentier had appeared in her life, and the wishing was worse than ever.

"I'll feed the baby." She pulled back a little. "If you want to rest, I can wake you when your breakfast is ready."

Something crossed his features. He hadn't shaved, and he'd gotten a lot less sleep than Sophie had. He was weary, but also... sad, Sophie decided. That was something, that he was sad too.

"I'll start on the paths. A hot breakfast would be appreciated once you get Kit fed."

She slipped from his side. "If you fall asleep in a snowdrift, I will not wake you until spring."

She was almost to the door before his voice stopped her. "There's a part of me that doesn't want to go, Sophie."

She nodded and left, closing the door quietly. He was trying to be kind again, but this time it didn't feel at all welcome.

❧

Vim shoveled a path to the garden gate then shoveled one across the alley to the mews. That done, he decided a path from the house to the jakes at the bottom of the garden only made sense, and one from the gate to the jakes, as well.

And Sophie would appreciate having her back

terrace shoveled off too, so he went about that, trying very carefully to keep his mind blank as he did.

Yes, he was procrastinating his leave-taking.

Yes, he felt guilty for leaving Sophie here to contend with the baby—and the possible consequences of having given shelter to a male stranger while unchaperoned. She might be a mere domestic—or she might be something else entirely—but her reputation would be precious to her in either event.

And yes, he felt an ache at the thought of never seeing her again, never seeing Kit discover the joy of independent locomotion, never hearing the boy chortle with baby-glee at capturing an adult nose in his tiny mitt.

But Vim also felt guilty for staying when he knew those who depended on him—those who had every right to depend on him—awaited him in Kent.

Something prickled along the back of his neck. He looked up to see Sophie standing on the back porch without so much as a shawl over her day dress, her expression puzzled.

He stopped shoveling and crossed the drifted garden to stand a few steps below her. "I didn't think Higgins and Merriweather would get much done, as cold as it is and as old as they are."

"You've shoveled half the garden out, Vim. Come in and eat something before you leave us."

He let the shovel fall to the side and wrapped his arms around her waist. Because she was standing higher than he, this put his face right at the level of her breasts. Oblivious to appearances and common sense, he laid his head on her chest.

"You will catch your death, Sophie Windham."

She wrapped her arms around him for one glorious moment, the scent of spices and flowers enveloping him as she did. She offered spring and sunshine with her embrace, and Vim felt an ache in his chest so painful he wondered if it was the pangs of inchoate tears.

"Come inside." Sophie dropped her arms and took him by the hand. "You haven't eaten yet today, and shoveling is hard work."

She was patronizing him. He allowed it, unable to ask her the mundane questions that might put aside the reality of his impending departure.

Did Kit eat his breakfast?

Will you do more baking today?

Do you need more coal for your fireplace?

Is there anything I can do to delay this parting?

"Drink some tea," Sophie said when she'd got him out of his outer clothes. "Kit demolished his breakfast, and I've already changed his nappy twice. I've wrapped up some food to take with you when you leave too, and I'm heating potatoes to stuff in your pockets."

She remained quiet while he ate toasted bread, a large omelet, a substantial portion of bacon, two oranges she'd peeled for him, some fried potatoes, and a piece of buttered Christmas bread.

And despite all the piping hot tea he washed it down with, fatigue hit Vim like an avalanche when he got to his feet.

"You're ready to go?" Sophie was kneading dough at the counter, kneading it with ferocious concentration. He watched her punch and fold the dough for a moment before her question registered.

"I'll get my things from upstairs and be on my way."

She said nothing, just nodded and kept pummeling the dough. Even watching her do that, he felt some of that ache near his sternum, so he dragged himself up the back steps.

Not two hours earlier, he'd awakened hard as a pikestaff, ready to make love to the first woman to share a bed with him in ages. More than ready—eager, throbbing, and held back only by the knowledge that today was the day he'd leave her.

But God, to have her looking at him like he was some holiday treat... He'd dealt with himself swiftly once he had the privacy to do so, but it hadn't helped much.

When he got to his guest room, he made short work of packing. His quarters had been commodious in the extreme, providing every comfort a weary traveler might long for. He hung the brocade dressing gown back on a hook in the wardrobe and sat on the unmade bed.

He needed a catnap before he tried to take on winter travel at its worst. Just forty winks, one more little taste of luxury and comfort before he froze his testicles to the size of raisins trying to reach a place he'd never enjoyed being.

Vim toed off his boots and lay back on the bed. His last thought was that he ought to ask Sophie to wake him in another thirty minutes.

He arose to consciousness three and a half hours later, still thinking he ought to ask Sophie to wake him in another thirty minutes.

❦

"What have you done with our baby brother?" Gayle Windham, Earl of Westhaven, put the question casually as he passed St. Just—never was a belted earl more reluctant to use his title—a mug of ale.

"We're not partaking of the local wassail?" St. Just studied the mug as he settled in beside his brother on the sofa of their private parlor.

"Your damned punch gave me a pounding headache that faded only after an entire pot of strong tea, which tea required a half dozen trips to the blasted freezing privy, each trip specifically designed to make man appreciate another tot of hot grog. All in all, I'd have to say your one day of waiting out the weather has been a trial and a half."

St. Just set the ale aside untasted. "You're worried about Anna?"

"Anna and the baby, who, I can assure you, are not worried about me."

"Westhaven, are you pouting?"

Westhaven glanced over to see his brother smiling, but it was a commiserating sort of smile. "Yes. Care to join me?"

The commiserating smile became the signature St. Just Black Irish piratical grin. "Only until Valentine joins us. He's so eager to get under way, we'll let him break the trail when we depart in the morning."

"Where is he? I thought you were just going out to the stables to check on your babies."

"They're horses, Westhaven. I do know the difference."

"You know it much differently than you knew it a year ago. Anna reports you sing your daughter to sleep more nights than not."

Two very large booted feet thunked onto the coffee table. "Do I take it your wife has been corresponding with my wife?"

"And your daughter with my wife, and on and on." Westhaven did not glance at his brother but, rather, kept his graze trained on St. Just's feet. Devlin could exude great good cheer among his familiars, but he was at heart a very private man.

"The Royal Mail would go bankrupt if women were forbidden to correspond with each other." St. Just's tone was grumpy. "Does your wife let you read her mail in order that my personal marital business may now be known to all and sundry?"

"I am not all and sundry," Westhaven said. "I am your brother, and no, I do not read Anna's mail. It will astound you to know this, but on occasion, say on days ending in y, I am known to talk with my very own wife. Not at all fashionable, but one must occasionally buck trends. I daresay you and Emmie indulge in the same eccentricity."

St. Just was silent for a moment while the fire hissed and popped in the hearth. "So I like to sing to my daughters. Emmie bears so much of the burden, it's little enough I can do to look after my own children."

"You love them all more than you ever thought possible, and you're scared witless," Westhaven said, feeling a pang of gratitude to be able to offer the simple comfort of a shared truth. "I believe we're just getting started on that part. With every child, we'll fret more for our ladies, more for the children, for the ones we have, the one to come."

"You're such a wonderful help to a man, Westhaven.

Perhaps I'll lock you in that nice cozy privy next time nature calls."

Which in the peculiar dialect known only to brothers, Westhaven took as thanks for service rendered. The door behind them banged open on a draft of cold air.

"That old bugger in the stables says he knows where there's a Guarneri, a del Gesù, not five miles from this stinking inn." Valentine tossed gloves, hat, and scarf on the table as he spoke. "I've only seen a couple Guarneris, and by God they are beautiful. One was a viola, by the old master, but this is supposed to be by Bartolomeo Guiseppe Guarneri himself."

"Guarneri sounds like a dessert." St. Just passed his ale up to Val, who was making a circuit of the small parlor. "I favor good English apple tarts, myself."

"It's a violin," Westhaven said. "Valentine, are you suggesting you met some instrument dealer in the stables?"

"I'm not suggesting. I'm telling you the old man offered to take me to see this thing and even hinted it might be for sale."

Westhaven kept his silence, because some things— like older brothers—were occasionally gratifyingly predictable.

"Correct me if I'm wrong, Valentine," St. Just said, "but wasn't it you who was cursing and stomping about here last night because I suggested we wait one day to see what the weather was going to do?"

"I wasn't cursing. Ellen frowns on it, and one needs to get out of the habit if one is going to have children underfoot."

"Doesn't exactly work that way," Westhaven muttered. "I'm willing to tarry a day if you're asking us to, Val. Devlin?"

"The horses can use the rest."

Val looked momentarily nonplussed at having won his battle without firing a shot then dropped down onto a sofa. "So, Westhaven, are you saying children don't inspire a man to stop cursing?"

"They most assuredly do not," Westhaven said, rising. "His Grace and I are agreed on this, which is frightening of and by itself. Let me order some toddies, and we can discuss exactly how the arrival of children changes an otherwise happily married man's vocabulary."

Seven

"THERE ARE FEW CONSOLATIONS IN MY PRESENT state—do not piss on the mounting block, for God's sake. How many times must I tell you?" Aethelbert Charpentier, Eighth Viscount Rothgreb, nudged his dog's backside with the end of a stout oak cane. Talking to old Jock—not Jacques—was one of those consolations, and one could hardly indulge in it if the dog was off in a snit somewhere for having been too harshly reprimanded.

Jock lifted his head from giving the sight of his last indiscretion a good sniff and trotted obediently to the viscount's side.

"As I was saying, there are few enough consolations in my life at present, you being one of them, such as you are, her ladyship's predictability being another."

The dog sneezed.

"Meaning no insult, old boy, but we're neither of us what we used to be."

Jock sidled over to the snow-dusted remains of a chrysanthemum and lifted his leg, his expression blasé while he heeded nature's call.

"Piss on it, you say? Handy enough sentiment." The viscount scanned the sky while he waited for the dog—nothing wrong with Jock's bladder, no matter the canine was older in dog years than the viscount in human years.

"Nasty weather up toward Town," the viscount remarked as they resumed their progress. "Must be why my nephew has yet to make an appearance. He cuts the holidays closer and closer in those years when he deigns to show up at all. Some people don't know the meaning of family loyalty, even if they can be counted on not to toss up their accounts on her ladyship's best carpets."

If this slight reference to a previous lapse made any impression, Jock was not inclined to acknowledge it when the frosty ground was so full of interesting scents.

The trip to the stables seemed to take longer each season, but when a man felt the cold wheeze of eighty years breathing down his neck, he was grateful to be making the distance on his own two legs at any speed.

"Then again, perhaps Wilhelm has been detained in the North, or his life lost at sea. The boy can't be bothered to write, but for his damned quarterly accountings."

Jock stopped to water another bush—the dog's abilities were still prodigious in some regards—and came quietly to heel as the viscount paused at the bottom of the swale upon which the Sidling stables sat in aging splendor.

"Noble hound, my ass," Rothgreb said, stroking his hand over the dog's head. There would be hell to pay for not putting on gloves before leaving the manor, but Essie had gone wandering again. With the weather threatening to turn miserable, retrieving her from the stables became urgent.

"Go find her ladyship," Rothgreb said, moving one hand toward the stables. "Go find Essie, Jock."

The beast bounded up the hill, ears flapping with an eagerness better suited to a puppy. Jock would find Essie where they always found her, sitting on some dusty old tack trunk, a cat or two in her lap, her expression serene despite the fact that of late she was wandering without gloves, bonnet, scarf, or—and this was truly worrisome—even a cloak.

Essie had always had her own kind of sense, which was fortunate when their daughters and granddaughters suffered an egregious lack of same.

But lately...

"My lady?" Rothgreb tottered into the barn aisle, leaning on his cane for a moment while his eyes adjusted to the gloom—he was not catching his breath, for God's sake, the stables being only a quarter mile from the manor.

"Rothgreb?" Essie rose from her perch, gently displacing a worthless excuse for a mouser as she did. "My lord, you are without gloves and scarf. This is not well advised."

"My lady, you are without a cloak, gloves, or scarf yourself."

He said it as gently as he could, but the woman was haring around in a dress and shawl, and at her age, lung fever could be the end of her. She patted snow white hair braided neatly into a coronet.

"Why so I am. What an awkward state. Come say hello to Drusilla as long as you're here."

She glided away, drawing Rothgreb along by the hand. They stopped outside the stall of an elegant gray mare—Dutch's Daughter was the only mare the viscount continued to breed, because her foals were nothing short of spectacular, just as her granddame Drusilla's foals had been.

"Such a pretty girl," Essie crooned, taking a lump of carrot from her pocket. The mare sidled over to the half door and craned her neck to take the treat from Essie's hand.

"She is pretty," the viscount said, watching as his wife of more than fifty years stroked her hand down the horse's furry neck. "She's beautiful, in fact, and she always will be. But we mustn't spoil her, my dear. May I escort you back to the house?"

She gave the horse one more pat and turned to regard her husband sternly. "You certainly shall. I do not know what you were thinking, coming out in this weather without your gloves. I should spank that hound of yours for allowing it."

"Yes, you should, but luncheon is long past, and I missed you, Essie." He offered her his arm and sent up a prayer that they made it back to the house before spring—or before death claimed them.

"Have we heard from Vim?" She took his arm, but he leaned on her as much as she leaned on him. Essie's wits might be wandering, though she was yet wonderfully spry.

"Beg your pardon, my dear?"

"Vim," she said, speaking a little more loudly. "Wilhelm Lucifer Charpentier, our nephew and your heir."

"No word yet, but I do expect him."

They tottered along in silence for a good long way, uneven ground being something neither of them negotiated carelessly anymore. The dog sniffed about here and there but never let them get very far from his notice.

"He'll come," Essie said quietly as they reached the back gardens. "Vim is a good boy; he's just sad, as Christopher was."

"Christopher was a damned sight worse off than sad," Rothgreb said. Stairs were the very devil when there was even a dusting of snow involved. "Essie, what say you beat me at a hand of cards?"

"Chess would make the time go faster—assuming we can locate your chess set?"

Rothgreb glanced away. For all she was growing quite vague about a few things, he had the sense his wife was more astute than ever about others.

"If we can't find the Italian set, we can play cribbage or checkers."

She snorted as she swept up the steps ahead of him. "Not checkers. For heaven's sake, Rothgreb. That is a game for dodderers who can no longer tell a pawn from a knight."

"So it is." He ascended the steps more slowly than she and took her hand when they reached the terrace. Her hand was warm, while his—an old man's gnarled paw—was cold.

"Come along, Rothgreb. I feel like giving your pride a trouncing."

She smiled the smile of a much younger wife, and Rothgreb followed her into the house. They did not find the Italian chess set—he'd known they wouldn't, and he suspected Essie had known they wouldn't, as well—but she beat him soundly using the everyday pieces left about for the servants to use.

Trounced him handily, as she had been doing for decades whenever the notion struck her.

⤜ঌe⤛

Sophie awoke to silence and near darkness, the warmth of Vim's length blanketing her back.

"You're awake." Vim spoke very quietly, likely in deference to the baby sleeping in his cradle near the hearth.

"I'll be back." He patted her arm, and Sophie felt the mattress bouncing. She really should be getting up herself, but she heard Vim behind the privacy screen and decided to stay put. When he came back to the bed, he sat on the opposite side then scooted under the covers.

"You tried to wake me," he said, still nearly whispering. "Budge up, Sophie. We'll both be warmer." Because neither one of them was going to risk making a racket building up the fire, not while My Lord Baby was still napping peacefully.

"I tried waking you twice then built up your fire enough so you wouldn't catch a chill," Sophie said. "When I realized Kit was taking his nap, I climbed in here to avoid moving him to my room and having to make up another fire."

As if he'd believe that.

His arm came around her middle. "One more day won't make a difference."

She heard that he was trying to convince himself, but she needed no convincing. A weight on her heart eased, though it couldn't lift entirely. Tomorrow would come all too soon.

"Vim?"

"Sweetheart?"

The whispered endearment spoken with sleepy sensuality had Sophie's insides fluttering. Was this what married people did? Cuddled and talked in shadowed rooms, gave each other bodily warmth as they exchanged confidences?

"What troubles you about going home?"

He was quiet for a long moment, his breath fanning across her neck. Sophie felt him considering his words, weighing what to tell her, if anything.

"I'm not sure exactly what's amiss, and that's part of the problem, but my associations with the place are not at all pleasant, either."

Was that...? His lips? The glancing caress to her nape made Sophie shiver despite the cocoon of blankets.

"What do you think is wrong there?"

Another kiss, more definite this time.

"My aunt and uncle are quite elderly, though Uncle Bert and Aunt Essie seem the type to live forever. I've counted on them living forever. You even taste like flowers."

Ah, God, his tongue... a slow, warm, wet swipe of his tongue below her ear, like a cat, but smoother than a cat, more deliberate.

"Nobody lives forever."

The nuzzling stopped. "This is lamentably so. My aunt writes to me that a number of family heirlooms have gone missing, some valuable in terms of coin, some in terms of sentiment."

His teeth closed gently on the curve of her ear.

What was this? He wasn't kissing her, exactly, nor fondling the parts other men had tried to grope in dark corners—though Sophie wished he might try some fondling.

"Do you think you might have a thief among the servants?"

He slipped her earlobe into his mouth and drew on it briefly. "Perhaps, though the staff generally dates back to before the Flood. We pay excellent wages; we pension those who seek retirement, those few who seek retirement."

"Is some sneak thief in the neighborhood preying on your relations, then?"

It was becoming nearly impossible to remain passively lying on her side. She wanted to be on her back, kissing him, touching his hair, his face, his chest...

"Or has some doughty old retainer merely misplaced some of the silver?" Vim muttered right next to her ear.

"You'll sort it out." Sophie did shift then, as quietly as she could. She lay on her back right next to Vim, while he remained on his side, peering down at her in the gloom.

"We ought to leave this bed, Sophie." The warmth of his palm stole across her midriff, a slow, sumptuous caress that, even through the fabric of her old house dress, left Sophie wanting so much more.

"Kiss me." She twined her arms around his neck, hitched a leg over his hips, and pulled herself snug against him. "Please."

"God help me."

He growled this prayer against her neck as he drew her flush against him, his arm lashing around her back. When his mouth fused to hers, Sophie was glad she was lying down, because the sensations were that dizzying.

Vim, all around her, his hand cupping her derriere to drag her more tightly against his rising erection. The taste of him flooding her mouth, the feel of his heat and strength all along her body.

The sound of him groaning quietly as Sophie ran her tongue along his lower lip.

She anchored a hand in his hair, trying to quell any fool notion he might have about leaving the bed.

Leaving her life, yes, she was prepared to accept that—but not yet.

"My God, Sophie, we have to stop."

He shifted so he was on all fours over her, then shifted again, wedging his body down between her spread legs. Sophie brought her knees up and locked her ankles at the small of his back, and when he might have spouted more ridiculousness, she levered up and kissed him with every ounce of frustration and desire she could muster.

"Vim, I want…" He kissed her before she could finish that thought, kissed her witless. His tongue creating a sinuous rhythm that had currents of heat ribboning down through Sophie's body.

"Sophie, we can't…"

"Can too." She was a duke's daughter, capable of a duke's determination. She got her hand under the waistband of his breeches and sank her fingers into the bare, muscular swell of his flank.

"Naughty…" Vim muttered the word, but it didn't

sound like a scold, so Sophie moved her hand over and grabbed him outright by the derriere.

He pushed himself against her sex, provoking a wonderful, awful conflagration of sensations. Sophie wedged herself against him, and was mentally cursing the invention of clothing when a small sound penetrated the fog of her arousal.

Vim must have heard it too, for he went utterly still, lifting his head.

"The baby." They spoke in unison, Vim with resignation and something that sounded like relief, Sophie with horror: she'd forgotten utterly that the child was in the room.

"Let me up." She pushed at his shoulder, which was about as effective as pushing at Goliath's shoulder when he was at his oats. "Vim, Kit's awake."

"He might go back to sleep." The little thread of hope in his voice was almost comical.

"He never goes back to sleep."

"I'll get him." Vim kissed her nose and lifted away, taking with him warmth and a world of unfulfilled wishes. Sophie was just getting up her nerve to toss the covers aside when Vim came back to the bed, the baby snuffling quietly against his shoulder.

"Make room. My Lord Baby is coming aboard for a progress on his royal barge."

"Is he dry?"

"The royal wardrobe is quite in order, for now." Vim climbed on the bed and arranged himself on his side, the baby propped against the pillows between the two adults.

"He'll be hungry soon enough," Sophie said, taking

a little foot and shaking it gently. Kit grinned at her and kicked out gleefully, so she did it again.

"He likes a change of scene." Vim was smiling at the baby as he tickled the child's belly.

Sophie would not have thought to bring the baby to bed with them; she would not have thought to kiss Vim's nose before she left the bed.

She would not have thought she could fall in love with a man because he put aside his lovemaking to tend to a baby, but as she watched Vim smiling at the child, enjoying the child, she realized she'd gotten one stubborn, long-despaired-of wish to come true: she'd fallen in love.

She tarried for a few moments, listening to Vim speak nonsense to the child about navigating the treacherous waters of pillows and blankets; then she climbed out of the bed and went to build up the fire.

❧

Vim heard Sophie mutter something about heating up some porridge as she slipped into her socks. She was out the door a moment later, leaving Vim with his nose in the grasp of one happy, refreshed, and—thank the gods—dry baby.

He arranged the infant on his chest, a warm little bundle of comfort in an otherwise abruptly bleak situation.

"Attend me, young Kit."

"Gah." Kit made another swipe at Vim's nose.

"I'll seek retribution if you persist at this nose-capturing business."

Kit thumped Vim's chest and levered up, grinning hugely.

"Go ahead and smile, you little fiend. Do you know why the aristocracy have large families? Several reasons, the first being that any man who can afford to fuck his way through life finds it tempting to do so, and babies like you are the frequent result."

"Fah!" Another thump. "Fah, fah, fahck!"

"Boy, you had better watch your language when Miss Sophie is about. Say damn. Much less vulgar."

"Bah!"

"Bah is acceptable, used judiciously. The aristocracy have large families not just because they can, but also because their babies are kept well away from any situation where the pleasurable business of procreation might ensue. Babies belong in nurseries."

"Bah-bah-bah-bah!"

Vim lifted Kit straight above his chest, which provoked much chortling and waving about of small limbs. "Perhaps you'll be a balloonist."

He brought the baby back down to his chest, cradling the child close.

"You saved me from folly, you know. Sophie Windham is dangerous to a man's best intentions."

No comment from the child, leaving Vim to realize if the baby hadn't interrupted, Sophie Windham's clothes would likely be tossed all over the bed and Vim buried inside her as deep as he could get, doing his utmost to make her scream with pleasure.

Make them both scream.

"There's no reason not to," he murmured against the baby's crown. "She's willing, I'm so willing my eyes are at risk of being permanently crossed, but I don't think it would serve her…"

He fell silent, trying to think through how a man—a gentleman—ought to act under the circumstances. If she were merely a domestic—and the clues pointed as much in this direction as any other—then Sophie was not in a position to pursue marriage, but she brought marriage, commitment, and permanence to Vim's mind.

Also hot, soul-shattering pleasure, a confusing combination if ever there was one.

Kit grabbed for Vim's lower lip.

"Since when do babies come with claws?" He gently peeled Kit's fingers away and examined tiny fingernails. So small, but Vim knew they grew quickly. "We'll have to find some embroidery scissors and render you weaponless, me hearty."

He lingered in the bed with the child for a few more minutes, but when a particular, determined look came across the baby's face, Vim got them both quickly down to the laundry and dealt with the requisite change of linen.

"Are you baking again?"

He kept his tone casual as he carried the infant into the kitchen. Sophie looked up from the sink where she was peeling an apple.

"Adding some apple to His Highness's porridge."

"We made a stop in the laundry. Kit's ready to tour the Ring at the fashionable hour."

"At this rate, I'll need to boil some laundry for him." Sophie dropped some apple quarters into a pot simmering on the stove, sliced another fat quarter in half, and passed both sections to Vim.

He gave one to the baby and ate the other. "I didn't finish telling you about the situation at Sidling."

"That's your family seat?"

She stirred the apples then stirred a second pot, as well. He could tell nothing about her mood from her expression, tone, or posture, her reserve being the equal of some monarchs Vim had encountered on his travels.

"Sidling has been in my family since Norman times, though the manor house itself is fairly modest."

She peered over at him from the stove while Kit started waving a thoroughly gummed piece of apple about like a sword. "The name Sidling is very familiar."

"It's not particularly distinctive, but my aunt and uncle have been comfortable there, as have my cousins." Or they'd grown comfortable there once Vim had been able to take over the finances.

"And this is the place that's losing its heirlooms to thievery or something underhanded?"

She was putting together a tea tray now, her movements competent, graceful, and unself-conscious. Maybe she was the cook, or an undercook? Vim had to listen to her words again in his mind to register her question.

"We've come close to losing my aunt a time or two, as well, if Uncle's letters can be believed."

"How does one lose an aunt? Is she in poor health?"

"Not physically, but she's growing… vague. She wanders the estate, though I've suggested a companion could be hired for her."

He'd insisted on it, in fact, with his uncle writing back angrily that a man who'd been married to a woman for more than half a century knew better than to assign that lady a nursemaid over the woman's own objections.

Sophie got a pitcher of milk from the window box. "My father had a heart seizure not long ago. It threw the entire family into a tizzy."

"How is he faring now?"

She set the milk on the counter and got a bread knife down from the rack built onto the rafter overhead. "Better than ever. The heart seizure was the excuse my mother needed to take him more firmly in hand, and I think the excuse he needed to allow her to do so."

She cut several slices of bread, wrapped up the loaf, and set a small bowl of porridge, a clean napkin, and Kit's little spoon at one end of the table. "If you'd see to the honors, I'll make us some sandwiches."

Kit put away a prodigious quantity of porridge and apples, necessitating another trip to the laundry. By the time Vim had changed the child, built up the fire in the parlor, and washed his hands, darkness had fallen.

Sophie brought a picnic to the servants' parlor while Vim arranged the baby on the nest of blankets before the fire.

"There was something more I wanted to tell you, Sophie, about things at Sidling."

She paused in the act of passing him a plate piled high was sandwiches. "This doesn't sound like we're about to have a cheerful conversation."

"It isn't cheerful, but it isn't that remarkable, either. I'm my uncle's heir, you see, and I'm expected to marry sooner rather than later." And why she needed to understand this when he would not see her after tomorrow, Vim could not say.

She lifted the top off a sandwich of her own and

added a dollop of butter. "I forgot to put on the butter, though there's mustard enough." The small silver knife looked elegant in her hand as she made neat little passes over the bread, spreading the butter just so.

"My uncle has three daughters, and each of them has at least two daughters," Vim went on. He didn't pick up his sandwich—his mouth for some reason had abruptly become dry. "I have seven of these cousins of some remove. At least two are old enough to marry, possibly more by now."

"Are you inclined to marry one of them?"

She was fussing the baby's blankets, folding over the satin binding around the edge of the blanket and smoothing her palm along its length.

"Sophie, I hardly know these women, but I'm responsible for them. At the very least, I need to dower them. My aunt and uncle hint strongly that it's time I settled down, though the thought fills me with…"

He trailed off, trying to put a name to the heavy, anxious feeling in his gut. The conversation wasn't going in the direction he might have intended, if he'd used enough forethought to *have* intentions about it.

"Yes?"

"Dread, the idea of dealing with those twittering, fluttering young girls fills me with dread." He lifted his sandwich in one hand but did not take a bite. "Have you ever considered marriage, Sophie?"

"Not seriously."

And she wasn't considering it seriously now, either. That much was evident from her casual tone and the way she didn't meet his eyes. His careful hinting around was getting him a clear response from her, just not the response he'd hoped for. Whatever she wanted from him, it was going to be temporary and quickly forgotten.

On her part.

"Eat your sandwich," Vim said. "You can see why I need to be on my way. The situation in Kent is troubling from many angles, and it's the very last place I want to be over the holidays."

She made no reply but ate her sandwich in silence while the fire burned merrily and the baby figured out how to put his toes in his mouth.

Eight

SOPHIE GOT THROUGH THE EVENING WITH A SORT OF bewildered resignation. She had waited her entire adult life and much of her girlhood, as well, to feel a certain spark, a lightening of her heart when a particular man walked into the room.

Vim was that man, but he wasn't the *right* man. For once in her life, Sophie wished she had an older brother on hand to explain to her how it was with men.

How could Vim kiss her like that and speak of marrying a stranger—or possibly a cousin—in the next breath?

How could life finally introduce her to the man she'd been hoping she'd meet, only to limit her time with him so terribly?

How could she endure another Christmas watching her family lark about in high spirits, graciously entertaining hordes of neighbors in equally high spirits, while Sophie's spirits were anything but high?

And how—how in the name of God—was she going to part with Kit when the time came?

"You're not listening, Sophie Windham." Vim

brushed his thumb along her cheekbone. "Shall I put His Highness to bed?"

Sophie glanced down at the child nestled in her arms. "He's almost asleep."

She sat beside Vim on the worn sofa in the servants' parlor while he read Wordsworth by the firelight. His arm wasn't around her, and she knew why: those cousins in Kent, that aunt and uncle in Kent, that dread Vim had of marriage, those travels he'd undertaken for most of his life.

"Sophie, is something amiss?"

The concern in his voice nearly undid her.

"I do not want to part from this child, Vim. I wanted a few days to myself in this house because the good cheer others take in the season deserted me several years ago. I planned and schemed to have some time alone because I thought solitude would yield some peace, but it has yielded something else entirely."

That much was honest. Kit let out a little baby-yawn and stuck his two middle fingers in his mouth as if aware of the weariness plaguing Sophie's spirit. He was such a wonderful baby.

"I will travel on in the morning, Sophie, and I doubt our paths will cross again, but if you need money for the child, I will happily…"

She shook her head. The last thing she needed or wanted from him was money.

"Let's get this baby into his bed, shall we?" She rose off the sofa, Kit cradled against her heart. Vim tidied up the blankets and folded them into the cradle, letting Sophie precede him up the main stairs, through the freezing hallways and into her bedroom.

In just a few days, they'd fallen into a routine around the child as if Kit had been theirs since birth. It comforted and it hurt terribly to feel that silent sense of synchrony with a man she wanted so much from.

Vim lit the candle by Sophie's bed using a taper from the glowing coals in the hearth, then built up her fire and turned to regard her as she laid Kit in the cradle.

"Will you be able to sleep? I'm at sixes and sevens myself, having slept late and napped substantially. I expect women in their childbearing years get used to such disruptions of schedule."

It struck Sophie that Vim didn't want to leave her room.

"I'm tired, and tomorrow will come soon enough." She wanted him gone, and she wanted him to hold her close, as he had in his bed that very afternoon. But more than that, she wanted him to want her in his arms.

So much wanting and wishing.

Vim sank into a chair by the fire. "I'll wait until His Highness has dropped into the arms of Morpheus. Come sit, Sophie, and tell me about your brothers."

She took the rocking chair near the cradle, though the topic was hardly cheering.

For a moment she rocked in silence, listening to the soft roar of the fire and the sound of the baby slurping on his fingers. "Bartholomew fought under Wellington. My brother Devlin went with him, though each had his own command. Still, they kept an eye on each other, and Dev was there when Bart died. The Iron Duke himself sent a note of condolence. He commended Bart's bravery, his devotion to duty."

"But you are a woman, a sister, and you wish your brother hadn't been so brave."

"I wish he hadn't been such an idiot. My mother was spared the details, but Devlin was honest with his siblings: Bart approached a woman he thought was available for his pleasure. His command of the language was so poor he did not understand he was insulting a lady until pistols were drawn. It's a surpassingly stupid way to die but entirely in keeping with Bart's nature."

"And you are angry with him for dying like that."

Vim's words, quietly spoken, no blame or censure in them at all, had the ring of truth. "I am angry with him for dying, simply for dying. Bart was the oldest, the one groomed for leadership, and he would have made a magnificent patriarch."

"Was he a magnificent brother?"

Had he been? What was a magnificent brother?

"He was. He could be awful—he threatened to chase me around with earthworms until Maggie told me to threaten to put horse droppings in his favorite pair of riding boots. I have a deathly horror of slimy things."

"All sisters do." He slid off his seat and took the place on the floor beside Sophie's rocking chair, sparing a glance for the baby. "He's not getting to sleep as quickly as I thought he would."

"Pondering the events of the day."

"Pondering his next bowl of porridge. So what does a magnificent brother do, Sophie?"

"Bart could make you laugh. He could make fun of our parents without being vicious, and he could make fun of himself. He could also keep a secret. My mother did not want me riding out without a groom from the time I was ten or so, and Bart knew I often eluded the grooms. He'd mount up and take off in a different direction, but I knew he was there, a few hundred yards away, shadowing me. Devlin did the same thing."

"And you let them look after you like that."

"I wasn't a complete ninnyhammer. One time my pony threw me—bolted at a rabbit or something—and I tore my riding habit when I fell. Bart caught the horse before it could go thundering back to the stables without me. Dev sneaked a sewing kit down the stables so I could repair the damage before anyone was the wiser."

She did not see him shifting, but one moment he was sitting placidly on the floor next to the cradle, his knees drawn up, his hands linked around them. The next, he'd moved a few inches so his shoulder pressed against Sophie's thigh.

"Just when I thought I was recovering from Bart's death, I realized Victor wasn't going to get better. Victor sensed it before we did, but he kept this unhappy truth to himself, letting each of us accept it at our own pace. My father never quite got around to acknowledging that his son would die, and if my mother did, she wasn't about to contradict her husband."

"Was it a wasting disease?"

"Consumption."

With just her fingers, she stroked his hair. His queue had come loose—it often did around Kit—and Sophie felt an ache in her middle to think she wouldn't have another night like this to speak quietly with him, to feast her eyes on his golden splendor, to hear his voice coaxing confidences from her.

"Bloody miserable way to go." He tilted his head so his temple rested on her leg. "He fought it, I'm guessing."

"He fought so hard... not to live exactly, but to keep us from seeing how awful it was, struggling for breath, not being free to laugh lest it mean he started coughing, not being free to run, to ride, to do anything really. I read to him by the hour."

"What was he like as a younger man?"

"Full of the devil." Sophie traced the shape of Vim's ear, a delicate, curious part of man's body she'd never considered before. "Victor got my father's charm and my mother's ability to smooth over an awkward moment. He was handsome—all my brothers have the audacity to be gorgeous men—urbane, witty, graceful on the dance floor and dashing in the saddle. Victor was..."

It hurt to recall all that Victor had been. It hurt awfully.

"And then he was ill," Vim said. He turned and rose up on his knees, slipping his arms around Sophie's waist. "He's the one who died at the holidays?"

She nodded, the lump in her throat making words too difficult. Vim's hand settled on her hair, gently pushing Sophie's forehead to his shoulder.

"Cry, Sophie. When it hurts this badly, a woman needs to cry."

She'd cried. She'd cried buckets every time she'd left Victor's room because he was feigning sleep just to get rid of her. She'd cried after she chased the damned leeches from his bedside, as if bleeding was going to do anything in the face of consumption. She'd cried when she heard her father railing at Victor to quit malingering and get the hell out of that damned bed. She'd cried until she wished she couldn't cry any more ever again.

"I never cried where Victor could catch me at it."

"You never cried where *anybody* could catch you at it." His hand made slow circles on her back; his chin rested against her hair. The simple comfort of it, the acceptance, was reason enough to start crying all over again.

"Men don't cry." What this had to do with losing her brothers, Sophie didn't know. Another one of life's injustices, she supposed.

"Have you asked the brother who came home from war about that?"

"Devlin doesn't like to speak of his years of command." She lifted her head. "I suppose I could ask him now—he's doing better since he married."

And she wished she hadn't used that word—married.

"Ask him. Men have no corner on dignity. Women aren't the only ones who cry, but I suspect fatigue has lowered your defenses, Sophie Windham. Get you to bed, and I'll wait for this naughty boy to fall asleep."

He wasn't going to come to bed with her, and Sophie wasn't going to beg him. She instead went about her routine as if he weren't there by her rocking chair, the firelight gilding his hair and shadowing the planes and hollows of his face. She used her tooth powder behind the privacy screen, traded her house dress for a quilted dressing gown, and took her hair down.

"I don't suppose the coaches will be running in the morning," she observed as she took the brush to her hair.

"Likely not. I'll hire a stout beast and make what progress I can toward Kent. We're bound to get some melting once the storm moves on, and then it will be nothing but mud on the lanes."

"I will miss you." She spoke as casually as she could, though the lump was back in her throat. "Kit and I will miss you."

"I'll miss you both, as well."

She could not find the resolve to view that as positive. As tired as she was, as bleak as the evening's discourse had been, she couldn't view much at all as positive.

She was certain of one thing, though: when next Christmas came around, as it inevitably would, she wasn't going to be making any fool wishes about falling in love and living happily ever after.

⁂

"It's late." Valentine said, toeing off his boots. "Can't you write letters some other night?"

Westhaven didn't look up immediately, but finished whatever profundity he was penning at the desk and then shot Val a look. "Have you considered that for our parents, seeing all three of us married in little over a year must be a little like losing us?"

Val had long since given up trying to figure out the labyrinthine corridors of his brother's mind. It was enough to conclude the man was quietly, sometimes very quietly, brilliant, and prevaricating with him would serve no purpose.

"It felt like I was losing you when you married

Anna. There I was, happily quartered with both of my brothers for once, safe from the ducal eye, well supplied with whatever treats and blandishments a bachelor might desire, your excellent Broadwood grand available for my constant delectation, and then all of a sudden, you're rusticating with your dear wife in Surrey, and Dev has gone clear to Yorkshire to brood. If seeing him off to the Peninsula and then Waterloo didn't feel like losing him, watching him plod north to Yorkshire certainly did."

Westhaven stared at his letter for a moment then sanded it. "You are saying you missed us."

"Probably trying not to say it. Next you'll have me admitting I miss our sisters."

Westhaven, damn him, did not accept the comment as a flippant aside.

"Your wife will help with that."

"Ellen? They aren't her sisters." And now that the topic of missing people had been raised, Val felt a low, lonely ache for his recently acquired wife.

"She'll correspond with them, she'll make you go visit, and she'll invite them to visit. You're going to be a papa, which means you'll have offspring to show off. Might even get Their Graces to make a progress out to Oxfordshire."

"Do I want them to?"

Westhaven's version of a smile appeared, a little turning up at the corners of his mouth, accompanied by a softening of his gaze. That smile had been a great deal more in evidence since the man had taken a wife.

"You want them to visit at least once," Westhaven said, pushing back in his chair and crossing his long legs at the ankle. "You want the memory of His Grace sizing up your entire operation in a sentence or two. You want to hear Her Grace's voice in the breakfast room as you come in from your stables. You want to see how your wife can handle your parents without so much as raising her voice. You want to see Her Grace cry when she holds your firstborn and see His Grace pass her the ducal hanky while he swears at nothing in particular and tries not to look anxious."

"The ducal hanky?" Val had to smile. "I knew about the strawberry leaves and the coat of arms, but a hanky?"

"All right, call it the marital hanky. I'm sure you have one."

"Two on my person at all times, at least. When I was first married, I wondered if women were simply much more prone to crying and our sisters an aberration in that regard. They don't cry, that I've noticed."

"They cry." Westhaven's smile faded.

"You are fretting about Maggie. It's thankless, that. She'll come calling with a copy of the financial pages in her hand, and every time you try to turn the conversation to a handsome single fellow who doesn't want to be leg-shackled to a simpering twit from the schoolroom, Mags will start nattering on about some shipping venture."

"I listen when she natters on, I hope you do likewise. I strongly suspect Worth Kettering listens to her, as well."

"Kettering has no sisters. I don't mind giving him the loan of one of ours."

Westhaven was quiet for a moment, sealing up

his letter, and replacing the cork in the inkwell, but Westhaven's silences were always the considering sort, so Val kept his peace, as well. "I worry about Maggie," Westhaven said quietly, "but lately I've started worrying about Sophie too."

"You find this worrying enjoyable, then. Nobody worries about Sophie. She's the salt of the earth and the only thing keeping the ducal household sane when Her Grace abdicates the duty. We don't worry because Sophie is on hand."

"She's not at Morelands as we speak, is she?"

That was a fact. Westhaven was a fiend for pouncing on bothersome little facts—the man had read law, being a younger son who'd expected to make his own way in the world. This had permanently deranged a portion of the fellow's otherwise excellent mind.

"Sophie is entitled to socialize on occasion," Val said, but it bothered him: why would Sophie be socializing with neighbors who lived directly across the square when she could be in the country with her entire family? What Val recalled of the Chattell sisters wasn't so endearing as to explain Sophie's decision.

"She socializes with perfect grace, as do all our sisters." Westhaven started tapping his missive on the desk, first one edge of the folded paper, a ninety-degree turn, then another edge. "But I don't like her remaining behind when she might be out in the country, singing carols, decking the hall, and keeping an eye on the rest of the family. Sophie's a mother hen at heart."

"So we'll collect her and get her to Morelands, and you'll see we have nothing to worry over where

Sophie's concerned. Not one damned thing. Now if you're done with that desk, I think I'll be writing a short epistle to my wife."

"It's late," Westhaven said, rising. "You could write to her tomorrow."

"Tomorrow we strike out for London, though I think it will be slow going the closer we get to Town."

"But we're in no real hurry," Westhaven said, stretching languidly. "Not unless you count the burning desire to be reunited with our wives once we've seen to this errand."

"Right," Val said, uncorking the ink bottle. "No damned hurry at all."

≈

Vim glanced down at the cradle only to see two not-very-sleepy blue eyes peering back up at him.

Babies did not go to sleep when it would suit others for them to do so. This was probably The First Law of Babyhood, the close corollary being that they didn't stay dry or tidy when it suited others, either.

The feel of Sophie Windham's fingers tracing the shape of Vim's ear would be enough to keep him awake for some while, as well. He did not allow himself to watch her getting ready for bed, though the sheer domesticity of it was riveting.

One glimpse of her hair unbound, a dark, silky fall of feminine beauty cascading right down to her hips, and he was remaining in his seat only so he might not embarrass himself with evidence of his arousal.

The entire situation made no sense whatsoever. Sophie had indicated her willingness to accommodate his lust—though nothing more than that—as genteelly as a woman could, and Vim had no doubt he desired her.

Desired her on a level new and not wholly comfortable to contemplate.

And because he desired her so, he was wary of what she offered. Anything that seemed too good to be true generally was too good to be true. Father Christmas did not exist except in the hearts of innocent children; rainbows did not sport pots of gold where they touched the earth.

And Sophie Windham wasn't meant to be a man's casual Christmas romp.

And yet... He did not want to disappoint her.

Vim glanced over to see the baby had finally, thank ye gods, gone to sleep. He adjusted the blankets around the cherubic little form and rose to tuck the hearth screen closer to the fire.

He moved over to the bed and stood in silent indecision for a long moment. There would be no recrimination in the morning if he joined Sophie in that bed, none if he merely spent the night in slumber beside her, none if they again took turns getting up with the baby.

And none if they made passionate love in the dark of night.

"Did you close these curtains to indicate I would not be welcome in there with you, Sophie?"

He kept his voice just above a whisper, allowing her to feign sleep if she wanted to spare them both embarrassment. In the moment that followed, a procession of emotions tumbled through him: hope, anticipation, desire... and when Sophie made no reply, a disappointment that had precious little of relief in it. Perhaps he'd misread the situation, or perhaps Sophie wasn't—

The curtain moved, revealing Sophie sitting up in the shadowy interior. "You are welcome."

He couldn't read her expression, and there was nothing particularly welcoming in her tone.

"I'll be right back, then." He drew the curtain closed and moved as quickly as he could without making a sound. He lifted the cradle, baby and all, and moved down the darkened corridor to his room, which was warm enough to serve as the child's temporary quarters.

Vim's clothes landed in a heap on the floor, his ablutions were made with cold water, and his use of the tooth powder was particularly thorough. As he pulled on the brocade dressing gown, he glanced at the cradle.

"If you know what's good for you and good for Miss Sophie's spirits, you will endeavor to sleep for at least the next hour. Two would be more gentlemanly. I'll see to it you get a pony just as soon as you learn your letters if you'll accommodate me on this."

He slipped into the corridor, leaving the door cracked just an inch—not enough to let in a draft, but enough to let a baby's cries be heard two doors down.

And when he quietly closed Sophie's door behind him, eagerness turned to something... less certain.

Perhaps he should have brought himself off first...

Perhaps this wasn't wise. Assuming Sophie's welcome was a sexual overture—and that *was* an assumption, regardless of how she kissed him—no matter what precautions were taken, there was always a chance of consequences...

He pushed the bed curtains aside, appallingly willing to take on such consequences if taking on Sophie were part of the bargain, as well. Sophie didn't roll over as Vim shed his dressing gown, which had him pausing, one knee on the mattress, one foot on the floor.

She reached behind her and flipped the covers up. Vim scooted into their warmth and arranged himself along the lovely, feminine curve of Sophie's back. She was in her nightgown, which he took for a minimal boon to his self-control, until he heard a funny hitch in her breathing.

Had she been crying while he was plotting seduction?

"You did not want to speak of your brothers," he said, drawing his hand down the elegant length of her spine and feeling remorse twist in his gut where arousal had been just moments before.

"We don't, generally."

"When my father died, I was a small child. I did not understand grieving in silence, but my mother seemed to need it. Fortunately, my aunt and uncle understood I needed to speak of my papa. Uncle had sketches of Papa hung in the schoolroom, which had a salubrious impact on my studies."

She craned her neck to peer at him over her shoulder. "I think that's the first positive thing you've said about anyone or anything associated with your home."

"It's a lovely place, settled, comfortable, and…"

"Yes?" She subsided, which meant he couldn't see her face—and she couldn't see him.

"Come here, Sophie Windham. If you're to interrogate me, at least let us be comfortable while you do." He tucked her close enough that she had to be aware of the remains of his erection snug against her backside.

"Mr. Charpentier, you are without clothing."

"And soon you will be too, if you want to be."

"Tell me about Sidling."

It was to be slow torture, then, unless he'd mistaken her invitation entirely. No matter, it was the loveliest form of torture, and he would do his utmost to make sure it was mutual.

"Sidling goes back nearly to the days of the Conqueror, at least to hear my grandfather tell it. We've a Norman ruin that was likely a watchtower of some sort. The land rolls, but not so you can't get a crop in. There's a drive about a half-mile in length, oaks on both sides, some of them huge. We had a big windstorm when I was a boy, and one toppled. I stopped counting the tree rings at four hundred, and in the middle, where the rings were almost too small to count, my grandfather said those were the hard, cold years."

"Cold makes for solid wood. My brother has studied violin construction and says northern wood is preferred for that reason."

"These brothers of yours are an interesting lot." Her hip was interesting too. A smooth, beautiful conjunction of leg, derriere, and woman that fit beneath his palm perfectly.

"Tell me of your uncle and aunt."

Had she sighed a little with that question? He leaned over and kissed her cheek to investigate. When he resumed speaking, he kept his cheek against her hair.

"Uncle is a tough old boot. He was the spare, the oldest son having died before I was born. My father was an afterthought produced to secure the succession, but I'm told he was never very healthy. Grandfather was a force of nature, on his fourth wife when he died. He had every confidence he'd have more sons of that one too."

"You come from fierce stock, then."

Fierce. This was an apt description for the sensation pooling in his groin. He brought his attention to the conversation with effort.

"Uncle is fierce, in his way, so is my aunt. Proud, independent. They've let me wander half my life away rather than ask me for anything."

His hand stilled on her flank as it occurred to him some of his feelings toward Sidling were explained by guilt. Not disgust for the events in his past, nor resentment, nor impatience... Guilt, for having turned his back on not just some bad memories—his worst memories, really—but on people who'd loved him since he was Kit's age.

Sophie caught his hand in hers and brought it around her waist. "And you're worried about them now, worried you've left them too long alone."

"Yes." She said it better than he could have. Vim wrapped her close and just held her for a long, thoughtful moment. He could visit and discuss and flirt the night away, or he could gather his courage in both hands and do the woman the courtesy of asking her a simple question.

"Shall I pleasure you, Sophie?"

Nine

THERE WAS A VOCABULARY BETWEEN MEN AND WOMEN, one Sophie had never needed to understand. It included glances, sly innuendo, subtle movements of the fan, and even particular flowers combined into bouquets and presented at certain angles. It was a different and darker vocabulary than she'd learned in the drawing rooms and ballrooms, one more fraught with meaning and emotion.

So the precise implication of a single, quiet question—"Shall I pleasure you, Sophie?"—was not entirely obvious to her mind, but her body was clear enough on its meaning.

That velvet baritone promised he would kiss her, hold her, and very likely join his body to hers.

"We shall pleasure each other," she said, lying in the circle of his arm. She'd made her decision not in the heat of their passionate kisses but rather in quiet moments, watching him tickle the baby, listening to him read poetry, or watching him shovel a walkway to the privy in the freezing wind and snow.

"Then the nightgown will have to go." He set

his hand on her shoulder, and Sophie's heart started hammering in her chest. It was dark behind the bed curtains, cozy, and warm, but she covered his hand with her own.

His fingers trailed down her arm. "Eventually," he said. "It can go eventually. Let me hold you."

Not a question this time, and yet Sophie was certain if she announced she'd changed her mind and decided to excuse Vim from the bed, he'd sigh, flop the covers back—likely kiss her nose—and leave for his own room.

In the morning, he'd be pleasant and considerate, affectionate even, and then he'd be gone.

Gone.

Sophie rearranged herself on her back. She couldn't ask questions, lest he fathom the degree of her ignorance, so she kissed him. Leaned up and pressed her lips to his, cradling his jaw with her hand.

A man's jaw at the end of the day was a rough, scratchy thing. She reveled in this realization, a little detail that was the stuff of adult intimacy. He'd used his tooth powder too, and probably washed off with bergamot-scented soap.

He turned his face into her palm. "You must tell me what pleases you, Sophie."

"Such words are not always easy to say." Particularly when the feel of him—his jaw, his lips, his nose, his hair, the exact shape of the back of his skull against her palm—was so absorbing.

"Then show me. Put my hands where you want them to go, touch me where it pleases you to touch me."

"All over. I want to touch you all over."

He might have chuckled a little, or growled with pleasure at her words, though she'd spoken only the simple truth. Vim was a healthy, naked male in his prime, and she wished she'd had the courage to leave a candle burning and the curtains drawn back.

But no matter, she'd see him with her hands. While he lay quietly beside her, she explored the terrain of his chest, a warm, smooth plane of bone, muscle, and beating heart. When she grazed her palm over one small male nipple, she heard him inhale.

"It's the same for me as for you," he said, moving his hand to cover one breast. "There's sensitivity in certain places. Marvelous sensitivity."

Marvelous, indeed. Through the fabric of her nightgown, the weight of his hand covering her breast spread a lovely warmth through her middle. Her back arched into the contact without Sophie's volition, and when he closed his fingers gently over her nipple, her breath caught in her throat.

"The same, you see." Vim stroked her breast through the fabric then lowered his head and used his teeth to apply the same gentle, arousing pressure.

She had to do something, lest his attentions destroy her reason, so she found his nipple and emulated his caress.

"Like that," he said, barely lifting his mouth from her. He'd wet the fabric of her nightgown with his mouth, a maddening, frustrating, altogether pleasurable sensation that had heat coursing out through Sophie's body.

Did he want her mouth on him in the same way?

"Stop trying to think, Sophie." He lifted his head from her breast and shifted to fuse his mouth to hers.

Marvelous, lovely, spectacular… She winnowed her hand through his hair and gave herself up to the sheer glory of being kissed by a man who knew exactly what he was about. His onslaught was delicate and voracious at once, tasting her, enticing her tongue with his own, and inspiring Sophie to hike her leg over his hips in a bid to draw him closer.

Ah, God, she wanted this to go on forever. She wanted him to show her all there was to know and then forge new ground with her, ground unique to the two of them. And God bless the man, while he was storming her very reason with his kisses, his hand, his wonderful, warm hand, settled back over her breast.

"Vim…"

"Tell me if you like it." He closed his hand around her breast, drawing a little on her nipple. "*I* like it. I like the feel of you in my arms, Sophie. I like the way you taste, I like how your hands feel on my naked body."

"Naked." Naked was wonderful too. She slid her hand down over his flank to grab him by his derriere and try to pull him closer. "I like that you're naked. I like it a lot."

He closed his mouth over hers, and Sophie just barely registered the sensation of her nightgown being slowly, slowly eased up her thigh.

Naked was wonderful, and she wanted to be naked too. This burning, searing closeness was another part of what she'd wished for, lighting bonfires in all the places her mind and body had been growing steadily colder for years. She put her hand over his where it was stealing up her leg.

"Let me take this off." She said the words right against his mouth and was thus able to feel him smile. He shifted back just a few inches.

"Be quick about it, lest I aid you and shred the thing to bits."

And that had her smiling too, to think of him literally tearing her clothes off. She wrestled the nightgown over her head and tossed it to the foot of the bed.

"I'm naked." It didn't seem like a foolish thing to say; it seemed like the most brave, delightful sentence ever uttered. She was naked, he was naked in the same bed, and her body was humming and tapping its figurative toe to the tune of some lovely new music.

"And now what shall I do with you in your naked state?" he mused. "What shall you do with me?"

He settled on his back, leaving Sophie momentarily puzzled.

"You were doing quite nicely a moment ago," she said, drawing the covers up around her.

"And I could kiss and pet you forever, love, but we must indulge *your* desires if I'm to consider myself properly acquitted in this bed."

"How can you sound so damnably composed?" The question came out all of its own, leaving Sophie to realize that parting with her clothes was creating other vulnerabilities and exposures completely beyond her experience.

His shifted so his hands could close on her shoulders. "Iron self-discipline alone keeps me from tossing the covers aside and rutting on you like a satyr."

A thread of darkness in his declaration suggested he was telling the truth.

"Satyrs seem like such happy creatures." Sophie made this observation as Vim shifted her over him, until she realized he wanted her to straddle him.

Good God, was this why ladies never rode astride? The very position, with him laid out beneath her like a banquet, her knees pressed to his hips, left her feeling naughty and bold.

"The satyrs likely expired from an excess of pleasure. Come here, Sophie, and kiss me."

With the shift in position, Vim had changed the game. Sophie perceived this at the level of instinct, but it took gazing down at him for a moment before she understood the nature of the change.

"You want me to make love to you." She trailed her hand over his chest. "When I was on my back, you were making love to me."

His hand closed over hers on his chest, and he brought her fingers to his lips. "We make love to each other, Sophie." No teasing, no flirting, but rather a quiet gravity infused his voice. "I am here for the sole purpose of giving you pleasure, and that will give me pleasure long after this night has passed."

She folded down onto his chest, abruptly needing to hide her face against his throat. His arms closed around her, and the game changed yet again.

It was no longer a game at all. He'd leave in the morning, and Sophie would let him go. That was how matters would conclude, no matter what joy or pleasure they wrung from the night.

She spent a long, sweet moment curled against him,

his hands making slow patterns on her back. Against her belly, she felt the length of his erection—firm, warm, and undeniable, but passive.

"I will miss you, Vim Charpentier."

"This comforts me a little, Sophie, though I'd never want to cause you upset. I will miss you too."

They'd said the same words just a few hours ago, but here in the dark, nothing between them at all, the sentiments took on a different, more poignant weight. Sophie pushed his hair off his forehead, and with her hand on his crown, set her lips to his.

She put as much longing and wishing into her kiss as she knew how, but as he tasted her in return, she felt Vim shift the kiss to something deeper, closer. His hand moved slowly on her bare back, mapping bone, muscle, and sinew.

Sophie had the sense he was memorizing the feel of her even as his tongue traced the shape of her lips.

"Go easy, Sophie." He murmured the words against her neck. Sophie felt his nose grazing her ear, then he was levering her up so she hung over him. That same nose nuzzled at her breast.

"Vim... I want..."

"Yes." He closed his mouth over her nipple, drawing in a slow, wicked rhythm that ignited all manner of need deep in Sophie's body.

In her womb. She cradled the back of his head in her palm, holding him to her as she tried to adjust to what cascaded through her.

Tenderness certainly, unbearable tenderness for the man giving her such pleasure, but also desire. Hot, needy, unfamiliar, and for the first time, *welcome*.

"Move on me, Sophie. Pleasure yourself."

He arched up, snugging the length of his erection right against her sex.

Move on me, Sophie.

She wanted to move; she wanted to grind herself down on him, to consume him bodily, to have him—to *have* him—deep inside her body.

"Like this." Vim's hands settled on her hips, and he guided her along his length, a slow, wet sweep and return that had Sophie groaning softly.

It wasn't tidy, but it was... God in heaven... It was beyond words.

When she'd found a rhythm, his hands glided away, one to her breast, one to wrap around her lower back. He guided her, and yet he exerted no demands at all.

"Take your time." The words were just above a whisper, sinking into Sophie's brain through a haze of pleasure and growing bewilderment. "Take all night if you need to."

This was not copulation. Sophie had been raised with five brothers, she'd spent plenty of time in the barns and stables and mews at her family's various holdings. This was not copulation.

She could not think beyond that, for her body was beginning to throb with a low, hot want that connected Vim's fingers on her nipples with his mouth on hers and with the hard length of his arousal tight against her sex.

She desperately tried to keep the sensations separate, to be catalogued and savored one body part and memory at a time, but her boundaries were collapsing.

"Vim, I can't... I'm not..." She couldn't think,

couldn't seize words from the maelstrom Vim's male body was brewing in hers.

"Let go, Sophie. Fly, soar—I'll catch you."

He touched her, used his thumb on a part of her Sophie did not know what to call, a small scrap of flesh at the apex of her sex that abruptly commanded every bit of her attention.

"What are you...?"

"Hush, Sophie, my love. I'll catch you..."

That simple, knowing caress of his thumb had Sophie catapulting right out of her body into a cataclysm of pleasure and wonder and light that went on and on. She heard herself making some sort of sound—a sigh, a groan, a wordless plea—but Vim did not cease his attentions until she was panting and limp where she hung above him, braced on her arms.

"My... Goodness. Oh, my goodness."

She had flown, she had soared; in his arms she had broken free of every earthly weight—sorrow, loneliness, propriety, familial expectations, her own body. Past, present, and future had all dissolved in the blinding pleasure of his embrace.

"Hold me tight, Sophie." The words were a hoarse whisper against her throat.

She mustered wits enough to anchor her arm under his neck, abruptly aware that while she had endured unimaginable pleasure, he had not.

This was still not copulation, but he moved against her as if it were, used the slick friction of her sex on his rigid length to pelt her body with aftershocks of sensation that made clinging to him not merely possible, but as necessary as breath. She felt the same blinding pleasure gathering again even as Vim's hand at the base of her spine anchored her tightly to him.

"God in heaven, Sophie…"

Damp heat spread between them as Sophie was again seized with convulsions low in her body—shorter, sharper, and if anything, more intense than the previous bout. He kept their bodies seamed tightly until Sophie was panting against his neck, reeling and dizzy even as a part of her still floated in a cloud of pleasure.

"You." Vim kissed her cheek, leaving Sophie to wonder what exactly she'd heard in his voice: Affection, most definitely, a little wonder, and maybe something else—regret?

She snuggled in closer, wanting nothing except to hold him to her and be held by him.

"You soared for me, Sophie Windham. Soared high, if I'm not mistaken."

"So high I could no longer see the earth."

"Good." His hand trailed over her hair. "That's good."

He fell silent, his hand moving on her in a languid caress that had Sophie's eyes drifting closed.

She did not want to fall asleep. She wanted to treasure these moments, this lovely, warm, undreamt of intimacy with a man who tickled a foundling baby just to see the child smile.

A man who would be leaving in the morning.

❧

Vim's mind fractured in the haze of sexual satiety, impressions coming to him piecemeal and yet with a certain immediacy: The weight of Sophie's body pressed to his chest as she fought sleep.

The softening length of his cock amid the heat and carnal mess he'd created between their bellies.

The sheer, sensual pleasure of stroking her hair.

From the morass of emotion and sensory information stewing in his brain, he discerned three reasons why he had not taken fullest advantage of the pleasures Sophie had offered.

First, to assure himself there had been no permanent consequences of such an act necessitating his having to stay in touch with her.

She was different from other women in several regards: he wanted to spend time with her, not just in bed, but in the parlor, in the kitchen, in the stables. He liked simply to watch her, whether she was tending the baby, puttering with her baking, or braiding up her hair by the light of the dying fire. This difference might have borne potential for a broader relationship, except Sophie wasn't looking for marriage.

And while Vim had to admit marriage to Sophie would be highly problematic—she would want to dwell here in the south, among her family, when just visiting in Kent was a rare act of will for him—her indifference in this regard still rankled.

When a man was best advised to forget a woman, staying in touch with her was not wise.

The second reason he'd denied them both the pleasure of intimate joining had to do with the first: it was going to be hard enough to put these days with Sophie in a memory box without adding to the list the recollection of spending his seed in her sweet female heat. The third reason was purely practical, and the most compelling: if he made love to her truly, fully, without restraint, he was nearly certain leaving her would be impossible.

He'd made a colossal fool of himself over a woman once before, and once was more than enough.

Sophie lifted her head and pushed the remains of her braid over her shoulder. "I should check on the baby."

"I'll do that. I need to tidy up, in any case."

She frowned at him. "I don't know what comes now with you. Do we roll over and go to sleep? Will you seek your own bed?"

He could sense her trying to make her brain function on the strength of mental determination, but he could also hear the vulnerability lurking in her question.

"I'll fetch you a cloth and check on Kit, and then we'll talk."

Relief registered in the way her mouth curved up. God in heaven, did she think he'd just wander off down the freezing hall and drift away to sleep when she was here, warm and cozy, his seed still scenting her flesh?

He fished at the foot of the bed for his dressing gown but didn't belt it, letting the cold air blow some sense into his befogged brain. For a woman intent on casual pleasures, Sophie Windham had a certain artlessness, as if it had been a long time between frolics, or as if her previous liaisons hadn't done much for her confidence.

He knew from experience all it took was a little bad fortune, and confidence could be hard to restore. Man, woman, old, young, it made no difference. Part of him wanted to ask her about it, and part of him refused to entertain the idea lest she pry reciprocal confidences from him.

He let himself into his room, pleased to find Kit was snoring gently in the cradle.

"A pony it is, then. A fat little piebald who'll jump anything, provided you've set a course for the barn. You shall call him something presuming, Bucephalus, or Orion, but he'll have a pet name when you're private."

Vim tidied himself up in a few brisk movements, lifted the cradle, and returned to Sophie's room.

He built up her fire, wrung out a flannel, and hung it on the screen to warm while trying not to contemplate what his pet names for Sophie would be.

Love. *My love.* He'd called her that already. Sweetheart. My dear.

When he parted the bed curtains, he half expected her to be asleep, but she lay on her back, regarding him solemnly in the shifting firelight. Vim moved the covers off her carefully and started swabbing at the stickiness drying on her belly.

"This is intimate." She spoke quietly, her gaze following the movements of his hand. "But we could have been more intimate, couldn't we?"

Vim tossed the cloth in the general direction of the privacy screen. "Women are the braver of the two genders." He climbed under the covers and settled on his back. "They will discuss anything quite openly, while men go to war to avoid the near occasion of these discussions. Come here."

She cuddled along his side, her head on his shoulder. "Not all men are such cowards."

"It isn't cowardice, exactly. We're just formed differently. It's manly reserve."

Her hand drifted over his abdomen, counting his ribs and threatening his manly reserve. There was a quality to Sophie Windham's touch he hadn't encountered before, as if her hand were attached to her thinking brain, sending it information in some form other than words and images.

It was a lovely touch—tender, sweet, soothing and arousing at once.

"We did not quite..." She drew in a breath. "You did not want to join with me."

"For God's sake." He buried his lips in her hair, wanting to both laugh and... something else. Throw something breakable, perhaps. Several somethings. "Of course I wanted to. I want to this very moment, but such behavior has consequences, Sophie. Sometimes those consequences are permanent, such as the consequence now slumbering in that cradle by the hearth."

She was quiet, placated, he hoped, though she was female, and silence could mean all manner of things where they were concerned.

"I care for you, Sophie. I care for you far more than I want a passing moment of oblivion in your arms." It came out irritably, but he felt her smile against the bare skin at the side of his chest. A peculiar sensation from a surprisingly sensitive place on his body.

Her hand drifted lower, cupping his stones then closing along his length.

"Go to sleep, Sophie Windham." But he didn't move her hand.

"We've talked, then?"

"I have talked. Bared my damned soul. Don't suppose there are confessions you'd like share with me?"

Another smile. "I care for you too."

"Excellent. Now may we go to sleep?"

"Of course."

And this was fortunate, because a few more minutes of her casual exploration, her fulminating silence, and Vim's own conscience hammering away at the remnants of sexual satisfaction, and he might have been telling the woman he loved her, which would not do at all.

He was leaving in the morning, and stirring declarations of heartfelt sentiment weren't going to make that parting any easier, no matter how true those declarations might be.

❧

Sophie was coming to the conclusion that a wish half granted was worse than a wish denied.

Vim cared for her. He would not lie about such a thing, but it was tantamount to saying he did *not* love her. There had been a little ironic satisfaction in giving the words back to him, but only a little.

And more than a little misery too. The physical glories he'd shown her had been magnificent, though contemplating such behaviors on a casual basis left Sophie bewildered. Such a thing could never be casual to her, and she wished—such a troublesome word— they could never be casual to Vim, either.

"Though the whole business means nothing to you, does it?" She lifted Kit from the sofa, where she'd seen to his nappy after a big breakfast of porridge with apples and stewed carrots. "Will you miss him too?"

Kit swung his tiny paw in the general direction of Sophie's nose, catching her chin.

"That much? You don't want him to go, either, do you?" She hugged the child to her, feeling foolishly comforted. The baby would be leaving too, though she would wait to face that loss until her brothers showed up.

Her brothers, who were already overdue.

"What has you looking so solemn?" Vim appeared in the parlor doorway, his traveling satchel in hand. He did not look solemn; he looked rested and ready to be on his way.

"I am concerned for you. I doubt the coaches are running clear to Kent."

"I'll find one leaving the city then hire a horse if I have to. For all we know, the storm was fairly local, and the going might get easier south of Town."

"You will be careful?"

My goodness, she sounded like a wife—fussing for form's sake when there was really no need to fuss. Vim set his satchel down and closed the parlor door behind him.

"Sophie Windham, put that child down and come here."

"You are forever telling me to come here," she replied, but she put the baby on the floor amid his blankets.

"And now I am going away, so humor me." He held out his arms, and she went into his embrace. "I will not forget you, Sophie. These few days with you and Kit have been my true Christmas."

"I will worry about you." She held on to him, though not as tightly as she wanted to.

"I will keep you in my prayers, as well, but, Sophie, I've traveled the world for years and come to no harm. A London snowstorm will not be the end of me."

Still, she did not step back. A lump was trying to form in her throat, much like the lumps that formed when she'd seen Devlin or Bart off after a winter leave. She felt his chin resting on her crown, felt her heart threatening to break in her chest.

"I must go to Kent," he said, his hands moving over her back. "I truly do not want to go—Kent holds nothing but difficult memories for me—but I must. This interlude with you..."

She hardly paid attention to his words, focusing instead on his touch, on the sound of his voice, on the clean bergamot scent of him, the warmth he exuded that seeped into her bones like no hearth fire ever had.

"...Now let me say good-bye to My Lord Baby."

He did not step back but rather waited until Sophie located the resolve to move away from him. This took a few moments, and yet he did not hurry her.

"Say good-bye to Mr. Charpentier, Kit." She passed him the baby, who gurgled happily in Vim's arms.

"You, sir, will be a good baby for Miss Sophie. None of that naughty baby business—you will remain healthy, you will begin to speak with the words 'please' and 'thank you,' you will take every bath Miss Sophie directs you to take, you will not curse in front of ladies, nor will you go romping where you're not safe. Do you understand me?"

"Bah!"

"Miss Sophie, you're going to be raising a hellion." He smiled at the baby and leaned down, so his adult beak was in range of Kit's failing hands. "I cannot leave. I'm about to be taken prisoner." He spoke with his nose in Kit's grasp. "I promised the boy a pony when he learns his letters."

"I'll see to it. My brothers will aid me in this if I ask it."

Vim straightened, gently tucking the child's hand away. "I wish I could be the one providing that aid, Sophie." He advanced on her, wrapping his free arm around her while he yet held the baby with the other. "I wish a great deal that isn't very practical."

She let herself be held for just a moment longer, for the last statement was marginally of more comfort than being told he cared for her. Sophie took one last whiff of the warmth and male fragrance of him. "Wishes can be quite inconvenient."

Vim passed her the baby, kissed her cheek, and picked up his satchel. "Don't see me out, Sophie. Stay here warm and snug, cuddle this baby, and know that I will never forget you."

She nodded, willing herself not to cry. "We'll be fine, but thank you so much for… for everything."

He kissed her cheek again and withdrew, quietly closing the parlor door behind him. A moment later, she went to the window and watched his progress across the snowy expanse of the back gardens. He moved easily, a man used to dealing with the elements, a man very likely relieved to be on his way.

The sun was out, making the snow sparkle with painful brightness. When Vim got to the back gate, he turned amid all that sunshine, and his gaze sought out the parlor window.

Sophie waved, and emulating the idiot gesture of mothers everywhere, raised Kit's hand in a little wave too. Vim blew them a kiss, slipped through the gate, and disappeared.

She could not stand there, staring at the gate, at the brilliant sunshine, and she could not remain in the parlor that held so many lovely memories. But then, there were memories in the kitchen too, and the bedrooms, and the pantries, and even the bathing chamber.

So she got the baby comfortable in the steamy confines of the laundry, where the windows did not look out on the garden, where she could boil up laundry until her shoulders ached and her hands were red.

Where she could cry in peace.

∼∾∼

"There is no goddamned way we're going to make London today, possibly not even tomorrow." St. Just checked his horse's girth and glanced at his brothers. For men who'd never been on campaign, they traveled well, even under the circumstances.

"Their Graces will worry," Val said, patting his chestnut's neck. "Sophie ought to be comfortable enough, though."

Westhaven's lips pursed where he sat on his horse. "My backside is not comfortable in the least. I tell myself to be grateful we're not dealing with rain and mud, but a cold saddle is only a little less miserable."

"You should have let me fit a sheepskin under the

ducal arse," St. Just said, swinging onto his horse. "Baby Brother wasn't so proud."

Val climbed aboard too, settling onto the sheepskin cushion St. Just had fashioned the night before. "It helps with that initial, ball-shriveling shock of cold when your backside first lands in the saddle. You ought to try it, Westhaven."

"Perhaps tomorrow, if we're indeed to be traveling another day."

"We could push it," St. Just said as they moved away from the inn where they'd eaten a luncheon of bread, cheese, and ale. "But everybody's tale is the same: move south, and the snow is navigable. Move west, and the drifts are several feet deep in places."

"So we give it another day to melt and continue working south." Val's gaze went to the perfect azure sky making the day appear much warmer than it was. "At least I got a violin out of it. A little Christmas present for having been a very good boy."

This comment was too worthy of reply to be ignored, so St. Just, cheerfully abetted by Westhaven, spent the next five miles teasing their baby brother about just how good he'd been. This led the way to a lengthy discussion regarding Christmases past, naughty deeds, pranks, and family memories.

St. Just watched the sun sink and gave thanks that this campaign was so much more joyous than others he'd endured in the past. No, they would not make London in the limited daylight available, and they possibly wouldn't on the next day, either, but he was with his brothers, traveling in relative comfort, and all was right with the world.

"Do you recall the year His Grace thought Sophie should have a pet rabbit for Christmas?" he asked his brothers.

"And Bart told her it was headed for the stew pot. I thought she'd brain him senseless," Westhaven supplied. "I do believe it's the only time I've heard Her Grace laugh out loud."

"But we didn't tease our sisters quite as mercilessly after that," Val pointed out.

"Sophie has her ways," St. Just said. "To this day, a man does not cross her with impunity."

The talk drifted to various neighbors and other sisters before Westhaven was again complaining that his ass had frozen to the saddle, and this was hardly how the heir to a dukedom expected to spend his holidays.

When next they paused to rest the horses, his brothers washed his handsome face with snow for that nonsense.

❧

All day long, as Vim's toes turned to distant, frozen memories, the wind chapped his cheeks and nose, and the food Sophie had packed for him disappeared into a bottomless well of cold and hunger, he mentally kicked himself.

He should not have left Sophie to contend with that baby by herself. She was brave and sensible but a novice when it came to babies.

He should have escorted her to the cozy, well-staffed home of some titled acquaintance and set about courting her—a display of his connections in polite society accompanied by discreet indications of his wealth would have been a nice place to start.

He should have waited for better weather to leave Town, weather fine enough that he could take Kit with him to Sidling, where the boy could be raised up secure and safe in any number of useful professions.

He should have told her that whatever her station in life—cook, housekeeper, companion, governess, *whatever*, it mattered naught to him so long as she exchanged it for the position of his baroness.

And for variety, he'd occasionally curse himself for tarrying in London, at all. If he hadn't put off going to Kent to the very last minute, he'd be cozy and snug at Sidling right now, listening to his aunt explain the subtleties of chess to a man who'd been letting his wife beat him at the game for half a century.

And finally, when he lost sensation in his fingers, the food was gone, and darkness starting to fall, he admitted he should have made love to Sophie when they'd had the chance. He should have put aside all the rotten memories he carried courtesy of the last female he'd pursued in the Yule season, gotten together his courage, and made such passionate love to Sophie that she couldn't bear to let him go.

This thought coalesced in his brain just as his foot went sideways beneath him in the snow and he pitched headfirst into a fluffy drift at least four feet deep.

Ten

"WESTHAVEN WRITES THAT VALENTINE IS ON THE trail of some sort of violin, but it will cost them a day's traveling time." His Grace passed his wife the letter, a terse, efficient little epistle, via messengers, from a man who'd taken the disarrayed finances of the duchy and set them to rights in about a year flat.

"A violin?" Her brow furrowed as she perused the single page where she sat in serene domestic splendor near the study's fire. "A Guarneri. No small find. Do you suppose Valentine is happy?"

Women. They were forever pondering the imponderables and expecting their menfolk to do likewise.

"Valentine delights in his music, the Philharmonic is ever after him to give up his ruralizing and come to Town to rehearse them. One must conclude his rustic existence appeals to him."

Her Grace set the letter aside. "Or being up in Oxfordshire appeals to him, or his wife appeals to him. I think Ellen is yet shy of polite society."

If their youngest son ran true to Windham form, he was spending the winter keeping his new wife warm and cozy, and perhaps seeing to the next generation of the musical branch of the family.

His Grace reached over and patted his wife's hand. "We'll squire her around next Season, put the ducal stamp of approval on Val's choice. Care for more tea, my love?"

"No, thank you."

She fell silent, leaving His Grace to go back to a daunting pile of correspondence from his cronies in the Lords. Damned fools were still yammering on about this or that bill, when they ought by rights to be with their own families, catching all the pretty parlor maids under the kissing boughs.

This thought, for some reason, connected two thoughts in His Grace's often nimble brain.

"You're fretting over Sophie," he said, pushing his chair back from his desk. "This means whatever mischief she's up to, her brothers will be yet another day in retrieving her from it."

The slight—very, very slight—tightening at the corners of Her Grace's mouth told him he'd scored a lucky hit. "For God's sake, Esther, I can saddle up and fetch the girl home. It's not that far, and I'm hardly at my last prayers."

She gave him a look such as a wife of many years gives the man who taught her the true meaning of patience. "It is the depths of winter, Percival Windham, and you would leave me here with four daughters to keep out of trouble by myself when every home in the neighborhood is full of mistletoe and spiked punch. Sophie is the sensible one. She's doubtless visiting elsewhere in Town, and her letter to us went astray in the bad weather."

"Very likely you're right." For appearances sake, he was compelled to add, "It really would be no trouble, my love. I'll take a groom or two if you insist."

She turned her head, giving him a view of her lovely profile as she gazed out the window. "Sophie will be fine. Perhaps I will have a spot more tea after all."

"Of course."

Except by now, Sophie would have sent more than one letter regarding her change of plans. His Grace was reminded that all those years ago, when he'd been an impecunious younger son bent on a career in the cavalry, Esther had been considered the sensible daughter too. This had allowed them all manner of ill-advised leeway in their flirting and courtship, and accounted for Lord Bartholomew's arrival something less than nine months after the nuptials.

It gave pause to a loving papa immured in the country drinking tea, and tempted him to saddle up his charger and head for Town, miserable weather be damned.

༄

Sophie's day dragged, the hours punctuated by Vim's absence more than by the chiming of the tall clocks throughout the house.

Vim wasn't there to help Sophie feed the baby.

He wasn't on hand to deal with some of the soiled nappies.

He wasn't offering the occasional opinion on the baby's situation, leaving Sophie to fret that the child was too warm, too cold, too tired, too everything.

Vim wasn't offering adult companionship at meals,

complimenting Sophie's pedestrian cooking as if it were the finest food he'd ever eaten.

He wasn't there when Sophie contemplated and discarded the notion of lying down for a nap while Kit caught his midafternoon forty winks, there being memories to haunt her in both her own bed and Vim's.

Vim wasn't there, and he would never be there again.

"I have both brothers and sisters," she told Kit as she laid him in the cradle near the kitchen hearth. "My oldest sister is named Maggie. She's several years my senior and very much a comfort to me, though she's technically a half sister."

Would Kit have brothers and sisters? Did Joleen's footman have other children he'd created with the same careless disregard for the child's future? That Kit might have siblings and never know them, or not even know of them, made her chest ache.

"Maggie explained certain things to me when I made my come out," she said, shifting the cradle to the worktable and putting it beside her baking ingredients. "Things no decent girl is supposed to know." And how Maggie came upon the knowledge was something Sophie had wondered.

"She explained that people like you get conceived at certain times and are less likely to be conceived at other times."

The baby kicked both feet and stuck the two middle fingers of his left hand in his mouth.

"I was hoping…"

She'd been hoping Vim would show her what the greatest intimacy between a man and a woman could be. She'd been hoping to be his lover, to know with him what she'd never know with any other man.

She'd been hoping a great deal more than that, actually, but hoping was as useless as wishing.

"I'll deal with Valentine's room tomorrow," she assured the baby. "I'll clean up the bathing chamber, and I'll send along a cheery note to Their Graces."

She wouldn't lie, exactly, but she wouldn't mention Vim Charpentier, either. Among her siblings, there was tacit acknowledgment of the occasional need to protect their parents from some unsavory detail or development. It was the kind thing to do, also the most practical, as some aspects of reality did not yield even in the face of ducal determination.

Like the reality that Vim was gone and Sophie would never see him again.

Tomorrow she'd tidy up Val's room and set the bathing chamber to rights. She'd remove every possible piece of evidence indicating Vim had been in the house.

Just… not… yet.

She started mixing another batch of stollen, though she had to pause occasionally to swipe the stray tears from her cheeks.

⤞

"My dear, I'm afraid it's gone."

Essie Charpentier watched her husband rise slowly from where he'd knelt on the carpet. One foot on the floor, then while he braced himself, the second foot. A pause, then a hearty shove to gain him his feet, and another pause to recover from the effort.

"Perhaps it is simply misplaced," she said as she'd

said on an appalling number of other occasions.
"Or maybe the servants have taken it downstairs for
cleaning in anticipation of the holidays."

He cast a glance at her, an indulgent glance laced
with a little worry and a tinge of… pity. She hated the
pity probably as much as he hated the ways she pitied
him in recent years too.

"It was just an olive dish," she said briskly. "We
have several such, and the olives don't taste any better
or worse for being in an antique silver dish or a piece
of the everyday." She laced her arm through his. "It's
sunny today. I'm of a mind to visit the ancestors, if
you'll escort me?"

"Of course, my dear." He patted her hand and
led her from the family parlor where they'd stored
various items of sentimental and commercial value for
years—the heirloom parlor.

"Perhaps we should take to locking the doors of
certain rooms," Essie said. "You lock the billiards
room when we're not entertaining."

"The gun cabinets are in there, my dear. I'm sure
the dish will turn up, and it wouldn't do to offend the
staff by locking the place up like some medieval castle.
Is there someone in particular you'd like to see?"

"Christopher, I think. We must tell him his son is
coming for a visit."

They made a slow, careful progress up the main
stairs, a majestic cascade of oak whose grandeur was
dimming in Essie's eyes as her knees increasingly
protested the effort of climbing it.

"We hope Wilhelm will grace us with his presence," the viscount said, pausing at the top of the

stairs. "There's been no word, Essie, and he should have been here by now."

She paused, as well, and surveyed the front hall below them. All was cheerfully laden with swags of pine. A wreath graced the inside of the front door, and a fat sprig of mistletoe wrapped with red ribbon was temporarily hanging from a coat rack in the corner.

"Kiss me, Rothgreb."

He smiled down at her, a trace of his old devilment in his blue eyes. "Naughty girl." But he bussed her cheek and patted her hand. "My lovely, naughty girl."

"Vim will be here," she said as they resumed their progress toward the portrait gallery. "He keeps his word."

"He keeps his word, but his associations with Sidling are not cheerful, particularly not his associations with Sidling at Yuletide. Watch the carpet, my love."

"His associations with Sidling *are* cheerful. He passed his early childhood here cheerfully enough."

Rothgreb held the door to the portrait gallery open for her. Down the length of the room, some eighty feet, a fire was laid but not lit in a huge fieldstone hearth, and the cavernous space was chilly indeed.

"Shall I fetch you a shawl, Essie?"

He was not going to argue with her about Vim's past, which was a small disappointment. Arguing warmed them both up.

At the rate they moved around the house lately, by the time he fetched the shawl, she'd be frozen to the spot she occupied. She smiled at him. "Bellow for Jack footman. Trotting around will keep him from freezing."

"He won't move any faster than I will, and you know it." Nonetheless, Rothgreb strode off and could be heard yelling in the corridor. The man had a good set of lungs on him, always had, and no amount of years was going to take away from the broad shoulders favored by the Charpentier menfolk.

"He misses you," Essie said to the portrait occupying the wall to the right. She let her eyes travel over blond hair, blue eyes, a teasing hint of a smile, and masculine features so attractive as to approach some standard of male beauty.

"Christopher was the best looking of us three boys," Essie's husband said, slipping his arm around her waist. "He would have made a wonderful viscount."

"You make a wonderful viscount, and to my eyes you were and still are the pick of the litter." She let her head rest on his shoulder, sending up a prayer of thanks that, for all their years, they still had each other and still had a reasonable degree of health.

"You need spectacles, my lady." He smiled down at her then resumed perusing his brother's portrait. "Vim never comes here, you know. When he visits, he doesn't come say hello to his old papa, nor to his grandfather, either."

"He will this time." She decided this as she spoke, but really, Vim was not a boy any longer, and certain things needed to be put in the past.

"No scheming, Essie, not without including me in your plans."

This was the best part of being married to Rothgreb for decades—though there were many, many good parts. Another man might have become indifferent to his wife, the wife who had been unable to provide him sons. Another man might have quietly or not so quietly indulged in all manner of peccadilloes when the novelty of marriage wore off.

Her husband had become her best friend, the person who knew her best and loved her best in the whole world, and Essie honestly believed she'd come to know him as well as she knew herself. It made up for advancing years, white lies, misplaced olive dishes, and all manner of other transgressions.

She hoped.

"Let's say hello to Papa while we're here," Rothgreb suggested. "He always did have great fun at the holidays."

Essie let him steer her down the gallery at a dignified pace. The point of the outing had been to get away from the family parlor and wipe the concern from Rothgreb's eyes. If she had to freeze her toes among previous generations of Charpentiers, then so be it.

"If Vim comes, we will have great fun again," Essie said. "His cousins will mob him, and the neighbors will come to call in droves. Esther Windham still has five unmarried daughters, Rothgreb. Five, and their papa a duke!"

"Now, Essie, none of that. The last thing, the very last thing Vim will be interested in is courting a local girl at the holidays, and given how his previous attempt turned out, I can't say as I blame him."

Essie made a pretense of studying the portrait of Rothgreb's father. The old rascal had posed with each of his four wives, the last portrait having been completed just a few months before the man's death.

He was a thoroughgoing scamp of the old school,

a Viking let loose on the polite society of old King George's court. She'd adored him but felt some pity for his successively younger wives.

"I believe I shall send Her Grace a little note," Essie said.

His lordship peered over at her, his expression the considering one that indicated he wasn't sure whether or how to interfere.

"Just a little note." She patted her husband's arm. "I do think Vim inherited the old fellow's smile. What do you think?"

"I would never argue with a lady, but I honestly can't say I've seen Vim's smile enough to make an accurate conclusion."

True enough. They tarried before a few other portraits, and by the time Essie's teeth were starting to chatter, Jack footman tottered in with a cashmere shawl for her shoulders.

※

Sophie's first day tending Kit without Vim's assistance went well enough as far as the practicalities were concerned. She made more holiday bread and a batch of gingerbread, as well, took care of the baby, folded the dry laundry, placed stacks of clean nappies and rags in strategic locations about the house, and successfully avoided going into the room where Vim had slept.

Tomorrow, maybe.

A fresh bout of tears threatened—my goodness, she hadn't cried this much in years—and she glanced over at where Kit was slurping on his fingers on the parlor rug. While she watched, he took his hand from his mouth and started twisting his body as if to look at the fire dancing in the hearth.

"You're getting grand ideas again."

His gaze went immediately to Sophie where she sat on the floor beside his blankets.

"Go ahead; amaze yourself with a change in scenery."

As if he'd understood her words, Kit squirmed and twisted and gurgled until he'd succeeded in pushing himself over onto his stomach. His head came up, and he braced himself on his hands, grinning merrily.

"This is how it begins with you men," she said, running her hand down the small back. "You have this urge to explore, to sally forth, to conquer the world. Next you'll be going for a sailor in the Royal Navy, shipping out for parts unknown, all unmindful of the people you leave behind, the people who love you and worry about you every moment."

Kit hiked his backside skyward and managed to get on all fours. Sophie wiped the drool from his mouth, but his grin was undiminished.

"Men. You must adventure; you must go; you must march and sail and charge about in the company of your fellows. No matter you could be killed, no matter you break hearts every time you leave."

Kit slapped his blankets with one small hand.

"I've never understood men. Bart would come home on winter leave, and nothing would do but he'd go off to Melton, riding to hounds, hell-bent, in all kinds of evil weather. It wasn't enough to taunt fate by charging into French lines. No, he must risk his neck even on leave."

She fell silent, frowning as Kit raised his second hand and slapped it down, as well, slightly ahead of where it had been previously. He bounced with pleasure, cooing and rocking, until he scooted one small chubby knee a little forward. He rocked on his knees more exuberantly, thrilled with himself for simply moving one small leg.

He was… crawling. Amid more noise and rocking and drooling, he shifted the second knee, then a hand, until he was shortly pitched forward onto his little chest, smacking the blanket and kicking his glee. He struggled up to all fours again and started rocking once more, while Sophie felt another damned tear slide down her cheek.

When it appeared Kit had tired of his newfound competence and Sophie had regained control over her wayward composure, she picked him up and hugged him close.

"I am proud of you. I am most, most proud of you, but these exertions will work up an appetite."

She herself had eaten quite enough, finding it did nothing to fill the sense of emptiness created by Vim's absence. The kitchen was toasty warm and full of the scent of gingerbread when Sophie repaired there to make Kit's dinner, but it was as if her usual misery at the holidays had descended manyfold.

"The house is decorated," she told the baby. "There are presents under the tree at Morelands, the servants are all enjoying their leave, and I want simply to sleep until all the merriment is over. But I mustn't sleep."

Kit spit out his last spoonful of mashed potatoes.

"I can't sleep because I must find a family to

love you, and I can't sleep now because both of the bedrooms hold too many memories, and besides, I let the fire go out in Vim's room. Except it isn't Vim's room. It is Valentine's room, or it was before he ran off and got married just like his brothers…"

She was babbling, babbling about her brothers leaving her, for death or marriage, it made no difference. They were all gone, her father had had a heart seizure, and he would be going in time too. Kit would soon be gone, and Vim…

Vim was gone. A sob, a true, miserable, from-the-gut sob welled up, propelled by the darkness falling outside, the effort of being good for an entire day, and God knew what else. Sophie caught herself around the middle and swallowed back the ugly sound which, should it escape her, she feared would signal a permanent loss of her self-control.

It did not stay subdued, though. No, her body was determined to have its unhappy say. But then the back door slammed shut, and despite her misery, Sophie heard the sound of booted feet stomping in the hallway.

Good heavens, Merriweather or Higgins would be coming to check on her. She rose, swiped at her cheeks, and set aside the baby's spoon and rag.

Then a thought hit her that had her sitting down hard on the bench again: her brothers. Oh, please God, *not those three*. Yes, she'd missed them terribly, but at that precise moment, she didn't want to see anybody, not one soul except the very person she would never see again.

Vim.

He stood in the doorway, looking haggard, chilled to the bone, and so, so dear. Sophie flew across the kitchen to embrace him, the sob escaping her midflight.

"I'm sorry," he said, his arms going around her. "There were no coaches going to Kent, no horses to hire for a distance that great. No horses to buy, not even a mule. All day... I tried all day."

He sounded exhausted, and the cold came off him palpably. His cheeks were rosy with it, his voice a little hoarse, and against his ruddy complexion, his blue eyes gleamed brilliantly.

"You must be famished." Sophie did not let him go while she made that prosaic, female observation. Despite all she'd eaten, she was famished—for the sight of him, for the sound of his voice, and oh, for the feel of his tall body against her.

"Hungry, yes. How fares Kit?"

Still they did not part. "He started crawling today. Not far, not quite well, but he'll figure it out quickly. He's just finished dinner."

Vim moved off toward the table but kept an arm around Sophie's shoulders.

"Clever lad." He smiled down at the baby propped amid blankets and towels on the table. "Making your first mad dash across the carpet, are you? And I missed it. You must have a demonstration for me before you retire, for it's a sight I would not miss."

"I missed you." Sophie hugged Vim close, burying her face against his chilly shoulder.

She felt a sigh go out of him and wished she could recall the words. Yes, they were the truth, a defining truth, but still, she should not have said the words.

When he did not give those unwise words back her to, she stepped away. "Put your wet things in the parlor to dry. I'll see about dinner."

≈≈

Vim did as ordered, spreading his sodden greatcoat over the back of a wing chair, adorning the mantel with his gloves, hat and scarf, peeling off the knit sweater he'd worn all day, and removing his boots and the soaked outer pair of trousers from his legs.

In his life, he'd been colder, more exhausted, and hungrier on many occasions, but he'd never been so glad to come in from the weather.

The picture Sophie had made, sitting in a faded brown velvet dress at the table—her dark hair gathered sleekly at her nape, her soft voice a low caress in Vim's mind as she'd spoken to the child—had been an image of heaven.

And then the feel of her…

No hesitance, no remonstrance for reappearing uninvited, nothing but her arms lashed around him in welcome, and those dangerous, wonderful words: *I missed you.*

"These are socks I knitted for my brother Devlin when he was wintering in Spain," Sophie said, closing the parlor door behind her. "I made several pairs for him and for Bart, as well, but Bart's things were distributed among his men, in accordance with his wishes. Devlin went north in summer, so all his winter socks were left behind."

"My thanks." He took the socks from her, letting his hand brush hers.

"You are chilled to the bone, Vim Charpentier. I cannot believe you wandered London the entire day."

He sat to peel off his soaked and chilled footwear, struck with the precious domesticity of the situation.

Sophie sank to her knees before him. "Allow me." She plucked the socks she'd just handed him from his grasp and scowled at his feet. "For heaven's sake, Mr. Charpentier, could you not have paused to warm your feet up at the occasional public house?" She went on scolding him, taking a kitchen towel from her shoulder and applying it briskly to his feet.

"Easy, Sophie, the feeling comes back in an uncomfortable rush."

She paused, the towel wrapped around his feet. "Did you really look all day for a horse?" She studied his feet while she posed her question, and Vim resisted the urge to stroke a hand over her hair.

"Not all day. First I made the rounds of the coaching inns in Mayfair, Soho, St. James, Knightsbridge, and halfway to the City. There were a few traveling due east, but I could not buy a place, even on the roof, not for any price. People are determined to join their loved ones for the holidays."

She nodded and hugged his feet. Hugged his big, cold, red, soon to be madly itching feet. Hugged them right to her breasts.

It was ridiculous, that gesture. Extravagantly generous, personal, and practical all at once, given her bodily warmth. He allowed it and realized his heart would never recover entirely from encountering Sophie Windham.

"I tried to rent a horse, but nobody wanted to part with a sound animal for so great a distance when many people were willing to pay dearly for a local hire. I tried the abattoirs and breweries, everywhere. No luck."

And no room at the inns he'd tried, either. He didn't tell her that.

"I'm glad." She let his feet go and resumed rubbing them gently. "I'm glad you came back where I can feed you properly and know you're warm and safe and well fed."

She did feed him, fed him thick slabs of smoked ham, steaming potatoes seasoned with herbs, cheese, and butter, and crusty slices of bread fresh from the oven. It was the best meal he'd ever eaten, and yet he tasted little of it because he was preoccupied watching her move around the kitchen, tidying up as he demolished his dinner.

And then he followed her down the hallway to where he'd never thought to be again, sprawled on the thick carpet of the servants' parlor, Kit on all fours between them, rocking and cooing and enjoying the life of a cosseted baby.

"Kit listened to your parting sermon this morning. He was a very good boy today." She lay on her back, her head turned to watch the baby.

"And he's thriving in your care. Sophie. You aren't really going to give him up, are you? If Their Graces were tolerant of the tweenie's situation, they might make allowances for you."

He regretted the words, because they opened the door for him to wonder again what exactly her position in the household was. He told himself it didn't matter—it *still* didn't matter—because again, he'd be leaving in the morning.

She curled over on her side, pillowing her cheek on her hand as she gazed at the fire. "Their Graces would indulge me, did I ask it of them, but Kit needs a real family, brothers and sisters, a mama, a papa. I would spoil him shamelessly, and there's much I do not know about raising a child."

He gave in to the temptation to touch her, reaching over and smoothing the side of his thumb along her hairline. "You're a quick study. Every mother and aunt and granny in Town would be happy to help you." Women were like that. They rallied around babies despite differences in age, class, standing, and even nationality.

She did not react to his caress, not that he could see. "I think the country is a better place to grow up, especially for boys."

It occurred to him to offer her a place at Sidling. His aunt and uncle were forever grousing about their aging staff, but they refused to pension off the duffers and dodderers on their payroll.

But then he'd never see her, for Sidling was one place he would not frequent if he could help it. Still, the idea was not without merit. It would be better than losing touch with her entirely.

"He's getting tired." Sophie spoke quietly as Kit let out a huge yawn, looking like a lion cub on all fours, roaring in sleepy silence.

"Shall we remove upstairs?"

She nodded, and they began the routine of folding up blankets, banking the fire, packing up the baby, and heading for the servants' stairs. The stairway and corridors were frigid, but Sophie's room was a cocoon of warmth.

"I let the fire in the other bedroom go out," she said, waiting for Vim to set the cradle near the hearth before depositing Kit in his bed. "We can get it going again, or you are welcome to stay with me."

She was fussing the baby in his cradle as she spoke, depriving Vim of the sight of her face. If it was an invitation, it was quite casually offered.

Carefully offered?

He lit the candle near her bed, blew out the taper, and moved to stand next to the cradle.

"I do believe that child is growing so quickly he'll soon no longer fit in his cradle. We'll wake to find the thing in pieces on the floor and Kit striding about the room, demanding his breakfast."

It wasn't at all what he'd intended say.

He dropped to his haunches and waited until Sophie peered at him. "Sophie Windham, if I share a bed with you ever again, I will make mad, passionate love with you through the night. We'll neither of us get any rest, though in the morning, I will leave, and I will not come back." He would *want* to come back though, and wanting sometimes turned into wishing, and wishing into making it so. Sometimes.

She appeared to consider his words calmly. "Mad, passionate love?"

"With you, dear lady, it could not be otherwise." He hadn't meant to say that, either, though it was true.

She sat back on her heels but continued studying the baby as he found two fingers to slip into his rosebud mouth. "I believe I'll use the bathing chamber. Mad, passionate love sounds quite agreeable."

Eleven

SOPHIE LEANED OVER AND KISSED VIM, A LINGERING, claiming kiss that had lust bursting into flame in his vitals. He'd purposely not kissed her, because to do so would have been presumptuous and stupid and dangerous and…

Wonderful. He groaned with pleasure at the taste of her, his hand finding her hair and holding her steady for the plundering his mouth demanded. "God in heaven, Sophie…"

"Uhn."

A small, female sound, one of satisfaction and pleasure that left Vim envisioning mad, passionate, semiclothed lovemaking on the hearth before the fire, Sophie making just such sounds beneath him, his cock buried—

She patted his cheek and broke the kiss. "I won't be long."

She wafted out of the room, and Vim was still sitting dazedly on his heels before the fire when he heard the door to the bathing chamber click shut across the hallway.

He again used cold water to wash off, and found his borrowed dressing gown was still draped across the foot of the bed. Kit was fast asleep by the time Vim had used the warmer on the sheets, banked the fire, then applied his naked self to the sheets to keep them from cooling before Sophie could join him.

Mad, passionate love? Had he ever in his life made mad, passionate love? He enjoyed sex, he enjoyed the friendships that could arise around a shared pleasure in sex, but mad, passionate love?

Sophie appeared in the doorway, wearing only a nightgown and wrapper, her hair curling down her back, her smile a trifle uncertain. The sight of her fresh from her ablutions had blood pooling in Vim's groin and more images dancing in his brain.

Mad, passionate love it would be. Vim propped himself on one elbow and patted the covers. "Come to bed. Kit will have us up and about before the night's half gone, and I have plans for you, my lady, that do not involve sleep."

She wandered over to the hearth. "He does seem to be sound asleep. Crawling is hard work."

He watched while she drifted to her vanity and sat before the mirror. "I recall when my youngest sister started to crawl. Papa insisted we have a party in the nursery, because his last little princess was up off the floor. I danced with him by standing on his shiny, tall boots."

"I can do that for you, you know."

"Let me dance on your boots?" She picked up a brush and tilted her head to the side so the mass of her hair fell over one shoulder.

"Brush your hair." He tossed the covers back, started across the room, and then caught sight of Sophie's fascinated expression in the vanity mirror. He snatched the dressing gown from the bed and belted it snugly around his waist.

When he stood directly behind her, she passed the brush back to him, letting their fingers barely touch.

Ah, so she was teasing him. The subtle teasing of a woman who understood the value of anticipation, but teasing all the same. Vim smiled at her in the mirror. "You have gorgeous hair, Sophie Windham." He drew the damp, curling length of it back over her shoulders in both of his hands and repeated the caress when she closed her eyes.

"Shall I braid it?"

"Please." She opened her eyes. "Over the right shoulder, because I like to sleep on my left side."

"What else do you like?"

She blew out a breath, her expression considering while Vim used the brush in long strokes from her crown to her hips. It was beautiful hair, thick, lustrous, and gleaming with an indication of basic health and sound living.

"I like music," she said, "and sweets. I am quite partial to sweets."

Vim took this answer for a deliberate and charming prevarication. "I meant, what do you like from your lovers? Shall I kiss you all over? Shall you bind my wrists and have your way with me?" He leaned down and nuzzled her neck, the braid he'd been fashioning forgotten. "Shall you put your mouth on me, Sophie, and make me forget myself utterly?"

She sat very still while Vim slid a hand over her shoulder and let it rest there, just above her breast while he pressed his cheek to hers.

"My love, are you blushing?"

"You are very bold, Mr. Charpentier."

He straightened, feeling it imperative that he braid up her hair, so he might have the pleasure of unbraiding it once they'd gained the bed.

"I like your hands on me," he volunteered. "There's a particular quality to your touch I can't quite describe. There's... meaning in it."

"Meaning?"

She regarded him in the mirror, her blush fading.

"That's not the right word. Some people can calm a nervous horse with their touch. They communicate to the animal with hands, tone of voice, and posture in ways more substantial than words. Your hands on me feel that way—more substantial than words."

She turned and pressed her forehead to his midriff. "You must not say such things."

He stroked his palm over her crown, holding her half-finished braid with the other hand. "Why not, Sophie?"

"You simply must not." She straightened, and he finished with her braid, using his own hair ribbon to tie it.

"Get in bed, my love. I'll be along in a minute."

She gave him a wary look but did as he bid, closing the bed curtains while Vim poured a glass of water and set it on the nightstand, along with a single, tall candle. He wanted to be able to see her face when their bodies joined, wanted to read her expression, gauge her pleasure.

But first things first. He picked up the cradle and crossed to the bathing chamber, making use of his tooth powder once again for good measure, and tucking the child in a warm corner. "Just for a bit. I can't guarantee you'd have peace and quiet otherwise."

Nothing from the infant, which was encouraging. He cracked the door enough that if the child fussed, the adults in the next room would hear him.

And now, for some mad, passionate lovemaking.

Except part of Vim was more inclined to take all the time in the world than to permit mindless hurry, to savor and draw out this pleasure for them both, because it was all they would have to keep of each other.

On that sobering thought, he climbed into bed and stretched out beside Sophie.

"Are you warm enough?"

She turned her head on the pillow to look at him. "I'm fine. Did you mean to leave the curtain open on your side?"

"Yes." The candle was on his side.

He reached under the covers for Sophie's hand. "Do you suppose the weather has delayed your brothers?"

"Very likely."

He could roll over and mount her, fuse his mouth to hers, and be inside her in moments. He wanted to. Badly.

And that simply would not serve. He cast around for a topic that might permit some affection without requiring that he concentrate on anything more than the clean, flowery scent of the woman in bed with him.

"Tell me about your brothers, Sophie."

"They are good men." She laced her fingers with his. "But they are men. They've married and gone their own ways. Two have started their families. One up in Yorkshire, another in Oxfordshire, and the other mostly in Surrey."

"Surrey isn't so far." He brought her hand to his mouth and gently bit her knuckle. "My brother Benjamin hares all over the kingdom. He's some sort of investigator for the high and mighty, which he tells me is not half so glamorous as it sounds, though it's lucrative."

"Benjamin Hazlit?"

"You know him?" He rolled to his side to peer at her in the gloom, wondering when the innocuous topic of her brothers had shifted to the more difficult subject of his own. "He says discretion is the first requirement of his profession."

"I know of him. I believe Their Graces have employed him in some administrative capacity. He doesn't look at all like you."

God in heaven, she knew his brother. She'd seen his brother. This knowledge pinned back the ears of Vim's lust and had him wishing he had simply initiated the lovemaking.

"Benjamin and I have different fathers. Polite society is such a small world. I can put into almost any port on the globe and find some tavern or watering hole where the Englishmen congregate. Within moments of meeting each other, they're engaged in an earnest attempt to find common social ground, and we've managed it without even trying."

"Are they trying to find common ground or trying

to find out which of them occupies the higher social ground?"

Interesting question, for some other day.

"Which of your brothers is your favorite, Sophie?" He stayed on his side and gave her back her hand so he might trace her hairline with his fingers.

"They're all my favorites. My sisters are my favorites too."

Would she never touch him?

"Which one tries your patience the most?"

"My papa. He means well, truly he does, but he is quite determined he knows best for everybody. My mama reasons with him behind closed doors, but other than that, he's quite unmanageable."

Mention of Sophie's papa was not at all conducive to satisfying the lust simmering Vim's gut. He cast around for yet another gambit.

"Is it hard, being here without your family at the holidays?"

"No." She answered quickly, the most decisive thing she'd said since getting into the bed. She also took his hand in her own and nuzzled his palm with her nose. "Even your hands smell good."

"When one washes his hands frequently…"

Her tongue, hot, wet, and delicate, traced the crease between his third and fourth fingers. Vim rolled up and over her, crouching on his forearms and knees. "For the love God, kiss me, Sophie."

He waited for a long moment while she cradled his jaw then framed his face with both hands. She kissed him on the mouth, a sweet, almost chaste kiss, then ran one hand back through his hair to anchor at his nape.

"You kiss me too," she whispered. "Madly, passionately."

Lust sprang from the starting blocks and raged through Vim's system. He opened his mouth over hers, desire a voracious force singing in his blood.

"Vim." Sophie's fingers on his chin were light, her grip in his hair secure without being painful. She spoke his name softly, as if pleading for something.

He hauled back hard on the reins of his lust and rested his forehead against hers. Passionate was not at all the same thing as heedless. Not with Sophie, not on their one shared night.

He tasted her slowly, one corner of her mouth then the other. She sighed, her breath fanning against his neck, and he thanked God for all the ladies who'd taught him restraint, timing, patience, and consideration.

All the ladies whose faces and names he could not recall and probably would never be able to recall again.

He slid his tongue into the soft heat of Sophie's mouth only to feel her grip on his hair tighten. She drew on him then came out to play in hesitant, teasing forays into his mouth.

"I could kiss you all night, Sophie. I shall kiss you all night."

She shifted to lock her ankles at the small of his back. "Not just kiss." She spoke against his mouth.

Vim smiled against hers. "Not just." Sophie arched up against him at the hips, reminding Vim that while he was naked, she was not. "Nightgown, Sophie."

She kissed him harder, one arm wrapping tightly around his back, the other lower, so her hand gripped his buttocks.

He drew his mouth back half an inch. "Sweetheart,

I want you naked." Her hand on his backside eased a trifle. "I want to feel your skin next to mine. I want to touch you all over. I want the scent of you on me everywhere."

Her hands fell away, and she unlocked her ankles. "Nightgown. Quickly please."

He sat back between her legs, and when she levered up, he got the thing off her, but he didn't immediately settle into the cradle of her body.

"What do you like, Sophie? How do you want me to love you?"

She blinked in the candlelight. "You were doing quite nicely a moment ago."

"I was about to go up in flames a moment ago." He crouched over her and brushed her hair back from her forehead. "I think you were getting a bit enthusiastic too."

"Is that bad?"

"God in heaven." He tucked himself closer but kept his cock from grazing her belly. "You do not dally often, do you, Sophie Windham?"

Her hand stroked over his hair slowly. "Not often at all. Then everybody assumes you are not interested in dallying, and the opportunities stop presenting themselves. Pretty soon it doesn't matter that you might be interested, because no one's going to ask."

And she was not designed to ask for what she wanted, for what she needed. He became determined to give it to her, to see that for once Sophie Windham's every wish came true.

"You have me for this night, Sophie, and I have you." He started over with the kissing, taking his time as if they'd never kissed before. He kissed her brow, finding that despite her bath, her hair still bore the faint scents of vanilla and cinnamon underscored with gingerbread. He kissed the tender spot below her ear; he kissed the juncture of her neck and shoulder, hearing her draw a slow inhale as he did.

"My love, you like that."

"I like it."

So he treasured her with his mouth for long, long moments, until he could detect the pulse in her throat beating more rapidly and feel some tension in the hand she had fisted in his hair.

He trailed his mouth lower, settling his lips over one puckered nipple then the other. She wrapped her legs around his back and used her fingers to trace his ears.

"I like that, what you're doing with my ears."

"You have lovely ears."

He smiled against her breast until she tugged on his earlobe, which created a resonating tug in his groin.

"Sophie?"

"Hmm?"

He went still above her. "I want you."

The words weren't said with any mad passion. He'd stated a simple, stark, undeniable reality, one more pressing by the instant.

"I want you too, Vim."

She brushed a hand down his chest and wrapped her fingers around the length of his cock. "I want this part of you to join us together. I want to feel you inside me." She squeezed him a little, and Vim felt it in all manner of wonderful places. .

"Guide me, Sophie."

She frowned and made no move to join them.

"Show me where you want me, love." And then she seated him snugly against the damp, hot opening to her body, her hand falling away, her body still.

"You're ready for me."

"I have waited a long time for you, Vim Charpentier. Don't make me wait any longer."

Words to make love by. Vim flexed his hips forward just a bit, just enough to effect that first, lush sensation of penetration.

"God in heaven, Sophie…" She was hot, wet, gloriously tight, and wise enough not to do anything to threaten his tenuous control. He advanced again and did not retreat, savoring the sensation of her body gloving his.

"You're all right?"

She nodded and opened her teeth against his shoulder. She didn't bite him, exactly, but the sensation helped keep him from completing their joining in one hard, luscious thrust.

He moved again, slowly, gaining just a little more depth, losing a little more of his sanity.

"More?"

Another nod, and the sensation of Sophie's hand gripping his buttock hard. He managed it like that, a little advance then a mental inventory of Sophie's reaction to it. She gripped his backside, then his hair, arched her breasts into his chest, ran her foot along the back of his knee.

And then, when he was just shy of his goal, she took a funny, hitching breath.

"Sophie? You're all right?" He pressed his cheek to hers then drew back. "My dear, are you crying?"

"No, not like that."

"Have I hurt you?" He could not stand it if he had. He started to withdraw, slowly, carefully, but she locked her legs around him.

"I didn't know how it would be."

He paused, keeping his cheek to hers. "How it would be?"

"I can't… it's wondrous. Sweet, dear, so intimate… glorious."

Ah, God… He wrapped his hand around the back of her head and pressed her face to his shoulder. He could feel her crying, feel it with his body, because he was inside her and around her and pressed to her over much of his body.

So intimate, she'd said. Glorious.

"Move with me, love."

He kept his pace slow, so she could follow his rhythm. Her focus was a palpable thing, gathering momentum as her body learned the give and take from his. When she was moving easily with him, the tempo picking up moment by moment, he dropped his head so his mouth was near her ear.

"Let it happen, Sophie. Take flight."

He felt the instant she stopped focusing on timing and movement and fell helplessly under the onrush of sensation.

"Vim…" His name on her lips was a whispered plea, one that had him driving into her in tight, hard strokes while she shook and clung and convulsed around him. She gave herself up to it, keening against his shoulder, meeting him thrust for thrust until she was panting and spent beneath him.

When he felt her hands slips from his body, when her legs untwined to rest passively at his flanks, Vim levered up on his arms. By the light of the single candle, he could see a rosy flush on her cheek and tears yet leaving a sheen on her eyes.

She reached up and brushed his hair back. "I don't know what to say."

"You say, 'Vim, give me a minute to recover my wits, and then do that again, please, only better.'"

She blinked, and then a slow, sweet smile bloomed on her lips. He lowered himself down onto her so they were chest to chest, as close as two people could be.

He felt her fingers stroking over the hair at his nape. "Vim, give me a minute to recover my wits, and then do that again, please, but if you do it any better, I won't possess wits to recover ever again."

"Then we shall both be loved witless."

He gave her a minute, but just a minute.

❧

Sophie watched as Vim climbed from the bed. He didn't tuck the bed curtains closed, but rather, moved behind the privacy screen. She heard the sound of a cloth being wrung out over a basin and wished he were tending to himself where she could see him.

"Stay in that bed, Sophie Windham." He spoke quietly as he emerged from the gloom and arranged the cloth on the hearth screen. "I'll be back in a moment."

Naked, firelight gilding his skin, he left the room only to appear shortly thereafter with the cradle in his arms. He set the thing by the hearth, carefully, so it didn't start rocking.

"Where was Kit?"

"Across the hall." Vim advanced on the bed, cloth in hand. "Spread your legs, my love."

"Why across the hall?"

"I can be loud, at certain times."

"You growl softly, Mr. Vim Charpentier. I like it."

He was thorough and gentle with her, finishing with a few passes directly over her intimate parts. "You growl too." He leaned forward and bit her earlobe. "I adore it. Scoot over."

He tossed the rag toward the hearth, missing the cradle by inches. Sophie scooted, much relieved they'd spend the balance of the night together.

Vim lay down beside her, wrapped an arm around her shoulders, and hiked her leg across his thighs. "You should have allowed me to withdraw, Sophie." He cradled her foot in his large, warm hand as he spoke. It brought the oddest comfort.

"I am not fertile now. I didn't want you to abandon me."

She cringed at her own word choice, given that he'd be moving on in the morning once and for all. He made no reply, though, so Sophie turned her attention to collecting memories: the feel of Vim's hard male chest rising and falling beneath her hand, the bergamot scent of his skin, the slightly salty taste of his shoulder, the transcendent sensation of him joining their bodies so very, very carefully...

"My business in Kent shouldn't take but a few weeks," he said, his tone thoughtful. His fingers smoothed her hair back, and Sophie understood exactly what he was working up to.

"You must not worry. I cannot conceive now, or I would not have been so... selfish."

"You can't be certain, Sophie. I'll leave you my direction when I go." There was just a hint of reproof in his voice, but he was wrong. Sophie was certain their paths needed to separate regardless of any unlikely consequences. She'd waltzed with his very own half brother, for heaven's sake, and Benjamin Hazlit's discreet assistance had been instrumental in keeping both Valentine's and Westhaven's wives safe from harm.

Vim would learn that—learn she was the daughter of a duke, no less—and think she'd been untruthful with him.

Which she had. He hadn't asked any awkward questions yet, but it was hardly likely Lady Sophia Windham would have been all alone, unchaperoned, without servants or family in the ducal mansion. She had contrived mightily to make it so. He would feel deceived and manipulated, and it would ruin everything, even the memories.

"Your brain is turning on a greased wheel, Sophie."

His voice was lazy in the darkness, as lazy as his hand stroking over her hair. If he'd been offering his direction in Kent out of something other than duty and guilt, she might have considered explaining the situation to him more fully.

"I am trying to recall each moment with you in this bed."

"There could be more such moments. I'll come back through Town when I'm done sorting out my relatives."

Ah, damn him. "I have my position to consider."

More silence, while in Sophie's heart, the glow of a wonderful sexual initiation and shared intimacy grew chilled by encroaching regret.

"I could offer you another position, one of substantial duration and considerable standing. One I have never offered another woman worthy of such a consideration."

She closed her eyes, lest more tears give her away. Vim was a good man, the kind of man wishes and dreams were made of, but she'd made such a tangle of things, he could never be the man for her, particularly not if all he was offering was a few years as his mistress between sea voyages.

And if he'd offered not a careful description of a discreet liaison, but marriage? No hope lay in that direction. Even if he proposed, when he learned she'd been dishonest with him about her position in the household and the world at large, the proposal would be withdrawn.

She fell asleep in his arms and did not recall her dreams in the morning.

⤜⤛

Vim was learning to read Miss Sophie Windham, learning that despite appearing serene and even sanguine, she was hurting. She was going about her morning routine calmly, her expression pleasant while she tidied up her hair and used her vanity mirror to watch Vim dressing and putting her bed to rights. The heartache was there in her eyes, in her posture, in her silences.

Kit started to fuss but was still in the happy stages of greeting his own toes when Vim picked up the rag he'd tossed aside so casually the night before.

The rag that in the light of another brutally bright day was sporting definite streaks of pinkish brown.

"Sophie?"

"Hmm?"

"Do your courses approach?"

Her hands paused in twining her braid into a bun at her nape, but other than that, she showed no reaction. "They always approach, unless they've descended. My mother has a lot of unflattering things to say about The Almighty's design in this regard. One's only respite is to carry a child, and that is hardly a fair trade, considering what's involved in birthing the child."

In the back of Vim's mind, he was recalling how very wonderfully snug Sophie's body had been, how she'd bit his shoulder as he'd sunk into her damp heat, how artless her lovemaking had been. *I didn't know how it would be...*

How virginal?

Twelve

IT WOULD CHANGE EVERYTHING, IF SOPHIE HAD BEEN A virgin—and it would mean she'd misrepresented her circumstances.

"Are you sore this morning?" he asked, picking Kit up and holding the baby high above his head. "Good morning, My Lord Baby."

"I am tired and hoping your journey to the country-side passes uneventfully." She watched as he raised and lowered the baby, her expression a trifle guarded.

"Sophie, am I the first man you've allowed carnal intimacies?" He put the question casually, keeping his attention to appearances on the baby.

She frowned, just a flicker over her features. "I am not a virgin, if that's what you're asking." It was exactly what he'd been asking, though her wording was in the present tense. "Does that child need his nappy changed?"

"He does." Vim lowered the baby, still dissatisfied with Sophie's answer but not knowing quite how to clarify matters without interrogating her very directly.

He was still uncomfortable when less than an hour

later they stood in the aisle of the stable, Sophie holding a bundled-up Kit in her arms.

"Goliath will see you safely to Kent," she said, stroking a hand down the beast's neck. "He delights in romping through the snow, and I know you will let no harm befall him."

Vim's pockets held piping hot potatoes; his traveling satchel sported a considerable quantity of bread, cheese, stollen, and even a stash of marzipan Sophie had produced from one of her pantries. His feet were warm and dry and likely to stay that way, as she'd insisted he keep a pair of her brother's marvelous wool stockings, and she'd even tucked a bottle of fine brandy among his belongings, as well.

And for all these comforts, his heart, which he'd long since considered beyond such nonsense, was aching. For her, for himself, for what was not going to be.

"This is the price we pay for our pleasures," he said, keeping his voice down so Higgins and Merriweather wouldn't overhear. "We part, and it's... difficult."

She nodded, her lips thinning in telltale self-discipline. Vim glanced over his shoulder and saw both grooms had taken themselves elsewhere. "Come here, Sophie Windham."

She went into his arms, a perfect bundle of woman and baby and warmth, and everything Vim's sojourning heart had ever wanted to come home to. She was home, she was...

Not interested in a permanent position as his wife. He'd almost considered asking her to be his mistress, but Sophie was too dear, too worthy of his respect for him to proffer such an arrangement.

"I'll send the horse back as soon as the roads clear."

Her shoulders dropped on a sigh. "Just send him over to Morelands."

"Morelands?" It was a large property less than four miles from Sidling. The Duke and Duchess of Moreland had been legendary for their hospitality even in his youth, though Vim had been in the family home only once and was at pains to recall the family name.

And wasn't it just divine irony that Sophie would be employed by the very family who'd hosted the scene of Vim's worst nightmares all those years ago?

"It lies in Kent," she said, resting her cheek against his chest. "You'll not overtax yourself today? You'll warm your feet before you do lasting damage to them?"

"I will warm my feet." He kissed her cheek and stepped back, lest he fall to his knees and start begging her to reconsider his proposal of marriage. She'd made her position gently but firmly clear, preferring the independence of her employment over what a stranger might offer her on appallingly short acquaintance.

"Sophie, if you need anything, anything for you or Kit, you'll send to me?"

She nodded but did not give him her word.

He would never hear from her again.

He kissed the top of the baby's fuzzy head and turned to check the girth on the makeshift saddle adorning the massive horse's back.

"Thank you." Sophie kept her voice low and her features from view by virtue of nuzzling the baby.

"For?"

"I made some Christmas wishes, foolish, extravagant wishes. You have made many of them come true."

"Then I am content."

It was the most resoundingly false lie he'd ever told.

❦

Down the barn aisle, Miss Sophie was pretending to groom her remaining precious, the one-eyed Sampson. What she was really doing was crying, crying like her heart would break, crying on the great beast's smelly neck, and hiding it like she always hid it.

"Don't pay no mind, nipper." Higgins grinned at the baby in his arms. "Lady Sophie is due a few tears, unlike some wee people who have their every need met before it needs meeting. She's spoiling you proper, she is."

"Miss Sophie said the nipper has taken to crawling already," Merriweather observed from where he was cleaning a muddy girth across the snug little tack room. "Best day of the lad's life was when that worthless Joleen went haring off."

"Spare the girl a prayer. That Harry was none too steady."

"Horny bastard. Bet he had her breeding again, and the nipper not even a year."

Which would explain why Joleen had taken the desperate and shrewd step of abandoning her child in Miss Sophie's care.

"Miss Sophie will do right by the lad."

Merriweather glanced up from the girth. "Be a bit of a surprise when her brothers show up and find her sporting a bebby on her hip."

Higgins used a gnarled finger to chuck the baby's wee chin. "Be some surprises all around before the sun sets this day. Mark me on this, nipper."

Merriweather winked, and they shared a grin while Kit chortled gleefully and grabbed for Higgins's nose.

♋

"You've grown ominously silent," Val observed.

Westhaven rode to his brother's left, because it was St. Just's turn to break the trail ahead. The merchants along The Strand had done what they could to clear a path, but with so much snow on the ground, there was simply nowhere to put it all. Two horses could pass comfortably most places, but not all.

"I'm trying to decide which part of me is the most frozen," Westhaven replied. "It's a toss-up between my bum-fiddle and my nose."

"I lost awareness of my nose before we hit London."

Westhaven glanced at Val's gloved hands. "Your fingers are not in jeopardy, I trust?"

"Heaven forfend! Ellen would be wroth, which I cannot allow."

"I cannot allow much longer in this perishing saddle."

"We've little enough light left." Val glanced at the sky, which was turning a chilly sunset turquoise. "The Chattells will likely be sitting down to dinner, and didn't Their Graces give the staff at the mansion holiday leave?"

"I gave them holiday leave." Which was an idiot notion when compared with imposing on the neighbors for hospitality. "They get four weeks off, we pay them for two, and everybody has pleasant holidays. The crew at Morelands takes leave in late summer, before harvest."

"I'll have to implement something like it at Bel

Canto, assuming I don't turn into an icicle before spring. I don't relish being Chattell's uninvited guests."

"You're married," Westhaven said, lips quirking up. "You're safe, Valentine. Of no interest to the debutantes at all."

"Yes, but they all come with mothers and aunts and older sisters… St. Just, halt if you please."

St. Just twisted in his saddle, his horse coming to a stop without a visible cue. "We're going to take in the fresh air, are we? It grows dark soon, in case you were too busy composing tunes in your head, Baby Brother."

"I want to drop off this violin. The repair shop is just down that alley." Val swung a leg over his horse's back and climbed down into the snow. "I won't be but a minute."

"Might as well rest the horses," St. Just said, nudging his beast out of the middle of the beaten path. "Westhaven, can you dismount?"

"I cannot. My backside is permanently frozen to the saddle; my ability to reproduce is seriously jeopardized."

"Anna will be desolated." St. Just waited while Westhaven swung down, then whistled at an urchin shivering in the door to a nearby church.

"We'll just get the feeling back into our feet, and the saddles will be chilled sufficiently to threaten even your lusty inclination." Westhaven led his horse to the side of the street, such as it was.

"Cold weather makes Emmie frisky." St. Just assayed his signature grin. "We have a deal of cold weather up in the West Riding, so I've learned to appreciate it. Let's at least find a tot of grog while Baby Brother sees to his precious violin."

"The George is just up the street. I'll be along in a minute."

But St. Just could not just toddle on and wet his whistle. No. He must turn to Westhaven, hands on his hips, and cock his head like a hound trying to place a far-off sound. "And what will you be about while I'm swilling bad ale?"

"I'll be stopping at that sweet shop yonder, before they close up for the day."

Fortunately, it was too cold for a man to blush creditably.

"You're thinking of sweets when the George will have a roaring fire and libation to offer?" The ragged child came trotting over from the church, and St. Just fished out a coin. "Keep an eye on the horses."

"Aye, g-guv. I'll watch 'em close."

"For pity's sake." Westhaven unwound his scarf and wrapped it around the child's neck. "We won't be long."

They couldn't be long, or Westhaven's ears would freeze off. "As it happens, I own that sweet shop. Go get your grog, and I'll meet you back here in ten minutes." He walked off, hoping his brother would for once take an unsubtle cue.

"You own a sweet shop?" St. Just fell in step beside Westhaven, all bonhomie and good cheer.

"Diversification of assets, Kettering calls it. Get your own sweet shop, why don't you?"

"My brother, a confectioner. Marriage has had such a positive impact on you, Westhaven. How long have you owned this fine establishment?"

It was a fine establishment, which was to say, it was warm. The scents of chocolate and cinnamon thick in the air didn't hurt, either.

Westhaven waited silently while St. Just peered around the place with unabashed curiosity. There was a prodigious amount of pink in the decor, and ribbon bows and small baskets and tins artfully decorated.

"You own a bordello for sweets," St. Just observed in a carrying voice likely honed on the parade grounds of Spain. "It's charming."

"Unlike you."

"You're just cold and missing your countess. One must make allowances."

Mercifully, those allowances meant St. Just kept quiet while Westhaven purchased a quantity of marzipan.

"You aren't going to tell the troops to carry on, God Save the King, and all that?" St. Just asked as they left the shop. He reached over and stuffed his fingers into the bag of sweets Westhaven was carrying.

"Help yourself, by all means."

"Can't leave all the heavy lifting to my younger brothers." St. Just munched contentedly on some of the finest German confection to be had on earth. "Why didn't they know you were the owner?"

"Because I don't bruit it about."

"You don't want to be seen as dabbling in trade?"

Westhaven took a piece of candy from the bag in his hand, wondering if the marzipan would freeze before his brothers consumed it all. "I do not want to be seen as owning a sweet shop. Sweet shops are not dignified."

He marched forward to meet Valentine at the horses, his older brother's laughter ringing in his ears.

❦

"Ouch, blast you!"

The blow to Sophie's chin was surprisingly stout, considering it had been delivered by a very small, chubby baby heel, but it left Sophie wanting to hurl the infant's bowl of porridge against the hearth stones.

"That hurt, Christopher Elijah." She grasped his foot and shook it gently. "Shame on you."

He grinned around the porridge adorning his cheeks and kicked again. Sophie tried one more spoonful, which he spat out amid another happy spate of kicking.

"Time for you to romp," she said, wiping his mouth off with a damp cloth. And then time to play with him, read to him, and tuck him up in his cradle, while she…

Sophie's gaze drifted to the window to see darkness had finally fallen. Yesterday had been a day for tears; today was a day beyond tears. She'd missed Vim yesterday; today she ached for him in places she could not name, even in Latin.

Personal, feminine, silent places she feared had the ability to ache without end.

She tidied up the baby's supper mess and lifted him into her arms. "You do feel heavier, sturdier, but this is doubtless my imagination."

That his nappy needed changing was by no means a product of her imagination. She tended to him in the laundry, realizing that in just a few days, the whole untidy business had become routine to her.

"You are a good baby," she said, picking him up and bringing him nose to nose. "You are a wonderful baby. Time for you to conquer the carpet, hmm?"

And time for her to tidy up Valentine's room,

because surely her brothers would be arriving tomorrow, and surely she did not want them asking any more awkward questions than necessary.

"They will honor my confidences," she said to the baby as she carried him to the parlor. "I will explain I needed solitude. Westhaven hid in his business endeavors, Valentine at the piano, and Devlin in the stables, but where was I to hide when I needed peace and quiet? Where was I to have any privacy? Taking tea with Her Grace? Shopping with my sisters? Parading about Town on the arm of my papa?"

Good heavens, she sounded almost... angry.

She sat on the sofa with the baby in her lap.

A lady never showed strong emotion, except she had shown strong emotion, with Vim... Weeping had been the least of it.

A bump sounded from the direction of the kitchen, making her jump, suggesting she'd spent the entire day half listening for just such a sound.

A sound suggesting Vim had once again returned?

Another bump, and the muted sound of voices.

She put Kit in his cradle. "I will be back momentarily. Behave." She put his hand up to his mouth, and he obligingly slipped two fingers between his lips. "Good baby."

Closing the parlor door behind her, Sophie hurried to the kitchen, only to find her three brothers stomping snowy boots, muttering, and bringing in the damp and cold as they shed outer garments.

"Sophie!" Val spotted her first and abandoned all ceremony to wrap his arms around her. "Sophie Windham, I have missed you and missed you." He held her tightly, so tightly Sophie could hide her face against his shoulder and swallow back the lump abruptly forming in her throat.

"I have a new étude for you to listen to. It's based on parallel sixths and contrary motion—it's quite good fun." He stepped back, his smile so dear Sophie wanted to hug him all over again, but St. Just elbowed Val aside.

"Long lost sister, where have you been?" His hug was gentler but no less welcome. "I've traveled half the length of England to see you, you know." He kissed her cheek, and Sophie felt a blush creeping up her neck.

"You did not. You've come south because Emmie said you must, and you want to check on your ladies out in Surrey."

Westhaven waited until St. Just had released her. "I wanted to check on you." His hug was the gentlest of all. "But you were not where you were supposed to be, Sophie. You have some explaining to do if we're to get the story straight before we face Her Grace."

The simple fact of his support undid her. Sophie pressed her face to his shoulder and felt a tear leak from her eye. "I have missed you so, missed all of you so much."

Westhaven patted her back while Valentine stuffed a cold, wrinkled handkerchief into her hand.

"We've made her cry." St. Just did not sound happy.

"I'm just…" Sophie stepped away from Westhaven and dabbed at her eyes. "I'm a little fatigued is all. I've been doing some baking, and the holidays are never without some challenges, and then there's the baby—"

"What baby?" All three men spoke—shouted, more nearly—as one.

"Keep your voices down, please," Sophie hissed. "Kit isn't used to strangers, and if he's overset, I'll be all night dealing with him."

"And behold, a virgin shall conceive," Val muttered as Sophie passed him back his handkerchief.

St. Just shoved him on the shoulder. "That isn't helping."

Westhaven went to the stove and took the kettle from the hob. "What baby, Sophie? And perhaps you might share some of this baking you've been doing. The day was long and cold, and our brothers grow testy if denied their victuals too long."

He sent her a smile, an it-will-be-all-right smile that had comforted her on many an occasion. Westhaven was sensible. It was his surpassing gift to be sensible, but Sophie found no solace from it now.

She had not been sensible, and worse yet, she did not regret the lapse. She would, however, regret very much if the lapse did not remain private.

"The tweenie was anticipating an interesting event, wasn't she?" Westhaven asked as he assembled a tea tray. While Sophie took a seat at the table, St. Just hiked himself onto a counter, and Val took the other bench.

"Joleen," Sophie said. "Her interesting event is six months old, a thriving healthy child named... Westhaven, what are you doing?"

"He's making sure he gets something to eat under the guise of looking after his siblings," St. Just said, pushing off the counter. "Next, he'll fetch the cream from the window box while I make us some sand-wiches. Valentine find us a cloth for the table."

"At once, Colonel." Val snapped a salute and sauntered off in the direction of the butler's pantry, while Westhaven headed for the colder reaches of the back hallway.

"You look a bit fatigued, Sophie." St. Just studied her with a brooding frown, all hint of teasing gone. His brows knit further as his gaze went to the hearth. "Is that a pair of my favorite socks set out to dry? They're a bit large for you, aren't they?"

Westhaven emerged from the back hallway, a small box in his hand. "Somebody has decimated my stash of marzipan. If His Grace has given up crème cakes for German chocolate, I'll be naming my seconds."

Valentine returned from the corridor. "Somebody left my favorite mug in the linen closet. I thought you favored more delicate crockery, Sophie."

In the ensuing moment of silence, Sophie was casting around desperately for plausible reasons why all this evidence of Vim's presence in the house was yet on hand, when the back door opened and slammed shut.

"Sophie, love! I'm back. Come here and let me kiss you senseless, and then, by God, we're going to talk."

Oh dear.

Oh, good heavens.

Vim emerged from the darkness looking weary, handsome, and very pleased—until his gaze traveled to each of the three men glowering at him.

"Who the hell are you?" Westhaven's voice was soft, but he did not sound sensible in the least.

"And what makes you think you're going to be kissing my sister?" St. Just added, hands on his hips.

"And what on earth could you have to speak with Lady Sophia about?" Valentine asked, crossing his arms.

Thirteen

THREE THINGS PENETRATED THE SURPRISE VIM FELT AT seeing Sophie in company with three large, undeniably attractive men.

First, they resembled her, each in a slightly different way. Around the eyes, for the darkest one; something about the chin in the one with lighter hair; and the shape of the nose for the leanest one. And green eyes. All four had green eyes.

Brothers. These were her brothers. The thought brought relief and resentment too: where had these stout fellows been when Sophie had been stranded here, trying to cope with a baby and a snowstorm and a stranger under her roof?

The second realization was that the mews had shown a number of hoofprints in the snow. He'd handed his horse off to Higgins and not remarked all the stable traffic. Had he paid attention, he might have been warned that Sophie was no longer alone.

But then the third realization sank into his brain: *Lady* Sophia.

"Your horse started off sound enough," he said,

addressing her directly and ignoring the glowering idiots cluttering up her kitchen. "The farther I got from the river though, the more he felt off. Not lame, exactly, but not sound, either. I did not want to leave him to the indifferent care of a coaching inn or livery, so I brought him back. Whatever the difficulty, he seemed to work out of it as we approached Town. How fares Kit?"

The teakettle started to whistle, but Vim kept his gaze locked on Sophie.

Lady Sophia. The implications reverberated through his mind: the daughters of earls, marquises, and dukes were ladies, as were the wives of peers. Wives were permitted a great deal of latitude unmarried women did not enjoy...

"Sophie, as you appear acquainted with this *person*"—the fellow with the chestnut hair put an edge of condescension on the word—"will you introduce us?"

From down the hall, an indignant squall sounded.

"I'll get him." Sophie sent Vim a pleading look when she brushed past him. "And there had better not be any broken crockery when I get back."

The brother who'd asked for introductions had a scholarly look to him, and he'd watched Sophie go with something like concern in his eye.

"Vim Charpentier." Vim stuck out a hand and tried not to make it a dare. He was outnumbered, for one thing, and Sophie did not want broken crockery, for another.

"Westhaven." The man nodded but did not extend his hand. "My brothers, Devlin St. Just, Earl of Rosecroft, and Lord Valentine Windham. We are assuredly not at your service until we get an explanation for your very presuming greeting to our sister."

And if Sophie's brother was Lord Valentine Windham, and she was Lady Sophia Windham, then that narrowed down the family title to a marquis or a...

God in heaven, it was almost funny.

"Explanations will wait until Lady Sophia rejoins us," Vim said just as she emerged from the hallway with Kit in her arms.

"Hello, lad." Vim had to smile at the way the baby started bouncing in Sophie's embrace and reaching his arms toward Vim. "I missed you too."

She passed him the baby, a gesture he was sure had more to do with preventing her brothers from putting out his lights than anything else. Still, it felt good to hold the child, to see that somebody was glad to know he'd not frozen in some snowbank.

Sophie spoke softly as she eyed the baby in his arms. "Westhaven, Rosecroft, Lord Valentine, may I make known to you Mr. Vim Charpentier, late of Cumbria and bound for Kent. The storm stranded him here, and I needed help..."

"Sophie." Vim spoke quietly and willed her to meet his gaze. "I suggest we see the child settled first and then have a civil discussion with your brothers. They are no doubt hungry, and you are entitled to a few moments to compose yourself."

She twisted her hands and said nothing, her gaze meeting his only fleetingly.

"A sound enough plan," the dragoon said— Rosecroft, or St. Just. "Valentine is stealing all your marzipan, Westhaven. I believe you mentioned naming your seconds?"

The tension eased fractionally at what Vim took for a jest—or sword rattling, but not a genuine threat. He turned with the baby. "We'll be in the parlor with Kit." He did not reach for Sophie's hand. He wasn't sure he wanted to.

Lady Sophia's hand.

"Leave the damned door open," Lord Valentine said. It was a marginal comfort that Sophie ignored her brother's admonition and closed the damned door when they reached the parlor.

"It will let in the worst draft. Valentine has no children yet, you see, and it wouldn't occur to him Kit will be on the carpet—"

"Sophie." He made no move to touch her. She fell silent and sank to her knees on the rug and blankets.

"They'll think the worst," she said. "I don't want them to think ill of me, Vim. Mr. Charpentier, oh—bother. What do I call you?"

He stopped short in the process of turning Kit loose among his blankets. "If I'm to call you Lady Sophia, you might consider calling me Lord Sindal."

Her brows flew up, then down. "You're titled?"

"A courtesy title, much like your own, but humbler. I'm heir to the Rothgreb viscountcy. Baron Sindal."

"Oh. My goodness." She did meet his gaze then, and he saw understanding and relief in her eyes. "You did not tell me because you thought I was just a what... a lady's companion? A housekeeper?"

"Something like that. Mostly I thought you were lovely." *He still did.* "What do we tell your brothers,

Sophie? They've left us these few moments out of respect for you, but they'll be in here any minute, crockery be damned."

"I suppose we tell them as little as possible."

It wasn't what he'd wanted to hear, though the constraints of honor allowed him one further attempt to secure his heart's desire. "I will offer for you, if that's what you want." Offer for her *again*. He kept the hope from his voice only with effort.

Though from the severe frown Sophie displayed, a renewed offer wasn't what she sought from him. "I won't ask it of you."

He was marshalling his arguments mentally when Lord Valentine came to the door, a tray in his hands. "You will pardon me for not knocking." He lifted the tray a few inches and shot Vim a challenging look. "Scoot over, Soph. Westhaven is counting his candies, and St. Just is fetching some libation. What's the little blighter's name?"

"Kit. Christopher Elijah Handel."

Valentine lowered himself to the sofa, which had the agreeable result that Sophie shifted closer to Vim on the carpet. "Any relation to the composer?"

"I doubt it."

"Relax, Sophie." Lord Val nudged her with his toe. "The elders will take their cue from you, or I'll make them wish they had. May I offer you a sandwich, Charpentier? Even a condemned prisoner is entitled to a last meal."

The smile accompanying this gracious offer would have suited one of the large feline denizens of the Royal Menagerie.

"My thanks. Sophie, would you care for a bite?"

"That's Lady Sophia, to you, Charpentier." Lord Valentine's reminder was quite, quite casually offered.

Sophie reached for the sandwich while she shot her brother a glare. "Thank you, Lord Sindal."

She took a ladylike nibble then passed the sandwich back to Vim as Lord Valentine placidly demolished his own portion.

"You might have waited for us," St. Just said. He, too, had arrived carrying a tray, but this one had a decanter and several glasses on it. Westhaven brought up the rear, closing the parlor door behind him.

One lowly servants' parlor had probably never held quite so many titles at one time nor so much tension. Sophie's expression would have suited a woman facing excommunication, but her brothers were apparently satisfied to put off her trial until they'd eaten.

"Another bite, Lady Sophia?" Vim held out the second half of his sandwich, mostly to aggravate her brothers.

"Thank you, no. I've had quite enough to eat today."

"Is he teething?" Westhaven asked the question as he took a place in the wing chair near the fire. His brothers—just the two of them—took up the entire sofa, leaving Vim, Sophie, and the baby on the floor.

"I don't know," Sophie said, passing out the remaining sandwiches.

"He drools a great deal," Westhaven observed. "If he hasn't sprouted fangs yet, he will soon, and you can forget forever after whatever pretenses you had to peace of mind. Where were you thinking of fostering him?"

Lord Val started to pour drinks. "The Foundling Hospital ought to take him. His namesake set the place up with a fine organ, and Kit probably fits their criteria."

St. Just looked preoccupied, and the sandwich Sophie had passed him only a moment ago was nowhere in sight. "What criteria are those?"

"He's a firstborn," Lord Val said. "His mother is in difficulties though otherwise of good character, and his papa is nowhere to be found." He passed Vim a drink as he spoke.

"He won't be going to the Foundling Hospital," Vim said. The relief on Sophie's face was hard to look on. "Soph—Lady Sophia will find him a family to foster with in the country."

St. Just sat forward to accept a drink from Lord Val. "Is that what you want, Sophie?"

Vim did not answer for her, though he saw the indecision in her eyes.

"I think that would be best for Kit. A fellow needs brothers and sisters, and fresh air, and a family." To a man, Sophie's brothers found somewhere else to look besides their sister's face.

"We have larger concerns to occupy us," Westhaven said, dusting his hands. "I'm sure Their Graces will assist in finding a situation for the child, but your circumstances here, Sophie, leave much to be explained."

He took a sip of his drink, letting the silence stretch with the cunning and calculation of a barrister. Vim wanted to put a staying hand on Sophie's arm, or even cover her mouth with his hand, but the sodding buggers were right: they needed to get their story organized if Sophie's reputation wasn't to be tarnished beyond all repair.

"The storm helps you," Lord Val said, lifting his sister's hand and putting a drink in it. "Nobody was out and about, nobody was socializing."

"Hardly anybody," St. Just said. "We called at the Chattell's, and a tipsy footman told us the family had departed for Surrey, and you were headed for Kent with your brothers."

"It's accurate," Westhaven said, "provided nobody inquires too closely about the timing."

Lord Val sat back, his drink cradled in his lap. "How do we explain *him*? If he's Sindal, that makes him old Rothgreb's heir, though a grown-up version compared to the one I recall from years ago."

"You're on your way to Kent?" St. Just asked.

"I am."

"Then to Kent you shall go, traveling in company with us." St. Just glanced over at Westhaven, suggesting Westhaven occupied a place of authority regarding family matters.

"That will serve," Westhaven said. "But confirm for us, first, Charpentier, or Sindal, that you are half brother to Benjamin Hazlit."

Benjamin, who according to Sophie had handled some administrative matters for Their Graces—which could mean anything. That these men would know of the connection between brothers was… curious.

"Hazlit is my half brother," Vim said. "He is not in Town at present, to my knowledge." There was no telling with Ben. The man never outright lied, but he raised discretion to a high, arcane art.

Lord Valentine cocked his head and regarded his sister. "Does this complicate matters, that he's related to Hazlit?"

"Watch him!" Westhaven was half out of his chair as all eyes turned to Kit. Sophie was calmly prying the dangling end of an embroidered table runner from the child's grasp, while the men in the room collectively sat back and took a sip of their drinks.

"He nearly brought the entire platter down on his head," Westhaven said. "It's a dangerous age, infancy."

"He's a wonderful baby," Sophie said, tucking the table runner out of reach. "He's just starting to crawl."

St. Just snorted. "Not in earnest, or that table runner would be nowhere in sight. Emmie and I have boxes of things, pretty, breakable, ornamental things that had to disappear from sight when my younger daughter started crawling."

Lord Valentine frowned at the baby. "I believe we were discussing Sindal's connection with Hazlit before Disaster Incarnate here upstaged the topic."

"My Lord Baby will do," Sophie said, sending Lord Valentine a reproving look.

"It's like this. Charpentier, Sindal, or whoever you are." Westhaven also regarded the child as he spoke, or perhaps he regarded Sophie and the baby both. "The Windham family owes your brother a debt of… consideration. Both Lord Valentine and myself would find ourselves removed from our wives' charity did we not extend Hazlit's relation some courtesy."

Vim passed Sophie a serviette to wipe the drool from Kit's little maw. For as much upheaval as the child had endured, he seemed to be enjoying a room full of Sophie's siblings.

"Your wives frown on dueling?" Vim asked.

"Her Grace frowns on dueling," Lord Valentine supplied. "Rather ruins a young man's reputation, when his fellows know his mama won't allow him to duel."

"But as we're no longer young," St. Just added, "we might be persuaded to make an exception for you, Sindal."

"Most kind of you."

Sophie rolled her eyes. "Don't encourage them. There's a child present."

"And a lady," Westhaven said. "I propose we simply proceed to Kent, and as far as the world is concerned, we're traveling with Sindal for the convenience of all parties. The three of us have been resting here for several days in the company of our sister before setting out for the country. Sindal did not join the household until Sophie's relations were already on the scene."

Vim watched Sophie carefully, trying to pick up a reaction from her to this planned deception. A ducal family could pull off such a subterfuge, particularly this ducal family, and particularly if there was only one tipsy footman to gainsay them.

"Soph?" Lord Valentine tapped her knee with the toe of his boot. "You want some time to consider your options?"

The baby chose that moment to toddle forth on his hands and knees, squealing with glee when he'd covered the two feet between Sophie's side and St. Just's boots.

"A headlong charge into enemy territory can see a fellow taken prisoner." St. Just lifted the baby under the arms and brought the child up to face level.

Kit grinned, swiped at St. Just's nose, and emitted such sounds as to establish beyond doubt that a certain fellow's nappy was thoroughly soiled.

"Gah!"

"Gah, indeed." St. Just kept the child at arm's length. "Westhaven, you have a son. I nominate you."

"Valentine needs the practice."

Vim took the baby from St. Just's grasp and headed for the laundry. As he left the parlor, he heard Lord Valentine softly observe, "You know, Soph, most men with any backbone can calmly accept the threat of a duel to preserve a lady's honor, but it's a brave man indeed who can deal with a dirty nappy without even being asked."

"Your timing is deplorable," Vim told the malodorous, grinning baby. "But I think you've given Sophie's brothers their first reason to pause before they call me out."

"Bah!"

❧

"They are up to something." Sophie kept her voice down as Vim handed her a clean nappy, lest they or someone else in the inn's common overhear her.

Vim tickled Kit's cheek. "I don't think your brothers are waiting to call me out, if that's what you're implying."

Sophie passed him the folded up soiled linen. "They might. Devlin used to kill people for his living.

Valentine arranged a very bad fate for one of his wife's relations, and Westhaven has been known to be ruthless where Anna's welfare is concerned. You can't trust them."

"They trust you, Sophie." Vim put his finger on the tape Sophie was tying into a bow. "They trust I'm not suicidal enough to make advances to you in their very company."

She wanted to ask him if that was why he'd kept his distance, but Valentine came sauntering up.

"Our meal will be served in the private dining room. The Imp of Satan smells a good deal better."

"You were just such an imp not so very long ago," Sophie reminded him. "Did you check on the horses?"

"Your precious friends are knee-deep in straw and munching contentedly on fresh hay. I watched with my own eyes while St. Just fed them their oats, which oats did not hit the bottom of the bucket but were consumed by a process of inhalation I've never seen before. I intend to emulate it if they ever serve dinner here."

Something passed between the men—a glance, a look, a particular way of breathing at each other.

"I'll take Kit." Vim lifted the child from the settle where Sophie had been changing the baby's nappy. "Does this place have a cradle?"

He addressed the question to Val, who shrugged. "I understand how to bed down a horse; I understand how to keep my wife safe and content. These creatures"—he gestured at Kit—"confound me entirely."

"But the King's English does not," Sophie said before the breathing got out of hand. "Go ask if they have a cradle, and if they do, have it placed in my chamber." She spun him by his prodigiously broad shoulders and gave the middle of his back a shove.

"St. Just or Westhaven will be along momentarily," Vim said, rubbing noses with the baby. "They aren't complete fools."

"Do they think I'm going to have my wicked way with you right here in the common?" Sophie hated the exasperated note in her voice, hated the way Vim slowly turned his head to assess her, as if he wasn't quite sure he recognized the shrew standing there, hands on her hips, hems soaked, hair a fright.

"Is it your courses?"

"I beg your pardon?"

"My sisters grow... sensitive when their courses approach." He went back to having his nose-duel with the baby, while Sophie fisted both hands and prayed for patience.

"I am traveling in the company of my three older brothers and the man with whom I violated every rule of polite society, as well as a baby whom I will have to give up when we reach Morelands, and all you can think is that my—"

He did not kiss her, though she hoped he might be considering it, even here, even with her brothers stomping around nearby. He regarded her gravely then passed her the baby.

"Because if it's not your courses, then perhaps it's all that rule violating we did that has you so overset. Or maybe it's that we got caught violating those rules. I am willing to answer for my part of it, Sophie, duke's daughter or not. I think your brothers know that."

He glanced around then leaned in and brushed his nose against hers.

Leaving Sophie not knowing whether to laugh or cry.

❧

"Lady Sophia sends her regrets. She'll be taking a tray in her room." Westhaven settled into a chair as he spoke, then reached across the table and appropriated a drink from his brother's ale while Vim watched.

Lord Valentine slapped his brother's wrist. "Which means we don't have to take turns passing Beelzebub around while we pretend we're having a civil meal. Is Sophie truly fatigued, or is she being female?"

"Can't tell," Westhaven said. "She's probably worn out, worrying about the child. Valentine, if you value your fingers, you will put that roll back until we've said the blessing."

Lord Valentine took a bite of the roll then set it back in the basket.

"Think of it as playing house," Devlin St. Just— also the Earl of Rosecroft, though he apparently eschewed use of the title—suggested. "Westhaven gets to be the papa, Val is the baby, and I am the one who refuses to indulge in such inanity. For what we are about to receive, as well as for infants and sisters who travel fairly well, and snowstorms that hold off for one more freezing damned day, we're grateful. Amen."

Before the last syllable was out of St. Just's mouth, Lord Val had retrieved his roll.

They ate in silence for a few moments, food disappearing as if it were indeed being inhaled. Vim figured it was some kind test too, and aimed his question at St. Just.

"To what do we attribute Goliath's miraculous recovery? He was off when I tried to take him from Town yesterday, and today he's dead sound."

St. Just lifted his mug and peered into the contents. "Higgins explained that Goliath is a horse of particulars. Westhaven, did Valentine spit in my mug?"

Westhaven rolled his eyes as he glanced at first one brother then the other. "For God's sake, nobody spat in your damned mug. Pass the butter and drop the other shoe. What manner of horse of particulars is Sophie's great beast?"

"He does not like to travel too far from Sophie. He'll tool around Town all day with Sophie at the ribbons. He'll take her to Surrey, he'll haul her the length and breadth of the Home Counties, but if he's separated from his lady beyond a few miles, he affects a limp."

"He affects a limp?" Vim picked up his mug and did not look too closely at the contents. "I've never heard of such a thing."

"I'll tell you what I've never heard of." Westhaven shot him a peevish look. "I've never heard of my sister, a proper, sensible woman, spending a week holed up with a strange man and allowing that man unspeakable liberties."

Lord Val paused in the act of troweling butter on another roll. "Kissing isn't unspeakable. We know the man slept in my bed, else he'd be dead by now."

And thank God that Sophie hadn't obliterated the evidence of their separate bedrooms.

"I have offered your sister the protection of my name," Vim said. "More than once. She has declined that honor."

"We know." Lord Val put down his second roll uneaten. "This has us in a quandary. We ought to be taking you quite to task, but with Sophie acting so out of character, it's hard to know how to go on. I'm for beating you on general principles. Westhaven wants a special license, and St. Just, as usual, is pretending a wise silence."

"Not a wise silence," St. Just said, picking up Lord Val's roll and studying it. "I wonder how many cows you keep employed with this penchant you have for butter. You could write a symphony to the bovine."

Lord Val snatched his roll back. "Admit it, St. Just, you've no more clue what's to be done here than I do or Westhaven does."

"Or I do." The words were out of Vim's mouth without his intention to speak them. But in for a penny... "I want Sophie to be happy. I do not know how to effect that result."

A small silence spread at the table, a thoughtful and perhaps not unfriendly silence.

"We want her happy, as well," Westhaven said, his glance taking in both brothers. He ran his finger around the rim of his mug twice clockwise then reversed direction. "When I wrested control of the finances from His Grace, things were in a quite a muddle—I hope I don't have to tell you that bearing the Windham family tales would not be appreciated?"

In other words, it would earn him at least that beating Lord Val had referred to.

"I can be as discreet as my brother."

"One suspected as much." Another reversal of direction. "I gradually got the merchants sorted out, the businesses, the shipping trade, the properties, the domestic expenses, but the one glaring area that defied all my attempts at management was the pin money allocated for my mother and sisters."

From Westhaven's tone of voice, this had been more than a mere aggravation. Pin money by ducal standards for that many women could be in the tens of thousands of pounds annually.

"Her Grace likes to entertain," Lord Val observed. "Monthlong house parties, shoots in the fall, a grand ball every spring. Gives one some sympathy for our dear papa."

And don't forget the Christmas parties, Vim thought darkly.

"And bear in mind," St. Just said, "we have five sisters of marriageable age. Five. Most of whom are quite social, as well."

"Dressing them alone was enough to send me to Bedlam," Westhaven said. "I'd end up shouting at them, shouting at them that even a seven-year-old scullery maid knew not to overspend her allowance, but then Her Grace would look so disappointed."

This was indeed a confession. Vim kept a respectful silence, wondering where the tale was going.

"Sophie does not overspend her pin money," Westhaven said. "Not ever. She did not want to offend me, you see, but she saw I was far more overset to be shouting at my sisters than they were to be shouted at—His Grace is a shouter—and she intervened. She asked me to turn the ladies' finances over to her, and a more grateful brother you never beheld. She passes the ledger back to me each quarter, the entries tidy and legible, the balances—may all the gods be thanked—positive. I don't know how she does it; I haven't the courage to ask."

"I'm a grateful brother too," Lord Valentine said after a short silence. "I got my year in Italy thanks to Sophie." His lips quirked into a sheepish smile. "I play the piano rather a lot, though composition has my interest these days, as well. His Grace does not—did not—approve of the intensity of my interest in music but was unwilling to buy me my colors with both Bart and St. Just already on the Peninsula. I was climbing the walls."

"I'm sorry I missed that," St. Just said.

"You should be glad you missed it," Lord Val replied. "Shouting doesn't begin to describe the rows I had with His Grace. Sophie sought me out one day after a particularly rousing donnybrook and jammed a sailing schedule under my nose. She'd researched the ships going to Italy, the conservatories in Rome, the cost of student lodging, the whole bit. Paris was out of the question, thanks to the Corsican, but Rome was... Rome was my salvation. She offered to give me her pin money. Not lend, give."

"Did you take it?" Vim had to ask, because a moment like this would not present itself again, of that he was certain.

"Of course not, but I took her idea, and for the first time in my life found myself among people who shared my passion for music. You cannot imagine what a comfort that was."

Yes, he could. He could well imagine wandering for years without any sense of companionship or belonging, then finding it in perfect abundance.

Only to have it snatched away again.

"I suppose I'll have to add my tuppence," St. Just said. He didn't look at anyone as he spoke, but stared at his empty plate. "I was not managing well when I came home from Waterloo."

"When I dragged you home," Lord Val interjected.

"Dragged me home kicking and screaming and clutching a bottle in each fist."

Vim had to stare at his plate too, because St. Just was the last man he could picture losing his composure. Westhaven was polished, Lord Val casually elegant. St. Just was a gentleman and no fool, but the man was also had the bearing of one who was physically and emotionally tough.

"I was quite frankly a disgrace," St. Just said. Westhaven looked pained at this summary but held his peace. "I'd left a brother buried in Portugal and seen more good men…" He took a sip of his ale, and Vim saw a hint of a tremor in the man's hand.

"I went to ground." He set his ale down carefully. "I holed up at my stud farm in Surrey, where I consumed more good liquor than should be legal. I could not sleep, yet I had no energy. I could not stand to be alone, I could not stand to be around people, I could not—"

"For God's sake, Dev." Lord Val glowered at the mug he cradled in his hands. "You don't have to—"

"I do. I do have to. For Sophie. She came tooling down to Surrey after a few months of this and took in the situation at a glance. She rationed my liquor, and I suspect she put you two on notice, for you began to visit periodically, as well. She called in my man of business and chaperoned a meeting between him and me. She had a stern talk with my cook so I'd get some decent nutrition. I hated her for this, wanted to wring her pretty, interfering neck, and contemplated it at length."

"Gads." Westhaven ran a hand through his hair. "I hadn't known."

"She didn't tell anybody. She was off visiting friends, supposedly, so you see there's precedent for her little detours from the agreed-upon itinerary. She stayed two weeks, and when she judged I was sober enough to listen to her, she pointed out that I had five sisters who were all in want of decent mounts. I owned a stud farm, and did I think my business would prosper if my own sisters could not find decent horses in my stables?"

Westhaven looked intrigued. "She lectured you?"

"She bludgeoned me with common sense, and when I told her to have His Grace pick out something from Tatt's she... she cried. Sophie hates to cry, but I made her cry. I was so ashamed I started selecting my training prospects that very afternoon."

"You made her cry." Westhaven smiled ruefully. "Rather like my shouting at our sisters."

"Or hollering at His Grace over my music," Lord Val observed. "I wanted to make beautiful sounds... and there I was, carrying on like a hung over fishwife."

"And Sophie put you all to rights?" Vim had siblings, he'd had parents and a loving stepfather, a grandfather and several grandmothers, cousins, and an aunt and uncle. Family interactions were seldom quite this dramatically simple, but clearly, in the minds of Sophie's brothers, the situation was not complicated at all.

"Sophie put us to rights," Westhaven said, "and my guess is we've never thanked her. We've gone off and gotten married, started our families, and neglected to thank someone who contributed so generously to our happiness. We're thanking Sophie now by not calling you out. If she wants you, Charpentier, then we'll truss you up with a Christmas ribbon and leave you staked out under the nearest kissing bough."

"And if she doesn't want me?"

"She wanted you for something," Lord Val said dryly. "I'd hazard it isn't just because you're a dab hand at a dirty nappy, either."

Vim didn't want to lie to these men, but neither was he about to admit he suspected Sophie Windham, for reasons he could not fathom, had gifted him with her virginity then sent him on his way.

"She lent you that great hulking beast of hers," St. Just pointed out. "She's very protective of those she cares for, and yet she let you go larking off with her darling precious—never to be seen again? I would not be so sure."

Vim had wondered about the same thing, except if a woman as practical as Sophie were determined to be shut of a man, she might just lend the sorry bastard a horse, mightn't she?

"I proposed to my wife, what was it, six times?" Westhaven said.

"At least seven," Lord Val supplied.

St. Just sent Westhaven a wry smile. "I lost count after the second hangover, but Westhaven is the determined sort. He proposed a lot. It was pathetic."

"Quite." Westhaven's ears might have turned just a bit red. "I had to say some magic words, cry on Papa's shoulder, come bearing gifts, and I don't know what all before Anna took pity on me, but I do know this: Sophie has been out for almost ten years, and she has never, not once, given a man a second look. You come along with that dratted baby, and she looks at you like a woman smitten."

"He's a wonderful baby."

"He's a baby," Westhaven said, loading three words with worlds of meaning. "Sophie is attached to the infant, but it's you she's smitten with."

All three of Sophie's brothers speared him with a look, a look that expected him to do something.

"If you gentleman will excuse me, I'm going to offer to take the baby tonight for Sophie. She's been the one to get up and down with him all night for better than a week, and that is wearing on a woman."

He left the room at as dignified a pace as he could muster and considered it a mercy Lord Val hadn't barked anything at him about leaving Sophie's damned door open.

❧

"That is just famous." Westhaven scowled at the empty basket of rolls, wanting nothing so much as to summon Sindal back into the room—but for what?

"Yes," Valentine said, though his expression was

more puzzled than thunderous. "If Sophie and Sindal were in separate bedrooms several doors apart, how does he know she was getting up and down all night with the child? I slept in one of those bedrooms for years and never heard Sophie stirring around at night."

St. Just smiled a little crookedly. "Because you sleep like the dead and snore accordingly. One wonders if Sindal has told Sophie about the debacle in his past. I don't think the man's forgotten it."

"She wouldn't hold it against him," Val said, frowning. "We don't hold it against him, do we?"

"His Grace thundered about it for weeks," St. Just said. "You two were more concerned with getting back to school, but Sindal is only a couple years older than I am. It isn't something a man would quickly forget."

Westhaven got up and crossed the room to hunker near the fire. "Like we can't forget he took liberties with our sister. His Grace will be calling for his dueling pistols if the truth should reach him."

"I don't think so." Val kept to his seat and rearranged the cutlery on his empty plate. "I've come to realize His Grace picks up a lot more than we thought he did, and he chooses to overlook it."

"Perhaps." St. Just shifted in his chair and crossed his legs at the ankle. "That leaves us only with Her Grace to worry about."

Westhaven rose from poking up the fire and regarded his brothers' unhappy expressions. "'Tis the season, you lot. Cheer up. At least the man can change a dirty nappy. If he and Sophie have anticipated their vows, he'll need to be handy in the nursery. Now, shall I beat you at cribbage seriatim or both at the same time?"

"And what if there are to be no vows?" St. Just asked.

Valentine answered as he crossed his knife and fork very precisely across his plate. "Then he'll need to learn how to disappear from Sophie's life and never show his miserable face in the shire again. We won't have him trifling with her."

Westhaven resumed his place at the table.

"But his family seat is in Kent," St. Just said. "He can't very well avoid that for the rest of his life, particularly not after he inherits."

Westhaven smiled, not a particularly pleasant smile. "Exactly so. Valentine, fetch the cards; St. Just, we'll need decent libation. As I see it, we really don't have very many options."

Fourteen

A QUIET KNOCK SOUNDED ON SOPHIE'S DOOR, no doubt one of her infernal, well-meaning brothers come to check on her.

Come to make sure she hadn't knotted her sheets and eloped with a stable hand to dance on café tables in Paris.

She opened the door and stepped back.

"I wasn't sure you'd still be awake." Vim didn't come into the room, just looked her up and down from where he stood in the drafty corridor.

"Come in, please. We're letting in the cold."

He advanced exactly three steps inside the door and still made no move to touch her. "I've come to spell you with Kit. I can take him tonight, and you can get some rest."

And wasn't that just fine? Vim would come for the baby but not to see how she fared or to speak with her privately.

"I'll let you take him. I must accustom myself to being without him, mustn't I?"

"Not necessarily." He shifted half a step as Sophie

closed the door behind him. "You can raise that child, Sophie. You're a duke's daughter, and your reputation has no doubt been spotless until now. Your family is of sufficient consequence you could take in a half-dozen children and nobody would take it amiss."

"You're wrong." She rummaged in her traveling bag for some clean nappies and a rag. "They would say: Like father, like daughter. They would say: Like brother, like sister."

"What does that mean?"

"Anna and Westhaven anticipated their vows, as did St. Just and Emmie. The proof is in their nurseries. I expect Val and Ellen did, as well, but time will tell. His Grace raised two bastards in the Moreland Miscellany, though I love my brother and sister dearly. I'm even named for the royal princess whom all believe to have whelped a bastard, though nobody will say it in public."

"Sophie, what's wrong?"

Now, he'd moved. He'd crossed the room silently to stand at her elbow. The bergamot scent of him, the Vim scent of him, tickled her nose.

"I'm tired," she said, shifting away to sink onto the raised hearth of her small fireplace. "Seeing my brothers is wonderful, but under the circumstances..."

He lowered himself to sit beside her. "Under the circumstances, I've ruined your holiday."

"Christmas is not my favorite time of year."

"Mine either, and hasn't been since a certain holiday gathering almost half my lifetime ago. I expect your parents will acquaint you with the details if your brothers haven't already."

This was news. She lifted her head to peer at him. "Is this why you dread coming to Kent? There is some scandal in your past?"

"My sisters were the victims of scandal, though I started the tradition well before they did, and I was not exactly a victim. I was a fool."

"Soph?" Valentine's voice called softly from the corridor. A moment later, a knock sounded on the door, and a moment after that, Val pushed the door open. Slowly—slowly enough she might have hastened to an innocent posture if she'd been, say, kissing the breath out of her guest. "Is the prodigy asleep yet?"

"You were a prodigy," she said, rising from the hearth. "Though now you're just prodigiously bothersome. Lord Sindal was coming by to collect Kit for a night among you fellows."

"We fellows?" Val's brows crashed down. "We fellows took turns the livelong freezing day, carrying that malodorous, noisy, drooling little bundle of joy inside our very coats. You should be missing him so badly you can't let him out of your sight for at least a week of nights."

"Ignore your brother, my lady." Vim rose off the hearth, and to Sophie's eyes, looked very tall as he glared at Valentine. "We will be pleased to enjoy My Lord Baby's company for the night, won't we, Lord Valentine?"

Valentine was not a stupid man, though he could be as pigheaded as any Windham male. Marriage was apparently having a salubrious effect on his manners, though.

"If Sophie says I'll be pleased to spend the night with that dratted baby, then pleased I shall be. Coming, Sindal?"

And then, then, Vim kissed her. On the forehead, his eyes open and staring at Valentine the entire lingering moment of the kiss. "Sleep well, Sophie. We'll take good care of Kit."

He lifted the cradle and departed. Sophie pushed the nappies at Valentine, ignored her brother's puzzled, concerned, and curious looks, and pointed at the door without saying one more word.

"Westhaven sent us a pigeon." His Grace waved the tiny scrap of paper at his wife. "Says they've retrieved Sophie, and all is well. The four of them are on their way."

Though it didn't say precisely that.

"In this miserable weather too," Her Grace replied. "I don't worry about the boys so much, but Sophie has never enjoyed winter outings. Come sit and have some tea."

He sat. He did not want tea, but he did want to share his wife's company. She was the picture of domestic serenity, plying her needle before the fire in their private sitting room.

"They're traveling in company with Rothgreb's nephew," His Grace said, flipping out his tails. "Is that a new piece?"

"A blanket for your grandson. Anna will be showing him off this spring in Town, and he must be attired to befit his station."

"Mighty small fellow to be so fashion-minded,"

His Grace remarked. "Have we seen the Charpentier boy since that awful scene all those years ago?" He'd tried to keep the question casual, but Her Grace was as shrewd as she was sweet.

And she was very, very sweet.

"We have not." She looked up to frown at him, the only manifestation of her frown in the corners of her lips. "The viscountess has mentioned him passing through from time to time, but he hasn't socialized when in the neighborhood. If he's going to be underfoot this year, we really must invite him to the Christmas party."

His Grace accepted a perfectly prepared cup of tea from his wife and made a show of putting the teacup to his lips. Insipid stuff, tea. Its saving purpose was to wash down crème cakes, of which there were exactly none in evidence, bless Her Grace's heart.

"You invite everybody and their granny, Esther. Don't expect him to come."

She said nothing while His Grace could hear her female mill wheel grinding facts together with intuition and maternal concern.

"Do you suppose Sophie has come to enjoy Mr. Charpentier's company?"

He thought his daughter had done a great deal more than that, given the nature of Westhaven's note. *Will explain in person* usually meant the news was too bad to be committed to writing.

"Charpentier has the courtesy title now, has had it since his grandfather died all those years back."

"A title." Her Grace appeared to consider this. "Sophie has never been much impressed with titles."

"He's only a baron."

They could hope. They could hope he was a hand-some, charming, single baron who had a penchant for quiet, spinsterly types given to charitable causes and taking in strays.

Christmas was the season of miracles, after all. His Grace downed his tea in one brave swallow and regarded his wife. "I believe you should invite the boy to the party, after all. It will make for an interesting evening."

"I will, then. It will be nice to see Essie and Bert, but you are not to get up to any tricks, Percival Windham. More tea?"

His Grace passed over his cup and saucer. "Of course, my love. Nothing would please me more."

❧

"We can stop for lunch at Chester," Vim said. "I'll split off a few miles the other side of town, or you can come with me to Sidling."

Beside him, Westhaven shifted in the saddle. "St. Just? You're the head drover. What do you say?"

"I'm the head nothing," Lord Valentine interjected, nudging his horse up beside Vim's. "I say we get out of this weather as soon as we can. Sophie's lips are blue, and I don't like the look of that sky."

St. Just looked up from where he'd been adjusting his greatcoat. "I say we move on and make that deci-sion when Sindal's fork in the road appears. The baby seems fine, though the damned clouds look loaded with more snow."

"It's my turn to take him." Vim shifted his horse to pull up beside St. Just.

"The lad's fine where he is." St. Just spoke mildly, while Vim endured a spike of frustration. He might be seeing the last of the child in the next two hours; the least St. Just could do was let a man have some—

"Unless you'd rather?" St. Just quirked a dark eyebrow. Vim was tempted to refuse on general principles, but something in St. Just's green eyes... not pity. A retired officer wouldn't offer insult like that, but maybe... understanding. "I have a stepdaughter, Sindal. Less than a day in her company, and I would have cheerfully cut out my heart for her. My younger daughter wasn't even born before I was making lists of reasons to reject her potential suitors."

He spoke quietly enough that his brothers could pretend they hadn't heard him. Vim accepted the child and ensconced the bundle of infant inside his greatcoat.

"Why are we stopping?" Sophie's cheeks were not pink; they were red. As her great beast trudged into their midst, Vim was relieved to see her lips were not truly blue, though they no doubt felt blue.

"Reconnoitering," Westhaven said. "The baron has offered us shelter before we travel the last few miles to Morelands."

"Is Kit managing?"

Four men spoke as one: "He's fine."

"Well, then." She urged her horse forward. "If we're to beat the next storm, we'd best be moving on."

She rode past Vim without turning her head. Even mounted on one of her pet mastodons, she looked elegant and composed, for all the cold had to be chilling her to the bone. He regretted mentioning his aversion to holiday gatherings, suspecting she'd spoken of it to her brothers and gleaned the details of his youthful folly.

For years, he'd tried to refer to it that way, *my youthful folly*, but completely losing one's dignity before every title and tattle in the shire—and Kent was rife with both—was more than folly. It was enough to send a man traveling around the world for years, enough to cost him his sense of home and connection with the people who'd known him and loved him since birth.

"In my head, I'm composing a new piece of music."

Vim turned to see Lord Val riding along beside him. "It will be called, 'Lament for a Promising Young Composer Who Died of a Frozen Bum-Fiddle.' I'll do something creative with the violins and double basses—a bit of humor for my final work. It will be published posthumously, of course, and bring me rave reviews from all my critics. 'A tragic loss,' they'll all say. It could bring frozen bum-fiddles into fashion."

"You haven't any critics." St. Just spoke over his shoulder, having abdicated the lead position to his sister. "Ellen won't allow it, more's the pity."

"My wife is ever wise—"

"Oh, famous." Westhaven's muttered imprecation interrupted his idiot younger brother.

Lord Val leaned over toward Vim. "There's another word, a word that alliterates with famous, that his-lordship-my-brother-the-heir has eschewed since becoming a father. Famous is his attempt at compromise."

"I'll say it, then." St. Just sighed as another flurry drifted down from the sky. "Fuck. It's going to snow again. Beg sincere pardon for my language, Sophie."

She did not so much as shrug to acknowledge this exchange.

They got the horses moving at a faster shuffle, but it occurred to Vim as they trudged and struggled and cursed their way toward Sidling, that Sophie's brothers—passing him the baby, making inane small talk with him, and even in their silences—had been offering him some sort of encouragement.

Would that her ladyship might do the same.

Inside Vim's coat, Kit gave a particularly hearty kick, connecting with the rib under Vim's heart.

While the snow started to come down in earnest.

❧

From a distance, Sidling looked to be in decent repair. The oaks were in their appointed locations, lining the long, curving driveway; the fences appeared to be in adequate condition; the half-timbered house with its many mullioned windows sat at the end of the drive, looking snug and peaceful in the falling snow.

"It's lovely." Sophie drew her horse to a halt and crossed her wrists on her knee. "It looks serene, content. You must have missed it terribly."

"It has a certain charm." Which at the moment was completely lost on Vim.

Would the hall be tidy enough for visitors? Would there be sufficient sheets for their beds? Would Uncle's antediluvian hound have chewed all the carpets to rags? Would Aunt be drifting about in dishabille, making vague references to friends no longer alive?

"You're very quiet, my lord."

He was anticipating more seasonal humiliation

already. "My aunt and uncle are elderly. I'm hoping I haven't overestimated their capacity for hospitality."

"I daresay my brothers could enjoy each other's company before a campfire with naught but horse blankets and a short deck of cards between them." She sent her horse forward, leaving Vim no option but to do likewise.

"Is that what all this bickering is about? Enjoying each other's company?"

"Of course." She peered at him, looking lovely, the snow clinging to her scarf, the cold putting a ruddy blush on her cheeks. "Isn't it the same for you? You come home for the holidays, and it's as if you never gave up your short coats. The feelings of childhood and youth are restored to you just like you never left."

"God, I hope not."

She fiddled with her reins. "Perhaps this year can give you some memories to replace the ones you find uncomfortable. Tell me about your aunt and uncle."

And now he'd hurt her feelings, which was just... famous, as Westhaven would have said. Bloody, famously famous.

"Sophie." He reached over and covered her hand with his own for just a moment. Her brothers were allowing them some privacy by dropping back a few dozen yards, probably because the entire party was in full view of the house. "I will treasure the memories I already have of this holiday season for all the rest of my days."

She urged her horse to a slightly faster walk, which meant Vim had to drop his hand or look as ridiculous as he felt. What had he been thinking, to offer hospitality to a litter of full-grown ducal pups who'd be used to only the best of everything?

He'd been thinking of spending just a few more hours with Sophie, of giving her another day or night before she had to face parting with Kit.

"Pretty place." Lord Valentine rode up on Vim's right. "I like the old-fashioned manors myself. I just finished restoring a lovely old place out in Oxfordshire. Don't suppose you have a piano on the premises?"

"It will likely need tuning." Unless the rats had chewed the thing to kindling.

"I always bring my tools with me. Soph! Wait up. St. Just and Westhaven have been picking on me without ceasing, and I want you to scold them properly."

He trotted up to his sister, only to be replaced by Westhaven and St. Just on either side of Vim's horse.

"It's wonderful to see Valentine back to his old self," Westhaven said. "The man was getting too serious by half."

"We all were." St. Just's observation was quiet as he watched Val steer his horse right into the flank of Sophie's larger mount, then threaten to drop his sister in the snow as he helped her dismount. "Her Grace was right to summon us home, even if means we don't see our wives until Twelfth Night."

"Maybe it was His Grace doing the summoning."

Before they could wax maudlin over that, as well, Vim spoke up. "I will apologize in advance for the state of the household here at Sidling. We'll keep you safe from the elements, but I can't vouch for the particulars my aunt and uncle might be able to offer."

Westhaven cocked his head when his horse came

to a halt. "Like that, is it? Always a bit sticky taking over the reins from the old guard. I wrested a power of attorney from His Grace not long ago." He swung down easily. "In hindsight, I'm not sure His Grace put up more than a token fight. Be a good lad and distract dear Sophie while I rub some feeling back into my abused fundament."

Vim dismounted, his frozen feet and ankles suffering agonies when they hit the driveway. "I have never heard so much about a grown man's miserable backside in all my days. How do your brothers put up with you?"

Westhaven paused in the act of running his stirrup irons up their leathers. "I do it for them, mostly." Westhaven's voice was low and devoid of humor. "They fret I'll become too much the duke. I won't ever be too much the duke if it costs me my siblings' friendship."

Vim was puzzling out what reply to make to such a confidence when his uncle's voice boomed from the main entrance. "Vim Charpentier, get yourself into this house this instant lest your aunt fly down these steps and break her fool neck welcoming you!"

"And you." Vim's aunt emerged from the house, wearing only a shawl to protect her from the elements. "You get back into this house, my lord, before you blow away in the next breeze. Come in, Wilhelm, and bring your friends."

His aunt pronounced his name in Scandinavian fashion: Villum. It was a small thing, but others typically used the English version: Will-helm.

"Come along." His uncle gestured to the assemblage.

"Let's get this pretty young lady ensconced before a fire so your aunt can quiz her properly. And you fellows can use a mug or two of wassail, I'll warrant."

His uncle sounded the same: bluff, gruff, and quite at home in his own demesne. When Aunt Essie presented her cheek for Vim to kiss, she bore the scent of lemon verbena, just as she had from his infancy.

Maybe things weren't so bad.

"Merciful powers!" Aunt Essie took a half step back. "Who have you got there in your coat, Vim?"

Presenting Kit upstaged the introductions, but Aunt and Uncle assumed a neighborly familiarity with Sophie's brothers, and even with Sophie herself.

By the time coats, hats, and gloves had been passed off to various footmen, Uncle Bert was holding the baby and bellowing for refreshments in the library. Kit nearly kicked the old man's chin, while Aunt Essie surrendered her shawl to swaddle the cooing, chortling infant.

"He'll need a change," Sophie said quietly. "He'll need to eat and romp, as well."

And she was telling *him*, not conveying it to her host or hostess. "I'll see to it."

He felt a slight pressure to his hand, a brief warmth where Sophie's fingers closed around his. She was smiling at his uncle, a gracious, soul-warming smile, but she'd kept her hand in Vim's for a palpable moment.

The tightness in his chest that had started growing the moment he'd realized weeks ago he couldn't avoid this trip eased a bit. Perhaps he might yet avoid disaster, despite the holiday season, despite the looming separation from Sophie and Kit, despite the disarray and trouble here at Sidling. Christmas was the season of miracles, after all.

❧

That Sophie hadn't done any of her brothers bodily injury was miraculous.

"They mean well, the lot of them," Sophie fumed as she lifted a naked, happy Kit from a laundry tub of warm water.

"Gah-bu-bu!"

"They're getting as meddlesome as His Grace, leaving me to ride by myself for most of the journey, dodging about so Vim must take me in to dinner, then shuffling around with the subtlety of elephants so he sits beside me, as well." She rubbed noses with the baby. "The worst part was deciding to spend the night here when Morelands is just a few miles farther down the road, and all without consulting me, of course. And Vim, ever so polite through it all."

"Ba-ba-ba." Kit grinned, and as soon as Sophie laid him on a folded-up bath sheet, he started kicking and squirming.

"You are no help at all, but you want to romp, don't you?"

Kit made no reply but applied himself assiduously to the task of rolling onto his stomach. Sophie's sitting room was cozy and well appointed, though the curtains and carpet were both a trifle faded. Lady Rothgreb hadn't batted an eye when Sophie had requested to keep the baby with her, but had directed one of the footmen to find a cradle among the furniture stored in the attic.

A soft tap on the door had Sophie hoping Vim was

stopping by. It didn't matter that he'd be coming to say good night to the baby; it mattered only that she missed him, and that every single word to come out of her mouth today had seemed the wrong thing to say if it was directed at Vim.

"Come in."

"Just me," the viscountess said. "Don't get up, my dear. Those young fellows are lingering over their port, and Rothgreb is so glad to have company, he's going to linger with them. How's the lad?"

"Relieved to be somewhere he can stretch his legs, so to speak."

Lady Rothgreb braced one hand on the arm of the settee and the other on the edge of the coffee table and slowly lowered herself to the floor. "Old bones," she said. "Winters are longer when you get old, but the years go more quickly, anyway. Someone should make a study of this. Is your room in order?"

"It's lovely. I'm sure Kit and I will be very comfortable here."

Lady Rothgreb brushed a veined hand over Kit's head. "If I'd known how having company would perk up the staff, I'd have sent over to Their Graces for the loan of a few of their grown children." Kit grabbed Lady's Rothgreb's finger and grinned at his hostess. "My, you're a strong little fellow, and my guess is you're about to cut some teeth too."

"Westhaven mentioned this. I gather it's something of an ordeal?"

"They get a little cranky." She withdrew her finger. "They can also get a cold to go with their fussiness—a runny nose, a touch of congestion."

"He had a runny nose last week."

"Are you sure you don't want to turn him over to a nursery maid, my dear? Nanny has long since retired, but our housekeeper has sixteen grandchildren."

"I'm sure your housekeeper is dealing with unexpected guests; that's challenge enough."

"She loves Vim's visits, rare though they are. We all do."

A silence fell, while Kit positioned himself to go a-Viking across the carpet, and Sophie wondered about Lady Rothgreb. Vim had suggested the older woman was growing vague, wandering both mentally and physically, and yet her ladyship had presided over a lively dinner conversation and handled unexpected guests with gracious good cheer.

"I have a motive for intruding on you, my dear."

"It's not an intrusion," Sophie said, shifting to sit between the baby and fireplace. "I can't imagine swilling port with my brothers has any appeal."

"Actually, it would—they are charming men, and it would allow me a little more time with my nephew. Rothgreb is entitled to play host, though, so we'll leave them to it."

"I should not have shut myself up with Kit," Sophie said, feeling defensive without any particular reason, "but he has had a great deal of upheaval lately, and I did not want to impose on—"

"May I exercise an old woman's prerogative and be blunt, my dear?"

"Of course." Something uneasy in Sophie's middle suggested this bluntness was going to be painful.

"You are attached to this child, Lady Sophia."

Sophie watched as Kit lurched and crawled and scooted over to Lady Rothgreb. "Anybody would be. He's that dear."

"He's a baby. Dear is their forte, but he's not your baby."

The old woman spoke very gently. Sophie kept her eyes on the child. "I will find a foster family for him soon."

"Vim said you were sensible."

Sensible. He'd said she was sensible. Not lovely, intelligent, dear, attractive, or capable of mad, passionate love. Not even an adequate cook, for goodness sake. *Sensible*. She added Vim to the list of men narrowly escaping bodily injury.

"I cannot encourage you strongly enough to place this baby with that foster family as soon as possible, my dear. To all appearances, he's in good health and will make the transition easily now. The longer you put it off, the harder it will be on both of you."

Sophie managed a nod, but her hostess's words cut like a winter wind. To think Kit would part from her easily hurt; to think he'd be pained to part from her was unbearable.

"Do you know of any families in a position to take on an infant?" She made herself ask the question but hoped in a selfish corner of her heart for a negative reply.

"Indeed I do. The curate's family has three half-grown girls, and they'd love to have a boy. Mrs. Harrad has remarked many times that a son would lighten her husband's load."

"Are they an older couple?" Sophie sternly suppressed

the notion that Kit would end up as some fire-and-brimstone preacher's glorified bond servant.

"They aren't old from my perspective, but they are humble, godly people who have always comported themselves charitably." Lady Rothgreb pushed to her feet, while Sophie picked Kit up and rose with him. "I think the boy would thrive in their care."

"I will consider what you've suggested, my lady, though I'd like to have my mother's wisdom on the matter, as well."

"Her Grace would agree with me, I'm sure of it." Lady Rothgreb eyed the infant. "The only person I know whose eyes are still that blue is my nephew. I hope he was pleasant company at dinner?"

"He was all that was gentlemanly." Sophie wrapped the baby in a receiving blanket as she spoke. "But tell me something, Lady Rothgreb, why is Lord Sindal so reluctant to visit his family seat over the holidays?"

It was spying, plain and simple, but spying on a man who'd had all day and then some to acquaint Sophie with details of his past—and had declined to do so.

"He was happy enough here as a toddler," Lady Rothgreb said. "We were happy to have him, though his papa did not enjoy good health. Vim's father married primarily because the old lord insisted on it, for all I don't think it was an unhappy union."

"You think his father's death overshadows Vim's memories of the place?"

Vim. She should not have called him Vim before his aunt, but he was Vim to Sophie. Vim changed nappies and read poetry and made mad, passionate love to her. Lord Sindal was a man at risk for injury.

"His early memories were happy ones, and his papa's death was not unduly difficult—Vim's mother took the boy north within the year." Lady Rothgreb tucked the blanket a little more carefully around the baby. "Wilhelm suffered some egregious and very public indignities, courtesy of a young lady, around the holidays the last year he was visiting here. We haven't seen much of him since."

"His heart was broken?"

"He'd be the one to ask about that, wouldn't he? You should also ask him to show you around the portrait gallery, if it's sunny tomorrow. The little fellow here might enjoy the outing, as well, but it's chilly up there this time of year."

Something in Lady Rothgreb's smile suggested this outing to the portrait gallery would be more than a way to pass the time or walk off breakfast. The older woman was being too casual, too... disinterested in her own suggestion?

"I'll ask him, though I'm fairly certain my brothers will want to push on to Morelands tomorrow."

Lady Rothgreb paused with one hand on the door latch. "Her Grace replied to our note. She says you're not to overtax yourselves hastening on to Morelands in dirty weather. Rothgreb is enjoying your visit very much, my dear, so I hope you won't hurry off too early."

She slipped out the door, a gracious hostess having checked on her guests.

Sophie cuddled the baby close, not knowing whether to pray for decent weather so she could get free of proximity to Lord Sindal, or to pray for the roads to be closed for days, that she might enjoy a little more time with the child she was bound to give up.

Fifteen

"Here you go." St. Just offered Vim a peculiar sort of smile as he handed over a carrying candle. "You'll want to light your uncle up to his room, won't you?"

He would? "Of course. Uncle, I'm sure Aunt is wondering what's become of you."

"She knows damned good and well what's become of me," Rothgreb said, tottering to his feet. "Haven't had so much fun swilling port and telling stories since I last rode to hounds."

"And you'll introduce me to Dutch's Daughter in the morning," St. Just said, shaking a finger at the viscount. "I've seen her offspring under saddle and coveted her bloodlines."

"No doubt about it, my boy, you'd be a lucky man to get your hands on such as her." The viscount winked and turned to his nephew. "Onward, young Vim. My bride awaits me."

Vim caught looks from Westhaven and Lord Val suggesting Rothgreb might need a steadying hand on the stairs, but when he accompanied his uncle into the corridor, the old man's step was brisk.

"Moreland sired some decent sons," Rothgreb remarked. "And that's a pretty filly they have for a sister. Not as brainless as the younger girls, either."

"Lady Sophia is very pretty." Also kind, intelligent, sweet, and capable of enough passion to burn a man's reason to cinders.

"She's mighty attached to the lad, though." His uncle shot him a look unreadable in the gloom of the chilly hallways. "Women take on over babies."

"He's a charming little fellow, but he's a foundling. I believe she intends to foster him. Watch your step." He took his uncle's bony elbow at the stairs, only to have his hand shaken off.

"For God's sake, boy. I can navigate my own home unaided. So if you're attracted to the lady, why don't you provide for the boy? You can spare the blunt."

Vim paused at the first landing and held the candle a little closer to his uncle's face. "What makes you say I'm attracted to Lady Sophia? And how would providing for the child endear me to her?"

"Women set store by orphans, especially wee lads still in swaddling clothes. Never hurts to put yourself in a good light when you want to impress a lady." His uncle went up the steps, leaning heavily on the banister railing.

"And why would I want to impress Lady Sophia?"

"You ogle her," Rothgreb said, pausing halfway up the second flight.

"I do not ogle a guest under our roof."

"You watch her, then, when you don't think anybody's looking. In my day, we called that ogling. You fret over her, which I can tell you as a man married for more than fifty years, is a sure sign a fellow is more than infatuated with his lady."

Vim remained silent, because he did, indeed, fret over Sophie Windham.

"And you have those great, strapping brothers of hers falling all over themselves to put the two of you together." Rothgreb paused again at the top of the steps.

Vim paused too, considering his uncle's words. "They aren't any more strapping than I am." Except St. Just was more muscular. Lord Val was probably quicker with his fists than Vim, and Westhaven had a calculating, scientific quality to him that suggested each of his blows would count.

"They were all but dancing with each other to see that you sat next to their sister." Rothgreb pushed away from the banister and headed off toward his room, Vim trailing a step behind him. "What are you about, boy? I know where my own room is. Lady Sophia's in the green guest bedroom."

The room right across from Vim's room. "I would not disrespect a guest in this house, Uncle."

"Youth! It's a wonder the aristocracy hasn't perished for sheer lack of brains. I'm not suggesting you disrespect anybody. Wish her a pleasant good night. Won't take but a minute, and I'm sure your aunt neglected this courtesy."

Vim passed his uncle the candle. "Good night, Uncle. Thank you for the suggestion."

The old man pointed with a gnarled finger. "Her room's that way, and for God's sake, don't wake the baby while you're wishing her good night."

❧

Valentine stepped over the hound drowsing on the hearth rug in Lord Rothgreb's study. "I can spend hours tuning that piano. Once I start on the harpsichord, we might be here all day." He settled onto the sofa beside Westhaven.

"That's fortunate," St. Just said from the other end of the couch. "Trying out the mare's paces was only going to take all morning, and that's assuming nobody in the stables moves faster than the staff here at the house."

"Which leaves me to do what?" Westhaven groused.

Valentine wedged himself a little lower on the sofa and propped his feet on a hassock. "You're a clever lad, being the heir and all, you'll think of something."

❧

Sophie put down her hairbrush, not even sure she'd heard a tap on the door. "Come in." She said it very softly, in deference to the baby sleeping in the cradle near the hearth.

Valentine was fearless to the point of recklessness. He would be the one foolish enough—

"I hope I'm not intruding?" Vim closed the door quietly behind him.

"You're not." Sophie gathered her wrapper around her a little more closely. It was borrowed from Lady Rothgreb's closet, a voluminous old thing more comfortable than attractive.

"Kit's asleep?"

She nodded and watched as Vim moved a few steps into the room. "You have everything you need,

Sophie? I'm not sure the staff has had to contend with visitors since the last time I passed through."

"I'm quite comfortable. How long has it been since you came to visit?" She picked up the brush with every intention of resuming her evening toilette. It would not do to fall upon the man as if she were starving for the sight of him, for the sound of his voice, for the exact shade of blue in his eyes.

"Shall I braid your hair for you?" He rose from where he'd been kneeling by the cradle and prowled over to the vanity.

Or maybe it just looked to her like he was prowling, because her mind was in such a muddle. He took the brush from her grasp, and shifted her shoulders gently with his hands so she was facing the mirror.

"I want you to do something for me." Sophie spoke quickly, lest she lose her nerve.

"Anything within my power, of course." He used both hands to scoop her hair over her shoulders so it flowed down her back, a sweet, soothing caress that made Sophie's insides melt.

"Are you familiar with the curate's family?"

"I am not." He started brushing her hair, long, slow strokes down the length of it. "Why?"

"Your aunt suggested they might be willing to take in a boy child. They have only girls and would likely dote on Kit." *Or work him to death.* She didn't say that. She closed her eyes lest Vim see the indecision she was wrestling with.

"Curates tend to move around, Sophie, at least until they gain a vicar's living. Are you sure that's what you want for Kit?"

She shook her head, and behind her, Vim went still.

He said nothing, not one word, while Sophie's mind fumbled around for some coherent phrases to explain something so difficult to express. "I am *not* sure, which is why I'm going to ask you to interview these people and see if they might suit Kit."

He hunkered at her side, so they were at eye level. Sophie forgot she wanted to do him bodily injury, forgot he'd been excruciatingly polite over dinner, forgot everything except the kindness once more in his eyes.

"You ought to be the one to make this decision, my dear." He did not touch her, but his voice touched her heart. "You love that baby as if he were your own, and this is too important a decision to make secondhand."

"But I can't..." She swallowed and looked away, emotion welling. "I simply cannot."

He rose and tugged her by the wrist over to the bed, then sat beside her holding her hand. "I will be your emissary, but you must tell me what my marching orders are."

She wanted to throw her arms around him in gratitude—or in some excess of emotion—but he was being so... reserved. She marshaled her dignity, though it was a struggle.

"You simply go and look the family over. See if their circumstances are adequate to take on another mouth, offer them whatever coin you think they'll need to provide for Kit. My pin money is lavish, and I'd spend it all to see Kit comfortable. Make sure the house is warm and the larder stocked. Look over their livestock and their root cellar, see if their children have shoes and warm clothes."

His arm came around her shoulders.

"And look to make sure the roof isn't leaking, and that the doors all close snugly. It would be nice if they had some toys... no, they *must* have toys. Sturdy toys a boy can't break by playing with them too vigorously, not just pretty things and dolls for little girls. And something musical. I don't expect a piano, but a guitar doesn't cost much, or even a wooden flute..."

She trailed off and pressed her face to Vim's shoulder as an awful thought occurred to her. "They'll change his name."

This struck her as more monstrous even than taking Kit on simply for the free labor he'd provide. To toss his very name aside, as if he were just a beast, a dog, an old horse passed from owner to owner...

"You can insist they address him as Kit, my dear, but for him to have a different last name from his family would raise uncomfortable questions."

She nodded against his shoulder, it being impossible to wedge words past the lump in her throat.

"I'll go first thing in the morning, if this is what you wish."

It wasn't what she wished. She *wished* she weren't Lady Sophia Windham. Wished she were just some goodwife and Vim her yeoman, able to take on another baby to go with their own brood. She wished she could provide Kit family—brothers and sisters to tease and grow up with and still be his people when Sophie was dead and gone.

She wished…

She pulled away from the sturdy comfort of Vim's body. Wishing never got anybody anywhere.

"I must do what's best for Kit." She untangled her fingers from Vim's. "I meant it about the money. Westhaven is very generous with us, and I have enough frocks and bangles and bonnets to last a lifetime."

She got up from the bed and returned to her vanity but didn't sit down.

To her relief, he remained on the bed. "I have never seen you in a bonnet, never seen you wear a single item of jewelry, never seen you in a dress that wasn't five years out of fashion."

"What has that to do with anything?" She picked up her hairbrush, and lest she throw it, started swatting at her hair.

"Sophie, I cannot help but think you should take more time with this decision."

He did move off the bed, then, and Sophie flipped her hair over the other shoulder so she wouldn't have to look at him.

"Time will only make it harder on both of us. It's been little more than a week, and already I grow confused about what should be a simple decision."

He was close enough that she could catch a whiff of the bergamot scent of him, close enough she could feel the tempting, muscular bulk of him looming near, and still she merely brushed her hair.

"I will wish you good night, then, Lady Sophia."

She paused and peered up at him. "I do not need to be Lady Sophia to you when we are private."

"Yes, you do."

He leaned down and kissed her forehead, lingering near for so long Sophie was tempted to throw her arms around his neck and beg him to stay, to hold her, to love her, to talk her out of this awful decision regarding Kit.

"Sweet dreams, Lady Sophia. I will be about your errand directly after breaking my fast."

And then he was gone, and Sophie had no one to talk her out of anything, not even the errand of placing her wonderful baby in the care of complete strangers.

Sixteen

"I THOUGHT YOU'D BE GONE TO MORELANDS BY NOW."

Vim stood in the doorway to Sophie's sitting room, watching as she played on the floor with a smiling Kit. They made such a lovely picture, thoroughly enthralled with each other, a picture no amount of practical reasoning could convince Vim should be drawn for Kit with any other family.

"I was outvoted," Sophie said, picking up the baby and getting to her feet. "Valentine must tune the piano, St. Just is dickering with your uncle over the mare, and Westhaven is claiming certain unmentionable parts are not up to another ride in the cold without soaking them for a bit first." She paused in her recitation and met his gaze. "Well?"

"The Harrads were from home." The relief in her eyes was painful to behold. "They'll be back this afternoon."

And then the dread again. She cuddled the baby closer and kissed his ear. Kit turned to swing his little paw at her, but Sophie drew back, only to kiss his ear again when he dropped his hand.

"That child likes to play." And Sophie adored to play with him, to lavish love and attention upon him.

"He's been singing today, as well," she said, taking a seat on the sofa with the infant. "Wonderful baby songs, odes to his toes, madrigals to his knuckles. I wonder when he'll begin to speak. Mrs. Harrad will no doubt know such things."

She was Lady Sophia this morning, a woman with no recollection of the glorious intimacies they'd shared. A duke's daughter determined on her cause. He sat beside her, missing plain Sophie Windham with a fierce ache.

"The livestock look well fed, the fences are in good repair, the chicken coop is snug, and the house looks tidy and spruce. The windows are clean, the wood-boxes are full, the porch is swept, and the walkway has been shoveled clear of snow. I hope this disappoints you as much as it did me."

She gave him a puzzled look.

"Sophie, I would foster the boy here, except my aunt and uncle are surrounded by the oldest domestics this side of the Flood, my aunt is growing vague, and my uncle can't keep track of the valuables. I will not be here enough to matter, and that is no situation to leave a child in."

"I meant to ask you about that." She bundled the child into a receiving blanket then folded a second, heavier blanket around the first. "Will you show me your portrait gallery?"

"Of course." But why would she want to see a bunch of old paintings, and what exactly was she going to ask him about?

She passed him the baby and wrapped a shawl around her shoulders. As they progressed through the house, Vim tried to hoard up some memories: Sophie trotting up the main staircase, Sophie pausing at the top to wait for Vim and his burden to catch up with her, while a shaft of sunlight gilded red highlights in her dark hair.

As they entered the cavernous portrait gallery—a space so cold Vim could see his breath before him—Sophie gathered her shawl around her.

"We ought not to stay long," he said. "You'll take cold with just a shawl."

"I'm warm enough." She glanced around the room, which was brightly lit with late morning sun pouring in the floor-to-ceiling windows and bouncing off the polished parquet floors. "This would be a marvelous place to hold a holiday reception."

"It would take days to heat it." But she had a point: when had his aunt and uncle stopped entertaining?

"Fill it with enough people, and it will heat easily enough. Who's this?"

She stood before a full-length portrait of a big, blond fellow standing beside a pretty, powdered lady lounging in a ladder-backed chair.

"My grandfather. He never took to wearing powder or wigs, though he liked all the other finery. That is his first wife. My grandmother is in the next portrait down."

Sophie moved along a few steps. "I see where you get your great good looks. These four are all of him?"

"With his various wives. He lived to a great old age and was expecting to get a passel of sons on them all."

She studied the portrait, while Vim wondered what, exactly, constituted great good looks.

"I can see Rothgreb in him," Sophie said, "about the eyes. They have a Viking quality to them, devil take the hindmost. Was your grandmother the only one to give him sons?"

"An heir and spare, and then years later, when the heir died of some wasting disease, my father as an afterthought. I think my father's death was particularly hard on the old man."

She moved to the last portrait of Vim's grandfather. "He had you by then, though. You should have been some consolation."

"I was not." Vim shifted to stand beside her but focused on Kit, not the painting of his grandfather. "My father had a weak heart. His lordship was convinced, because I look like my father, I would be a similar disappointment."

Sophie perused him up and down, her lips compressed in a considering line, then she gestured to the next portrait. "This is your father?"

"Christopher Charpentier, my sainted father."

"He's quite handsome, but I have to say, you look as much like your grandfather as you do your sire."

"I do not." Not one person had ever told him he looked like his grandfather.

She crossed her arms. "By the time you came along, his hair had likely gone white, but it was the exact shade of golden blond yours is now. As a younger man, his eyes were the exact shade of baby blue yours are too."

"If I am the spit and image of him, I wonder why, when I told him I was leaving for a life at sea, he did nothing to stop me."

She gave him another visual inspection. "Was this declaration made after your heart was broken?"

"Shall we move on? The older portraits are over here."

Sophie crossed the room with him and took a seat beside him when he lowered himself to one of the padded benches between paintings.

"I never liked this room," he said, shifting so Kit sat on his lap. "Never liked the sense the eyes of the past are upon me."

"Some of the people in this room loved you, I should hope." She reached over and loaned Kit her finger to wrestle into his mouth.

"And I loved them, but they're dead all the same." He paused to take a breath and marshal his composure. "It wasn't my heart that was damaged so much as it was my pride, and on the occasion of a gathering attended by the entire neighborhood. A young lady made it dramatically apparent she preferred another, and I did not handle the situation well. In hindsight, I made far too much of the entire matter. Would you like to hold the baby?"

As gambits went to change the subject, it ought to have been foolproof, but Sophie shifted to look out over the room, taking her finger from Kit's maw.

"He's comfortable where he is, and if I'm dreading my leave-taking from him, you can't be looking forward to losing him, either. Are you still in love with your young lady?"

"For God's sake, Sophie." He set the baby, blankets and all, in her lap and rose, pacing off a half-dozen feet. "I haven't seen the woman in years, and she preferred another. No sane man would allow himself to hold on to tender feelings under such circumstances."

"We're not necessarily sane when we're in love." Her smile was wistful, as if recalling her own first love.

"Then I'm happy the condition has since not befallen me. Shall we go? I'm sure I heard the first bell for luncheon, and we don't want Kit taking a chill."

She looked peevish, as if she might argue with him, which was about what he deserved for being so short-tempered. Fortuitously, the baby started bouncing in her lap and carrying on in baby-language about God knew what.

"Come." Vim scooped the child up and extended a hand to Sophie. "We'll bring him to the table and entertain your brothers with his singing. Aunt will be delighted, and Uncle will start telling stories again."

❧

"Do you know, Percy, my eyes are not what they used to be." Esther, the Duchess of Moreland, kept her tone mild, but her spouse was no fool. After more than thirty years of marriage, he could sniff out an uxorial interrogation just in the way she said his name, and she could tell from his very posture he was already maneuvering charm into place to avoid it.

"Your eyes are as lovely as ever, my dear. Hold a minute." He pointed upward, to where a fat sprig—nigh a sheave—of mistletoe was suspended from the rafters over the Morelands main entrance. She smiled while he bussed her cheek.

"Your behavior is wonderfully decorous, husband. I don't know whether I approve."

"The girls are all underfoot, save Sophie. It doesn't do to set a bad example. I wish you could have seen young Deene's expression when he realized he was going to have to kiss four Windham sisters in succession if he wanted to leave the house with his reputation intact."

"And did you treat him to a ducal glower?"

"Permit me my entertainments, my love, but I could hardly glower when the girls were the ones who ambushed him under the kissing bough."

And as distractions went, the image of four of Esther's daughters kissing the handsome Marquis of Deene ought to have sufficed—except Esther did not allow it to.

"What else did Westhaven have to say?" She tucked her arm through her husband's, lest he try to nip into his study for something he'd forgotten or pop down to the kitchen to snitch a crème cake or go on some other ducal frolic and detour.

"Westhaven?"

"Yes, you know. Earl of, also known as Gayle Windham, your heir and our son. He sent you another little epistle this morning from Sidling."

His Grace paused outside the door to Esther's personal parlor. "How do you know these things, Esther? The children swear you have eyes in the back of your head, but I suspect it's supernatural powers."

"I saw the Sidling groom coming up from the stables. The man isn't young, and his progress took some time. Perhaps the note wasn't from Westhaven."

"It was from Westhaven. He said old Rothgreb was pressing them to stay an extra day, claiming his viscountess hasn't been so animated since Sindal's last visit. St. Just is negotiating the sale of that mare Rothgreb is so proud of, our very own Mozart is tuning their piano, and Sophie might be taking notice of young Sindal."

"Sindal is a bit older than St. Just."

"A veritable relic, though still barely half my age. Would you mind if she took an interest in him?"

In the studied casualness of her husband's inquiry, Esther understood very clearly that His Grace would not mind. His Grace was encouraging the association, in fact. Esther passed into the cozy little parlor overlooking the wintry landscape of Morelands' park, waited until her husband had joined her, and closed the door behind him.

"This room always smells lovely," he said, glancing around. "Flowers in summer and spring, and spices in the fall and winter. How do you do it?"

Now that they were behind closed doors, his arms slipped around her, and she leaned against him.

"It's a secret. Do you want to know what was in the viscountess's note to me?"

He rested his chin against her hair. "I wasn't going to pry."

Nothing wrong with His Grace's eyesight. "It seems our Sophie has become enamored of a foundling. The tweenie did not catch her coach for Portsmouth, but left the child in Sophie's care and hasn't been heard from since. Esmerelda gleaned this from things Rothgreb winkled from his nephew over port. She is concerned Sophie is too smitten with the baby to realize she's made a conquest of young Wilhelm."

"Oh my." His Grace stepped back and went to the sideboard, lifting a quilted cozy from the teapot. "It seems we have an intrigue going on, my love. The temptation to meddle is very strong."

She crossed her arms and considered her husband, the man she loved, the father of her children, and a man who would never have enough grandchildren. "My very thought, Percival. Perhaps we should sit down and discuss the situation."

"No 'perhaps' about it."

❧

Already, after only a handful of days and nights, Vim *knew* her. Half asleep, deep in the night, without even touching her, he knew she was there.

"Sophie, what are you doing in my bedroom?"

The shadows beside his bed shifted, and he felt a weight beside him on the mattress.

"I don't want to talk."

"Sophie, this is not in the least wise. You're leaving tomorrow—" Two soft, rose-scented fingers settled over his mouth then slowly moved up along his jaw to caress the outer contour of his ear.

"You can send me away." Her weight came closer on the expanse of the mattress. "I wish you would not, because you're right. Tomorrow, *I will leave*."

There was such desolation in three words, desolation that echoed in the very chambers of Vim's own heart. She'd turned down a lifetime with him but was apparently willing to steal another hour in the dead of night. Then too, in the morning, she would give up the child.

"This is not wise, Sophie."

She kissed him. Her lips connected first with his cheek, then wandered over to the corner of his mouth, then grazed the edge of his jaw.

"My dear, where is Kit?"

"Fast asleep in my room. Kiss me, Vim, please."

It was the last thing she said for a long, long time—with words—but he sensed she'd come to *know* him too. Her hands as they skimmed over his chest and arms were sure on his body; her kisses on his skin were cherishing and unhurried.

For all she'd turned down his proposals, Vim was certain this was not mad, passionate lovemaking from Sophie, but *loving*. Maybe it was born of grief in anticipation of parting from the baby; maybe it was an indulgence before she fully resumed the mantle of Lady Sophia Windham.

Whatever her reasoning, it would be his privilege to accommodate her wishes on this one, unlooked for, final occasion.

"Straddle me, Sophie." A whisper, only. She replied by arranging herself over him in the darkened confines of the canopy bed. His hands told him she was naked, not a stitch on her, and his heart told him it would be blasphemy to hurry.

He palmed her nape and levered up to find her mouth with his. For long, lazy moments, he kissed her. Chaste kisses at first, kisses that politely invited her to tenderness and flirtation, then—with a sinuous slide of his tongue—hinted at something more intimate and carnal.

For a time, she seemed content to be seduced, to be tasted and teased and coaxed, but then Vim heard a small sound of longing from her and felt her sigh against his mouth. He took this as a request and slid both hands down her sides, slowly, one rib at a time, savoring the feel of her as he mapped her with his hands.

She broke off the kiss as if listening for what his hands would do next, or perhaps to decide on her own strategy while he measured the span of her hips.

He moved his hands back up, settling them over her breasts so her nipples puckered against his palms.

Another sigh, while she let him have just a hint of her weight on his erection. Not enough to comfort, but more than enough to encourage. He rewarded her generosity by playing with her breasts, stroking them lightly, kneading gently, until she brought her hands up to cradle his grip more snugly to her.

More, then. His lady wanted more of him, so he obliged by arching his hips up, caressing her damp sex with his rigid flesh.

"Vim?"

"Soon. Kiss me, Sophie."

She leaned forward, her breasts pressing into his chest, and settled her mouth over his. He shifted his grip to explore the length of her spine, the graceful sweep of muscle and bone that was her back. When she gave him her tongue, he steadied himself with two hands on her derriere and gave her his in return.

She groaned softly and found him with her sex again, moving over his length in a slow, hungry push and retreat. "Vim, I need…"

"Your wish, my lady…"

She went still, and he angled himself for penetration, pausing just at the point where their bodies would join.

"Is this what you wished for, Sophie Windham?"

The question had slipped out uncensored by reason, a genuine inquiry for all it was ill timed. At this instant, she wanted him for something, not for marriage but for comfort or passion or simple carnal oblivion.

She made a sound, perhaps of sexual frustration, and shifted her hips forward enough to capture him by half his length. The pleasure of it stunned him, sent all his questions flying from his mind, and had him gripping the back of her head less than gently as he sought her mouth with his own.

He withdrew slowly then set up a torturously languid rhythm—torturous to him—while he plundered her mouth and built the conflagration of their desire.

The first time, she came silently, her body convulsing around his while she hung over him and submitted to his relentless thrusting. His objective had not been to gratify her arousal but to intensify it, to share the pleasurable torture.

When she eased up off his chest, he gave her the space of exactly three deep, shuddery breaths before he started up again, this time attending to her breasts as he resumed the push and drag of his cock inside her body.

He loved her, he wanted her to be happy, but he wanted her to burn, as well, to spend the rest of her life wishing and regretting and remembering.

God knew, he would.

"This is too much." Sophie panted the words, her voice conveying bewilderment and heat.

"Hold on to me." He rolled them so he was above her, inside her, and in a better posture to devour her sexually. "I will never have too much of you, Sophie Windham."

She brought her hands up, anchoring herself by gripping his wrists as he started to thrust with purpose. The second time she came, she whimpered with the pleasure and burden of it. He showed her no mercy, bearing down hard when she shuddered and arched and convulsed around him.

And still, he gave her but a moment to go quiet and motionless beneath him, to reach up and brush his hair back with one hand before he began moving again.

"I did not know it could be like this. I didn't know... *anything*."

Behind the wonderment in her voice, there was pain. He slowed his hips despite the desire and darkness clamoring for release, lowered his body over hers, and cradled her face to his shoulder.

"Shall I stop?"

It would *kill* him, slay him for all time, devastate him on some level a man never acknowledged in daylight if he had to withdraw from her at that moment. He braced himself on his arms, prepared to die rather than indulge his selfishness any longer.

"Love me. Please, Vim, just love me."

Yes. That was what he'd been trying and failing to comprehend—that the gift of this final joining was about loving, not about regrets or erotic arguments or his own wishes. Sophie's body had understood that even if her mind would not let her explain it to him in words.

This time when he moved, he moved gently, gathering her to him, cherishing her with everything in him. He meant to withdraw, to give her one more increment of pleasure, to *love* her and protect her.

But the third time when she came, her body seizing up with desire so fiercely and sweetly around him, he was helpless not to join her, not to let his grip on discipline and determination slip so he might instead hold on to love.

❦

The day Sophie learned her brother Bart was dead dwelled in her memory as a black, miserable stretch of hours. A man gone for a soldier was always at risk of death, and she'd reconciled herself to Bart's choice in the matter. As a ducal heir, no one would have thought less of him for remaining a civilian.

He'd wanted his colors, wanted them badly, and Sophie had had the consolation that Bart had died doing more or less as he pleased.

The worst pain of the day had been not her brother's death but her parents' utter paralysis with the loss. His Grace's bluster and rough good humor had gone abjectly silent, Her Grace had, for the first time in Sophie's life, looked lost and more old than dignified. Her parents had embraced repeatedly in her sight, an upsetting rarity.

Victor's death had been a similar ordeal—a relief for her ailing brother, perhaps, but a loss of more than a sibling for Sophie. She'd given up a little more of the illusion that her parents and her position could protect her from both grief and harm.

And today, there would be no one to protect her from the loss of a baby she'd grown to love ferociously in such a short time.

And no one to protect her from the loss of the man she'd come to love, as well. He'd been generous last night, passionate, tender, lavish with the intimacies he'd afforded her. To know she could be married to him if only she'd settle for passion...

But she'd wished not for a man to take to bed every night, but a man to love.

A man who would *love her* as his wife and the mother of his children.

"You will be fine." She held a grinning, drooling Kit up before her. "You are charm personified, and they will love you before the sun sets. Lord Sindal has assured me the Harrads are decent, hardworking people devoted to their children and their church. You'll thrive there, tease your sisters, and be a comfort to your parents."

They'd call him Christopher, though, Kit being too far removed from the theological origins of his given name.

"Chris-to-pher. That shall be your name."

She cuddled him close when he squirmed. "You shall be Christopher Harrad, and you shall want for nothing."

"Sophie, the horses are saddled, and your brothers are waiting." Vim stood in the doorway of her sitting room, looking handsome and grave. In his eyes, Sophie saw concern but no hint of the passionate lover she'd held just a few hours previously.

The man she'd said good-bye to with every kiss and caress she'd given him.

"I'm ready." She would never be ready.

"Come." He held out a hand to her, and Sophie expected him to wing his arm and provide her a proper escort from the house. Or perhaps he'd take

the baby and steal a few minutes more of Kit's smiles
and sweetness.

His arm slid around her shoulders, his chin rested
on her crown. "I wish you'd reconsider this. He can
always join the Harrads in spring or when he's started
to walk or speak."

He meant this as a kindness, but Sophie felt the
suggestion as something like a betrayal, sloshing about
amid all the other pain she was carrying around in her
heart. "If I don't do this today, *now*, I won't ever be
able to. Not ever."

She felt him nod, but he didn't let her go, and
she didn't step back. For a long moment, she leaned
against him and took for herself some of his strength
and warmth. "I don't want to do this."

"My dear, I know."

It was as much comfort as she'd have, the consolation that Vim knew exactly what this decision would
cost her. Kit fussed and kicked between them, and
Sophie moved away.

Or tried to. Vim kept his arm around her shoulders
as they traveled through the house, then took the
baby from her when they walked out into a sunny,
cold day.

"At least it's still. You should make Morelands easily."

Sophie paused at the bottom of the front steps.
"You're not accompanying us?"

"He is." St. Just led a big bay horse up to the mounting
block. "We took the liberty of having a mount saddled
for you, Sindal. It's a pleasant day for a ride."

"I'd thought to look over account books with my
uncle this morning."

And the winter day was about as pleasant as the coldest circle of hell by Sophie's lights.

St. Just smiled a smile sporting more teeth than charm. "To hear your aunt tell it, the account books have languished for years without your attention to them. Surely you'd rather accept our invitation for a short jaunt on this sunny day?"

Valentine and Westhaven rode up, halting their horses on either side of St. Just.

"It'll clear the cobwebs," Westhaven said.

"And you can tell us all why you've been such a stranger at Morelands these last years," Valentine added. "Sister, I can take the infant up with me."

Vim glanced from one brother to the other, something like a smile lurking at the corners of his mouth. "I would be pleased to join you, and Kit rides with me."

He passed Kit to St. Just, gave Sophie a leg up, mounted and retrieved the baby, and then they were moving down the driveway, a silent cavalcade in the sunny, bitter morning.

It took no time at all to reach the curate's little house beside the church, a mere span of minutes by Sophie's reckoning, while she tried not to watch Vim holding Kit, occasionally speaking to the child, cradling him close against the brisk air.

Already, she felt an empty place under her heart, a place that ought to be filled with gummy smiles, baby-songs, and a tiny flailing hand intent on capturing the nearest adult nose, chin, or heart.

"Take him for just a moment." Vim was regarding her with steady blue eyes, while Sophie's throat closed and her chest began a slow miserable tattoo of impending loss. She shook her head.

"Just while I dismount." Vim passed the baby over, despite another shake of her head, and then Sophie was cradling Kit close, shutting her eyes to memorize the sweet, baby scent of the child, to block out the sight of a tidy, tired young woman coming from the house in a plaid shawl.

"Sophie." Vim, standing by her horse, waiting for her to give him the child. "You can come by later and visit with Mrs. Harrad. We should get Kit out of this weather." He spoke gently, his voice pitched so the others would not hear.

This was why her brothers had impressed Vim into coming with them: so Sophie could hand the child to *him*, not to the woman shivering at the bottom of her steps, trying to look anywhere but at Sophie or the baby.

She handed Kit down and looked away, off toward the rolling terrain of Morelands just outside the village. She forced herself to take in air, then expel it, take in air, then expel it.

She counted her breaths—four, five, six... while Vim passed the child into the waiting woman's arms and out of Sophie's life.

"I'll ride to the Morelands gates with you." Vim swung up and shifted his horse so he was alongside Sophie's mount, but he kept his silence while they rode.

"You've made the best decision, Soph." Valentine shot her a glance that held a world of understanding, and all Sophie could do was nod and stare straight ahead, lest her brother's compassion destroy her composure. He seemed to comprehend how tenuous her nerves were, because he rode on, joining their brothers in the lead.

"I can tell you it will ease," Vim said very quietly. "I pray for you that the hurt will ease, Sophie Windham. Some things just take a great deal of time."

He didn't castigate her, didn't try to reason with her or cheer her up, but Sophie was grateful for his presence nonetheless. All too soon, they were at the Morelands gates, the wrought iron wings standing open in welcome.

Vim drew his mount to a halt. "I'll turn back here and thank you all for both your companionship on the journey and your willingness to provide my relations their first houseguests in quite some time."

He was leaving her *now*? *Now* when there was no compulsion, no urgency whatsoever, and her heart was never going to mend? "You won't come in for a cup of tea?"

"Sophie." Westhaven sounded serious indeed. Val and St. Just looked equally grave. St. Just shook his head subtly, but the message was clear.

She was not to push Morelands hospitality on Baron Sindal.

Vim moved his horse right next to Sophie's, leaned over, and there—before her three solemn brothers—gave her a lingering kiss on the cheek. "You will send to me if there's need." He spoke very quietly, and it was not a question. Then he turned his mount and steered it in the direction of Sidling.

While Sophie watched Vim walk out of her life, her brothers maneuvered so their horses were beside her,

Valentine to her immediate right, Westhaven and St. Just to her left.

"Shall we?" St. Just kneed his horse forward, and Sophie's mount walked on, as well. All too soon, they were ambling up the drive to Morelands, the house sitting in winter splendor just a hundred yards ahead.

"I don't know how I'll face Their Graces."

Sophie realized she'd spoken aloud when all three brothers were looking at her with concern.

"A headache might do," Westhaven said.

"Fatigue would be convincing," St. Just added.

Valentine cocked his head, his expression hard to read. "You're a grown woman. We'll make your excuses, Soph. Just go to your room and leave orders you're not to be disturbed until dinner."

She realized as Val helped her dismount that her brothers had been right to suggest Vim avoid an encounter with Their Graces. Sophie's parents were perceptive people, and who knew what innuendos and looks they might have picked up on between Sophie and the man who'd made half her wishes come true?

"Back so soon?" Rothgreb surveyed his nephew, not needing spectacles to see the boy was preoccupied.

Not a boy, a man grown, and a handsome—if somewhat thick-witted—man at that. Love made such fools of young people.

Vim slid into the chair across from his uncle's desk. "The distance we covered wasn't great. You have the ledger books out?"

"You just let that pretty filly go?"

Vim looked up, and Rothgreb could see him trying to balance respect for his elder with the urge to throttle an interfering old busybody.

"She refused my suit on more than one occasion, Uncle. I don't suppose you've made a list of all the things that have gone missing?"

"Refused your suit! Did you go down on bended knee? Shower her with compliments and pretty baubles? Did you slay dragons for her and ride through drenching thunderstorms?"

"I changed dirty nappies for her, got up and down all night with the child, and offered her the rest of my life."

"Dirty nappies? Bah! In my day, we knew how to court a woman."

This provoked a sardonic smile. "In your day, you married for convenience and were free to chase any panniered shirt that caught your eye."

"Little you know." Rothgreb tossed his spectacles on the desk. "Your aunt would have had my parts fed to the hogs if I'd done more than the requisite flirting with the dowagers. And she knew better than to share her favors elsewhere too, b'gad."

"About my aunt." Vim sat up, his expression grim. "She does not seem in the least vague to me, Uncle. I must conclude your descriptions of her conditions were exaggerated, and I have to wonder for what purpose."

Damn the boy. Love had made him stupid about some things, but not nearly stupid enough.

"She has good and bad days, and having people around seems to help. She's particularly glad to see you and glad to see you've an interest in the Windham girl."

Let the young rascal chew on that. "Don't suppose you'd be willing to take Essie calling over at Morelands? These old bones don't weather a chill like they used to."

The truth of that admission didn't make it any easier to state, and Vim didn't look like he was taking the bait.

"If I never set foot on Moreland property again, it will be too soon."

Oh, the boy had it bad. Rothgreb shoved to his feet, a shift too ponderous to have the requisite dramatic impact, but it did allow him to glower down at his beef-witted nephew. "For God's sake, when are you going to let a youthful peccadillo go? The Holderness girl was a wrong turn, nothing more. We all make them, and most of us, thanks be to The Deity, get over them."

"I'm over the girl," Vim said, springing to his feet with enviable ease. "I was over the girl before the packet left Bristol, but I will never get over being refused the opportunity to seek satisfaction for the slur to her honor *and mine.* I'll expect a list of missing items on my desk after dinner."

He stomped out, all indignation and frustration, the picture of thwarted love. Rothgreb lowered himself into the chair and reached out a hand to the hound who'd come blinking awake at Vim's departure.

"The boy is an ass. My wife would say he takes after me."

The hound butted Rothgreb's hand.

"Let's go find Essie, shall we? We must do something, my friend. I'm not sure what, but we must do something."

Seventeen

"YOU'D BEST COME DOWN TO DINNER, SOPH."
Maggie's green eyes held compassion and a hint of
stubbornness too. "Her Grace is being patient, though
I suspect that's just because our brothers are charming
her for all their worth."

"I'm not hungry." Sophie rose from her escritoire,
where she'd been trying to write a list of Kit's likes
and dislikes for Mrs. Harrad, but this allowed Maggie
to walk over to the desk and start snooping.

"Sophia Windham, when did you become an
expert on changing an infant's linen?"

"Vim showed me the way of it—quick and calm."

"About this Vim…" Sophie realized her mistake
too late, because Maggie had put the list down and
was regarding Sophie very directly. "A dozen years
ago—when you had barely begun wearing your hair
up—I was introduced to him as Wilhelm Charpentier,
a younger relation with more good looks than consequence. He danced well enough but disappeared
without a word after some to-do at one of Her Grace's
Christmas parties."

"I know him as Vim, but he's Baron Sindal now, Rothgreb's heir." Sophie kept her voice diffident, very carefully diffident.

Maggie crossed her arms, a martial light coming into her eyes. "And how does the baron know about caring for babies?"

Older siblings knew family history worth learning, but they could also be damnably protective.

"Put down your guns, Maggie. Vim has younger sisters, and I think he simply has an affection for babies. He hasn't mentioned any offspring. What was the to-do about?"

Maggie pursed her lips and peered at Sophie as if torn by indecision. "I don't know. Socializing was never my forte, but whatever it was, nobody said a word about it afterward. Tell me about this baby of yours."

Sophie turned her back on her sister, ostensibly to rearrange things on the vanity tray. Vim had used that brush on her hair.

"You're being nosy, Mags."

And now Maggie was beside her, her expression hard to read. Maggie was the second born, a half sibling like St. Just, and her mother's influence showed in flaming red hair, more height than any other Windham sister, and an occasional display of temper.

"You changed this child's napkin, Sophie Windham—many times. Her Grace is a devoted mother, but I am willing to bet my favorite boar hog she never changed dirty linen for any of you."

Siblings were the very devil when a woman needed some privacy to regain her composure.

"Needs must," Sophie said softly, blinking at her hairbrush.

"It isn't just this dratted baby, is it?" Maggie gently took the brush from Sophie's grip. "You've gone and fallen in love with Sindal, and all over a basket of dirty laundry."

"It wasn't quite like that." It was exactly like that, and on the carpet in the servants' parlor, no less.

"I overheard the boys talking. St. Just was muttering something about Sophie's mad scheme and that idiot Sindal. Did something happen, Soph?"

Maggie, being the duke's oldest daughter and illegitimate, had not had an easy road. When she'd turned thirty, she'd moved into her own household in Town. This had created a paradoxical opportunity for closeness between the sisters, allowing Maggie's pretty little house to become a place of refuge for her younger siblings.

"I don't know what to do." Sophie picked up the brush again, then put it down and reached for a handkerchief neatly folded on the vanity tray. Vim's handkerchief—how had she come by this? She brought it to her nose, caught a whiff of bergamot, and began to cry.

"Damn all men forever to a place in hell so cold their nasty bits shrivel up and fall off," Maggie muttered. She slid her arm around Sophie's waist and walked her to the chaise by the hearth. "Shall I have the boys deal with Baron Sindal? They all love a good scrap, even Westhaven, though he'll think it's unbecoming of the Moreland heir to gang up on a man or even go at him one at a time. They'll likely draw straws, and Dev and Gayle will rig it so Valentine's hands—"

"Stop it, Maggie. You must not aggravate the menfolk," Sophie said, laying her head on her sister's shoulder. "Sindal offered for me, but it wasn't…"

Maggie brushed Sophie's hair back, hugging her where they sat on the chaise. "It wasn't an offer of marriage?"

Sophie shook her head. "Not at first. I let him think I was a h-housekeeper, or a companion, or something, and I wanted…"

"You wanted *him*."

Sophie pulled away a little. "Not just him. I wanted a man who loved me, Mags. A man who wanted to be with me, and Vim seemed so…"

"Oh, they all seem *so* when the moon is full and passion is in the air. I at least hope you enjoyed this lapse?"

Sophie's head came up at this question. It wasn't at all what she would have expected from socially retiring, financially minded, no-nonsense Maggie. "I did, Mags. I enjoyed it *immensely*."

A nonplussed expression flitted across Maggie's pretty features. "So what is the problem? He acquitted himself adequately in the manner you desired, and now you can have him to keep if you want. It requires only a word to bring him up to scratch."

"He isn't the man I wished for, though he was very definitely the man I desired."

Maggie sat back, a frown gathering between her brows. "Desire isn't a bad thing, Sophie Windham, particularly not between spouses. Many a marriage goes stale for lack of it."

This wasn't like any conversation Sophie had had with her older sister. It was both uncomfortable and a relief, to speak so openly about such a delicate subject. "You've been married so many times you can speak with authority?"

"I've been propositioned so many times by other women's husbands, men who think questionable birth and red hair mean I'll be grateful for any man's attentions."

"Oh, Mags." Sophie hugged her sister. "I've been so wrapped up in myself these past few years. I am sorry."

"Since Bart and Victor died, since the boys started marrying, since His Grace's heart seizure, we've all been a little bit widdershins." Maggie sighed and rested her chin on Sophie's temple. "I think you're being narrow-minded where Sindal is concerned."

"He offered marriage only when he realized he'd been trifling with Lady Sophia Windham. I don't want my husband served up on a platter of duty and obligation, Mags."

"You might have to take him that way." Maggie rose from the chaise and started pacing. "You could be carrying, Soph. All bets are off, then. I won't let my niece or nephew bear the stigma St. Just and I have put with our entire lives. I'll march Sindal up the aisle at gunpoint, and St. Just will load the thing for me. I'll see his—"

"Hush." Sophie brought Vim's handkerchief to her nose, finding his scent an odd comfort. "It shouldn't come to that, and even if it did, Vim is not going to tarry in Kent any longer than necessary. He'd be one of those husbands gone for years at a time—he hates Kent—and I am bound to stay here as long as Kit is here for me to love.

"And then twenty years from now, I can see how marriage to Vim would work: we'd pass each other on the street in Paris, and he'd exchange the most civil and considerate pleasantries with me. I couldn't bear that. Then too, something is amiss at Sidling, and now is not when Vim ought to be thinking of marriage to inconvenient ducal daughters who practice subterfuge for the worst reasons."

Maggie stopped abruptly midpace. "Loneliness seldom inspires us to our most rational choices. Is Sindal's allergy to the family seat related to that to-do all those years ago?"

"I think so. I could ask St. Just. He'd tell me."

"Or he might not. Men have the oddest sense of loyalty to each other."

They shared a look, a look such as only adult women could exchange regarding adult men, or the facsimiles thereof strutting about the livelong day in boots and breeches.

"You should call at the curate's," Maggie said. "It will distract you from your other problems and assure you the little creature is thriving."

"What if he isn't?" Awful, *awful* thought.

"Do we dote on our brothers?"

"Shamelessly."

"His foster sisters will be doting on him."

"I'll think about it." The idea tantalized, and Sophie would have been halfway to the stables, except the notion of having to once again part with the child stopped her.

"Come down to dinner while you think about it. The last thing you need is His Grace getting wind you've got trouble involving a man. Sindal will leave the shire once and for all, if that's the case."

Sophie stuffed Vim's handkerchief in her pocket, rose, and accompanied her sister to dinner.

❧

"For God's sake, Uncle, what can you be about?"

Vim did not raise his voice, for the old man was at the top of a rickety ladder that was held in place by two equally rickety footmen, while the positively ancient butler hovered nearby.

"Hanging the damned kissing bough," Rothgreb barked. "Your aunt will have it, and until somebody else sees fit to take over the running of this household, I will see that she gets it."

Guilt, thick and miserable, descended like a cold, wet blanket on Vim's shoulders as Rothgreb teetered down the ladder.

"I might have done that for you. You had only to ask." Vim glanced up to see half a bush worth of mistletoe dangling over Sidling's entrance hall.

"Ask? Bah. I've been asking you to come home now for years. What has it gotten me? You lot." Rothgreb glared at his servants. "You'll be dusting in here until this thing comes down." He waved a hand toward the mistletoe. "Only the homely maids and the married ladies will be tarrying in here as long as that's up there. I'll not have my house looking neglected when company's about to descend."

"Company?" The cold sensation slithered down to Vim's innards. "I wasn't aware you and Aunt were entertaining much these days."

"For a man who's been my heir for more than ten years, you're not aware of much when it comes to this place, except the ledgers, my boy." Rothgreb stepped back so the ladder could be removed. This entailed the combined efforts off all three underlings, who departed at an almost comically deliberate pace.

"They're deaf as posts when I'm calling for my coat but can hear gossip at fifty paces without missing a word."

"What company, Uncle? Your letters never mentioned you'd be entertaining over the holidays." Vim crossed his arms and widened his stance, aware the gestures were defensive even as he made them.

"Not company, then." Rothgreb rested a hand on the newel post. "Family. Your cousins, all three girls and their delightful offspring. And then we've invited a few of the local families over tomorrow afternoon so the girls will have some fellows to catch here in the entrance hall. I'll make my special punch; her ladyship will hold forth over more cookies and crumpets than His Majesty's regiments could consume in a week. You'll attend."

He would. His uncle wasn't issuing an order, he was stating a fact. Familial obligations were not something Vim would ever shirk with impunity.

"What time?"

"We usually start after luncheon, so everybody can get home before dark. I expect old Moreland might put in an appearance. He's grown more sociable with his neighbors in recent years, or perhaps the maids here have grown prettier."

And that last was offered with cheerful glee, as if Rothgreb knew damned good and well Vim was dying for even a glimpse of Sophie. "I'm going for a ride, Uncle. Don't wait tea on me."

"Wouldn't dream of it." Rothgreb started up the stairs, moving not exactly quickly, but with some purpose. Going off to plot treason with Aunt Essie or make pronouncements to the old hound, no doubt.

As Vim ambled down to the stables, he considered that for all Sidling wasn't where *he* wanted to be, his aunt and uncle seemed abundantly happy with their circumstances. The house was in fine shape, the estate books were in fine shape, and Vim was sure when he rode the land, he'd see it was being carefully tended, as well.

He did not need to appoint a new steward, not yet.

"Aunt?"

She sat on a tack trunk, wrapped in an old horse blanket, a carrot in her hands.

"Merciful Powers!" She hopped off the trunk, the blanket falling from her shoulders. "Wilhelm. I wasn't expecting you."

"You came down here in just your shawl? Need I remind you, Esmerelda Charpentier, it's the dead of winter?" Though the stable was protected from the wind, and the horses themselves, particularly the enormous draft teams and the sturdy coach horses, kept the place well above freezing.

"I know what season it is, young man."

"Then perhaps you'll allow me to escort you to the house?" He peered at her, unable to read her expression. It might have been some sort of veiled exasperation; it might have been embarrassment at having been caught out wandering.

"I can find my own way up to the house, thank you very much." She bustled off, only to come to a halt when Vim laid a hand on her arm.

"Humor me, Aunt." He draped his riding coat over her shoulders and winged his arm at her. She'd either been waiting for her husband to come fetch her back to the house, or she'd been waiting for somebody— anybody—to show her the way home.

❧

"What is that particularly irritating little air you're determined to vex our ears with?"

Valentine stopped whistling to smirk at Westhaven's question and started singing instead. "*All we like sheep, have gone astraaaaaay.*"

"More Handel." Sophie interrupted her brother's little concert. "Seasonally appropriate. You two did not have to accompany me, you know."

"Nonsense." Westhaven shot some sort of look at Valentine, who'd lapsed into humming. "I needed to call on the vicar since I'm in the area, and Valentine must tune the piano before the Christmas service."

"I'm getting very good at tuning pianos," Valentine said. "A skill to fall back on if my wife ever casts me to the gutter."

"She won't," Sophie replied, patting her mare. "She'll send you visiting your siblings and get her revenge on the whole family."

"Now, children," Westhaven started, only to provoke Valentine back into a full-throated baritone recital.

"*All we like sheep, have gone astraaaaaaaaaaaaaay.*"

Westhaven rolled his eyes. "To think my tiny

son is all that stands between this braying ass and the Moreland dukedom."

"I made Sophie smile," Val said, abruptly ceasing his braying. "My Christmas holiday is a success because I made Sophie smile." He smiled at her too, a particularly sweet and understanding smile. "Go visit the Demon Seed, Sophie. You'll feel much better when you've changed a nappy and My Lord Baby has cast his accounts upon your dress."

"Don't stay too long," Westhaven said as he helped her off her horse. Sophie went still before her brother's arms had dropped from her waist.

"That's Kit." She listened for a moment more. "That's his hungry cry. Let me go, *now*."

"Sophie." Westhaven's grip shifted to her shoulders. "He's not your baby, and they aren't going to starve him. There? You see? Already somebody must be stuffing porridge into the bottomless pit located where his stomach ought to be. Calm yourself. You're Percival and Esther Windham's sensible daughter, and you're merely calling as a courtesy."

Westhaven had the knack of conveying calm with just his voice, but still, Sophie had to rest her forehead on his shoulder for a moment.

"Your package?" Valentine stood beside them, holding out a parcel wrapped in paper. "I'll be most of the day, wrestling with that old curmudgeon in the church vestibule, but my guess is Westhaven will limit himself to one plate of cookies and two cups of tea."

A warning. She wasn't to linger, or her brothers would forcibly remove her from the curate's little house.

"Come along." Westhaven put her hand on his arm while Valentine led the horses over to the livery. "Thirty minutes, no more."

She nodded. They meant well, and right now, Sophie could not trust her own judgment when it came to Kit.

When it came to much of anything.

Westhaven knocked on the door, which was opened by a girl of about six. She grinned, revealing two missing front teeth to go with her two untidy blond braids. "Mama! There's a man here and a lady!"

Sophie smiled down at the child, who opened the door wide enough to let them pass into the house. "I'm Lady Sophia, and this is Lord Westhaven."

"I'm Lizbeth! We got a new baby for Christmas, Papa said. His name is Christian, but he's not really my brother. Mama! The lady's name is Sophie!" She peered up at Westhaven. "I forget your name."

Christian? His name was Kit, or even Christopher. Westhaven did not meet Sophie's eyes.

"You may call me Lord Westhaven."

"Mama! The man's name—"

"Elizabeth Ann Harrad. What have I told you about bellowing in the house?" Mrs. Harrad arrived to the foyer, hands on hips. "I beg your pardon, my lady, my lord. Elizabeth, make your curtsy."

The child flung her upper half forward and down in a bow.

"Very nice," Sophie said, retuning the gesture in more recognizable form. "Mrs. Harrad, I don't mean to impose, but my brothers were going this way, and I thought I'd drop a little something off for—Baron Sindal?"

Vim sauntered up behind Mrs. Harrad, Kit perched on his shoulder.

"Sindal." Westhaven's greeting was cool. "Mrs. Harrad, felicitations of the season. I'll be collecting Lady Sophia when I've called upon the vicar, if you'll excuse me?"

He was out the door before Sophie could stop him.

"Lady Sophia." Vim nodded at her, his smile genial. "We were just having a bit of early luncheon in the kitchen, weren't we, Mrs. Harrad?"

"If your lordship says so. I'll fetch Mr. Harrad to make his bow to you, Lady Sophia." She bustled off as an argument started up elsewhere in the house between two girl children.

Sophie stood there in her cloak, the argument fading, the various smells of the house fading— baking bread, a faint odor of tomcat, coal smoke, and unwashed baby linen. All she perceived was Vim, standing there with his shirtsleeves turned back to the elbows, his eyes the exact shade of blue as Kit's.

"His dress is dirty." Sophie glanced around, hoping Mrs. Harrad wasn't close at hand to overhear her.

"These things will happen when man flings his porridge in all directions," Vim said. "Perhaps you'll have better luck with him?"

"Mary and Louise are arguing again," Elizabeth reported, her gaze going from Sophie to Vim. "That's why Papa must keep the door to his study closed *all the time*. Because they always argue, and Mama yells at them, but they *never* stop."

Vim smiled at the child. "Tell them Lady Sophia complimented your curtsy. Then you can argue with them too." He winked at the child, and she scampered off.

And thus, for a moment, Sophie was alone with Vim and Kit, her gaze devouring the sight of them.

"How are you?"

"It's good to see you."

They spoke at the same time, and as each took one step toward the other, Mr. Harrad came bustling up the hallway, followed by his wife.

"Lady Sophia, my apologies. I wasn't aware we had more company. Do come in. My dear, can you take Lady's Sophia's wrap?"

He spoke pleasantly, but a hint of rebuke laced his tone. An instant's hesitation on Mrs. Harrad's part could have become awkward, but Kit chose that moment to start waving his arms in Sophie's direction and babbling.

"Here." Sophie shrugged out of her cloak. "May I hold him?"

"He seems to like being carried about," Mrs. Harrad said, hanging Sophie's cloak on a peg. "My girls weren't quite as demanding."

Sophie ignored the word choice, ignored whatever currents were passing between husband and wife, ignored even the pleasure of brushing her hand over Vim's as they passed the baby between them.

"My Lord Baby," she said softly, cuddling him close. "You were about to wake the watch with your racket." She glanced up at Vim. "Was he done eating?"

"Not nearly," Vim said. "Perhaps we might take

our tea in the kitchen? I'm sure Lady Sophia would enjoy spending some time with her young friend."

Mr. Harrad shrugged; his wife looked resigned. They were both blond, a little on the slight side, and had a tired, harried look to them.

"Has he been running you ragged?" Sophie asked Mrs. Harrad. "Kit, I mean."

Mrs. Harrad glanced at the baby in Sophie's arms. "It's just that he's a boy. My husband wanted a boy, but they're not the same as girls, and this one is fussy."

He wasn't the least fussy, Sophie wanted to retort. Kit was curled happily in her arms, his little fingers batting at her chin and mouth. "Has he been crawling much?"

Mrs. Harrad looked down, and before she could answer, they'd arrived to a big, warm kitchen redolent with the scent of baking bread. "I can offer you fresh bread with your tea."

"Don't go to any bother, please." Sophie sat so she could put Kit on her lap. "Lord Westhaven will be collecting me before I could do your bread justice." She picked up an adult-sized teaspoon and frowned at it. Had they been feeding Kit with this?

"It suffices," Vim said quietly from his seat beside her. "You just have to give him a moment to work at it."

The sound of his voice had Kit grinning and bouncing on Sophie's lap.

The next minutes passed in a blur, with Kit slurping down a quantity of plain, cold porridge, Vim making small talk with their host and hostess, and Sophie trying to store up a pleasant memory of spending time with Kit.

It was difficult. The baby's dress was dirty, which, true enough, could happen in five minutes flat, but his fingernails were also dirty, and the fat little creases of his baby-neck were grimy. There was a red scratch down the length of one arm, and when all three girls came bellowing and stampeding into the kitchen, Kit began to cry.

He cried more loudly when Mrs. Harrad began to scold, and Sophie herself felt an urge to cry.

"…So we'll just be going." Vim held her chair as he spoke, but the last thing Sophie wanted was to abandon Kit in the middle of this pandemonium.

She tried to communicate this to Vim with a look, but he remained standing above her, his gaze steady, while one of the girls pulled the other's hair and ran from the room. Mrs. Harrad followed in high dudgeon, and Mr. Harrad stood at the door to the hallway looking stoic.

"It isn't always quite this lively," he said when they'd reached the foyer. "The children are very excited to have young Christian with us, and then too, I'm a bit preoccupied. Vicar has given me the sermon for Christmas Day, which is quite an honor."

"I'm sure things will settle down once the girls get used to having a baby brother," Vim said, holding Sophie's cloak out to her.

But if she took the cloak, she'd have to give Kit up.

"Is there a reason you've changed his name?" she asked while Vim arranged the cloak around her shoulders.

"I'm a curate, Lady Sophia. A son named Christian seemed fitting, if a bit optimistic, given this one's origins." He nodded at the baby, his gaze speculative.

"Missus says he's more demanding than the girls, but we'll be patient with him."

He smiled at Sophie, a tired, charitable smile that made her want to scream. Vim took the child from her, and she gave him up, feeling as if the heart had been torn from her chest.

"We appreciate all you're doing for the boy," Vim said. "My regards to your wife. Lady Sophia?"

He passed the baby to the curate, who looked a little surprised. By the time Vim had Sophie bustled out the door, Kit was beginning to fuss again.

"I can't bear this." The words were out of her mouth before Vim had dragged her two steps from the door. "Kit is not thriving there. He's barely noticed amid all the squabbling and noise. He isn't bathed, he isn't clean, they aren't patient enough with him at feeding, those girls are jealous of him. He'll never—"

Right there on the curate's tidy little porch, Vim's arm came around her waist. Not exactly a hug, but a half embrace that let Sophie lean against him.

"Hush, my dear. Kit isn't crying now, is he? A man with three daughters knows a few things about dealing with babies. Let me walk you to the livery, and I'll wait with you until Westhaven is done making the pretty with vicar."

Across the cold, sunny air, Sophie heard one repetitive piano note being struck in the lower register again and again in slow succession. Over at the church, Valentine was tuning the curmudgeon, but the single repetitive tone felt like a bell tolling somewhere in Sophie's heart.

"I don't want to leave him. I should not have come."

"I can understand that sentiment." Vim led her down the steps as he spoke. "All my relations are about to descend, and I feel… ambushed, like I was lured here under false colors. I'm tempted to ride in the direction of Bristol rather than return to Sidling."

"Is that what you did all those years ago? Rode for Bristol?"

His step didn't falter as they moved across the frozen green toward the livery. "Have you asked your brothers about my past, then?"

"I have not. I'm asking you."

Abruptly, it seemed the thing to do. If this was what made it impossible for Vim to settle down at his family seat, if this was part of what made any hope of a future with him a ridiculous wish, then she wanted to hear it, and hear it from him.

For a time, they walked in silence, and Sophie thought if there was something worse than a crying baby, it was the silence of a man figuring out how to explain why he'd never be gracing the neighborhood again.

"Let's take a seat, shall we?"

He led her to a bench carved from a single oak tree trunk. The thing was huge and beautiful in a rough way. It had probably been there when Good Queen Bess had been on the throne.

"You're sure you want to hear this?" He waited for her to choose her seat then came down on her left. "The tale quite honestly flatters no one."

"Scandals usually don't, but you said it wasn't quite a scandal."

She wasn't at all sure she did want to hear an old and sordid tale, but she most assuredly wanted to hear his voice, to have a chance to study his features. In the bright, wintry sunshine, his eyes looked tired.

"Not a scandal. I was finishing up at university, trying to figure out how I was to go on in life." He paused, and Sophie saw him glance at her left hand. She was wearing riding gloves, which did not provide a great deal of warmth.

Did he want to take her hand? To make a physical connection to her? She made a pretense of gathering her cloak a little more closely and moved so their sides touched.

"You were here for the holidays?" she asked.

"For the holidays, yes, but I was down here a lot that fall, because Grandfather was old enough that at any point, he might be taken from us. He was hale at the time, and there was speculation he and his fourth wife had finally succeeded where the second and third hadn't been as lucky."

Sophie remained silent. Old men siring babies wasn't a subject she was equipped to converse on, not even with Vim.

"I became infatuated, Sophie." Vim said softly. Sophie could not tell if he was being ironic. She feared he was perfectly serious. "At the hunt ball, the first of October thirteen years ago, I fell in love with the most beautiful, witty, kind, attractive woman in the shire, an innocent girl with the promise of all manner of pleasures in her eyes, and she accepted my suit. I was over the moon, ready to move mountains, willing to conquer pagan armies to impress my lady."

"You were smitten." She watched his lips moving, forming words that seemed to hurt him as much as they hurt Sophie. He was in all likelihood still smitten, and *that* was why he absented himself from his own home for years at a time.

"The fall assembly had passed, and we were to be married early in the New Year, so we'd had no opportunity to make an announcement. She'd asked me to wait until after Yuletide to speak to her father, but there was no young man more optimistic than I. My lady allowed me the occasional taste of her charms, but I esteemed her too greatly to fully anticipate our wedding vows. She was delicate in this regard, and I respected that."

And what a lucky young lady she must have been, to have Vim's affections at such an earnest and tender time of life. Sophie smoothed a hand down her skirts, wishing she'd never asked for this recitation.

"So imagine my chagrin, Sophie, when I took my handsome young self in my best courting finery off to one of the most prestigious holiday gatherings in the shire, and my lady's father called for all to attend him, as he had an important and felicitous announcement to make. My chest filled with pride, for I was certain he was going to announce the impending nuptials and spare me an awkward interview."

Vim paused, and Sophie watched as his glance scanned the green. He looked like he never wanted to see the place again.

"Her papa announced that she'd be marrying the Baronet Horton's heir. Tony Horton was ten years my senior, in definite expectation of a title, and a man reputed to know his way under a woman's skirts, if I might be vulgar. I could not believe her father had cast her into the arms of such a worthless bounder."

"What did you do?"

"I tried to call the man out, right there at the men's punch bowl. I'd held my tongue until the prospective groom was among his confreres and away from the eyes and ears of the ladies. I accused him of poaching on an understanding, of enticing a gently bred lady with his charm and his expectations, and being the ruin of her happiness."

"Plain speaking." Egregiously plain speaking. Tony Horton's family was well settled in the area, though his holding was not known to be particularly prosperous.

"I would have slapped him soundly before all and sundry, but the host of the gathering caught me by the arm and prevented the blow."

"This is significant?"

"When a blow has been struck, no apology should prevent the duel, not if honor is to be maintained by both parties."

"Men."

His lips quirked, a fleeting hint of his smile. "Yes, men. The host made a joke of my outburst, said half the shire was going to go into mourning because Tony had taken my intended out of consideration, said young men were prone to such overreactions as mine, and with a few more cups of punch, I'd likely be falling in love with mine host's best milk cow. The man was and is well respected, and the others were all too happy to follow his lead. They ended up toasting His Grace's milk cow before I was hustled out of the room by three of my burlier neighbors."

Oh, my goodness. "His Grace?" There were other dukes in Kent, several, in fact.

"Your father, Sophie Windham, His Grace, the Duke of Moreland. Your father was the one who heaped such ridicule and scorn on my head, made a laughingstock of me before my peers, and saw to it an engagement undertaken in bad faith obliterated one made in good faith. I've crossed paths with him since in Town, and it's almost a greater insult that he treats me with great good cheer, as if a defining moment in my life meant nothing at all in his."

Sophie felt physically ill. Her father, particularly as a younger man, had been capable of callous, calculating behavior but this crossed a line to outright meanness.

"You never married?"

He stretched his legs out and crossed them at the ankle. "I'm English, Sophie. I always envisioned myself with an English bride to go with my English title and my English family, and yet, I've spent precious little of my adult life in England until recently. Then too, I was content to dwell in Cumbria when I had to be somewhere in the realm, but that option has been precluded now, as well."

Sophie blinked in the bright sunshine, hurting for him and feeling a hopelessness close around her. Not only had Vim chosen to leave the area never to dwell here again, her own father had been the author of his difficulties.

"Sophie, are you ready to go?"

How long Westhaven had been standing there, Sophie did not know. Vim got to his feet and extended a hand to Sophie. "I'll walk you to the livery."

When she put her hand in his, he bowed over it then wrapped her fingers over his arm, as if they were strangers promenading in some drawing room.

"Looks like we might get yet more snow," Westhaven remarked.

Neither Sophie nor Vim replied.

Eighteen

VIM BOOSTED SOPHIE ONTO HER HORSE, ARRANGED HER habit over her boots, and stepped back.

"Sindal, good day." Westhaven touched his hat brim and urged his horse forward, then checked the animal after a half-dozen steps and brought it around to face Vim. "Might we see you at Her Grace's Christmas gathering?"

Vim shook his head, wondering if the man had asked the question as a taunt, though Westhaven's expression suggested it had merely been a polite query. Rather than elaborate on his refusal, Vim turned to make his farewell to the second woman to cause him to associate Kent at Yuletide with heartbreak.

"Lady Sophia, good day. And if I don't see you before I depart on my next journey, I wish you a pleasant remainder to the holidays."

She nodded, raised her chin, fixed her gaze on her brother's retreating back, and tapped her heel against the mare's side.

Vim tortured himself by watching their horses canter down the lane, the thud of hooves on the frozen ground resonating with the ache in his chest. Her silence told him more plainly than words he was watching her ride out of his life.

As loyal as Sophie was to her family, there was no way she'd plight her troth to a man who'd given such an unflattering recitation regarding His Grace, and no way Vim would make the attempt to persuade her at this point, in any case.

"So you're still bungling about with my sister's affections?"

Valentine Windham, coat open, mouth compressed into a flat line, sidled up to Vim outside the livery.

"The lady has made her wishes known. I am merely respecting them."

Windham studied him, and not for the first time, Vim had the sense that this was the brother everybody made the mistake of underestimating. In some ways—his utter independence, his highly individual humor, his outspokenness, his virtuosic shifts of mood—this Windham son put Vim most in mind of the old duke.

"You are being an ass." Windham hooked his elbow through Vim's as if they were drinking companions. "Humor me, Sindal. If I spend another minute wrestling with that monster at the church, I will for the first time in my life consider tuning a keyboard instrument with a splitting ax."

Vim let himself be walked back toward the bench, mostly because the prospect of returning to Sidling and the plethora of female relations about to descend was unappealing in the extreme. Then too, Val Windham adored his pianos, suggesting the man wasn't going to do anything foolish—like, for example, obliging Vim's inclination to engage in a rousing bout of fisticuffs—if it might damage his hands.

"On second thought"—Windham switched directions—"let's drop in for a tot of grog."

They appropriated the snug at the local watering hole, steaming mugs of rum punch in their hands before Windham spoke again.

"You sip your drink, and I will violate a sibling confidence."

"I don't want you violating Sophie's confidences," Vim said, bristling at the very notion.

Windham's lips quirked. "Oh, very well, then. I won't tell you she screams like a savage if you put a frog in her bed. I was actually going to pass along a little something told me by an entirely different sister, one not even remotely smitten with you."

"Windham, are you capable of adult conversation? For the sake of your wedded wife, one hopes you are, and I do appreciate the drink. Nonetheless, I am expecting a great lot of family this afternoon at Sidling, and charming though your company is, I have obligations elsewhere."

Windham lifted his mug in a little salute. "Duly noted. Now shut up and listen."

Vim took a sip of his drink, lest by some detail he betray that he was almost enjoying Windham's company. The man had the look of his sister around the eyes and in the set of his chin.

"While Westhaven was haring about tidying up the family business affairs, and St. Just was off subduing the French, it befell me to escort my five sisters to every God's blessed function for years on end. I was in demand for my ability to be a charming escort, so thoroughly did my sisters hone this talent on my part."

"I am in transports to hear it. Alas, I am not in need of an escort."

"You are in *need* of a sound thrashing, but St. Just has said such an approach lacks subtlety. My point is that I know my sisters in some ways better than my brothers do." Windham studied his mug, a half smile playing about his lips. "They talk to me."

"Then at least you serve some purpose other than to delight your tailor with your excellent turnout."

"I delight my wife even in the absence of any raiment whatsoever."

"For God's sake, Windham—"

"My sisters talk to me," Windham resumed, "and as a male, I am always torn by the question: why are they telling me such things? Am I supposed to offer to thrash a fellow or lecture a shopkeeper, or am I merely to listen and make sympathetic noises?"

"Your capacity for making noise is documented by all and sundry."

Green eyes without a hint of humor narrowed on Vim. "Do not insult my music, Sindal."

"I wasn't. I was insulting your talent for roundaboutation."

"Oh. Quite. In any case, I've concluded that in the instant case, I am not to offer to do something nor to make sympathetic noises. I am to *act*. Don't neglect your drink."

"At the moment, it would serve me best emptied over your head."

The half smile was back, and thus Vim didn't see the verbal blow coming. "Sophie thinks you were offering her a less than honorable proposition before we came to collect her, and modified your proposal only when her station became apparent."

Windham took a casual sip of his drink while Vim's brain fumbled for a coherent thought. "She thinks *what*?"

"She thinks you offered to set her up as your mistress and changed your tune, so to speak, when it became apparent you were both titled. I know she is in error in this regard."

Vim cocked his head. "How could you know such a thing?"

"Because if you propositioned my sister with such an arrangement, it's your skull I'd be using that splitting ax on."

"If Sophie thinks this, then she is mistaken." Windham remained silent, reinforcing Vim's sense the man was shrewd in the extreme. "You will please disabuse her of her error."

Windham shook his head slowly, right to left, left to right. "It isn't my error, and it isn't Sophie's error. She's nothing if not bright, and you were probably nothing if not cautious in offering your suit. The situation calls for derring-do, old sport. Bended knee, flowers, tremolo in the strings, that sort of thing." He gestured as if stroking a bow over a violin, a lyrical, dramatic rendering that ought to have looked foolish but was instead casually beautiful.

"Tremolo in the strings?"

"To match the trembling of her heart. A fellow learns to listen for these things." Windham set his mug down with a thump and speared Vim with a *look*. "I'm off to do battle with the treble register. Wish me luck, because failure on my part will be apparent every Sunday between now and Judgment Day."

"Windham, for God's sake, you don't just accuse a man of such a miscalculation and then saunter off to twist piano wires." Much less make references to failure being eternally apparent.

"Rather thought I was twisting your heart strings. Must be losing my touch."

Vim watched as Windham tossed a coin on the table. "It makes no difference, you know, that your sister is mistaken. I did offer for her subsequently. She understood clearly I was offering marriage, and she turned me down."

Windham glanced around the common then met Vim's gaze. "As far as she's concerned, you offered her insult before you offered her marriage. An apology is in order at the very least, and Her Grace's Christmas party seems to be the perfect time to render it."

And then he did saunter off, and the blighted, bedamned, cheeky bastard was whistling "Greensleeves."

Westhaven's subtlety had failed, Valentine's bullying charm had met with indifferent success, so Devlin St. Just, Colonel Lord Rosecroft, saddled up and rode into battle on his sister's behalf.

"I'll collect the mare when I've signed the appropriate documents up at the manor," he said, stroking a hand down the horse's long face. The wizened little groom scrubbing out a wooden bucket showed no sign of having heard him, so St. Just repeated himself, speaking more slowly and more loudly.

"Oh, aye. Be gone with ye, then. I'll make me fare-wells to the lady and get her blanketed proper while ye and their lordships congratulate each other." The groom's eyes went to the mare, the last of Rothgreb's breeding stock, and in the opinion of many, the best.

"May I ask you something?" St. Just knew better than to watch the man's good-byes to the horse. He directed his gaze to the tidy manor a quarter mile away.

"Ask, your lordship."

"Why is there no young stock among the servants here? Why is everybody working well past the time when they've earned some years in high pasture?"

The old fellow turned to glare at St. Just. "We manage well enow."

"It isn't smart, letting the entire herd age," St. Just replied. "You need the elders to keep peace and maintain order, but you don't put your old guard in the traces beyond a certain point. The young ones need to learn and serve their turn."

"Tell that to yon strappin' baron."

The groom shuffled away, muttering in the Irish—which happened to be St. Just's mother tongue—about young men too happy to gallivant about the globe when they were needed to look after their family at home.

"Madame." St. Just addressed the mare. "I'll come for you soon. The grooms at Morelands are bedding your stall with enough oat straw for an entire team. Nonetheless, try to look downcast when you take your leave here, hmm?"

She regarded him out of large, patient eyes, her mental workings as unfathomable as any female's.

St. Just made his way to the manor, noting the number of horses in the Sidling paddocks and the several conveyances outside the carriage house. Her Grace said the Charpentier family gathered for the holidays, and it looked like what ought to be a quick exchange of coin, documents, and a toast in the viscount's study was going to require some seasonal socializing to go with it.

He looked at the sky, which bore the same sun as was shining at that very moment on his wife and daughters in Yorkshire. A comforting thought.

"Rosecroft! Come ye in and sing wassail!" Rothgreb stood grinning at the front door, his nose a bright red contrast to his green velvet jacket. "The place hasn't been this full of noise since the old lord's third wedding breakfast."

"My lord." St. Just stopped just inside the door and bowed to the older man. "I didn't mean to impose, but came to fetch the mare and thought I'd—"

"Here they come!"

St. Just looked up to see a half-dozen very young ladies trotting up the hallway in a giggling, laughing cloud of skirts and smiles.

"Another guest, girls! This is Lord Rosecroft. Make your curtsies and then line up." The ladies assembled with an alacrity that would have done St. Just's recruits in Spain proud. "All right, Rosecroft, best be about it. They get bold if you make 'em wait."

St. Just looked askance at his host, who was grinning like a fiend.

"It's the kissing bough," Vim Charpentier said as he emerged from the hallway, a tumbler in his hand. "You have to kiss them each and every one, or they'll pout. And, Rosecroft, they've been collecting kisses all afternoon between trips to the punch bowl, so you'd be well advised to acquit yourself to the best of your ability. They will compare notes all year. So far, I believe I'm your competition." He took a sip of his drink, eyeing his cousins balefully.

"I've charged headlong into French infantry," St. Just said, smiling at the ladies, "praying I might survive to enjoy just such a gauntlet as this." He went down the line, leaving a wake of blushes, kissing each cheek until he got to a little girl so small he had to hunker down to kiss her.

"What's your name, sweetheart?"

"Cynthia Weeze Simmons."

"The prettiest has been saved for last." He kissed a delicate cheek and rose. "Any more? I was cavalry, you know, legendary for our charm and stamina." This was said to tease the young ladies, but they all looked at their grandfather without breaking ranks.

"Once with you lot is enough," the old man barked. "Shoo." They departed amid more giggles.

Sindal looked disgruntled. "You made that look easy."

"I have daughters, and I'm half Irish. It was easy, also fun. Rothgreb, can we repair somewhere private to transact a little business?"

"What? Business? Sindal can deal with those details. I'm going to find my viscountess and tell her she missed a chance to kiss Moreland's war hero."

Sindal passed St. Just the tumbler. "It helps if you're

as half seas over as the rest of the household. I have never longed more ardently for sunset. Uncle has set himself up as the Lord of Misrule until then."

"And you're not feeling the seasonal cheer?"

"Bah, to quote my uncle." An odd smile flitted across Sindal's face. "Among others. Let's repair to the study. There's a bill of sale and a decanter—and no damned mistletoe."

"I rather like mistletoe."

"I rather like a fine brandy."

They dealt with the documents quickly, but Sindal had to hunt up the sand with which to blot them. "It should be in here some damned where. The old fellow is nothing if not—" He fell silent, peering into a low cupboard behind the estate desk.

"Something amiss?"

Sindal straightened, a divided serving dish in his hands. "What would an olive dish be doing secreted in my uncle's study?"

St. Just sipped at his brandy while Sindal withdrew a ceremonial sword, a carved chess set of ivory and onyx, an ivory-inlaid cribbage board, an antique pair of dueling pistols, a small crossbow, and several other curiosities from the same low cupboard.

"Is somebody putting away the valuables while company's underfoot?"

Sindal shot him a look, a speculating, cogitating sort of look. "Would a woman growing vague and easily disoriented know to stop by the kitchen for carrots and sugar before she wandered off toward the stables?"

The question made no sense and had no discernible context. "Sindal, have you spent a little too much time at the punch bowl fortifying yourself for the kissing bough?"

"There is no adequate fortification for such an ordeal. It's enough to make a man repair to heathen climes permanently." He set the contents of the cupboard out on Rothgreb's estate desk, came around the desk, and took the seat beside St. Just. "I have been manipulated by a pair of old schemers. The question is why?"

"Finish your drink." St. Just pushed a glass closer to his host. "You are not going to remove to distant parts, but I gather you divine some sort of conspiracy from what's here?"

"My aunt's letters suggested Rothgreb was misplacing valuables; his letters informed me my aunt had started wandering."

"And you came home to investigate?"

"Exactly. I suppose that was the point, though one wonders if they were conspiring with each other or intriguing individually."

"And until you come home to stay, the old guard will not retire nor step aside for any younger replacements. Your uncle's regiment has decided they're going to fight this battle as a team."

"One suspected such faulty reasoning was at work."

They fell into a companionable silence while St. Just tried to formulate a question that would pique but not quite offend. "I've wondered something."

Sindal turned to regard him. "If you're going to invite me to Her Grace's Christmas party, spare your breath. That is the very last place I'd seek to spend time."

"Yes, but one wonders why. If His Grace did you

a disservice by preventing you from dueling with Horton all those years ago, then why not take the opportunity to read the old boy the Riot Act? Why not beard the lion in his very own den?"

"The *old boy* is one of the most powerful men in the Lords, the highest title in the shire, and the father of the woman I happen to l—"

St. Just went on as if he hadn't heard the very thing no man ever admitted to another. "And every year that you dodge and skulk about, avoiding His Grace's hospitality, you enlarge the magnitude of what was not intended to do you any harm whatsoever. I was there, Sindal, and I saw exactly what happened. Come over tomorrow night, have a cup of eggnog, smile, and hang about in your finery under the mistletoe until Sophie comes swanning down the steps. You need a chance to make a grand exit with your head held high."

Sindal scrubbed a hand over his face and stared at his drink. "What do you mean, there was no intent to do me harm? The lady and I had an understanding, and half the shire knew it. His Grace might have handled the thing a thousand different ways that didn't involve making me a laughingstock. I regretted the loss of the lady's hand at the time, but more I bitterly resented that Moreland prevented me from defending my own honor."

The man believed he'd simply been elbowed aside by the collective papas of the shire for the better title, which would have been a bitter blow indeed, had that been the case.

"So demonstrate your backbone and make a short

social call. You deserve the chance to put your own conclusion to the matter. Then too, Horton is afflicted with gout. He can no longer even stand up with his own lady."

Sindal rose and went to stand facing the window. "I need a chance to apologize to your sister for a small misunderstanding, but I fail to see why a note won't suffice."

A fellow was not a coward who sought to avoid armed confrontation in the enemy camp. St. Just didn't judge his host, but he wasn't about to fail his sister, either.

"I kissed all seven of your cousins, including the fair Cynthia Louise. Are you saying you can't abide the thought of kissing five of my sisters, at least one of whom has already succumbed to your dubious charms?"

"For God's sake, St. Just, this isn't a schoolyard rivalry. I have no confidence whatsoever Sophie won't run from the sight of me. She thinks…"

"She thinks her swain capable of a less than gallant proposition," St. Just said, rising to stand by his host. "But here's what will happen if you fail to speak up. Today, the ladies are busy with preparations at Morelands, and they are not receiving. Tomorrow is the Christmas Party—an excellent opportunity to set matters to rights with His Grace, and your only real opportunity to sort things out with Sophie.

"Christmas Day will be spent at services, opening a few gifts, and starting on the Boxing Day rounds. We have too many tenants to distribute all the baskets in a single day, but on the following day, I will depart for Yorkshire, and I intend that Sophie accompany me."

Sindal turned to scowl at him. "You'd make her travel north at this time of year?"

"Nobody makes Sophia Windham do anything. I've extended the invitation because my womenfolk would love to have her for a long stay, and there are lots of lonely bachelors in the north who'd give their left testicle to stand up with a duke's daughter as pretty and well dowered as my sister. Then too, Sophie's associations with the holidays will soon be as miserable as your own, unless you clear the air with her. I bid you good day and extend one final invitation to the party."

St. Just picked up the bill of sale and left Sindal staring out the window, the family heirlooms in a dusty jumble on the desk behind him.

❧

"That style is quite becoming on you, my dear." The duchess advanced into Sophie's room, eyeing her daughter in Christmas party finery. Her very quiet, grown daughter. "You should start wearing your hair like that more often."

"Hello, Your Grace." Sophie frowned in her mirror at a coiffure that was half up, half tumbling down around her shoulders, a splendid compliment to the red velvet of her dress. "This is an experiment."

Esther's sons called her mama when they wanted to flatter, wheedle, or comfort, but her daughters were far less in the habit. *How had that happened?*

"It's a pretty experiment, but I have to wonder if experimentation hasn't become something of a new pastime with you, Sophia."

It was slight, but Sophie squared her shoulders before she turned to face her mother. "Can you be more specific, Your Grace?"

"I received correspondence from the Chattells, Sophia. You manipulated events to be alone without servants or chaperone in Town and then found yourself caring for that baby into the bargain. Your brothers assure me there will be no breath of scandal attached to this... departure from good sense, but I am left to wonder."

Sophie's face gave away nothing, not guilt nor remorse, not chagrin, not even defiance. "I wanted to be alone."

"I see." Except she didn't, exactly. *When had this child become a mystery to her own mother?*

"Why?"

Sophie glanced at herself in the mirror, and Esther could only hope her daughter saw the truth: a lovely, poised woman—intelligent, caring, well dowered, and deserving of more than a stolen interlude with a convenient stranger and an inconvenient baby—Sophie's brothers' assurances notwithstanding.

"I am lonely, that's why." Sophie's posture relaxed with this pronouncement, but Esther's consternation only increased.

"How can you be lonely when you're surrounded by loving family, for pity's sake? Your father and I, your sisters, your brothers, even Uncle Tony and your cousins—we're your family, Sophia."

She nodded, a sad smile playing around her lips that to Esther's eyes made her daughter look positively beautiful. "You're the family I was born with, and I love you too, but I'm still lonely, Your Grace. I've wished and wished for my own family, for children of my own, for a husband, not just a marital partner…"

"You had many offers." Esther spoke gently, because in Sophie's words, in her calm, in her use of the present tense—"I am lonely"—there was an insight to be had.

"Those offers weren't from the right man."

"Was Baron Sindal the right man?" It was a chance arrow, but a woman who had raised ten children owned a store of maternal instinct.

Sophie's chin dropped, and she sighed. "I thought he was the right man, but it wasn't the right offer, or perhaps it was, but I couldn't hear it as such. And then there was the baby… It wouldn't be the right marriage."

Esther took her courage in both hands and advanced on her daughter—her sensible daughter—and slipped an arm around Sophie's waist. "Tell me about this baby. I've heard all manner of rumors about him, but you've said not one word."

She meant to walk Sophie over to the vanity, so she might drape Oma's pearls around Sophie's neck, but Sophie closed her eyes and stiffened.

"He's a good baby. He's a wonderful baby, and I sent him away. Oh, Mama, I sent my baby away…"

And then, for the first time in years, sensible Lady Sophia Windham cried on her mother's shoulder as if she herself were once again a little, inconsolable baby.

❧

"What I don't understand is why you didn't simply ask me to come back to Sidling?" Vim shifted his gaze from his uncle to his aunt and back to his uncle. He'd waited a day to let his temper cool, but if anything, he was angrier than ever. They were looking at each other, though, and not at him, leaving Vim with the sense volumes were passing between them unsaid.

"I'd like to speak with your aunt in private." Rothgreb's tone was tired, quiet, and completely out of character.

"So the two of you can plot and scheme and get your stories straight?"

His aunt looked at him then. It took Vim a moment to decipher the emotion banked in her pale blue eyes: disappointment.

In him. He shifted his gaze back to Rothgreb.

"No, young man, I do not want to plot and scheme with your aunt. I want to apologize to her for trying to plot and scheme without her assistance." The viscount aimed a small smile at Aunt Essie. "Though I suspect she was getting up to tricks quite nicely on her own, weren't you, my dear?"

Aunt Esmerelda rose from her chair and began to stalk around the cozy parlor. "I was not managing quite nicely, but I was trying to do *something* to stop your nephew from charging off to God knows where yet again. Wilhelm, we have *tried* asking you to come home."

Vim's rejoinder was automatic, if a bit unkind. "Sidling is not my—"

"Not your home," she interrupted him. "Oh, we know it's not your home, except you were born here, you're going to inherit the place, and except for three rackety half siblings, your entire family is here in Kent. Your father and mother are buried here, your grandfather and all four of his wives. Your uncle, and very likely *you* will be buried here, as well, but for some stupid, known-only-to-your-pigheaded-self reason, this is not your home. I have a question for you, Wilhelm Lucifer Charpentier."

"My dear," Rothgreb said softly from his wing chair.

"*Not now*, Aethelbert. I want to hear from your buffle-brained, stubborn, idiot, errant nephew just where his home might be if it isn't here with the people who love him and pray for him every night? Where must you wander off to next, Wilhelm? I need to know where to send the letter that tells you you've missed the last opportunity to ride these acres with your uncle. I want to know what godforsaken heathen port you'll be in when I have to run the death notice. Tell me, and then hope a merciful God sustains me in my grief long enough to post the blessed thing."

She swished out of the parlor, the door latch closing with a definitive click in her wake.

And now it was Vim who didn't want to meet his uncle's gaze.

A silence started up while Rothgreb scooted to the edge of his chair, braced his hands on the padded arms, and pushed himself to his feet. "Don't worry. At breakfast tomorrow she'll be apologizing and cramming strawberry crepes down your gullet." He knelt to poke up the fire while Vim stood there, his aunt's tirade ringing in his ears.

"You did ask me to come home, didn't you?"

His uncle paused, the poker across his bony knee where he genuflected before the hearth. "A time or two. I don't want Essie to be alone if anything should happen to me. She's probably reasoning along the same lines. Your cousins will be some comfort, but they won't manage the place as it should be managed."

Rothgreb rose, teetered, and caught the mantel to finish pulling himself erect. "Your aunt is a dear, dear woman, but she is protective of me."

"Don't apologize for her when she was merely stating a few home truths."

"Apologize? I was explaining." Rothgreb peered at him. "She has a knack for walloping a man between the eyes on those rare occasions when she gets her dander up. Makes marriage to her a lively proposition."

Vim turned to stare out the window at the late afternoon landscape. "I don't suppose you want to take that ride now?"

"Ah, youth. If you want to freeze your arse off tooling about the shire in this weather, be my guest. Talk to me about riding out come spring, and I might take you up on the offer. I'm going to find your aunt and assure her you'll still speak to her when next she meets you." He frowned. "You will, won't you?"

Rothgreb was gruff, irascible, cantankerous, and sometimes even cussed, but in Vim's experience, his uncle was never, ever uncertain.

"Of course I will, and if she's not careful, I'll be sure we meet up under the mistletoe."

Rothgreb nodded slowly. "Not a bad approach. Puts the ladies in a fine humor when they get their regular share of kisses. Enjoy your ride."

He shuffled out, looking to Vim for the first time like a very old man. A very old and very dear man.

Nineteen

"He's not coming." Valentine kept his voice down and his smile in place, even managing to nod at some little pretty across the room who apparently hadn't gotten word he'd recently acquired a wife.

"He'll be here." Westhaven smiled, as well, as if Val had just said something amusing.

"I could always go fetch him." St. Just wasn't smiling. He was looking thoughtful, which generally did not bode well for somebody.

"We should send Her Grace," Val said. "She'd sort the bugger out in a hurry."

St. Just glanced at him. "She's too busy dispensing good cheer to every yeoman and goodwife ever to pass through the village."

"Sophie's being even more gracious than our mother." Westhaven did not sound happy about this in the least.

Maggie glided up to them, looking striking in a green velvet dress. "I thought you three said you had Sindal under control. Sophie's smiling so hard her jaw must hurt, and he's nowhere in sight."

"Oh, for God's sake." Westhaven sounded most displeased. "Evie just switched her glass of wassail for Deene's, and the idiot man didn't even notice."

Maggie's brows knit. "Why does that matter?"

"Because," St. Just said as Westhaven moved off, "Deene's is spiked with a dose of the loveliest white rum ever to knock a grown man on his arse."

Maggie took a little sip of her drink. "So's mine."

Val reached over and plucked her glass from her hand. "Then you'd better share, sister dear, or I'm going to go fetch Sindal here myself."

༄

A summer evening could be quiet, peaceful even, but it could never compete with the utter stillness of a winter night. No birds flitted from branch to branch; no insects sang to their mates; no soft breezes stirred leafy green boughs.

As Vim let his horse trot down the Sidling drive, all was still, and a fat moon was about to crest the horizon. The silence was as dense as the air was cold, but for the life of him, Vim could not have remained indoors with his silly young cousins, his fuming aunt, his oddly quiet uncle, and the aging retainers on every hand.

As the horse loosened up at a ground-eating trot beneath him, Vim started composing a note in his head to Lady Sophia Windham.

He was sorry—more sorry than he could say—that their paths were diverging.

Except that wasn't an apology, and he owed her an apology. He'd leapt to convenient conclusions, made mad, passionate love for what felt like the first time in his life, then bungled the aftermath badly. He should have gone down on his damn bended knee, should have made her heart tremble, or whatever that word was Windham had used.

At the foot of the drive, he turned the horse toward the village and started his note over: Dear Sophie…

My dear Sophie…

Dearest Sophie…

Sophie, my love…

The horse's ears swiveled forward, and Vim drew the beast up. The last thing he needed was to land on his arse on the cold, hard ground because some damned fox was out hunting his dinner.

"What is it?" He smoothed a hand down the gelding's neck and let the horse walk on. "You hear some hound baying at the moon?"

But as they approached the village, Vim heard it too: a baby crying.

He halted the horse and simply listened. This was the sound that had drawn his path to Sophie's, a purely unhappy, discontent sound, but unmistakably human.

Kit, and he wasn't hungry. He wasn't tired, either; this was his lonely cry, the lament he sent out when he needed to be held and cuddled and reassured. This was the simplest and most sincere form of a human being demanding to be loved.

The boy wanted Sophie, and he didn't second-guess his entitlement to her, didn't stop to fret about long-ago insults and innuendos and violins, didn't worry about titles or any other damned thing that stood between him and what he needed to be happy.

Mercifully, the crying ceased.

Before Vim could change his mind, he wheeled the horse in the direction of Morelands and set the beast to a brisk canter.

※

"Her Grace dispatched me to figure out what has you lot glowering like a matched set of gargoyles." Percival, the Duke of Moreland, surveyed his three sons, all of whom were clutching their drinks with the grim resignation of grown men being sociable under duress. This was odd, since all of his children were more than comfortable in social settings.

"We're that obvious?" Valentine asked.

"To Her Grace, all is transparent when it comes to her family. I suppose we're waiting for Sophie's swain to come to his senses and gallop up the drive on his white charger?"

St. Just stood by the window, peering through a crack in the drapes. "It's a bay, actually, and the idiot man is finally here. Somebody needs to warn Sophie."

"Not just yet," His Grace said. "I'm to have a word with Sindal first, Her Grace's orders. You three look after your sister, and for God's sake, find somebody to dance with Evie before she drags Deene under the mistletoe by his hair. She holds his liquor better than he does."

He left his sons to deal with their sisters while he moved to receive his latest guest.

"Sindal, glad you could join us." He passed the man's greatcoat to a footman and noted that Sindal's expression was wary and his cheeks were flushed, as if he'd galloped the entire distance from Sidling. "Stop peering around to see if Sophie's here. I assure you she's about somewhere."

Sindal passed his gloves and hat to the footman and waited until the servant had bustled away. "And you would not object to my socializing with Lady Sophia?"

"Such a bold fellow you have become." Emboldened by love, apparently, which made the situation both simpler and more delicate. "You would not give a tinker's damn if I objected, would you?"

Sindal's lips quirked. "I would not, Your Grace, but Sophie would."

"Thank God for small favors, then. Are we to stand around here in this draft and exchange innuendos, or will you let me get you a glass of punch?"

And still, Sindal's gaze was darting surreptitiously into every corner of the vast entrance hall. "No punch for me, thank you, Your Grace."

Oh, for God's sake. His Grace leveled a look at his guest that wasn't the least congenial. Love made young men daft—old men too, though that didn't signify at the moment.

"Perhaps a small glass," Sindal allowed.

And just when His Grace was certain they were going to gain the privacy of the men's punch bowl, who should come wafting by but dear little Sophia herself?

"Lord Sindal?" She stopped, her gaze fixed on Sindal's face.

"I'm fetching him a glass of punch, Sophie." His Grace took Sindal by the arm. "I believe Her Grace said something about Westhaven decimating the marzipan trays. You might want to have a look, hmm?"

He had to drag the boy away bodily. "You can lurk under the mistletoe later, Sindal. I want no more than five minutes of your time." *And grandchildren.* He most assuredly wanted grandchildren, though based on the way Sophie and her swain made eyes at each other, this happy outcome was a foregone conclusion.

Legitimate grandchildren would be a shade easier to explain to Her Grace.

"To your health." He passed a glass of spiked punch to Sindal. "Drink up, sir. I have a hunch you'll need the fortification."

Sindal took a sip of his drink, his eyes going to the door and the entrance hall beyond. "And your health, as well, Your Grace. Now if you're done demonstrating your ducal forbearance, I've something to say to your daughter that can't—"

His Grace plucked the glass from Sindal's hand. "You will listen to me first, young fellow." He saw his wife glide past the door and understood that she'd ensure they had a measure of privacy. "You have been notably absent from our Christmas gatherings in years past."

"I've been notably absent from England, but I don't foresee that being necessary in future."

"Glad to hear it. Stop that infernal mooning for Sophie and take a look at the woman standing at the foot of the stairs."

Sindal did stop scanning the environs long enough to shoot his host a look mixing irritation with vague curiosity. "The heavyset, older woman?"

"The one standing next to the bald fellow leaning on his cane." The woman obligingly turned, which ought to confirm, even to Sindal's preoccupied and besotted eyes, that she wasn't just heavyset, she'd graduated from matronly to something less flattering two stone ago.

"Do you recognize her?"

"She looks vaguely familiar, as does the older fellow with her."

"There is your thwarted dream, Sindal. Why don't you stand under the mistletoe and ambush her for old times' sake? Horton can barely stand on his own now, so bad is his gout and so seldom is he sober. I suppose if you called him out now, you could arm wrestle."

To his credit, Sindal did not gape.

"Then again"—His Grace paused to take a sip of his drink—"if I had six little heifers the likes of his to dower and launch, I might be driven to drink myself."

Sindal swung his gaze back to meet His Grace's. "Her present situation does not excuse your interfering with a man's defense of her honor and his own years ago, Your Grace."

"No, they do not." His Grace set his drink down. "But her oldest daughter? Born perhaps six and a half months after the wedding." He spoke very quietly—there was no need to bruit the woman's folly about again after all these years. "Your grandfather lamented the situation to me over many a brandy, Sindal. She was leading you about by the... *nose* and had her eye on the more highly titled prize the entire time. She even cornered my son Bartholomew a time or two, but he was a canny sort and not about to be taken advantage of. If it's any consolation, Horton was more effectively manipulated than you were."

As they watched, Horton staggered a little, sloshing some of his drink on his wife's sleeve. A silence spread and spread, underlain with the genial sounds of the party and a piano thumping out a Christmas tune somewhere in the house.

"I have been made a fool of, but not by you, Your Grace." Sindal spoke quietly too. His Grace put the man's drink back in his hand.

"No more so than most other young men can be made fools of. I had a few close calls myself before Her Grace took me in hand."

But it appeared Sindal wasn't even listening. He continued to watch as Horton's lady tried to look like she was enjoying herself, though all the while, her expression was pinched with fatigue, anxiety, and what looked to His Grace like a suppressed fury at her lot in life.

"She looks at least ten years older than she should."

"I don't think her situation has been easy. She's received—Her Grace saw to that—but her indiscretion is common knowledge. Some mathematical calculations are easy to recall. Your grandfather assured me the child could not have been yours."

"How could he have known such a thing? I was devoted to that woman for a span of several months." And still, Sindal did not take his eyes off the unfortunate woman and her sorry spouse.

"He knew you." The duke spoke not as the wealthy, titled aristocrat he was, nor even as Sindal's neighbor and a friend to his late grandfather. He spoke as a father, and most particularly as Sophie's father.

"I owe you an apology, Your Grace." Sindal

extended his hand, and they shook, which put a curious little sense of unfinished business to rest in His Grace's mind.

"None needed, to me at least. St. Just said something about you owing Sophie an apology, though. Might want to be about that posthaste, hmm?"

Sindal put his drink down, nodded once, and strode off like a man very determined on his mission, while His Grace went to the door of the small parlor. Across their crowded main hall, he found his wife's gaze, noted the slight anxiety in her eyes, and eased it with a small, private smile intended just for her.

❧

"He walked right past me." Sophie turned before the harpsichord, skirts swishing, and paced back to Val's side. "He barely looked at me, Valentine. Am I not even worth a glance?"

She veered off and marched over to the great harp. "Maggie offered to poison his drink. What has the blessed punch bowl got that I haven't got? What is that?"

"Your cloak. Some fresh air will settle you down, Soph."

"I don't want to *settle down*!"

He held her gaze, thinking his wife would be proud of him. Only a brave—or perhaps very foolish man—tried to console a woman with a heart in the process of breaking. "I rather think you do want to settle down, preferably with Sindal and a brace of offspring."

Her head came up, and Valentine was grateful he'd be leaving in a couple days. Much more of this drama, and he'd be swearing off family holidays for the next decade.

"I tossed aside a perfectly good baby. A wonderful baby," she said. "Placed him with *strangers*."

"That dratted baby has nothing to do with Sindal cutting you." He draped her cloak over her shoulders, even risking a small hug while he did. "Let's go for a little walk, Soph. It will put the roses back in your cheeks."

When he pulled away, she clung. He felt the instant when her ire turned to sorrow, felt her spine sag with impending grief. "I tossed away the baby, but Valentine, I'm beginning to wonder if I didn't toss away the man, as well. I never really explained to him what I was about—I didn't know what I was about."

"And I'm not sure I *want* to know. Come along, Soph. We can amble down to the church and make sure the curmudgeon hasn't gone rogue on me. The damned weather is hard on the old soldiers."

"You and your blessed pianos." But she let him tug her through the French doors to the terrace. St. Just was still keeping vigil by the windows, and he started when Val pulled Sophie along on the terrace. Val just shook his head when St. Just beckoned them back inside, all without Sophie noticing a thing in her increasing upset.

"He's a good baby," she was saying. "And the Harrads are good people, but Kit is special, he's unique, and they've raised only girls."

"You spent two weeks with the infant, and you know him better than an experienced mother of three would?"

She turned to glare at him in the moonlight. "You are a blockhead, Valentine Windham. Just wait until

Ellen presents you with a baby. Vim knew exactly what to do with Kit. *Exactly*. It has nothing to do with time or experience."

He knew he was taking a risk, but Val opted for goading her rather than comforting her. "Vim knew what he was doing with you too, sister dear. The question is, what are the two of you going to do about it now? I'm told he's leaving for the Americas again, and that is some distance from merry olde England."

"I hate you."

"Dear heart, I know this."

She stomped along beside him then stopped abruptly, dropped his arm and drew in a shuddery breath. Well, hell. He put his arms around her and silently vowed to give up his career as a charming escort. "What hurts the worst, Soph? Tell me."

"You'll bear tales to Her Grace and to our odious brothers."

"I'm your only odious brother."

She nodded. "You're the worst of a bad lot." She was stalling, but a lady was entitled when her heart was breaking. "I love him."

"Sindal hasn't earned that honor—" He fell abruptly silent when Sophie drew back and rolled her eyes at him.

"I meant I love Kit, though I love Vim, as well."

Val dropped his arms, feeling the last of his fraternal patience slipping its leash. "It's no wonder Sindal is uncertain of his reception with you, Sophie Windham, for I'm beyond confused myself. Have you told the man you love him?"

"Of course not."

Val resumed their walk. "Then how is he to know?"

"Because I'm going to insist he take Kit." Sophie followed after Val at a brisk pace. "Vim needs somebody to love, and to love him, and he's perfect with Kit. He said he'd consider fostering him at Sidling. The viscountess doted on Kit, and I think old Rothgreb was fond of him too."

Val kept on walking. "You have taken leave of your senses. Sindal is off to parts unknown. He can't be dragging your dratted baby with him."

"All manner of children are born on shipboard. Most merchant captains who can afford to take their wives and children with them do so. Then too, if Kit is at Sidling, Vim will have an excellent reason to be home more frequently. Rothgreb and his lady will like that."

"Sophie, I love you, but this plan has nothing to recommend it, except that it puts the two fellows you seem to love with your whole heart where they're either gallivanting about the globe without you or right under your nose where you can look but not touch."

She just shook her head and kept moving along with him.

"All right, then, go visit your Holy Terror and explain to the Harrads that no, you'll be haring off in a different direction now, playing skittles with a child's life while you completely ignore your own needs. I'm going to have a sane argument with a piano while I can still reason."

He marched off—he was *not* retreating—and left Sophie in the middle of the village green, her fists clenched at her sides while the sounds of the Christmas party drifted around in the frigid night air.

A man could not aspire to the status of man at all unless he admitted to himself he'd been mistaken.

And Sophie had apparently known this. She'd known Vim had spent more than a dozen years racketing around the world, laying up treasures on earth, all in the mistaken belief His Grace had treated him shabbily, when all the while…

"I beg your pardon." The very object of his youthful folly stepped back and peered at him through tired eyes. Louise Holderness Horton smiled tentatively. "I know you, sir, or I believe I do."

He leaned forward and kissed her cheek. "It's Sindal, Louise. Wilhelm Charpentier. Happy Christmas." He bowed and left her standing there under the mistletoe, her hand to her a cheek and a ghost of her old smile on her lips.

And now to deal with what really mattered. He took a quick leave of his hostess, whose serene mature beauty reminded him all too strongly of Sophie.

Sophie, who was discreetly maintaining an absence when he'd come expressly to mend his fences with her. He gave the place one more visual inspection and didn't see her anywhere, so he signaled for his hat and coat.

"Where are you off to?" Westhaven was doing a poor job of masking a glower. "If I'm not mistaken, you haven't made your bow to Sophie."

"I have not, and if that's how she wants it, that's how it will be. Excuse me."

"You're really leaving." The glower faded to puzzlement, though Westhaven's hand stayed on Vim's arm.

"I'm leaving for the curate's house, if you must know, and then, if Sophie still won't give me an audience, I am heading for Yorkshire, or wherever else you lot think you can secret her."

"What's at the curate's house?"

"Not a what, a who. The love of Sophie's life, who should at least be with her if she won't allow me to be. Happy Christmas, Westhaven."

He slipped out the door and didn't bother retrieving his horse. It was a short walk down to the village, and he'd need the time to clear his head.

❧

"Where was Sindal going?" St. Just growled.

"I'm not sure, but he mentioned the curate's house." Westhaven's brow knit. "He sounded a bit like he'd gotten into Deene's white rum, but he had only the one drink with His Grace."

"His Grace is involved now?"

The brothers exchanged a look, and they spoke in unison. "Let's go."

❧

Vim was composing a speech, having failed utterly with his note to Sophie. He sought a means of explaining to the Harrads that he'd like to have the baby back, thank you very much, because Sophie Windham loved the child, and she should have whom and what she loved.

And if he cleared that hurdle without landing on his arse, he might, apology in hand, point out to the lady that a growing boy could use a man's influence.

It was a shaky plan, but it had the advantage of sparing one and all trips to the West Riding in the dead of winter. Surely she'd see the wisdom of that?

"Vim?"

He stopped dead in his tracks. There *she* stood in the middle of the green, not fifteen feet away, resplendent in moonlight and velvet.

Twenty

"SOPHIE. WHY AREN'T YOU AT THE CHRISTMAS REVELS?"

She stared at Vim for so long he thought perhaps she hadn't heard him. But then a sigh went out of her, and she seemed to grow smaller where she stood.

"I'm fetching Kit to you."

What? "Why would you do such a thing?"

Her smile was wan, not a smile he'd seen on her before, and it tore at his heart.

"It's the right thing," she said, rubbing her hands up and down her upper arms. "It's the right thing for you and the right thing for Kit. I can't raise him—*Lady* Sophia and all. I can have my charities, but I cannot actually keep a child to raise. I understand that."

"Can we talk about this?"

Her chin came up. "You didn't want to talk to me at the party."

The strains of some old Handel came floating over the sounds of the Moreland gathering, the same pastoral lullaby Sophie had sung to Kit days ago, but this time rendered with mellow beauty on the church piano. The music was soothing, but sad too.

"Your father had something to explain to me, Sophie. I apologize if it seemed as if I was avoiding you." But she was avoiding him, standing there trying not to shiver in the frigid night air. "Can we not find somewhere to sit? Because I do want to speak with you; I want it badly."

"You're taking the baby," she said, visually scanning the green. "My brother is an idiot."

He wasn't sure which brother she referred to. "If you say so. I find them all likeable when they're not threatening to thrash me."

She scowled. "They're still making threats?"

"Not lately." He took her by the arm and started walking in the direction of the Harrads' tidy porch. "I'm not inclined to take on the responsibility for the child, Sophie. Not in my present circumstances."

"Because you're going to China?"

"I was supposed to go to Baltimore." And she was going to Yorkshire, for God's sake.

"Wherever. Children usually travel well, particularly when they're as small as Kit. He can't stay with the Harrads, though. They're decent people, but it was foolish of me to think strangers would love him the way we do."

"So you love Kit?"

She stopped at the foot of the Harrads' steps. "I do. I think you love him too, though, and you're in a position to provide for him. I am prepared to be stubborn about this."

"Formidable threat, my dear, but I am prepared to be stubborn too. Do you know what your papa wanted to discuss with me so urgently?"

This time when she looked him up and down, Vim

had the sense she might be *seeing* him. "Papa is prone to queer starts. He does not confide in anybody that I can tell, except possibly Her Grace."

He believed her. He believed she'd no more notion of who and what had been involved in Vim's great humiliation all those years ago than he had himself. To this extent, then, His Grace—and likely the ducal consequence, as well—had been guarding Vim's back, not driving daggers into it.

"It is a night for revelations. Can we take a seat?"

There was nowhere to sit, except the Harrads' humble wooden stoop. He lowered himself to it and patted the place beside him. "Cuddle up, Sophie. It's too cold to stand on pride much longer, and we have a dilemma to solve."

She sat, and he let out a sigh of relief.

"What is our dilemma?" She might have tucked herself just a bit closer to him, or she might have been trying to get comfortable on their hard wooden seat.

"If Kit is to have the best start possible in life, he needs two parents who love him and care for him."

She focused on something in the distance, as if trying to see the notes her brother's playing was casting into the chilly darkness. "I cannot be both mother and father to him; neither can you."

"I suggest a somewhat more conventional arrangement. You be his mother, and I'll be his father."

The arrangement was conventional in the extreme: one baby, a mama, a papa. It was the most prosaic grouping in the history of the species. The slow pounding of Vim's heart was extraordinary, though. He fought to speak steadily over it.

"I owe you an apology, Sophie Windham."

She closed her eyes. "You are speaking in riddles, Mr. Charpentier."

Not my lord, not baron, not Sindal. "Vim. I would be Vim to you, and I will start with the apology. When we were in Town—"

She shook her head. "That was then; this is now. That time was just a silly wish on my part, and we stole that time for ourselves despite all sound judgment to the contrary. If you are going to apologize to me for what took place there, I will not accept it."

He thought she might get up and walk away, and that he could not bear. Not again, not *ever* again. Not for himself, and not for the child, either. He found her hand and took it in both of his.

"You took the notion I was offering you a sordid arrangement before we left Town."

She ducked her face to her knees. "Must we speak of this?"

"I must." It was his only real hope, to give her the truth and pray it was enough. "You were not wrong, Sophie."

Her head came up. "I wasn't?"

"I was offering you any arrangement you'd accept. Marriage, preferably, but also anything short of that. I was offering anything and everything I had to keep a place in your life."

"No." She wrestled her hand free and hunched in on herself. "You were being gallant or honorable or something no woman wants to have as the sole motivator of a man's marriage proposal before she watches her husband go boarding a ship for the high seas. That wasn't what I wished for. It wasn't what I wished for, at all."

He shifted so he was kneeling before her on the hard ground, as much to stop her from leaving as because it seemed the only thing left to do.

"Tell me what you wished for, Sophie. Tell me, please."

"I wanted—" She paused and dashed the back of her hand against her cheek. "I wished for some Christmas of my own. I wished for a man who will care for me and stand by me no matter what inconvenient baby I've attached myself to. A man who will *love* me, love our children, and sojourn through life with me. I wished, and then you appeared, and I wished—"

"What did you wish, Sophie?"

"I wished you were my Christmas, wished you could be all my Christmases."

He wondered if maybe those shepherds on that long ago, faraway hillside had heard not the beating wings of the heavenly hosts but nothing more celestial than the beating of their own hearts, thundering with hope, wonderment, and joy.

"Happy Christmas, Lady Sophie." He framed her face in his hands and kissed her, slowly, reverently. "Be all my Christmases, mine and Kit's, forever and ever."

She wrapped her fingers around his wrists and tried to draw his hands away when he brushed his thumbs over her damp cheeks.

"I cannot," she said. "It isn't enough that we both care for the child or that I care for you."

He kissed her, kissed to silence her, kissed her to gather his courage. "Then let it be enough that I love you, you and the child both, and I will always love you. Please, I pray you, let it be enough."

She drew back and studied him, and he could not stop the words from forming. "I don't want to go to Baltimore. I don't want to leave my aunt and uncle to continue managing when I should have been here years ago. I don't want to avoid my neighbors because of some sad contretemps a dozen years ago, but I have wishes too, Sophie Windham."

"What do you wish for?"

"A place in your heart. A permanent place in your heart. I wish for my children to have you as their mother. I wish for your idiot brothers to be doting uncles to our children and your sisters to be the aunts who spoil them shamelessly. I wish to make a home with you for our children, where your parents can come inspect our situation and criticize us for being too lenient with our offspring. I want one present, Sophie Windham—a future with you. That is my Christmas wish. Will you grant it?"

Lord Valentine's impromptu recital came to a close as Vim posed his question, and silence filled the air.

"Please, Sophie?"

Vim was on his knees in the freezing darkness, and he reached for her. He reached out his arms for her just as she—thank God and all the angels—reached for him.

"Yes. *Yes*, Mr. Charpentier, I will be your Christmas, and you shall be mine, and Kit shall belong to us, and we shall belong to him, and my bro—"

He growled as he hugged her to him, and now, over in the church, Valentine's choice was an ebullient, thundering chorus from the old master's oratorio:

"*For unto us a child is born, unto us a son is given… unto us, a son is given.*"

❧

How long she stayed in Vim's arms there on the miserable cold steps Sophie could not have said. Spring could have come and gone and still she'd be reeling with joy and relief and hope.

Most of all with hope.

"Are you *bothering* our sister?"

Sophie raised her head to peer over Vim's shoulder. Valentine, Westhaven, and St. Just were standing not ten feet away, and she hadn't even heard them. St. Just had posed the question in that particularly calm tone that meant his temper could soon make an appearance.

Vim helped her to her feet and yet he kept an arm around her shoulders too.

"He was not bothering me. If you three can't tell the difference between a man bothering an unwilling woman and kissing his very own intended, then I pity your wives."

St. Just's expression didn't change, though Valentine was grinning, and Westhaven was quietly beaming at her. "And what of the child?" St. Just asked. "Sindal, do your good intentions encompass the child, as well?"

Vim's arm tightened around her marginally. "Of course they do." There was such a combination of ferocity and joy in his tone, Sophie couldn't help but smile.

"That's fortunate," St. Just said, sauntering toward them. "You'll be wanting this, then." He withdrew a piece of paper from his coat pocket and passed it to Vim, who didn't even unfold it.

"What is it?"

St. Just's teeth gleamed in the darkness. "It's the bill of sale for the mare and her unborn progeny."

Vim glanced at Sophie, but she had no idea what her brother was about and was quite frankly too happy to care.

"It's for the boy," St. Just said. "I can't exactly take the mare north in her present condition, and I don't want to have come back south for her next fall, do I?"

"I suppose you don't."

Valentine cleared his throat. "The last thing I need is another violin. Once it's restored, talented people will pay for the use of it in concert. Or given his moniker, the dratted baby might grow up with some musical inclinations."

Vim looked a little puzzled. "A violin?"

"That's very sweet of you, Val." Sophie wrapped her arm around Vim's waist. "We accept on Kit's behalf."

"Don't suppose you'd hold a sweet shop in trust for him?" Westhaven looked positively gleeful to be making the offer. "I will always be his favorite uncle, if you do, and his cousins will hold him in particular esteem. It might also stand him in good stead when it comes time for him to court—"

"That is diabolical," Valentine expostulated, scowling ferociously.

"It's *ducal*," St. Just agreed. "Worthy of the old man himself, Westhaven, and not well done of you."

"We accept," Sophie said, smiling at the dearest brothers in the world. "Don't we?"

"Of course, we do," Vim said. "But before our son has more wealth than his parents, I think I'd best be having another little chat with His Grace."

"Excuse me, my lords, my lady." Mr. Harrad stood in the doorway to his home, his slender frame exuding a certain self-consciousness. "I heard voices, and as it happens, my wife and I were hoping to speak with Lady Sophia and Lord Sindal in the near future."

"We'll leave you," Westhaven said, stepping forward to kiss Sophie's forehead. "Don't stay out too long in this weather. Sindal, welcome to the family."

"Welcome," Valentine said, "but if you so much as give Sophie reason to wince, I will delight in thrashing you." He kissed Sophie's cheek and stepped back.

"And then I'll stand you to a round," St. Just said, extending a hand to Vim then drawing Sophie forward into the hug. "You'll send the boy to me when it's time to learn how to ride."

It wasn't a request, but it was sufficiently controversial that as they walked off in the direction of Morelands, all three brothers could tear into a rousing good argument about who would teach the lad to ride, to dance, to flirt, to shoot...

With a particular ache in her chest, Sophie watched them disappear into the night but realized she had one more bit of business to conclude before she could bring Vim home to her family. "Mr. Harrad, would now be a good time to chat?"

He glanced from Sophie to Vim, looking sheepish and tired. "As good as any."

࿔

"The boy got through the whole service without making a peep."

Vim watched as His Grace, Percival, the Duke of Moreland, beamed at the baby in his arms. "Not one peep, my love! I cannot say the same for my own boys."

"Nor for yourself," Her Grace muttered from her place beside her husband in the ducal carriage.

Vim exchanged a look with Sophie, to which Their Graces—eyes riveted on Kit in his gorgeous little receiving blankets—were oblivious.

"I can tell you this, Sindal." His Grace did not glance up from the child. "Your grandfather and I discussed a match between you and one of my girls. He'd approve. He'd approve of this little fellow too."

Her Grace looked like a woman who would very much like a turn holding the baby, but she instead posed a question to Sophie. "How did you ever talk Mrs. Harrad into parting with him?"

"We didn't have to." Sophie slipped her hand into Vim's, so he took over the explanations.

"Mrs. Harrad is again in expectation of a blessed event," Vim said. "She had not told her husband when he agreed to foster Kit, and they had rather a lot of difficult discussions once Kit was put in their keeping."

"So things worked out all around," His Grace said, brushing the ducal nose along Kit's cheek. "He has my eyes, Esther."

"Percival Windham, for pity's sake."

But His Grace was in great good spirits, and before Vim helped Sophie from the coach, the duke was making a list of pocket boroughs where Kit might stand for a seat in the Commons.

"Will you join me in the study for a tot, Sindal?" His Grace *still* had not given up the baby, and Kit was smiling and babbling as if the he and duke had been in the same form at public school.

"My uncle anticipates my company at Sidling, Your Grace. Perhaps another time."

"We'll see you at dinner, then," the duchess said. "I daresay His Grace will at least let me feed the child sometime this afternoon."

"Of course you can feed him," His Grace replied. "But he's joining me for a nip in the study first. Come along, Esther, the boy doesn't need to be out in this weather, particularly when it looks like more snow will descend any moment." They made a dignified progress to the house, leaving Sophie and Vim standing in the drive.

"You'll travel back here in time for dinner tonight?"

"Assuming Uncle permits me to leave the grounds. Now that he knows we'll be residing primarily at Sidling, he's come up with all manner of projects and ideas requiring lengthy discussion."

And to Vim's pleasure and surprise, those lengthy discussions were enjoyable.

"I'm looking forward to seeing your property in Surrey." Sophie slipped her hand in his and started walking with him toward the stables. "The sky does not look very promising."

When they gained the relative privacy of the barn aisle, Vim treated the horses to the sight of a man kissing his intended with almost desperate focus. When he managed to step back, the secretive smile playing about Sophie's lips made a dip in an icy horse trough loom with desperate appeal.

"I will be back for dinner, and I'll be back tomorrow morning to ride out with you. If the weather's foul, we can bake bread or listen to your brother practice his pianoforte."

Her smile faded while she rested her check against Vim's chest. "They'll be leaving soon, all three of them. They've promised their ladies to be home by Twelfth Night."

"They'll come for the wedding." Vim hoped they would. Sophie hadn't set a date, and he hadn't pressed her to, though tomorrow would suit him admirably. That very afternoon would suit even better.

Sophie smoothed her hand down his chest. "You'd best be going. I have to rescue Kit from Papa, lest the two of them get to sampling the brandy. Mama will not forgive me if Kit is a bad influence on the duke."

Kit was a wonderful influence on His Grace, but Vim took the hint. The sooner he got to Sidling, the sooner he could return to Morelands. He kissed his intended *again*, mounted up, and rode out into the chilly air.

When he got to Sidling, not just his uncle but also his aunt waited for him in the estate office. They had plans, it seemed, for a reception in the portrait gallery in recognition of Vim's engagement. And while Vim eyed the clock and the lowering sky, and his Uncle prattled on about the next full moon or possibly the one following, pretty little snow flurries began to dance in the air.

~⁘~

"Your swain came to you despite the weather." Evie Windham kept her voice down, which was a mercy, because with three brothers in residence and Sophie being the first sister to become engaged, the situation was ripe for teasing.

"I don't expect he'll stay long." Though with the way the snow had picked up, Sophie *wished* he'd stay at least until morning.

Evie looked like she might be the first to begin the teasing, when His Grace approached his daughters.

"If I'm to lose my dear Sophie to the charms of Rothgreb's heir, then I must at least insist on accompanying her into dinner, mustn't I?"

Evie patted her father's arm. "You must, and you must protect her from our brothers, who have taken to dispensing advice on how to raise boy children, though between them they have about a year's experience at it themselves."

His Grace smiled. "They get this propensity for dispensing unwarranted advice from their mother."

"Of course they do, Papa." Evie swanned off, leaving Sophie the perfect opportunity to put a few quiet questions to her dear papa, questions she made very, very certain nobody—not a brother, not a sister, not even a duchess—overheard.

And if her questions perturbed His Grace, it wasn't evident at dinner. The duke presided over a genial family meal, while Sophie sat next to Vim and tried to ignore the urge to surreptitiously explore the exact contours of her intended's lap.

"My love." His Grace addressed his wife down the length of the table. "We must not be sending young

Sindal out into the elements tonight. There's been entirely too much of that sort of thing in his courtship of our Sophie for an old man's peace of mind."

"Baron?" Her Grace aimed a smile at Vim where he sat beside Sophie. "Can we prevail upon you to accept our hospitality? I wouldn't want to tempt fate by asking you to travel yet again in a worsening storm."

Sophie slid her hand up from where it had been resting on Vim's muscular thigh beneath the table. She squeezed the burgeoning length of him gently but firmly.

"I'm pleased to accept such friendly overtures, Your Graces." His voice sounded only a little strained, and that was probably because Sophie was listening attentively. "My aunt and uncle urged me to tarry here if the weather became challenging."

He settled his hand over hers, giving her fingers—and thus himself—another little squeeze as he said the last word.

And then, damn and blast, Her Grace gave the signal for the ladies to rise and join her for tea in the parlor, while Sophie's brothers started exchanging the kinds of grins that assured her Vim would not be retiring yet for hours.

Sophie kept her features placid, even when Evie winked at her, Maggie rolled her eyes, and Her Grace rang for the cordials instead of the teapot.

❧

Just knowing Sophie was down the hall—Vim's room was in the family wing—was both a torture and a pleasure. He wanted to go to her, but God knew which brother, sister, or *parent* Vim might meet in the corridor.

He sighed, and for the twentieth time since retiring, rolled over in the vast bed.

A slow creak came to his ears. The creak repeated itself—a door opening then closing.

A scent drifted to his nose, a flowery, clean fragrance he was coming to treasure.

"Sophia Windham, you have developed a lamentable penchant for sneaking into gentlemen's bedrooms."

"I'm going to sneak into your bed, as well," she said, parting the bed curtains. "It's chilly out here."

Trying to formulate a stern lecture about propriety was an utter waste of time as Sophie unbelted her wrapper, tossed it to the foot of the bed, and drew her chemise over her head.

"Can't have you catching your death." He flipped up the covers and admonished himself to plead shamelessly for the wedding to be held sooner rather than later—much sooner. The Good Lord was going to bestow only so many providential snowstorms on a man and his bride.

"I would rather catch my prospective husband at his slumbers." She tucked herself against Vim's side, a warm, lovely bundle of female. His arm came around her shoulders to gather her closer, and she sighed.

"I suppose, being a woman in contemplation of matrimony, you came here to talk?" He tried not to sound long-suffering, but her brothers had lectured him at great length about the adult woman's need for, and entitlement to, private conversation with her spouse.

Sophie's hand drifted across his bare abdomen. "Of course I came to talk. I love talking with you."

He'd work the conversation around to the wedding date, then. Work the situation to his advantage while he tried not to take advantage of Moreland's hospitality. And then, who knew where the conversation might lead them?

Sophie's hand trailed up across his chest then traced his sternum down to his navel. "I came here to talk, because snowstorms are not a very reliable means of acquiring time with one's beloved." Her hand moved south and closed gently around Vim's straining erection. "But I didn't come here *merely* to talk."

&

"The snow has stopped." His Grace dropped the curtain and turned back to regard his wife as she sat at her escritoire.

She set her pen down, her serene countenance giving little clue to her emotional state, though His Grace noted the shadows in her eyes. "Then I suppose the boys will be traveling on sooner rather than later."

"And in spring, we can go on a progress." He crossed the room and bent to poke up the fire. "We'll inspect Sindal's place in Surrey, drop in on Westhaven and Viscount Amery—wouldn't want Rose to feel neglected by her grandparents—head up to Oxfordshire to see Val and Ellen, then toddle on to the West Riding, if you like."

She nodded. A man offers to spend weeks jaunting about the countryside imposing on one child after another, and his wife merely nods. "Esther, is something troubling you?"

"Not troubling me." She rose and crossed to their bed, the bed where they'd conceived their children and made up after their increasingly rare fights. "Come sit with me, Husband."

Husband. She rarely called him that, almost never before others. He sat with her and took her hand. "Tell me, Wife. I cannot have you troubled while I yet draw breath."

"Our dear sensible Sophie, the daughter whom we never think to fret over—"

"We fret over every damned one of them, excuse my language."

"—We do, but our Sophie, whom we don't fret over so very much, that Sophie…" She turned and pressed her face to his shoulder, which caused His Grace to feel a frisson of unease. Esther was the kindest woman on God's earth, but when it came to family, she was neither sentimental nor cowardly.

"Tell me about Sophie, Esther."

"She cast up her accounts—as your sons would say—after breakfast. *Again.*"

His Grace put an arm around his wife's shoulders and kissed her hair, mostly to hide his smile. "All will be well, Esther. You are not to worry. Sophie is a Windham. Of course she'd indulge in certain liberties with her intended. Probably got the tendency from her mother."

Her Grace drew back, a frown creasing her pretty features. "You are not wroth? You're not going to call Sindal out or ring a peal over their heads?"

"I am not, not when our own marriage began on similar terms—and look how well that turned out. Come to bed. If the weather has truly let up, then the rider should have no trouble getting back from Town posthaste."

She climbed under the covers and curled into his arms, the same as she had almost every night of their married life. "What rider would that be?"

"The one procuring the special license Sophie asked me to obtain with all possible speed. Sent the poor messenger out in this weather with nothing less than my best bottle of whiskey to speed him on his way."

His duchess sighed and snuggled closer. "Happy Christmas, Percival. I do love you."

"Happy Christmas, Duchess, and I love you."

"We'll talk later, then." Vim shifted so he was crouched over Sophie, his erection brushing her belly. "Now, we'll anticipate marital privileges *again*, unless you march yourself right out that door this instant, Sophie Windham."

"Your enthusiasm for these priv—gracious sakes!" She sighed as he kissed her, her hand landing in his hair, her hips tilting invitingly against him. Sophie already wore one of the heirloom Charpentier rings, and a part of Vim had half hoped with an official engagement, his hunger for his bride might abate to something closer to fondness, something that admitted of restraint and decorum, and of church services and family meals that didn't feel like they lasted for days.

It was a vain, stupid hope. The more he loved her, the more he wanted to love her.

"Mr. Charpentier, why is it you locate your reserves of patience only when I am desperate for you to be impulsive?" Sophie purred her question into his ear, swiping at his lobe with her tongue then drawing it into her mouth and biting just firmly enough to tempt Vim to the impulsiveness she was trying to provoke.

"I am patient," he growled while nudging at her sex with his cock, "because I am considerate of your pleasure, Sophie."

"Such consideration usually has me yelling and moaning, and—" She grabbed his hair and used that to leverage her hips into a more accommodating angle. "I do love anticipating marriage to a considerate man."

She loved making love with him, as well, something Vim had come to appreciate in their few though passionate encounters. Sophie Windham was every inch a lady, but also every inch a bride in love with her prospective husband.

He sank slowly into her willing heat, the pleasure of it nigh causing his ears to roar.

"Stop that, Sophie." He slowed down more to make his point, but this just allowed her to use internal muscles to greater advantage. "For God's sake, you'll unman me."

"For about ten minutes maybe." She set up a rhythm that had Vim's resolve crumbling and the old bed creaking. When she started to make a telltale little whimper in the back of her throat, he gave up and let passion consume them both. It wasn't his imagination, either. As they became more familiar with each other as lovers, as each learned the other's sensitivities and preferences, the pleasure became greater and greater. He'd come to expect the roaring in his ears and the boiling pleasure that exploded out from his vitals and tore through his body each and every time they made love.

When he hung over her, panting and sated, when her fingernails had left an imprint on his backside, he lifted his head to peer around the room. "You really must stop accosting me like this, Sophie. I'm going to have to insist on a New Year's wedding, lest our next child be born prematurely."

"New Year's is a lovely holiday—or Twelfth Night." She sounded so satisfied, Vim had to smile.

"Stay put. I'm going to hold you to a date, my lady, if I have to be found sharing a bed with you to do it." He eased from her body, knowing her eyes would be on him as he climbed from beneath the covers.

When he came back to the bed as naked as God had made him, his intended had considerately obeyed him—for once—and remained on her back, a rosy flush fading from her cheeks.

"You are tired," he observed, sitting on the edge of the bed. "I do believe you were dozing during Vicar's sermon too."

"My eyes were closed the better to revere the wisdom he was imparting. Do not tickle me, else I shall have to seek revenge on you."

He swabbed delicately at her intimate parts, wishing he'd lit more candles. "I love it when you seek revenge, and did I hear you mention that you must wait ten minutes while I regain my manly vigor? Surely that was an exaggeration intended to provoke me."

"To inspire you." She held the covers up so he could rejoin her in the bed.

"You're going to love the place in Surrey, Sophie. We won't be far from Westhaven, but if he presumes to call before February, I'm going to sign his blasted sweet shop back over to him."

Vim would not allow her to miss her brothers. It was badly done of them to neglect her, but now she had a husband who knew all about traveling the realm, though of course he and Sophie would make Sidling their base.

"Hold me, please." She pulled his arm around her middle to emphasize her point, and Vim had to wonder if any pleasure on earth compared with cuddling with his very own Sophie.

"Will you fall asleep on me now, Miss Windham?"

"No, but I will avail myself of this fifteen-minute interval to speak with you privately."

"Five minutes." He palmed her breasts—her marvelously sensitive breasts—and heard her sigh with the pleasure of it.

He was not alarmed that she had something on her mind to discuss. When she'd accepted his heart into her keeping, Sophie Windham had earned his trust, as well—but he was curious.

"Why do we need privacy, my love?" He levered up on his elbow to watch as a predictable softness came over her features at the endearment. He used it with shameless frequency for his own pleasure, but also for hers.

"I have some questions for you."

Serious, indeed. He brushed her hair back from her

forehead with his thumb. "I will answer to the best of my ability."

"You know about changing nappies."

"I do."

"You know about feeding babies."

"Generally, yes."

"You know about bathing them."

"It isn't complicated."

She fell silent, and Vim's curiosity grew when Sophie rolled to her back to regard him almost solemnly. "I asked Papa to procure us a special license."

He'd wondered why the banns hadn't been cried but hadn't questioned Sophie's decision. "I assumed that was to allow your brothers to attend the ceremony."

"Them? Yes, I suppose."

She was in a quiet, Sophie-style taking over something, so he slid his arm around her shoulders and kissed her temple. "Tell me, my love. If I can explain my youthful blunders to you over a glass of eggnog, then you can confide to me whatever is bothering you."

She ducked her face against his shoulder. "Do you know the signs a woman is carrying?"

He tried to view it as a mere question, a factual inquiry. "Her menses likely cease, for one thing."

Sophie took Vim's hand and settled it over the wonderful fullness of her breast then shifted, arching into his touch. "What else?"

He thought back to his stepmother's confinements, to what he'd learned on his travels. "From the outset, she might be tired at odd times," he said slowly. "Her breasts might be tender, and she might have a need to visit the necessary more often than usual."

She tucked her face against his chest and hooked her leg over his hips. "You are a very observant man, Mr. Charpentier."

With a jolt of something like alarm—but not simply alarm—Vim thought back to Sophie's dozing in church, her marvelously sensitive breasts, her abrupt departure from the room when they'd first gathered for dinner.

"And," he said slowly, "some women are a bit queasy in the early weeks."

She moved his hand, bringing it to her mouth to kiss his knuckles, then settling it low on her abdomen, over her womb. "A New Year's wedding will serve quite nicely if we schedule it for the middle of the day. I'm told the queasiness passes in a few weeks, beloved."

To Vim's ears, there was a peculiar, awed quality to that single, soft endearment.

The feeling that came over him then was indescribable. Profound peace, profound awe, and profound gratitude coalesced into something so transcendent as to make "love"—even mad, passionate love—an inadequate description.

"If you are happy about this, Sophie, one tenth as happy about it as I am, then this will have been the best Christmas season anybody ever had, anywhere, at any time. I vow this to you as the father of your children, your affianced husband, and the man who loves you with his whole heart."

She cupped his jaw with her hand and blinded him with her smile. "The best Christmas," she said. "The best anybody has ever had, anywhere, at any time, until *our* Christmas, with our children, next year."

It did not take Vim five minutes to commence celebrating their impending good fortune—it did not take him one minute, in fact. And Sophie was right: their family's ensuing Christmases were the best anybody ever had, anywhere, at any time.

Acknowledgments

A number of elves and angels are responsible for getting this book into your hands, primary among them is the team at Sourcebooks who had the insight to see how a Christmas story could fit into the Windham family's plans. I wish (Sophie's word is so useful) I could say I thought this one up on my own, but I did not. Deb Werksman, my editor, called one Thursday late in October and asked if I could add a Christmas book to my Works In Progress.

What author wouldn't be thrilled to receive such a call?

And what author wouldn't panic immediately and repeatedly thereafter?

Many things about writing come to me easily—the solitude, the trips to the fridge, the imaginary friends—but plotting is a challenge. Deb took time from her busy Sunday to sit with me over pancakes along the Long Island Sound and brainstorm story lines. She called to check in on me at two precise moments when I was ready to turn the writing over to my cats because what, after all, hasn't been said, written, and rewritten about Christmas, one of the oldest love stories on the planet?

That sense of not being alone with a heap of straw to spin into gold pervades all the books I've written with Deb and the elves in the Sourcebooks shop: Cat, Susie, Danielle, Heather, Skye, Madame Copy Editor, and our publisher, Dominique, among others I haven't even met.

This turned out to be one of the most enjoyable books I've written, a holiday present from Sourcebooks to me. I hope it's a present to you, as well.

About the Author

New York Times bestselling author Grace Burrowes's debut novel, *The Heir*, was named one of *Publishers Weekly*'s Top Five Romances for 2010, and the sequel, *The Soldier*, was named one of *Publishers Weekly*'s Top Ten Romances for Spring 2011. Both are *New York Times* and *USA Today* bestsellers. As the final book in The Duke's Obsession trilogy, *The Virtuoso*, hits the shelves, Grace will be hard at work on the remaining stories of the five Windham sisters, of which *Lady Sophie's Christmas Wish* is the first.

Grace is a practicing attorney specializing in child welfare law. She lives and works in rural Maryland. She loves to hear from her readers and can be reached through her website at graceburrowes.com, her email at graceburrowes@yahoo.com, or through her fan page on Facebook.

READ ON FOR A SNEAK PREVIEW OF
GRACE BURROWES'S

THE Virtuoso

COMING NOVEMBER 2011
FROM SOURCEBOOKS CASABLANCA

One

"MY BEST ADVICE IS TO GIVE UP PLAYING THE PIANO."

Lord Valentine Windham neither moved nor changed his expression when he heard his friend—a skilled and experienced physician—pronounce sentence. Being the youngest of five boys and named Valentine—for God's sake—had given him fast reflexes, abundant muscle, and an enviable poker face. Being called the baby boy any time he'd shown the least tender sentiment had fired his will to the strength of iron and given him the ability to withstand almost any blow without flinching.

But this... This was diabolical, this demand David made of him. To give up the one mistress Val loved, the one place he was happy and competent. To give up the home he'd forged for his soul despite his ducal father's ridicule, his mother's anxiety, and his siblings' inability to understand what music had become to him.

He closed his eyes and drew breath into his lungs by act of will. "For how long am I to give up my music?"

Silence, until Val opened his eyes and glanced

down at where his left hand, aching and swollen, lay
uselessly on his thigh.

David sat beside him, making a polite pretense of
surveying the surrounding paddocks and fields. "You
are possibly done with music for the rest of your life,
my friend. The hand might heal but only if you rest it
until you're ready to scream with frustration. Not just
days, not just weeks, and by then you will have lost
some of the dexterity you hone so keenly now. If you
try too hard or too soon to regain it, you'll make the
hand worse than ever."

"Months?" One month was forever when a man
wanted only to do the single thing denied him.

"At least. And as long as I'm cheering you up,
you need to watch for the condition to arise in the
other hand. If you catch it early, it might need less
extensive treatment."

"Both hands?" Val closed his eyes again and hunched
in on himself, though the urge to kick the stone wall
where they sat—hard, repeatedly, like a man beset with
murderous frustration—was nigh overwhelming.

"It's possible both hands will be affected," David
went on. "Your left hand is more likely in worse
condition because of the untreated fracture you
suffered as a small boy. You're right-handed, so it's
also possible the right hand is stronger out of habit."

Val roused himself to gather as many facts from
David as he could. "Is the left weak, then?"

"Not weak, so much." David, Viscount Fairly,
pursed his lips. "It seems to me you have something
like gout or rheumatism in your hand. It's inflamed,
swollen, and painful without apparent cause. The test

will be if you rest it and see improvement. That is not the signal to resume spending all hours on the piano bench, Valentine."

"It's the signal to what? All I do is spend hours on the piano bench and occasionally escort my sisters about Town."

"It's the signal you're dealing with a simple inflammation from overuse, old son." David slid a hand to Val's nape and shook him gently. "Many people lead happy, productive lives without gluing their arses to the piano bench for twenty hours a day. Kiss some pretty girls; sniff a few roses; go see the Lakes."

Val shoved off the wall, using only his right hand for balance. "I know you mean well, but I don't *want* to do anything but play the piano."

"And I know what you want." David hopped down to fall in step beside Val. "What you want has gotten you a hand that can't hold a teacup, and while that's not fair and it's not right, it's also not yet permanent."

"I'm whining." Val stopped and gazed toward the manor house where David's viscountess was no doubt tucking in their infant daughter for the evening. "I should be thanking you for bothering with me."

"I am flattered to be of service. And you are not to let some idiot surgeon talk you into bleeding it."

"You're sure?"

"I am absolutely sure of that. No bleeding, no blisters, no surgery, and no peculiar nostrums. You tend it as you would any other inflammation."

"Which would mean?" Val forced himself to ask. But what would it matter, really? He might get the use of his hand back in a year, but how much conditioning and skill would he have lost by then? He loved his mistress—his muse—but she was jealous and unforgiving as hell.

"Rest," David said sternly as they approached the house. "Cold soaks, willow bark tea by the bucket, and at all costs, avoid the laudanum. If you can find a position where the hand is comfortable, you might consider sleeping with it splinted like that. Massage, if you can stand it."

"As if I had some tired old man's ailment. You're sure about the laudanum? It's the only thing that lets me keep playing."

"Laudanum lets you continue to aggravate it," David shot back. "It masks the pain, it cures nothing, and it can become addictive."

A beat of silence went by. Val nodded once, as much of an admission as he would make.

"Christ." David stopped in his tracks. "How long have you been using it?"

"Off and on for months. Not regularly. What it gives in ability to keep playing, it takes away in ability to focus on what I'm creating. The pain goes away, but so does both manual and mental dexterity. And I can still see my hand is swollen and the wrong color."

"Get rid of the poppy. It has a place, but I don't recommend it for you."

"I comprehend."

"You think your heart's breaking," David said, "but you still have that hand, Valentine, and you can do many, many things with it. If you treat it right now, someday you might be able to make music with it again."

"Is there anything you're not telling me?" Val asked, his tone flat.

"Well, yes," David replied as they gained the back terraces of the manor house. "There's another possibility regarding the onset of the symptoms."

"More good news?"

"Perhaps." David met his gaze steadily, which was slightly disconcerting. In addition to height and blond good looks, David Worthington, Viscount Fairly, had one blue eye and one green eye. "With a situation like this, where there is no immediate trauma, no exposure to disease, no clear cause for the symptoms, it can be beneficial to look at other aspects of well-being."

"In the King's English, David, please." Much more of David's learned medical prosing on, and Val was going to break a laudanum bottle over his friend's head.

"Sickness can originate in the emotions," David said quietly. "The term 'broken heart' can be literal, and you did say the sensations began just after you buried your brother Victor."

"As we were burying Victor," Val corrected him, not wanting to think of the pain he'd felt as he scooped up a symbolic fistful of cold earth to toss on Victor's coffin. "What in the hell does that have to do with whether I can ever again thunder away at Herr Beethoven's latest sonata?"

"That is for you to puzzle out, as you'll have ample time to ponder on it, won't you?"

"Suppose I will at that."

Val felt David's arm land across his shoulders and made no move to shrug it off, though the last thing he wanted was pity. The numbness in his hand was apparently spreading to the rest of him—just not quickly enough.

⤛⤜

"You seem to be thriving here, Cousin."

"I am quite comfortable." Ellen FitzEngle smiled at Frederick Markham, Baron Roxbury, with determined *pleasantness*. The last thing she needed was to admit vulnerability to him or to let him see he had any impact on her existence at all. She smoothed her hair back with a steady hand and leveled a guileless gaze at her guest, enemy, and de facto landlord.

"Hmm." Frederick glanced around the tidy little cottage, a condescending smile implying enormous satisfaction at Ellen's comedown in the world. "Not quite like Roxbury House, is it? Nor in a league with Roxbury Hall."

"But manageable for a widow of limited means. Would you like more tea?"

"'Fraid I can't stay." Frederick rose, his body at twenty-two still giving the impression of not having grown into his arms and legs, despite expensive clothing and fashionable dark curls. She knew he fancied himself something of a Corinthian, paid punctilious attention to his attire, boxed at Gentlemen Jackson's, fenced at Alberto's, and accepted any bet involving his racing curricle.

And still, to Ellen, he would always be the gangly, awkward adolescent whose malice she had sorely underestimated. Only five years difference separated their ages, but she felt decades his senior in sorrow and regret.

"I did want to let you know, though"—Frederick paused with his hand on the door latch—"I'll likely be selling the place. A fellow has expenses, and the solicitors are deuced tightfisted with the Roxbury funds."

"My thanks for the warning." Ellen nodded, refusing to show any other reaction. Selling meant she could be homeless, of course, for she occupied a tenant cottage on the Markham estate. The new owner might allow her to stay on. Her property was profitable, but she didn't have a signed lease—she'd not put it past Freddie to tamper with the deed—and so the new owner might also toss her out on her backside.

"Thought it only sporting to let you know." Frederick opened the door and swung his gaze out to his waiting vehicle. A tiger held the reins of the restive bays, and Ellen had to wonder how such spirited horses navigated the little track leading to her door. "Oh, and I almost forgot." Freddie's smile turned positively gleeful. "I brought you a little something from the Hall."

Dread seeped up from Ellen's stomach, filling her throat with bile and foreboding. Any present from Frederick was bound to bring ill will, if not worse.

Frederick bent into his curricle and withdrew a small potted plant. "You being the gardener in the family, I thought you might like a little cutting from Roxbury. You needn't thank me."

"Most gracious of you, nonetheless." Ellen offered him a cool smile as he put the clay pot into her hands and then climbed aboard. "Safe journey to Town, Frederick."

He waited, clearly wishing she'd look at the little plant, but then gave up and yelled at his tiger to let the horses go. The child's grasp hadn't left the reins before Frederick was cracking the whip, the horses lunging forward and the curricle slewing around in

Ellen's front yard as the boy scrambled up onto his post behind the seat.

And ye gods, ye gods, was Ellen ever glad to see the last of the man. She glanced at the plant in her hand, rolled her eyes and walked around to the back of her property to toss it, pot and all, on her compost heap.

How like Frederick to give her an herb often used to settle the stomach, while he intimated he'd be tearing the roof from over her head. He'd been threatening for several years now, as winters in Portugal, autumn at Melton, a lengthy stint in London each spring, and expensive friends all around did not permit a man to hold on to decrepit, unentailed estates for long.

She should be grateful she'd had five years to settle in, to grieve, and to heal. She had a few friends in nearby Little Weldon, some nice memories, and some satisfaction with what she'd been able to accomplish on this lovely little property.

And now all that accomplishment was to be taken from her.

She poured herself a cup of tea and took it to her back porch, where the vista was one of endless, riotous flower beds. They were her livelihood and her solace, her greatest joy and her most treasured necessity. Sachets and soaps, herbs for cooking, and bouquets for market, they all brought a fair penny, and the pennies added up. Fruits and vegetables created still more income, as did the preserves and pies made from them.

"And if we have to move"—Ellen addressed the fat-headed orange tom cat who strolled up the porch steps—"we have a bit put by now, don't we, Marmalade?"

Himself squeezed up his eyes in feline inscrutability,

which Ellen took for supportive agreement. The cat had been abandoned at the manor house through the wood and had gladly given up a diet of mice for the occasional dish of cream on Ellen's porch.

His company, though, combined with Frederick's visit and the threat to her livelihood, put Ellen in a wistful, even lonely mood. She sipped her tea in the waning afternoon light and brought forth the memories that pleased her most. She didn't visit them often but saved them for low moments when she'd hug them around her like a favorite shawl, the one that always made a girl feel pretty and special.

She thought about her first pony, about the day she'd found Marmalade sitting king-of-all-he-surveyed in a tree near the cottage, like a welcoming committee from the fairy folk. She thought about the flowers she'd put together for all the village weddings, and the flowers on her own wedding day. And she thought about a chance visit from that handsome Mr. Windham, though it had been just a few moments stolen in the evening sunshine, and more than a year had passed since those moments.

Ellen set her chair to rocking, hugged the memory closer still, and banished all thoughts of Frederick, homelessness, and poverty from her mind.

THE HEIR
GRACE BURROWES

AN EARL WHO CAN'T BE BRIBED...

Gayle Windham, Earl of Westhaven, is the first legitimate son and heir to the Duke of Moreland. To escape his father's inexorable pressure to marry, he decides to spend the summer at his townhouse in London, where he finds himself intrigued by the secretive ways of his beautiful housekeeper...

A LADY WHO CAN'T BE PROTECTED...

Anna Seaton is a beautiful, talented, educated woman, which is why it is so puzzling to Gayle Windham that she works as his housekeeper.

As the two draw closer and begin to lose their hearts to each other, Anna's secrets threaten to bring the earl's orderly life crashing down—and he doesn't know how he's going to protect her from the fallout...

A *PUBLISHERS WEEKLY* BEST BOOK OF THE YEAR

"A luminous and graceful erotic Regency...a captivating love story that will have readers eagerly awaiting the planned sequels."

— *Publishers Weekly* (starred review)

978-1-4022-4434-6 • $6.99 U.S. / £4.99 UK

New York Times and *USA Today* Bestseller

THE

GRACE BURROWES

EVEN IN THE QUIET COUNTRYSIDE, HE CAN FIND NO PEACE...

His idyllic estate is falling down from neglect and nightmares of war give him no rest. Then Devlin St. Just meets his new neighbor...

UNTIL HIS BEAUTIFUL NEIGHBOR IGNITES HIS IMAGINATION...

With her confident manner hiding a devastating secret, his lovely neighbor commands all of his attention, and protecting Emmaline becomes Devlin's most urgent mission.

> "Burrowes's straightforward, sensual love story is intelligent and tender, rising above the crowd with deft dialogue and delightful characters."
>
> — *Publishers Weekly* (starred review)

978-1-4022-4567-1 • $6.99 U.S. / £4.99 UK